Son of the religious philosopher Henry James, Sr., and brother of the psychologist and philosopher William, Henry James was born in New York City, April 15, 1843. His early life was spent in America; on and off he was taken to Europe, especially during the impressionable years from twelve to seventeen. After that he lived in Newport, went briefly to Harvard, and, in 1864, began to contribute both criticism and tales to the magazines. In 1869, and then in 1872–74, he paid visits to Europe and began *Roderick Hudson*. Late in 1875 he settled in Paris, where he met Turgenev, Flaubert, and Zola, and wrote *The American*. In December 1876 he moved to London, where two years later he achieved international fame with *Daisy Miller*. Other famous works include *Washington Square* (1880), *The Portrait of a Lady* (1881), *The Princess Casamassima* (1886), *The Aspern Papers* (1888), *The Turn of the Screw* (1898), and the three large novels of the new century, *The Wings of the Dove* (1902), *The Ambassadors* (1903), and *The Golden Bowl* (1904). In 1905 he revisited the United States and wrote *The American Scene* (1907). He also wrote many works of criticism and travel. Although old and ailing, he threw himself into war work in 1914; and in 1915, a few months before his death, he became a British subject. In January 1916 King George V conferred the Order of Merit on him. He died in London in February 1916, and his ashes were buried in the James family plot in Cambridge, Massachusetts.

HENRY JAMES

THE TURN OF THE SCREW

AND OTHER SHORT NOVELS

With an Introduction by
Perry Mcisel

A SIGNET CLASSIC

SIGNET CLASSIC
Published by the Penguin Group
Penguin Books USA Inc., 375 Hudson Street,
New York, New York 10014, U.S.A.
Penguin Books Ltd, 27 Wrights Lane,
London W8 5TZ, England
Penguin Books Australia Ltd, Ringwood,
Victoria, Australia
Penguin Books Canada Ltd, 10 Alcorn Avenue,
Toronto, Ontario, Canada M4V 3B2
Penguin Books (N.Z.) Ltd, 182–190 Wairau Road,
Auckland 10, New Zealand

Penguin Books Ltd, Registered Offices:
Harmondsworth, Middlesex, England

Published by Signet Classic, an imprint of Dutton Signet,
a division of Penguin Books USA Inc.

First Signet Classic Printing, May, 1995
10 9 8 7 6 5 4 3

 REGISTERED TRADEMARK—MARCA REGISTRADA

Library of Congress Catalog Card Number: 87–072886

Printed in the United States of America

BOOKS ARE AVAILABLE AT QUANTITY DISCOUNTS WHEN USED TO PROMOTE
PRODUCTS OR SERVICES. FOR INFORMATION PLEASE WRITE TO PREMIUM
MARKETING DIVISION, PENGUIN BOOKS USA INC., 375 HUDSON STREET, NEW
YORK, NEW YORK 10014.

CONTENTS

INTRODUCTION:

THE TURN OF THE SCREW
and Other Short Novels

Henry James's short novels provide a representative account of James's career as a whole, and serve as an excellent introduction to the peculiar unity of his singular imagination. Although the difference between James's early and later fiction is alone striking—simply compare the opening paragraphs of *The American* (1877) and *The Ambassadors* (1903) to see the movement from Victorian realism to the modern psychological realism of which James is the acknowledged master—it is probably more accurate to say that James's career is one of continuity and refinement rather than one of abrupt changes. Whether in his long novels or his shorter ones—nouvelles, as he liked to call the latter, six of which are collected in the pages that follow—James's fiction is always concerned with the play of impressions upon the mind and heart. While a gradual shift in perspective over the years heightens point of view and diminishes the description of faces, objects, and scenes at which the early James grudgingly excels, James's focus remains the extraordinarily specific circumstances that structure the self, and the ways in which the structure of experience and the structure of narrative are very often the same.

In the autumn of 1897, the year before *The Turn of the Screw* was first published, James had moved to Lamb House, Rye, after more than twenty years of residence in London. James had settled in England in 1876 (he became a British subject in 1915, the year before his death), and soon achieved critical triumph within the same English tradition that had once burdened him as a young American writer. The influence of James's own writing upon twentieth-century fiction is, of course, inestimable. James's psychological realism remains so influential even today that it is, to use James's own description of the success of the fictional poet Jeffrey Aspern in *The Aspern Papers* (1888), "part of the light by which we walk." Almost every modern writer of fiction in English carries the scars of James's influence, and almost every major English and American novelist in the generation following James's own—E. M. Forster, Virginia Woolf, Edith Wharton, Willa Cather, even Hemingway and Fitzgerald—can be measured by their respective turns from a strength at once enabling and potentially fatal in the decisiveness with which it reinvents the writing of fiction.

Why is James so influential? What is the nature of his power? The short novels collected here allow us to see what it is in efficient and delicious miniature. *The Turn of the Screw* (1898) is James's most famous and widely read short novel. Despite its unique extravagance, it contains the principal elements of James's customary world both early and late: interpretative uncertainty and an uncannily vivid sense of solitary and reflective human sadness. *The Turn of the Screw* shows us a writer fully at home with his powers, and one consciously concerned with central questions about the imagination and its determinations. Bly, the tale's country house, is a haunted house, and the tale a haunted tale. But haunted by what? Are the former governess and the former valet who loom as apparitions fantastic projections of the new governess's imagination? Or are they genuine ghosts, spirits of a past day? Ghosts represent both the past and a past way of thinking in as decisively secular a world as James's is. Surely the ironic brother of the philosopher William James, notorious freethinker and pragmatist, little fancied ghosts as such. Why, then, are we afraid? By means of what power does the tale promote the shudders that it does? We are afraid not only because James has the powers of illusion to do with us whatever he likes, but also because he has the power to do so while suspending all judgment as to what these witnesses of his power may mean. Testimony to James's audacity as a writer, the tale is poised between a series of interpretative alternatives that raise more questions than James thinks it right to answer. *The Turn of the Screw* is the turn, as it were, that reveals the archaeology or the unconscious of James's own sense of himself as a writer.

As a literary allegory, the tale is also poised between two very real alternatives as it meditates upon questions of imaginative priority. Is James's writing merely a ghost of past writing, or is it testimony to the splendid originality of his own imagination? As a writer of fiction who began in the last quarter of the nineteenth century, James had to control Romanticism itself. Like his unnamed governess-narrator (what, by the way, is the status of gender in James?), James is tormented by Romanticism's representatives. Who are Peter Quint and Miss Jessel? They are strangely familiar figures; he is the Romantic male in the visionary tower and she the house-haunting madwoman, whose only place of repose seems to be the attic. Leon Edel, James's biographer, notes the indirect allusions to *Jane Eyre* in *The Turn of the Screw*, and the narrator herself wonders out loud whether "an insane, an unmentionable relative" is being "kept in unsuspected confinement." As the governess's fear and malaise attest, however, James himself is interested in neither figure; these Romantic counterparts represent ghostly and offensive burdens that his own fiction will circumvent in favor of a new kind of literary character based upon figures like the depressive governess-narrator here or the scholar-narrator of *The Aspern Papers* ten years earlier, milder figures for whom vision and madness alike are unacceptable, even unavailable alternatives. Life is after all too sedentary an affair for prose realism to give the glamor of either stance any credibility.

What is left, then, for the novelist to do? Uncertainty and its causes and effects are the major and unifying concerns of James's career, and his use of them as materials allows him to link style and subject, form and theme in dauntingly clear ways. What James's other short novels share with *The Turn of the Screw* is the pressure of situations and the overriding question within them of what the truth in each case may be. Of course, what the truth is in

James's world is a legal or juridical question—a question of evidence, argument, and negotiation among alternatives—not a metaphysical one.

In *The Aspern Papers* (1888), the question of what the truth may be is the narrative's overt theme. Are the poet Aspern's papers hidden in the Misses Bordereau's house in Venice or not? What is the effect of each move planned by the now shrewd, now bumbling narrator as he tries to extract the truth from the situation? Toward the possession of what objects, as he himself wonders, are these feints directed? The very components of the story sound like the techniques involved in writing one. What frustrates the narrator thickens the illusion for the reader. It is the wonder that the story itself creates—the secret that it puts in place by not disclosing—that is both its motive force and its very subject. Concealing a secret is proof that there must be one. The sense of a fugitive truth gives the narrative and the lives of the characters within it goals that structure and organize both alike whether or not either receives a proper resolution. Tita Bordereau's admission at tale's end that she has burned the papers after her aunt's death is part of the mystery, not an answer to it.

If James's career is one of continuity and refinement, then even the early *Daisy Miller* (1878)—the book that made James famous—must, like Daisy herself, be far less plain and innocent than it seems to be. Here the early James is already exploring the interior as he paints a world presumably external to private states of mind, a world to which characters seem only to react. But the legendary split between an omniscient early James and an entirely subjective later James is partly a myth. Like all of James's work, *Daisy Miller* is a moral tale. Its lesson is that form does indeed matter; its nonobservance can lead, quite literally, to death. Daisy's flouting of the customs of Rome results in her dying from malaria. But this experiential moral is of a piece with the epistemological lesson that the story also presents, the kind of lesson we tend to associate only with the James of the late phase. With the "ruin" and "inscriptions" of Rome's archaeology serving as the story's site, James shows that "the common forms," as he calls them in *The Aspern Papers,* are essential to everyone's interior life, the shared assumptions or "pretexts," as he calls them in *Daisy Miller,* that are one's unconscious connection to the external world. There is some irony in the fact that even solitude and loneliness are made up of social materials (how do I measure myself, for example, except in relation to others?), but it is also this kind of irony that makes James so inconsolable and his world often so torpid.

An International Episode (1878), as early a work as *Daisy Miller,* is by contrast a tale of ambiguity and questioning despite its fierce realism. What happens between the lovers at tale's end? It is hard to tell; many explanations are implied, but none confirmed. Ten years before *The Aspern Papers,* James is already writing a kind of interactive fiction, asking the reader to get involved in construing the story itself even though the reader may feel that he or she is simply observing it. However politically incorrect, one reacts, says James, according to one's "preconceptions." Thus "reference," he says, speaking technically of his use of language in the tale, is "reference to a fund of associations," "associations" or "preconceptions" that implicate the reader in the same network of assumption (the figure of the web or mesh is among James's favorite metaphors in his criticism) as the text and its characters.

While *The Altar of the Dead* (1895) is likely James's most moribund tale of human loneliness and uncertainty, it is also among his frankest, since it provides an undisguised model for what narrative and subjectivity actually share. In the process, James's fiction also comes to discover the nature of its own technique, and dramatizes it with even greater clarity than usual. Its key is temporality, and it is the structure of temporality that identifies experience and narrative so exactly. When George Stransom, James's dubious hero, realizes that his female friend has been grieving for the old mutual friend who did him an unspecified wrong many years before, the shock of belated recognition changes his perspective, requiring him to drop her. "It had been all right so long as she didn't know," reflects Stransom, "and it was only now that she knew too much." The slightest difference can make an enormous one. Belated knowledge that alters one's view of the past is the crucial link between the structure of experience and the structure of narrative. Let Stransom explain:

> There were subtle and complex relations, a scheme
> of cross reference.... In this way, he arrived at a
> conception of the total, the ideal....

Whether it is the self, a story, or an idea, if the parts shift
their relation to one another, the whole shifts, although
one sees it all only "afterward," as James not infrequently
describes it. So efficient has James become that story and
technique coincide with remarkable ease. The structure of
Jamesian subjectivity is identical with the structure of Jamesian narration, and with the structure of the Jamesian sentence in particular. Like the relations among the elements
in a character's life or among those in a porous Jamesian
story, the components of a Jamesian sentence don't make
entire sense or show surpassing beauty until the reader
completes them. James's style and the effect of impressions
upon the mind are structured the same way. This is James's
reflexive realism, a realism whose representation of the self is
at one with the active logic of the writing that describes it.

If an early tale like *Daisy Miller* is epistemological as
well as moral, a late one like *The Beast in the Jungle* (1903)
is moral as well as epistemological. Indeed, *The Beast in
the Jungle* joins the two, showing how the later James really
is the refinement of the identity between narrative and experience, between the reflexive and the realistic, the formal
and the thematic. The belatedness of John Marcher's shock
of recognition is its primary characteristic, and the source
of both the story's sadness and Marcher's own. What is the
beast, the secret that Marcher fruitlessly awaits his whole
life long? That there is no secret, that all is as blank as the
face of a grave? Or is there also another, plainer meaning?
Like Stransom (François Truffaut combines *The Beast in
the Jungle* and *The Altar of the Dead* in his film *The Green
Room*), Marcher has also grown old with a friend and companion without having the brains or the nerve to see that
there is a durable love between them. *"She,"* says James,
"was what he had missed." Marcher is "fit indeed," says
James in his postscripted preface to *The Altar of the Dead*
in the complete edition of his works, "to mate with Stransom." The story shows us that Marcher is, in his own words,
"an ass." Like the luster of the Jamesian sentence, the
shock of Jamesian recognition comes only after the fact,

securing some shard of memory and desire, but leaving behind forever, as the price of knowing it, the possibility of ever having actually held it. Even the most painful cases offer the sole and ironic compensation of belated appreciation for the losses involved. "Belated," writes James, the "pain ... at least ... had something of the taste of life."

THE TURN
OF
THE SCREW

AND OTHER SHORT NOVELS

AN INTERNATIONAL
EPISODE

❧

Four years ago—in 1874—two young Englishmen had occasion to go to the United States. They crossed the ocean at midsummer, and, arriving in New York on the first day of August, were much struck with the fervid temperature of that city. Disembarking upon the wharf, they climbed into one of those huge high-hung coaches which convey passengers to the hotels, and with a great deal of bouncing and bumping, took their course through Broadway. The midsummer aspect of New York is not, perhaps, the most favorable one; still, it is not without its picturesque and even brilliant side. Nothing could well resemble less a typical English street than the interminable avenue, rich in incongruities, through which our two travelers advanced—looking out on each side of them at the comfortable animation of the sidewalks, the high-colored, heterogeneous architecture, the huge white marble façades glittering in the strong, crude light, and bedizened with gilded lettering, the multifarious awnings, banners, and streamers, the extraordinary number of omnibuses, horsecars, and other democratic vehicles, the vendors of cooling fluids, the white trousers and big straw hats of the policemen, the tripping gait of the modish young persons on the pavement, the general brightness, newness, juvenility, both of people and things. The young men had exchanged few observations; but in crossing Union Square, in front of the monument to Washington—in the very shadow, indeed, projected by the image of the *pater pat-*

riae—one of them remarked to the other, "It seems a rum-looking place."

"Ah, very odd, very odd," said the other, who was the clever man of the two.

"Pity it's so beastly hot," resumed the first speaker after a pause.

"You know we are in a low latitude," said his friend.

"I daresay," remarked the other.

"I wonder," said the second speaker presently, "if they can give one a bath?"

"I dare say not," rejoined the other.

"Oh, I say!" cried his comrade.

This animated discussion was checked by their arrival at the hotel, which had been recommended to them by an American gentleman whose acquaintance they made —with whom, indeed, they became very intimate—on the steamer, and who had proposed to accompany them to the inn and introduce them, in a friendly way, to the proprietor. This plan, however, had been defeated by their friend's finding that his "partner" was awaiting him on the wharf and that his commercial associate desired him instantly to come and give his attention to certain telegrams received from St. Louis. But the two Englishmen, with nothing but their national prestige and personal graces to recommend them, were very well received at the hotel, which had an air of capacious hospitality. They found that a bath was not unattainable, and were indeed struck with the facilities for prolonged and reiterated immersion with which their apartment was supplied. After bathing a good deal—more, indeed, than they had ever done before on a single occasion—they made their way into the dining room of the hotel, which was a spacious restaurant, with a fountain in the middle, a great many tall plants in ornamental tubs, and an array of French waiters. The first dinner on land, after a sea voyage, is, under any circumstances, a delightful occasion, and there was something particularly agreeable in the circumstances in which our young Englishmen found themselves. They were extremely good natured young men; they were more observant than they appeared; in a sort of inarticulate, accidentally dissimulative fashion, they were highly appreciative. This was, perhaps, especially the case with the elder, who was also, as I have said, the man of talent. They sat down at a little table, which was a very different affair from the great clattering seesaw in the saloon of the steamer. The wide doors and windows of the restaurant stood open, beneath large awnings, to a wide pavement, where there were other plants in tubs, and rows of spreading trees, and beyond which there was a large shady square, without any palings, and with marble-paved walks. And above the vivid verdure rose other façades of white marble and of pale chocolate-colored stone, squaring themselves against the deep blue sky. Here, outside, in the light and the shade and the heat, there was a great tinkling of the bells of innumerable street-cars, and a constant strolling and shuffling and rustling of many pedestrians, a large proportion of whom were young women in Pompadour-looking dresses. Within, the place was cool and vaguely lighted, with the plash of water, the odor of flowers, and the flitting of French waiters, as I have said, upon soundless carpets.

"It's rather like Paris, you know," said the younger of our two travelers.

"It's like Paris—only more so," his companion rejoined.

"I suppose it's the French waiters," said the first speaker. "Why don't they have French waiters in London?"

"Fancy a French waiter at a club," said his friend.

The young Englishman stared a little, as if he could not fancy it. "In Paris I'm very apt to dine at a place where there's an English waiter. Don't you know what's-his-name's, close to the thingumbob? They always set an English waiter at me. I suppose they think I can't speak French."

"Well, you can't." And the elder of the young Englishmen unfolded his napkin.

His companion took no notice whatever of this declaration. "I say," he resumed in a moment, "I suppose we must learn to speak American. I suppose we must take lessons."

"I can't understand them," said the clever man.

"What the deuce is *he* saying?" asked his comrade, appealing from the French waiter.

"He is recommending some soft-shell crabs," said the clever man.

And so, in desultory observation of the idiosyncrasies of the new society in which they found themselves, the young Englishmen proceeded to dine—going in largely, as the phrase is, for cooling draughts and dishes, of which their attendant offered them a very long list. After dinner they went out and slowly walked about the neighboring streets. The early dusk of waning summer was coming on, but the heat was still very great. The pavements were hot even to the stout boot soles of the British travelers, and the trees along the curbstone emitted strange exotic odors. The young men wandered through the adjoining square —that queer place without palings, and with marble walks arranged in black and white lozenges. There were a great many benches, crowded with shabby-looking people, and the travelers remarked, very justly, that it was not much like Belgrave Square. On one side was an enormous hotel, lifting up into the hot darkness an immense array of open, brightly lighted windows. At the base of this populous structure was an eternal jangle of horsecars, and all round it, in the upper dusk, was a sinister hum of mosquitoes. The ground floor of the hotel seemed to be a huge transparent cage, flinging a wide glare of gaslight into the street, of which it formed a sort of public adjunct, absorbing and emitting the passersby promiscuously. The young Englishmen went in with everyone else, from curiosity, and saw a couple of hundred men sitting on divans along a great marble-paved corridor, with their legs stretched out, together with several dozen more standing in a queue, as at the ticket office of a railway station, before a brilliantly illuminated counter of vast extent. These latter persons, who carried portmanteaus in their hands, had a dejected, exhausted look; their garments were not very fresh, and they seemed to be rendering some mysterious tribute to a magnificent young man with a waxed mustache, and a shirtfront adorned with diamond buttons, who every now and then dropped an absent glance over their multitudinous patience. They were American citizens doing homage to a hotel clerk.

"I'm glad he didn't tell us to go there," said one of our Englishmen, alluding to their friend on the steamer, who had told them so many things. They walked up the Fifth Avenue, where, for instance, he had told them that all the first families lived. But the first families were out of town, and our young travelers had only the satisfaction of seeing some of the second—or perhaps even the third—taking the evening air upon balconies and high flights of door-steps, in the streets which radiate from the more ornamental thoroughfare. They went a little way down one of these side streets, and they saw young ladies in white dresses—charming-looking persons—seated in graceful attitudes on the chocolate-colored steps. In one or two places these young ladies were conversing across the street with other young ladies seated in similar postures and costumes in front of the opposite houses, and in the warm night air their colloquial tones sounded strange in the ears of the young Englishmen. One of our friends, nevertheless—the younger one—intimated that he felt a disposition to interrupt a few of these soft familiarities; but his companion observed, pertinently enough, that he had better be careful. "We must not begin with making mistakes," said his companion.

"But he told us, you know—he told us," urged the young man, alluding again to the friend on the steamer.

"Never mind what he told us!" answered his comrade, who, if he had greater talents, was also apparently more of a moralist.

By bedtime—in their impatience to taste of a terrestrial couch again our seafarers went to bed early—it was still insufferably hot, and the buzz of the mosquitoes at the open windows might have passed for an audible crepitation of the temperature. "We can't stand this, you know," the young Englishmen said to each other; and they tossed about all night more boisterously than they had tossed upon the Atlantic billows. On the morrow, their first thought was that they would re-embark that day for England; and then it occurred to them that they might find an asylum nearer at hand. The cave of Aeolus became their ideal of comfort, and they wondered where the Americans went when they wished to cool off. They had not the least idea, and they determined to apply for information to Mr. J. L. Westgate. This was the name inscribed in a bold hand on the back of a letter carefully preserved in the pocketbook of our junior traveler. Beneath the address, in the lefthand corner of the envelope, were the words, "Introducing Lord Lambeth and Percy Beaumont, Esq." The letter had been given to the two Englishmen by a good friend of theirs in London, who had been in America two years previously, and had singled out Mr. J. L. Westgate from the many friends he had left there as the consignee, as it were, of his compatriots. "He is a capital fellow," the Englishman in London had said, "and he has got an awfully pretty wife. He's tremendously hospitable—he will do everything in the world for you; and as he knows everyone over there, it is quite needless I should give you any other introduction. He will make you see everyone; trust to him for putting you into circulation. He has got a tremendously pretty wife." It was natural that in the hour of tribulation Lord Lambeth and Mr. Percy Beaumont should have bethought themselves of a gentleman whose attractions had been thus vividly depicted; all the more so that he lived in the Fifth Avenue, and that the Fifth Avenue, as they had ascertained the night before, was contiguous to their hotel. "Ten to one he'll be out of town," said Percy Beaumont; "but we can at least find out where he has gone, and we can immediately start in pursuit. He can't possibly have gone to a hotter place, you know."

"Oh, there's only one hotter place," said Lord Lambeth, "and I hope he hasn't gone there."

They strolled along the shady side of the street to the number indicated upon the precious letter. The house presented an imposing chocolate-colored expanse, relieved by facings and window cornices of florid sculpture, and by a couple of dusty rose trees which clambered over the balconies and the portico. This last-mentioned feature was approached by a monumental flight of steps.

"Rather better than a London house," said Lord Lambeth, looking down from this altitude, after they had rung the bell.

"It depends upon what London house you mean," replied his companion. "You have a tremendous chance to get wet between the house door and your carriage."

"Well," said Lord Lambeth, glancing at the burning heavens, "I 'guess' it doesn't rain so much here!"

The door was opened by a long Negro in a white jacket, who grinned familiarly when Lord Lambeth asked for Mr. Westgate.

"He ain't at home, sah; he's downtown at his o'fice."

"Oh, at his office?" said the visitors. "And when will he be at home?"

"Well, sah, when he goes out dis way in de mo'ning, he ain't liable to come home all day."

This was discouraging; but the address of Mr. Westgate's office was freely imparted by the intelligent black and was taken down by Percy Beaumont in his pocketbook. The two gentlemen then returned, languidly, to their hotel, and sent for a hackney coach, and in this commodious vehicle they rolled comfortably downtown. They measured the whole length of Broadway again and found it a path of fire; and then, deflecting to the left, they were deposited by their conductor before a fresh, light, ornamental structure, ten stories high, in a street crowded with keen-faced, light-limbed young men, who were running about very quickly and stopping each other eagerly at corners and in doorways. Passing into this brilliant building, they were introduced by one of the keen-faced young men—he was a charming fellow, in wonderful cream-colored garments and a hat with a blue ribbon, who had evidently perceived them to be aliens and helpless—to a very snug hydraulic elevator, in which they took their place with many other persons, and which, shooting upward in its vertical socket, presently projected them into the seventh horizontal compartment of the edifice. Here, after brief delay, they found themselves face to face with the friend of their friend in London. His office was composed of several different rooms, and they waited very silently in one of them after they had sent in their letter and their cards. The letter was not one which it would take Mr. Westgate very long to read, but he came out to speak to them more instantly than they could have expected; he had evidently jumped up from his work. He was a tall, lean personage and was dressed all in fresh white linen; he had a thin, sharp, familiar face, with an expression that was at one and the same time sociable and businesslike, a quick, intelligent eye, and a large brown mustache, which concealed his mouth and made his chin, beneath it, look small. Lord Lambeth thought he looked tremendously clever.

"How do you do, Lord Lambeth—how do you do, sir?" he said, holding the open letter in his hand. "I'm very glad to see you; I hope you're very well. You had better come in here; I think it's cooler," and he led the way into another room, where there were law books and papers, and windows wide open beneath striped awning. Just opposite one of the windows, on a line with his eyes, Lord Lambeth observed the weathervane of a church steeple. The uproar of the street sounded infinitely far below, and Lord Lambeth felt very high in the air. "I say it's cooler," pursued their host, "but everything is relative. How do you stand the heat?"

"I can't say we like it," said Lord Lambeth; "but Beaumont likes it better than I."

"Well, it won't last," Mr. Westgate very cheerfully declared; "nothing unpleasant lasts over here. It was very hot when Captain Littledale was here; he did nothing but drink sherry cobblers. He expressed some doubt in his letter whether I will remember him—as if I didn't remember making six sherry cobblers for him one day in about twenty minutes. I hope you left him well, two years having elapsed since then."

"Oh, yes, he's all right," said Lord Lambeth.

"I am always very glad to see your countrymen," Mr. Westgate pursued. "I thought it would be time some of you should be coming along. A friend of mine was saying to me only a day or two ago, 'It's time for the watermelons and the Englishmen.'"

"The Englishmen and the watermelons just now are about the same thing," Percy Beaumont observed, wiping his dripping forehead.

"An, well, we'll put you on ice, as we do the melons. You must go down to Newport."

"We'll go anywhere," said Lord Lambeth.

"Yes, you want to go to Newport; that's what you want to do," Mr. Westgate affirmed. "But let's see—when did you get here?"

"Only yesterday," said Percy Beaumont.

"Ah, yes, by the Russia. Where are you staying?"

"At the Hanover, I think they call it."

"Pretty comfortable?" inquired Mr. Westgate.

"It seems a capital place, but I can't say we like the gnats," said Lord Lambeth.

Mr. Westgate stared and laughed. "Oh, no, of course you don't like the gnats. We shall expect you to like a good many things over here, but we shan't insist upon your liking the gnats; though certainly you'll admit that, as gnats, they are fine, eh? But you oughtn't to remain in the city."

"So we think," said Lord Lambeth. "If you would kindly suggest something——"

"Suggest something, my dear sir?" and Mr. Westgate looked at him, narrowing his eyelids. "Open your mouth and shut your eyes! Leave it to me, and I'll put you through. It's a matter of national pride with me that all Englishmen should have a good time; and as I have had considerable practice, I have learned to minister to their wants. I find they generally want the right thing. So just please to consider yourselves my property; and if anyone should try to appropriate you, please to say, 'Hands off; too late for the market.' But let's see," continued the American, in his slow, humorous voice, with a distinctness of utterance which appeared to his visitors to be part of a humorous intention—a strangely leisurely, speculative voice for a man evidently so busy and, as they felt, so professional—"let's see; are you going to make something of a stay, Lord Lambeth?"

"Oh, dear, no," said the young Englishman; "my cousin was coming over on some business, so I just came across, at an hour's notice, for the lark."

"Is it your first visit to the United States?"

"Oh, dear, yes."

"I was obliged to come on some business," said Percy Beaumont, "and I brought Lambeth along."

"And *you* have been here before, sir?"

"Never—never."

"I thought, from your referring to business___ " said Mr. Westgate.

"Oh, you see I'm by way of being a barrister," Percy Beaumont answered. "I know some people that think of bringing a suit against one of your railways, and they asked me to come over and take measures accordingly."

Mr. Westgate gave one of his slow, keen looks again. "What's your railroad?" he asked.

"The Tennessee Central."

The American tilted back his chair a little and poised it an instant. "Well, I'm sorry you want to attack one of our institutions," he said, smiling. "But I guess you had better enjoy yourself *first!*"

"I'm certainly rather afraid I can't work in this weather," the young barrister confessed.

"Leave that to the natives," said Mr. Westgate. "Leave the Tennessee Central to me, Mr. Beaumont. Some day we'll talk it over, and I guess I can make it square. But I didn't know you Englishmen ever did any work, in the upper classes."

"Oh, we do a lot of work; don't we, Lambeth?" asked Percy Beaumont.

"I must certainly be at home by the 19th of September," said the younger Englishman, irrelevantly but gently.

"For the shooting, eh? or is it the hunting, or the fishing?" inquired his entertainer.

"Oh, I must be in Scotland," said Lord Lambeth, blushing a little.

"Well, then," rejoined Mr. Westgate, "you had better amuse yourself first, also. You must go down and see Mrs. Westgate."

"We should be so happy, if you would kindly tell us the train," said Percy Beaumont.

"It isn't a train—it's a boat."

"Oh, I see. And what is the name of—a—the—a—town?"

"It isn't a town," said Mr. Westgate, laughing. "It's a —well, what shall I call it? It's a watering place. In short, it's Newport. You'll see what it is. It's cool; that's the principal thing. You will greatly oblige me by going down there and putting yourself into the hands of Mrs. Westgate. It isn't perhaps for me to say it, but you couldn't be in better hands. Also in those of her sister, who is staying with her. She is very fond of Englishmen. She thinks there is nothing like them."

"Mrs. Westgate or—a—her sister?" asked Percy Beaumont modestly, yet in the tone of an inquiring traveler.

"Oh, I mean my wife," said Mr. Westgate. "I don't suppose my sister-in-law knows much about them. She has always led a very quiet life; she has lived in Boston."

Percy Beaumont listened with interest. "That, I believe," he said, "is the most—a—intellectual town?"

"I believe it is very intellectual. I don't go there much," responded his host.

"I say, we ought to go there," said Lord Lambeth to his companion.

"Oh, Lord Lambeth, wait till the great heat is over," Mr. Westgate interposed. "Boston in this weather would be very trying; it's not the temperature for intellectual exertion. At Boston, you know, you have to pass an examination at the city limits; and when you come away they give you a kind of degree."

Lord Lambeth stared, blushing a little; and Percy Beaumont stared a little also—but only with his fine natural complexion—glancing aside after a moment to see that his companion was not looking too credulous, for he had heard a great deal of American humor. "I daresay it is very jolly," said the younger gentleman.

"I daresay it is," said Mr. Westgate. "Only I must impress upon you that at present—tomorrow morning, at an early hour—you will be expected at Newport. We have a house there; half the people in New York go there for the summer. I am not sure that at this very moment my wife can take you in; she has got a lot of people staying with her; I don't know who they all are; only she may have no room. But you can begin with the hotel, and meanwhile you can live at my house. In that way—simply sleeping at the hotel—you will find it tolerable. For the rest, you must make yourself at home at my place. You mustn't be shy, you know; if you are only here for a month that will be a great waste of time. Mrs. Westgate won't neglect you, and you had better not try to resist her. I know something about that. I expect you'll find some pretty girls on the premises. I shall write to my wife by this afternoon's mail, and tomorrow morning she and Miss Alden will look out for you. Just walk right in and make yourself comfortable. Your steamer leaves from this part of the city, and I will immediately send out and get you a cabin. Then, at half past four o'clock, just call for me here, and I will go with you and put you on board. It's a big boat; you might get lost. A few days hence, at the end of the week, I will come down to Newport and see how you are getting on."

The two young Englishmen inaugurated the policy of not resisting Mrs. Westgate by submitting, with great docility and thankfulness, to her husband. He was evidently a very good fellow, and he made an impression upon his visitors; his hospitality seemed to recommend itself consciously—with a friendly wink, as it were—as if it hinted, judicially, that you could not possibly make a better bargain. Lord Lambeth and his cousin left their entertainer to his labors and returned to their hotel, where they spent three or four hours in their respective shower baths. Percy Beaumont had suggested that they ought to see something of the town; but "Oh, damn the town!" his noble kinsman had rejoined. They returned to Mr. Westgate's office in a carriage, with their luggage, very punctually; but it must be reluctantly recorded that, this time, he kept them waiting so long that they felt themselves missing the steamer, and were deterred only by an amiable modesty from dispensing with his attendance and starting on a hasty scramble to the wharf. But when at last he appeared, and the carriage plunged into the purlieus of Broadway, they jolted and jostled to such good purpose that they reached the huge white vessel while the bell for departure was still ringing and the absorption of passengers still active. It was indeed, as Mr. Westgate had said, a big boat, and his leadership in the innumerable and interminable corridors and cabins, with which he seemed perfectly acquainted, and of which anyone and everyone appeared to have the entree, was very grateful to the slightly bewildered voyagers. He showed them their stateroom—a spacious apartment, embellished with gas lamps, mirrors *en pied,* and sculptured furniture—and then, long after they had been intimately convinced that the steamer was in motion and launched upon the unknown stream that they were about to navigate, he bade them a sociable farewell.

"Well, goodbye, Lord Lambeth," he said; "goodbye,

Mr. Percy Beaumont. I hope you'll have a good time. Just let them do what they want with you. I'll come down by-and-by and look after you."

The young Englishmen emerged from their cabin and amused themselves with wandering about the immense labyrinthine steamer, which struck them as an extraordinary mixture of a ship and a hotel. It was densely crowded with passengers, the larger number of whom appeared to be ladies and very young children; and in the big saloons, ornamented in white and gold, which followed each other in surprising succession, beneath the swinging gaslight, and among the small side passages where the Negro domestics of both sexes assembled with an air of philosophic leisure, everyone was moving to and fro and exchanging loud and familiar observations. Eventually, at the instance of a discriminating black, our young men went and had some "supper" in a wonderful place arranged like a theater, where, in a gilded gallery, upon which little boxes appeared to open, a large orchestra was playing operatic selections, and, below, people were handing about bills of fare, as if they had been programs. All this was sufficiently curious; but the agreeable thing, later, was to sit out on one of the great white decks of the steamer, in the warm breezy darkness, and, in the vague starlight, to make out the line of low, mysterious coast. The young Englishmen tried American cigars—those of Mr. Westgate—and talked together as they usually talked, with many odd silences, lapses of logic, and incongruities of transition; like people who have grown old together and learned to supply each other's missing phrases; or, more especially, like people thoroughly conscious of a common point of view, so that a style of conversation superficially lacking in finish might suffice for reference to a fund of associations in the light of which everything was all right.

"We really seem to be going out to sea," Percy Beaumont observed. "Upon my word, we are going back to England. He has shipped us off again. I call that 'real mean.'"

"I suppose it's all right," said Lord Lambeth. "I want to see those pretty girls at Newport. You know, he told us the place was an island; and aren't all islands in the sea?"

"Well," resumed the elder traveler after a while, "if his house is as good as his cigars, we shall do very well."

"He seems a very good fellow," said Lord Lambeth, as if this idea had just occurred to him.

"I say, we had better remain at the inn," rejoined his companion presently. "I don't think I like the way he spoke of his house. I don't like stopping in the house with such a tremendous lot of women."

"Oh, I don't mind," said Lord Lambeth. And then they smoked a while in silence. "Fancy his thinking we do no work in England!" the young man resumed.

"I daresay he didn't really think so," said Percy Beaumont.

"Well, I guess they don't know much about England over here!" declared Lord Lambeth humorously. And then there was another long pause. "He was devilish civil," observed the young nobleman.

"Nothing, certainly, could have been more civil," rejoined his companion.

"Littledale said his wife was great fun," said Lord Lambeth.

"Whose wife—Littledale's?"

"This American's—Mrs. Westgate. What's his name? J. L."

Beaumont was silent a moment. "What was fun to Littledale," he said at last, rather sententiously, "may be death to us."

"What do you mean by that?" asked his kinsman. "I am as good a man as Littledale."

"My dear boy, I hope you won't begin to flirt," said Percy Beaumont.

"I don't care. I daresay I shan't begin."

"With a married woman, if she's bent upon it, it's all very well," Beaumont expounded. "But our friend mentioned a young lady—a sister, a sister-in-law. For God's sake, don't get entangled with her!"

"How do you mean entangled?"

"Depend upon it she will try to hook you."

"Oh, bother!" said Lord Lambeth.

"American girls are very clever," urged his companion. "So much the better," the young man declared.

"I fancy they are always up to some game of that sort," Beaumont continued.

"They can't be worse than they are in England," said Lord Lambeth judicially.

"Ah, but in England," replied Beaumont, "you have got your natural protectors. You have got your mother and sisters."

"My mother and sisters——"began the young nobleman with a certain energy. But he stopped in time, puffing at his cigar.

"Your mother spoke to me about it, with tears in her eyes," said Percy Beaumont. "She said she felt very nervous. I promised to keep you out of mischief."

"You had better take care of yourself," said the object of maternal and ducal solicitude.

"Ah," rejoined the young barrister, "I haven't the expectation of a hundred thousand a year, not to mention other attractions."

"Well," said Lord Lambeth, "don't cry out before you're hurt!"

It was certainly very much cooler at Newport, where our travelers found themselves assigned to a couple of diminutive bedrooms in a faraway angle of an immense hotel. They had gone ashore in the early summer twilight and had very promptly put themselves to bed; thanks to which circumstance and to their having, during the previous hours, in their commodious cabin, slept the sleep of youth and health, they began to feel, toward eleven o'clock, very alert and inquisitive. They looked out of their windows across a row of small green fields, bordered with low stone walls of rude construction, and saw a deep blue ocean lying beneath a deep blue sky, and flecked now and then with scintillating patches of foam. A strong, fresh breeze came in through the curtainless casements and prompted our young men to observe, generally, that it didn't seem half a bad climate. They made other observations after they had emerged from their rooms in pursuit of breakfast—a meal of which they partook in a huge bare hall, where a hundred Negroes, in white jackets, were shuffling about upon an uncarpeted floor; where the flies were superabundant, and the tables and dishes covered over with a strange, voluminous in-

tegument of coarse blue gauze; and where several little
boys and girls, who had risen late, were seated in fastidious solitude at the morning repast. These young persons had not the morning paper before them, but they
were engaged in languid perusal of the bill of fare.

This latter document was a great puzzle to our friends,
who, on reflecting that its bewildering categories had relation to breakfast alone, had an uneasy prevision of an
encyclopedic dinner list. They found a great deal of entertainment at the hotel, an enormous wooden structure,
for the erection of which it seemed to them that the
virgin forests of the West must have been terribly de-
flowered. It was perforated from end to end with immense bare corridors, through which a strong draught
was blowing—bearing along wonderful figures of ladies
in white morning dresses and clouds of Valenciennes
lace, who seemed to float down the long vistas with
expanded furbelows, like angels spreading their wings. In
front was a gigantic veranda, upon which an army might
have encamped—a vast wooden terrace, with a roof as
lofty as the nave of a cathedral. Here our young Englishmen enjoyed, as they supposed, a glimpse of American society, which was distributed over the measureless
expanse in a variety of sedentary attitudes, and appeared
to consist largely of pretty young girls, dressed as if for
a *fête champêtre,* swaying to and fro in rocking chairs,
fanning themselves with large straw fans, and enjoying an enviable exemption from social cares. Lord Lambeth had a theory, which it might be interesting to trace
to its origin, that it would be not only agreeable, but
easily possible, to enter into relations with one of these
young ladies; and his companion (as he had done a
couple of days before) found occasion to check the
young nobleman's colloquial impulses.

"You had better take care," said Percy Beaumont, "or
you will have an offended father or brother pulling out
a bowie knife."

"I assure you it is all right," Lord Lambeth replied.
"You know the Americans come to these big hotels to
make acquaintances."

"I know nothing about it, and neither do you," said
his kinsman, who, like a clever man, had begun to per-

ceive that the observation of American society demanded a readjustment of one's standard.

"Hang it, then, let's find out!" cried Lord Lambeth with
some impatience. "You know I don't want to miss anything."

"We will find out," said Percy Beaumont very reason-
ably. "We will go and see Mrs. Westgate and make all
proper inquiries."

And so the two inquiring Englishmen, who had this
lady's address inscribed in her husband's hand upon a
card, descended from the veranda of the big hotel and
took their way, according to direction, along a large
straight road, past a series of fresh-looking villas em-
bosomed in shrubs and flowers and enclosed in an ingenious variety of wooden palings. The morning was
brilliant and cool, the villas were smart and snug, and
the walk of the young travelers was very entertaining.
Everything looked as if it had received a coat of fresh
paint the day before—the red roofs, the green shutters,
the clean, bright browns and buffs of the housefronts.
The flower beds on the little lawns seemed to sparkle
in the radiant air, and the gravel in the short carriage
sweeps to flash and twinkle. Along the road came a hundred little basket phaetons, in which, almost always, a
couple of ladies were sitting—ladies in white dresses and
long white gloves, holding the reins and looking at the
two Englishmen, whose nationality was not elusive,
through thick blue veils tied tightly about their faces as if
to guard their complexions. At last the young men came
within sight of the sea again, and then, having interro-
gated a gardener over the paling of a villa, they turned
into an open gate. Here they found themselves face to
face with the ocean and with a very picturesque structure, resembling a magnified chalet, which was perched
upon a green embankment just above it. The house had
a veranda of extraordinary width all around it and a
great many doors and windows standing open to the
veranda. These various apertures had, in common, such
an accessible, hospitable air, such a breezy flutter within
of light curtains, such expansive thresholds and reassuring interiors, that our friends hardly knew which was the
regular entrance, and, after hesitating a moment, pre-

sented themselves at one of the windows. The room within was dark, but in a moment a graceful figure vaguely shaped itself in the rich-looking gloom, and a lady came to meet them. Then they saw that she had been seated at a table writing, and that she had heard them and had got up. She stepped out into the light; she wore a frank, charming smile, with which she held out her hand to Percy Beaumont.

"Oh, you must be Lord Lambeth and Mr. Beaumont," she said. "I have heard from my husband that you would come. I am extremely glad to see you." And she shook hands with each of her visitors. Her visitors were a little shy, but they had very good manners; they responded with smiles and exclamations, and they apologized for not knowing the front door. The lady rejoined, with vivacity, that when she wanted to see people very much she did not insist upon those distinctions, and that Mr. Westgate had written to her of his English friends in terms that made her really anxious. "He said you were so terribly prostrated," said Mrs. Westgate.

"Oh, you mean by the heat?" replied Percy Beaumont. "We were rather knocked up, but we feel wonderfully better. We had such a jolly—a—voyage down here. It's so very good of you to mind."

"Yes, it's so very kind of you," murmured Lord Lambeth.

Mrs. Westgate stood smiling; she was extremely pretty. "Well, I did mind," she said; "and I thought of sending for you this morning to the Ocean House. I am very glad you are better, and I am charmed you have arrived. You must come round to the other side of the piazza." And she led the way, with a light, smooth step, looking back at the young men and smiling.

The other side of the piazza was, as Lord Lambeth presently remarked, a very jolly place. It was of the most liberal proportions, and with its awnings, its fanciful chairs, its cushions and rugs, its view of the ocean, close at hand, tumbling along the base of the low cliffs whose level tops intervened in lawnlike smoothness, it formed a charming complement to the drawing room. As such it was in course of use at the present moment; it was occupied by a social circle. There were several ladies and two or three gentlemen, to whom Mrs. Westgate proceeded to introduce the distinguished strangers. She mentioned a great many names very freely and distinctly; the young Englishmen, shuffling about and bowing, were rather bewildered. But at last they were provided with chairs—low, wicker chairs, gilded, and tied with a great many ribbons—and one of the ladies (a very young person, with a little snub nose and several dimples) offered Percy Beaumont a fan. The fan was also adorned with pink love knots; but Percy Beaumont declined it, although he was very hot. Presently, however, it became cooler; the breeze from the sea was delicious, the view was charming, and the people sitting there looked exceedingly fresh and comfortable. Several of the ladies seemed to be young girls, and the gentlemen were slim, fair youths, such as our friends had seen the day before in New York. The ladies were working upon bands of tapestry, and one of the young men had an open book in his lap. Beaumont afterward learned from one of the ladies that this young man had been reading aloud, that he was from Boston and was very fond of reading aloud. Beaumont said it was a great pity that they had interrupted him; he should like so much (from all he had heard) to hear a Bostonian read. Couldn't the young man be induced to go on?

"Oh no," said his informant very freely; "he wouldn't be able to get the young ladies to attend to him now."

There was something very friendly, Beaumont perceived, in the attitude of the company; they looked at the young Englishmen with an air of animated sympathy and interest; they smiled, brightly and unanimously, at everything either of the visitors said. Lord Lambeth and his companion felt that they were being made very welcome. Mrs. Westgate seated herself between them, and, talking a great deal to each, they had occasion to observe that she was as pretty as their friend Littledale had promised. She was thirty years old, with the eyes and the smile of a girl of seventeen, and she was extremely light and graceful, elegant, exquisite. Mrs. Westgate was extremely spontaneous. She was very frank and demonstrative and appeared always—while she looked at you delightedly with her beautiful young eyes—to be making sudden confessions and concessions, after momentary hesitations.

"We shall expect to see a great deal of you," she said to Lord Lambeth with a kind of joyous earnestness. "We are very fond of Englishmen here; that is, there are a great many we have been fond of. After a day or two you must come and stay with us; we hope you will stay a long time. Newport's a very nice place when you come really to know it, when you know plenty of people. Of course you and Mr. Beaumont will have no difficulty about that. Englishmen are very well received here; there are almost always two or three of them about. I think they always like it, and I must say I should think they would. They receive ever so much attention. I must say I think they sometimes get spoiled; but I am sure you and Mr. Beaumont are proof against that. My husband tells me you are a friend of Captain Littledale; he was such a charming man. He made himself most agreeable here, and I am sure I wonder he didn't stay. It couldn't have been pleasanter for him in his own country, though, I suppose, it is very pleasant in England, for English people. I don't know myself; I have been there very little. I have been a great deal abroad, but I am always on the Continent. I must say I'm extremely fond of Paris; you know we Americans always are; we go there when we die. Did you ever hear that before? That was said by a great wit, I mean the good Americans; but we are all good; you'll see that for yourself. All I know of England is London, and all I know of London is that place on that little corner, you know, where you buy jackets—jackets with that coarse braid and those big buttons. They make very good jackets in London, I will do you the justice to say that. And some people like the hats; but about the hats I was always a heretic; I always got my hats in Paris. You can't wear an English hat—at least I never could—unless you dress your hair *á l'Anglaise*; and I must say that is a talent I have never possessed. In Paris they will make things to suit your peculiarities; but in England I think you like much more to have—how shall I say it?—one thing for everybody. I mean as regards dress. I don't know about other things; but I have always supposed that in other things everything was different. I mean according to the people—according to the classes, and all that. I am afraid you will think that I don't take a very favorable view; but you know you can't take a very favorable view in Dover Street in the month of November. That has always been my fate. Do you know Jones's Hotel in Dover Street? That's all I know of England. Of course everyone admits that the English hotels are your weak point. There was always the most frightful fog; I couldn't see to try my things on. When I got over to America—into the light—I usually found they were twice too big. The next time I mean to go in the season; I think I shall go next year. I want very much to take my sister; she has never been to England. I don't know whether you know what I mean by saying that the Englishmen who come here sometimes get spoiled. I mean that they take things as a matter of course—things that are done for them. Now, naturally, they are only a matter of course when the Englishmen are very nice. But, of course, they are almost always very nice. Of course this isn't nearly such an interesting country as England; there are not nearly so many things to see, and we haven't your country life. I have never seen anything of your country life; when I am in Europe I am always on the Continent. But I have heard a great deal about it; I know that when you are among yourselves in the country you have the most beautiful time. Of course we have nothing of that sort, we have nothing on that scale. I don't apologize, Lord Lambeth; some Americans are always apologizing; you must have noticed that. We have the reputation of always boasting and bragging and waving the American flag; but I must say that what strikes me is that we are perpetually making excuses and trying to smooth things over. The American flag has quite gone out of fashion; it's very carefully folded up, like an old tablecloth. Why should we apologize? The English never apologize—do they? No; I must say I never apologize. You must take us as we come—with all our imperfections on our heads. Of course we haven't your country life, and your old ruins, and your great estates, and your leisure class, and all that. But if we haven't, I should think you might find it a pleasant change—I think any country is pleasant where they have pleasant manners. Captain Littledale told me he had never seen such pleasant manners as at Newport, and he had been a great deal in European society. Hadn't he been in the diplomatic service? He told me the dream of his life was to get appointed to a diplomatic post in Washington. But he doesn't seem to have succeeded. I suppose that in England promotion—and all that sort of thing—is fearfully slow. With us, you know, it's a great deal too fast. You see, I admit our drawbacks. But I must confess I think Newport is an ideal place. I don't know anything like it anywhere. Captain Littledale told me he didn't know anything like it anywhere. It's entirely different from most watering places; it's a most charming life. I must say I think that when one goes to a foreign country one ought to enjoy the differences. Of course there are differences, otherwise what did one come abroad for? Look for your pleasure in the differences, Lord Lambeth; that's the way to do it; and then I am sure you will find American society—at least Newport society—most charming and most interesting. I wish very much my husband were here; but he's dreadfully confined to New York. I suppose you think that is very strange—for a gentleman. But you see we haven't any leisure class."

Mrs. Westgate's discourse, delivered in a soft, sweet voice, flowed on like a miniature torrent, and was interrupted by a hundred little smiles, glances, and gestures, which might have figured the irregularities and obstructions of such a stream. Lord Lambeth listened to her with, it must be confessed, a rather ineffectual attention, although he indulged in a good many little murmurs and ejaculations of assent and deprecation. He had no great faculty for apprehending generalizations. There were some three or four indeed which, in the play of his own intelligence, he had originated, and which had seemed convenient at the moment; but at the present time he could hardly have been said to follow Mrs. Westgate as she darted gracefully about in the sea of speculation. Fortunately she asked for no especial rejoinder, for she looked about at the rest of the company as well, and smiled at Percy Beaumont, on the other side of her, as if he too must understand her and agree with her. He was rather more successful than his companion; for besides being, as we know, cleverer, his attention was not vaguely distracted by close vicinity to a remarkably interesting young girl, with dark hair and blue eyes. This was the case with Lord Lambeth, to whom it occurred after a while that the young girl with blue eyes and dark hair was the pretty sister of whom Mrs. Westgate had spoken. She presently turned to him with a remark which established her identity.

"It's a great pity you couldn't have brought my brother-in-law with you. It's a great shame he should be in New York in these days."

"Oh, yes; it's so very hot," said Lord Lambeth.

"It must be dreadful," said the young girl.

"I daresay he is very busy," Lord Lambeth observed.

"The gentlemen in America work too much," the young girl went on.

"Oh, do they? I dare say they like it," said her interlocutor.

"I don't like it. One never sees them."

"Don't you, really?" asked Lord Lambeth. "I shouldn't have fancied that."

"Have you come to study American manners?" asked the young girl.

"Oh, I don't know. I just came over for a lark. I haven't got long." Here there was a pause, and Lord Lambeth began again. "But Mr. Westgate will come down here, will not he?"

"I certainly hope he will. He must help to entertain you and Mr. Beaumont."

Lord Lambeth looked at her a little with his handsome brown eyes. "Do you suppose he would have come down with us if we had urged him?"

Mr. Westgate's sister-in-law was silent a moment, and then, "I daresay he would," she answered.

"Really!" said the young Englishman. "He was immensely civil to Beaumont and me," he added.

"He is a dear good fellow," the young lady rejoined, "and he is a perfect husband. But all Americans are that," she continued, smiling.

"Really!" Lord Lambeth exclaimed again and wondered whether all American ladies had such a passion for generalizing as these two.

He sat there a good while: there was a great deal of talk; it was all very friendly and lively and jolly. Everyone present, sooner or later, said something to him, and seemed to make a particular point of addressing him by name. Two or three other persons came in, and there was a shifting of seats and changing of places; the gentlemen all entered into intimate conversation with the two Englishmen, made them urgent offers of hospitality, and hoped they might frequently be of service to them. They were afraid Lord Lambeth and Mr. Beaumont were not very comfortable at their hotel; that it was not, as one of them said, "so private as those dear little English inns of yours." This last gentleman went on to say that unfortunately, as yet, perhaps, privacy was not quite so easily obtained in America as might be desired; still, he continued, you could generally get it by paying for it; in fact, you could get everything in America nowadays by paying for it. American life was certainly growing a great deal more private; it was growing very much like England. Everything at Newport, for instance, was thoroughly private; Lord Lambeth would probably be struck with that. It was also represented to the strangers that it mattered very little whether their hotel was agreeable, as everyone would want them to make visits; they would stay with other people, and, in any case, they would be a great deal at Mrs. Westgate's. They would find that very charming; it was the pleasantest house in Newport. It was a pity Mr. Westgate was always away; he was a man of the highest ability—very acute, very acute. He worked like a horse, and he left his wife—well, to do about as she liked. He liked her to enjoy herself, and she seemed to know how. She was extremely brilliant and a splendid talker. Some people preferred her sister; but Miss Alden was very different; she was in a different style altogether. Some people even thought her prettier, and, certainly, she was not so sharp. She was more in the Boston style; she had lived a great deal in Boston, and she was very highly educated. Boston girls, it was propounded, were more like English young ladies.

Lord Lambeth had presently a chance to test the truth of this proposition, for on the company rising in compliance with a suggestion from their hostess that they should walk down to the rocks and look at the sea, the young Englishman again found himself, as they strolled across the grass, in proximity to Mrs. Westgate's sister. Though she was but a girl of twenty, she appeared to feel the obligation to exert an active hospitality; and this was, perhaps, the more to be noticed as she seemed by nature a reserved and retiring person, and had little of her sister's fraternizing quality. She was perhaps rather too thin, and she was a little pale; but as she moved slowly over the grass, with her arms hanging at her sides, looking gravely for a moment at the sea and then brightly, for all her gravity, at him, Lord Lambeth thought her at least as pretty as Mrs. Westgate, and reflected that if this was the Boston style the Boston style was very charming. He thought she looked very clever; he could imagine that she was highly educated; but at the same time she seemed gentle and graceful. For all her cleverness, however, he felt that she had to think a little what to say; she didn't say the first thing that came into her head; he had come from a different part of the world and from a different society, and she was trying to adapt her conversation. The others were scattering themselves near the rocks; Mrs. Westgate had charge of Percy Beaumont.

"Very jolly place, isn't it?" said Lord Lambeth. "It's a very jolly place to sit."

"Very charming," said the young girl. "I often sit here; there are all kinds of cozy corners—as if they had been made on purpose."

"Ah! I suppose you have had some of them made," said the young man.

Miss Alden looked at him a moment. "Oh no, we have had nothing made. It's pure nature."

"I should think you would have a few little benches—rustic seats and that sort of thing. It might be so jolly to sit here, you know," Lord Lambeth went on.

"I am afraid we haven't so many of those things as you," said the young girl thoughtfully.

"I daresay you go in for pure nature, as you were saying. Nature over here must be so grand, you know." And Lord Lambeth looked about him.

The little coast line hereabouts was very pretty, but it was not at all grand, and Miss Alden appeared to rise to

Henry James

a perception of this fact. "I am afraid it seems to you very rough," she said. "It's not like the coast scenery in Kingsley's novels."

"Ah, the novels always overdo it, you know," Lord Lambeth rejoined. "You must not go by the novels."

They were wandering about a little on the rocks, and they stopped and looked down into a narrow chasm where the rising tide made a curious bellowing sound. It was loud enough to prevent their hearing each other, and they stood there for some moments in silence. The young girl looked at her companion, observing him attentively, but covertly, as women, even when very young, know how to do. Lord Lambeth repaid observation; tall, straight, and strong, he was handsome as certain young Englishmen, and certain young Englishmen almost alone, are handsome; with a perfect finish of feature and a look of intellectual repose and gentle good temper which seemed somehow to be consequent upon his well-cut nose and chin. And to speak of Lord Lambeth's expression of intellectual repose is not simply a civil way of saying that he looked stupid. He was evidently not a young man of an irritable imagination; he was not, as he would himself have said, tremendously clever; but though there was a kind of appealing dullness in his eye, he looked thoroughly reasonable and competent, and his appearance proclaimed that to be a nobleman, an athlete, and an excellent fellow was a sufficiently brilliant combination of qualities. The young girl beside him, it may be attested without further delay, thought him the handsomest young man she had ever seen; and Bessie Alden's imagination, unlike that of her companion, was irritable. He, however, was also making up his mind that she was uncommonly pretty.

"I daresay it's very gay here, that you have lots of balls and parties," he said; for, if he was not tremendously clever, he rather prided himself on having, with women, a sufficiency of conversation.

"Oh, yes, there is a great deal going on," Bessie Alden replied. "There are not so many balls, but there are a good many other things. You will see for yourself; we live rather in the midst of it."

"It's very kind of you to say that. But I thought you Americans were always dancing."

"I suppose we dance a good deal; but I have never seen much of it. We don't do it much, at any rate, in summer. And I am sure," said Bessie Alden, "that we don't have so many balls as you have in England."

"Really!" exclaimed Lord Lambeth. "Ah, in England it all depends, you know."

"You will not think much of our gaieties," said the young girl, looking at him with a little mixture of inter-rogation and decision which was peculiar to her. The interrogation seemed earnest and the decision seemed arch; but the mixture, at any rate, was charming. "Those things, with us, are much less splendid than in England."

"I fancy you don't mean that," said Lord Lambeth, laughing.

"I assure you I mean everything I say," the young girl declared. "Certainly, from what I have read about English society, it is very different."

"Ah well, you know," said her companion, "those things are often described by fellows who know nothing about them. You mustn't mind what you read."

"Oh, I *shall* mind what I read!" Bessie Alden rejoined. "When I read Thackeray and George Eliot, how can I help minding them?"

"Ah well, Thackeray, and George Eliot," said the young nobleman; "I haven't read much of them."

"Don't you suppose they know about society?" asked Bessie Alden.

"Oh, I daresay they know; they were so very clever. But these fashionable novels," said Lord Lambeth, "they are awful rot, you know."

His companion looked at him a moment with her dark blue eyes, and then she looked down in the chasm where the water was tumbling about. "Do you mean Mrs. Gore, for instance?" she said presently, raising her eyes.

"I am afraid I haven't read that, either," was the young man's rejoinder, laughing a little and blushing. "I am afraid you'll think I am not very intellectual."

"Reading Mrs. Gore is no proof of intellect. But I like

reading everything about English life—even poor books. I am so curious about it."

"Aren't ladies always curious?" asked the young man jestingly.

But Bessie Alden appeared to desire to answer his question seriously. "I don't think so—I don't think we are enough so—that we care about many things. So it's all the more of a compliment," she added, "that I should want to know so much about England."

The logic here seemed a little close; but Lord Lambeth, made conscious of a compliment, found his natural modesty just at hand. "I am sure you know a great deal more than I do."

"I really think I know a great deal—for a person who has never been there."

"Have you really never been there?" cried Lord Lambeth. "Fancy!"

"Never—except in imagination," said the young girl.

"Fancy!" repeated her companion. "But I daresay you'll go soon, won't you?"

"It's the dream of my life!" declared Bessie Alden, smiling.

"But your sister seems to know a tremendous lot about London," Lord Lambeth went on.

The young girl was silent a moment. "My sister and I are two very different persons," she presently said. "She has been a great deal in Europe. She has been in England several times. She has known a great many English people."

"But you must have known some, too," said Lord Lambeth.

"I don't think that I have ever spoken to one before. You are the first Englishman that—to my knowledge—I have ever talked with."

Bessie Alden made this statement with a certain gravity —almost, as it seemed to Lord Lambeth, an impressiveness. Attempts at impressiveness always made him feel awkward, and he now began to laugh and swing his stick. "Ah, you would have been sure to know!" he said. And then he added, after an instant, "I'm sorry I am not a better specimen."

The young girl looked away; but she smiled, laying

aside her impressiveness. "You must remember that you are only a beginning," she said. Then she retraced her steps, leading the way back to the lawn, where they saw Mrs. Westgate come toward them with Percy Beaumont still at her side. "Perhaps I shall go to England next year," Miss Alden continued; "I want to, immensely. My sister is going to Europe, and she has asked me to go with her. If we go, I shall make her stay as long as possible in London.

"Ah, you must come in July," said Lord Lambeth. "That's the time when there is most going on."

"I don't think I can wait till July," the young girl rejoined. "By the first of May I shall be very impatient." They had gone further, and Mrs. Westgate and her companion were near them. "Kitty," said Miss Alden, "I have given out that we are going to London next May. So please to conduct yourself accordingly."

Percy Beaumont wore a somewhat animated—even a slightly irritated—air. He was by no means so handsome a man as his cousin, although in his cousin's absence he might have passed for a striking specimen of the tall, muscular, fair-bearded, clear-eyed Englishman. Just now Beaumont's clear eyes, which were small and of a pale gray color, had a rather troubled light, and, after glancing at Bessie Alden while she spoke, he rested them upon his kinsman. Mrs. Westgate meanwhile, with her superfluously pretty gaze, looked at everyone alike.

"You had better wait till the time comes," she said to her sister. "Perhaps next May you won't care so much about London. Mr. Beaumont and I," she went on, smiling at her companion, "have had a tremendous discussion. We don't agree about anything. It's perfectly delightful."

"Oh, I say, Percy!" exclaimed Lord Lambeth.

"I disagree," said Beaumont, stroking down his back hair, "even to the point of not thinking it delightful."

"Oh, I say!" cried Lord Lambeth again.

"I don't see anything delightful in my disagreeing with Mrs. Westgate," said Percy Beaumont.

"Well, I do!" Mrs. Westgate declared; and she turned to her sister. "You know you have to go to town. The phaeton is there. You had better take Lord Lambeth."

At this point Percy Beaumont certainly looked straight at his kinsman; he tried to catch his eye. But Lord Lambeth would not look at him; his own eyes were better occupied. "I shall be very happy," cried Bessie Alden. "I am only going to some shops. But I will drive you about and show you the place."

"An American woman who respects herself," said Mrs. Westgate, turning to Beaumont with her bright expository air, "must buy something every day of her life. If she can not do it herself, she must send out some member of her family for the purpose. So Bessie goes forth to fulfill my mission."

The young girl had walked away, with Lord Lambeth by her side, to whom she was talking still; and Percy Beaumont watched them as they passed toward the house. "She fulfills her own mission," he presently said; "that of being a very attractive young lady."

"I don't know that I should say very attractive," Mrs. Westgate rejoined. "She is not so much that as she is charming when you really know her. She is very shy."

"Oh, indeed!" said Percy Beaumont.

"Extremely shy," Mrs. Westgate repeated. "But she is a dear good girl; she is a charming species of girl. She is not in the least a flirt; that isn't at all her line; she doesn't know the alphabet of that sort of thing. She is very simple, very serious. She has lived a great deal in Boston, with another sister of mine—the eldest of us—who married a Bostonian. She is very cultivated, not at all like me; I am not in the least cultivated. She has studied immensely and read everything; she is what they call in Boston 'thoughtful.'"

"A rum sort of girl for Lambeth to get hold of!" his lordship's kinsman privately reflected.

"I really believe," Mrs. Westgate continued, "that the most charming girl in the world is a Boston superstructure upon a New York *fonds*; or perhaps a New York superstructure upon a Boston *fonds*. At any rate, it's the mixture," said Mrs. Westgate, who continued to give Percy Beaumont a great deal of information.

Lord Lambeth got into a little basket phaeton with Bessie Alden, and she drove him down the long avenue, whose extent he had measured on foot a couple of hours before, into the ancient town, as it was called in that part of the world, of Newport. The ancient town was a curious affair—a collection of fresh-looking little wooden houses, painted white, scattered over a hillside and clustered about a long straight street paved with enormous cobblestones. There were plenty of shops—a large proportion of which appeared to be those of fruit vendors, with piles of huge watermelons and pumpkins stacked in front of them; and, drawn up before the shops, or bumping about on the cobblestones, were innumerable other basket phaetons freighted with ladies of high fashion, who greeted each other from vehicle to vehicle and conversed on the edge of the pavement in a manner that struck Lord Lambeth as demonstrative, with a great many "Oh, my dears," and little quick exclamations and caresses. His companion went into seventeen shops—he amused himself with counting them—and accumulated at the bottom of the phaeton a pile of bundles that hardly left the young Englishman a place for his feet. As she had no groom nor footman, he sat in the phaeton to hold the ponies, where, although he was not a particularly acute observer, he saw much to entertain him—especially the ladies just mentioned, who wandered up and down with the appearance of a kind of aimless intentness, as if they were looking for something to buy, and who, tripping in and out of their vehicles, displayed remarkably pretty feet. It all seemed to Lord Lambeth very odd, and bright, and gay. Of course, before they got back to the villa, he had had a great deal of desultory conversation with Bessie Alden.

The young Englishmen spent the whole of that day and the whole of many successive days in what the French call the *intimité* of their new friends. They agreed that it was extremely jolly, that they had never known anything more agreeable. It is not proposed to narrate minutely the incidents of their sojourn on this charming shore; though if it were convenient I might present a record of impressions nonetheless delectable that they were not exhaustively analyzed. Many of them still linger in the minds of our travelers, attended by a train of harmonious images—images of brilliant mornings on lawns and piazzas that overlooked the sea; of innumerable pretty girls; of infinite lounging and talking and laughing and flirting and

lunching and dining; of universal friendliness and frankness; of occasions on which they knew everyone and everything and had an extraordinary sense of ease; of drives
and rides in the late afternoon over gleaming beaches,
on long sea roads, beneath a sky lighted up by marvelous
sunsets; of suppers, on the return, informal, irregular,
agreeable; of evenings at open windows or on the perpetual verandas, in the summer starlight, above the warm
Atlantic. The young Englishmen were introduced to everybody, entertained by everybody, intimate with everybody.
At the end of three days they had removed their luggage
from the hotel and had gone to stay with Mrs. Westgate
—a step to which Percy Beaumont at first offered some
conscientious opposition. I call his opposition conscientious, because it was founded upon some talk that he had
had, on the second day, with Bessie Alden. He had indeed
had a good deal of talk with her, for she was not literally
always in conversation with Lord Lambeth. He had meditated upon Mrs. Westgate's account of her sister, and he
discovered for himself that the young lady was clever,
and appeared to have read a great deal. She seemed
very nice, though he could not make out that, as Mrs.
Westgate had said, she was shy. If she was shy, she
carried it off very well.

"Mr. Beaumont," she had said, "please tell me something about Lord Lambeth's family. How would you say it
in England—his position?"

"His position?" Percy Beaumont repeated.

"His rank, or whatever you call it. Unfortunately we
naven't got a *Peerage*, like the people in Thackeray."

"That's a great pity," said Beaumont. "You would find
it all set forth there so much better than I can do it."

"He is a peer, then?"

"Oh, yes, he is a peer."

"And has he any other title than Lord Lambeth?"

"His title is the Marquis of Lambeth," said Beaumont;
and then he was silent. Bessie Alden appeared to be looking at him with interest. "He is the son of the Duke of
Bayswater," he added presently.

"The eldest son?"

"The only son."

"And are his parents living?"

"Oh yes; if his father were not living he would be a duke."

"So that when his father dies," pursued Bessie Alden with more simplicity than might have been expected in a clever girl, "he will become Duke of Bayswater?"

"Of course," said Percy Beaumont. "But his father is in excellent health.

"And his mother?"

Beaumont smiled a little. "The duchess is uncommonly robust."

"And has he any sisters?"

"Yes, there are two."

"And what are they called?"

"One of them is married. She is the Countess of Pimlico."

"And the other?"

"The other is unmarried; she is plain Lady Julia."

Bessie Alden looked at him a moment. "Is she very plain?"

Beaumont began to laugh again. "You would not find her so handsome as her brother," he said; and it was after this that he attempted to dissuade the heir of the Duke of Bayswater from accepting Mrs. Westgate's invitation. "Depend upon it," he said, "that girl means to try for you."

"It seems to me you are doing your best to make a fool of me," the modest young nobleman answered.

"She has been asking me," said Beaumont, "all about your people and your possessions."

"I am sure it is very good of her!" Lord Lambeth rejoined.

"Well, then," observed his companion, "if you go, you go with your eyes open."

"Damn my eyes!" exclaimed Lord Lambeth. "If one is to be a dozen times a day at the house, it is a great deal more convenient to sleep there. I am sick of traveling up and down this beastly avenue."

Since he had determined to go, Percy Beaumont would, of course, have been very sorry to allow him to go alone; he was a man of conscience, and he remembered his promise to the duchess. It was obviously the memory of this promise that made him say to his companion a

couple of days later that he rather wondered he should be
so fond of that girl.

"In the first place, how do you know how fond I am
of her?" asked Lord Lambeth. "And, in the second
place, why shouldn't I be fond of her?"

"I shouldn't think she would be in your line."

"What do you call my 'line'? You don't set her down
as 'fast'?"

"Exactly so. Mrs. Westgate tells me that there is no
such thing as the 'fast girl' in America; that it's an English
invention, and that the term has no meaning here."

"All the better. It's an animal I detest."

"You prefer a bluestocking."

"Is that what you call Miss Alden?"

"Her sister tells me," said Percy Beaumont, "that she
is tremendously literary."

"I don't know anything about that. She is certainly very
clever."

"Well," said Beaumont, "I should have supposed you
would have found that sort of thing awfully slow."

"In point of fact," Lord Lambeth rejoined, "I find it
uncommonly lively."

After this, Percy Beaumont held his tongue; but on
the 10th of August he wrote to the Duchess of Bayswater.
He was, as I have said, a man of conscience, and he
had a strong, incorruptible sense of the proprieties of life.
His kinsman, meanwhile, was having a great deal of talk
with Bessie Alden—on the red sea rocks beyond the lawn;
in the course of long island rides, with a slow return in
the glowing twilight; on the deep veranda late in the evening. Lord Lambeth, who had stayed at many houses, had
never stayed at a house in which it was possible for a
young man to converse so frequently with a young lady.
This young lady no longer applied to Percy Beaumont
for information concerning his lordship. She addressed
herself directly to the young nobleman. She asked him a
great many questions, some of which bored him a little;
for he took no pleasure in talking about himself.

"Lord Lambeth," said Bessie Alden, "are you a hereditary legislator?"

"Oh, I say!" cried Lord Lambeth, "don't make me call
myself such names as that."

"But you are a member of Parliament," said the young girl.

"I don't like the sound of that, either."

"Don't you sit in the House of Lords?" Bessie Alden went on.

"Very seldom," said Lord Lambeth.

"Is it an important position?" she asked.

"Oh, dear, no," said Lord Lambeth.

"I should think it would be very grand," said Bessie Alden, "to possess, simply by an accident of birth, the right to make laws for a great nation."

"Ah, but one doesn't make laws. It's a great humbug."

"I don't believe that," the young girl declared. "It must be a great privilege, and I should think that if one thought of it in the right way—from a high point of view—it would be very inspiring."

"The less one thinks of it, the better," Lord Lambeth affirmed.

"I think it's tremendous," said Bessie Alden; and on another occasion she asked him if he had any tenantry. Hereupon it was that, as I have said, he was a little bored.

"Do you want to buy up their leases?" he asked.

"Well, have you got any livings?" she demanded.

"Oh, I say!" he cried. "Have you got a clergyman that is looking out?" But she made him tell her that he had a castle; he confessed to but one. It was the place in which he had been born and brought up, and, as he had an old-time liking for it, he was beguiled into describing it a little and saying it was really very jolly. Bessie Alden listened with great interest and declared that she would give the world to see such a place. Whereupon—"It would be awfully kind of you to come and stay there," said Lord Lambeth. He took a vague satisfaction in the circumstance that Percy Beaumont had not heard him make the remark I have just recorded.

Mr. Westgate all this time had not, as they said at Newport, "come on." His wife more than once announced that she expected him on the morrow; but on the morrow she wandered about a little, with a telegram in her jeweled fingers, declaring it was very tiresome that his business detained him in New York; that he could only hope the

Englishmen were having a good time. "I must say," said
Mrs. Westgate, "that it is no thanks to him if you are."
And she went on to explain, while she continued that
slow-paced promenade which enabled her well-adjusted
skirts to display themselves so advantageously, that unfortunately in America there was no leisure class. It was
Lord Lambeth's theory, freely propounded when the
young men were together, that Percy Beaumont was having
a very good time with Mrs. Westgate, and that, under the
pretext of meeting for the purpose of animated discussion,
they were indulging in practices that imparted a shade of
hypocrisy to the lady's regret for her husband's absence.

"I assure you we are always discussing and differing,"
said Percy Beaumont. "She is awfully argumentative.
American ladies certainly don't mind contradicting you.
Upon my word I don't think I was ever treated so by a
woman before. She's so devilish positive."

Mrs. Westgate's positive quality, however, evidently
had its attractions, for Beaumont was constantly at his
hostess's side. He detached himself one day to the extent
of going to New York to talk over the Tennessee Central
with Mr. Westgate; but he was absent only forty-eight
hours, during which, with Mr. Westgate's assistance,
he completely settled this piece of business. "They certainly do things quickly in New York," he observed to his
cousin; and he added that Mr. Westgate had seemed very
uneasy lest his wife should miss her visitor—he had been
in such an awful hurry to send him back to her. "I'm
afraid you'll never come up to an American husband, if
that's what the wives expect," he said to Lord Lambeth.

Mrs. Westgate, however, was not to enjoy much longer
the entertainment with which an indulgent husband had
desired to keep her provided. On the 21st of August Lord
Lambeth received a telegram from his mother, requesting
him to return immediately to England; his father had been
taken ill, and it was his filial duty to come to him.

The young Englishman was visibly annoyed. "What the
deuce does it mean?" he asked of his kinsman. "What am
I to do?"

Percy Beaumont was annoyed as well; he had deemed it
his duty, as I have narrated, to write to the duchess,
but he had not expected that this distinguished woman

would act so promptly upon his hint. "It means," be said, "that your father is laid up. I don't suppose it's anything serious; but you have no option. Take the first steamer; but don't be alarmed."

Lord Lambeth made his farewells; but the few last words that he exchanged with Bessie Alden are the only ones that have a place in our record. "Of course I needn't assure you," he said, "that if you should come to England next year, I expect to be the first person that you inform of it."

Bessie Alden looked at him a little, and she smiled. "Oh, if we come to London," she answered, "I should think you would hear of it."

Percy Beaumont returned with his cousin, and his sense of duty compelled him, one windless afternoon, in mid-Atlantic, to say to Lord Lambeth that he suspected that the duchess's telegram was in part the result of something he himself had written to her. "I wrote to her—as I explicitly notified you I had promised to do—that you were extremely interested in a little American girl."

Lord Lambeth was extremely angry, and he indulged for some moments in the simple language of indignation. But I have said that he was a reasonable young man, and I can give no better proof of it than the fact that he remarked to his companion at the end of half an hour, "You were quite right, after all. I am very much interested in her. Only, to be fair," he added, "you should have told my mother also that she is not—seriously—interested in me."

Percy Beaumont gave a little laugh. "There is nothing so charming as modesty in a young man in your position. That speech is a capital proof that you are sweet on her."

"She is not interested—she is not!" Lord Lambeth repeated.

"My dear fellow," said his companion, "you are very far gone."

In point of fact, as Percy Beaumont would have said, Mrs. Westgate disembarked on the 18th of May on the British coast. She was accompanied by her sister, but she was not attended by any other member of her family. To the deprivation of her husband's society Mrs. Westgate was, however, habituated; she had made half a dozen journeys to Europe without him, and she now accounted for his absence, to interrogative friends on this side of the Atlantic, by allusion to the regrettable but conspicuous fact that in America there was no leisure class. The two ladies came up to London and alighted at Jones's Hotel, where Mrs. Westgate, who had made on former occasions the most agreeable impression at this establishment, received an obsequious greeting. Bessie Alden had felt much excited about coming to England; she had expected the "associations" would be very charming, that it would be an infinite pleasure to rest her eyes upon the things she had read about in the poets and historians. She was very fond of the poets and historians, of the picturesque, of the past, of retrospect, of mementos and reverberations of greatness; so that on coming into the great English world, where strangeness and familiarity would go hand in hand, she was prepared for a multitude of fresh emotions. They began very promptly—these tender, fluttering sensations; they began with the sight of the beautiful English landscape, whose dark richness was quickened and brightened by the season; with the carpeted fields and flowering hedgerows, as she looked at them from the window of the train; with the spires of the rural churches peeping above the rook-haunted treetops; with the oak-studded parks, the ancient homes, the cloudy light, the speech, the manners, the thousand differences. Mrs. Westgate's impressions had, of course, much less novelty and keenness, and she gave

54

but a wandering attention to her sister's ejaculations and rhapsodies.

"You know my enjoyment of England is not so intellectual as Bessie's," she said to several of her friends in the course of her visit to this country. "And yet if it is not intellectual, I can't say it is physical. I don't think I can quite say what it is, my enjoyment of England." When once it was settled that the two ladies should come abroad and should spend a few weeks in England on their way to the Continent, they of course exchanged a good many allusions to their London acquaintance.

"It will certainly be much nicer having friends there," Bessie Alden had said one day as she sat on the sunny deck of the steamer at her sister's feet on a large blue rug.

"Whom do you mean by friends?" Mrs. Westgate asked.

"All those English gentlemen whom you have known and entertained. Captain Littledale, for instance. And Lord Lambeth and Mr. Beaumont," added Bessie Alden.

"Do you expect them to give us a very grand reception?"

Bessie reflected a moment; she was addicted, as we know, to reflection. "Well, yes."

"My poor, sweet child," murmured her sister.

"What have I said that is so silly?" asked Bessie.

"You are a little too simple; just a little. It is very becoming, but it pleases people at your expense."

"I am certainly too simple to understand you," said Bessie.

"Shall I tell you a story?" asked her sister.

"If you would be so good. That is what they do to amuse simple people."

Mrs. Westgate consulted her memory, while her companion sat gazing at the shining sea. "Did you ever hear of the Duke of Green-Erin?"

"I think not," said Bessie.

"Well, it's no matter," her sister went on.

"It's a proof of my simplicity."

"My story is meant to illustrate that of some other people," said Mrs. Westgate. "The Duke of Green-Erin is what they call in England a great swell, and some five years ago he came to America. He spent most of his time in New York, and in New York he spent his days and his nights at the Butterworths'. You have heard, at least, of the Butterworths. *Bien.* They did everything in the world for him—they turned themselves inside out. They gave him a dozen dinner parties and balls and were the means of his being invited to fifty more. At first he used to come into Mrs. Butterworth's box at the opera in a tweed traveling suit; but someone stopped that. At any rate, he had a beautiful time, and they parted the best friends in the world. Two years elapse, and the Butterworths come abroad and go to London. The first thing they see in all the papers—in England those things are in the most prominent place—is that the Duke of Green-Erin has arrived in town for the Season. They wait a little, and then Mr. Butterworth—as polite as ever—goes and leaves a card. They wait a little more; the visit is not returned; they wait three weeks—*silence de mort*—the Duke gives no sign. The Butterworths see a lot of other people, put down the Duke of Green-Erin as a rude, ungrateful man, and forget all about him. One fine day they go to Ascot Races, and there they meet him face to face. He stares a moment and then comes up to Mr. Butterworth, taking something from his pocketbook—something which proves to be a banknote. 'I'm glad to see you, Mr. Butterworth,' he says, 'so that I can pay you that ten pounds I lost to you in New York. I saw the other day you remembered our bet; here are the ten pounds, Mr. Butterworth. Goodbye, Mr. Butterworth.' And off he goes, and that's the last they see of the Duke of Green-Erin."

"Is that your story?" asked Bessie Alden.

"Don't you think it's interesting?" her sister replied.

"I don't believe it," said the young girl.

"Ah," cried Mrs. Westgate, "you are not so simple after all! Believe it or not, as you please; there is no smoke without fire."

"Is that the way," asked Bessie after a moment, "that you expect your friends to treat you?"

"I defy them to treat me very ill, because I shall not give them the opportunity. With the best will in the world, in that case they can't be very offensive."

Bessie Alden was silent a moment. "I don't see what makes you talk that way," she said. "The English are a great people."

"Exactly; and that is just the way they have grown great—by dropping you when you have ceased to be useful. People say they are not clever; but I think they are very clever."

"You know you have liked them—all the Englishmen you have seen," said Bessie.

"They have liked me," her sister rejoined; "it would be more correct to say that. And, of course, one likes that."

Bessie Alden resumed for some moments her studies in sea green. "Well," she said, "whether they like me or not, I mean to like them. And happily," she added, "Lord Lambeth does not owe me ten pounds."

During the first few days after their arrival at Jones's Hotel our charming Americans were much occupied with what they would have called looking about them. They found occasion to make a large number of purchases, and their opportunities for conversation were such only as were offered by the deferential London shopmen. Bessie Alden, even in driving from the station, took an immense fancy to the British metropolis, and at the risk of exhibiting her as a young woman of vulgar tastes it must be recorded that for a considerable period she desired no higher pleasure than to drive about the crowded streets in a hansom cab. To her attentive eyes they were full of a strange picturesque life, and it is at least beneath the dignity of our historic muse to enumerate the trivial objects and incidents which this simple young lady from Boston found so entertaining. It may be freely mentioned, however, that whenever, after a round of visits in Bond Street and Regent Street, she was about to return with her sister to Jones's Hotel, she made an earnest request that they should be driven home by way of Westminster Abbey. She had begun by asking whether it would not be possible to take the Tower on the way to their lodgings; but it happened that at a more primitive stage of her culture Mrs. Westgate had paid a visit to this venerable monument, which she spoke of ever afterward vaguely as a dreadful disappointment; so that she expressed the liveliest disapproval of any attempt to combine historical researches with the purchase of hairbrushes and notepaper. The most she would consent to do in this line was to spend half an hour at Madame Tussaud's, where she saw several dusty wax effigies of members of the royal family. She told Bessie that if she wished to go to the Tower she must get someone else to take her. Bessie expressed hereupon an earnest disposition to go alone; but upon this proposal as well Mrs. Westgate sprinkled cold water.

"Remember," she said, "that you are not in your innocent little Boston. It is not a question of walking up and down Beacon Street." Then she went on to explain that there were two classes of American girls in Europe —those that walked about alone and those that did not. "You happen to belong, my dear," she said to her sister, "to the class that does not."

"It is only," answered Bessie, laughing, "because you happen to prevent me." And she devoted much private meditation to this question of effecting a visit to the Tower of London.

Suddenly it seemed as if the problem might be solved; the two ladies at Jones's Hotel received a visit from Willie Woodley. Such was the social appellation of a young American who had sailed from New York a few days after their own departure, and who, having the privilege of intimacy with them in that city, had lost no time, on his arrival in London, in coming to pay them his respects. He had, in fact, gone to see them directly after going to see his tailor, than which there can be no greater exhibition of promptitude on the part of a young American who has just alighted at the Charing Cross Hotel. He was a slim, pale youth, of the most amiable disposition, famous for the skill with which he led the "German" in New York. Indeed, by the young ladies who habitually figured in this Terpsichorean revel he was believed to be "the best dancer in the world"; it was in these terms that he was always spoken of, and that his identity was indicated. He was the gentlest, softest young man it was possible to meet; he was beautifully dressed— "in the English style"—and he knew an immense deal about London. He had been at Newport during the previous summer, at the time of our young Englishmen's visit, and he took extreme pleasure in the society of Bessie Alden, whom he always addressed as "Miss Bessie." She immediately arranged with him, in the presence of her sister, that he should conduct her to the scene of Anne Boleyn's execution.

"You may do as you please," said Mrs. Westgate. "Only—if you desire the information—it is not the custom here for young ladies to knock about London with young men."

"Miss Bessie has waltzed with me so often," observed Willie Woodley; "she can surely go out with me in a hansom."

"I consider waltzing," said Mrs. Westgate, "the most innocent pleasure of our time."

"It's a compliment to our time!" exclaimed the young man with a little laugh, in spite of himself.

"I don't see why I should regard what is done here," said Bessie Alden. "Why should I suffer the restrictions of a society of which I enjoy none of the privileges?"

"That's very good—very good," murmured Willie Woodley.

"Oh, go to the Tower, and feel the ax, if you like," said Mrs. Westgate. "I consent to your going with Mr. Woodley; but I should not let you go with an Englishman."

"Miss Bessie wouldn't care to go with an Englishman!" Mr. Woodley declared with a faint asperity that was, perhaps, not unnatural in a young man, who, dressing in the manner that I have indicated and knowing a great deal, as I have said, about London, saw no reason for drawing these sharp distinctions. He agreed upon a day with Miss Bessie—a day of that same week.

An ingenious mind might, perhaps, trace a connection between the young girl's allusion to her destitution of social privileges and a question she asked on the morrow as she sat with her sister at lunch.

"Don't you mean to write to—to anyone?" said Bessie.

"I wrote this morning to Captain Littledale," Mrs. Westgate replied.

"But Mr. Woodley said that Captain Littledale had gone to India."

"He said he thought he had heard so; he knew nothing about it."

For a moment Bessie Alden said nothing more; then, at last, "And don't you intend to write to—to Mr. Beaumont?" she inquired.

"You mean to Lord Lambeth," said her sister.

"I said Mr. Beaumont because he was so good a friend of yours."

Mrs. Westgate looked at the young girl with sisterly candor. "I don't care two straws for Mr. Beaumont."

"You were certainly very nice to him."

"I am nice to everyone," said Mrs. Westgate simply.

"To everyone but me," rejoined Bessie, smiling.

Her sister continued to look at her; then, at last, "Are you in love with Lord Lambeth?" she asked.

The young girl stared a moment, and the question was apparently too humorous even to make her blush. "Not that I know of," she answered.

"Because if you are," Mrs. Westgate went on, "I shall certainly not send for him."

"That proves what I said," declared Bessie, smiling—"that you are not nice to me."

"It would be a poor service, my dear child," said her sister.

"In what sense? There is nothing against Lord Lambeth that I know of."

Mrs. Westgate was silent a moment. "You *are* in love with him then?"

Bessie stared again; but this time she blushed a little. "Ah! if you won't be serious," she answered, "we will not mention him again."

For some moments Lord Lambeth was not mentioned again, and it was Mrs. Westgate who, at the end of this period, reverted to him. "Of course I will let him know we are here, because I think he would be hurt—justly enough—if we should go away without seeing him. It is fair to give him a chance to come and thank me for the kindness we showed him. But I don't want to seem eager."

"Neither do I," said Bessie with a little laugh.

"Though I confess," added her sister, "that I am curious to see how he will behave."

"He behaved very well at Newport."

"Newport is not London. At Newport he could do as he liked; but here it is another affair. He has to have an eye to consequences."

"If he had more freedom, then, at Newport," argued Bessie, "it is the more to his credit that he behaved well; and if he has to be so careful here, it is possible he will behave even better."

"Better—better," repeated her sister. "My dear child, what is your point of view?"

"How do you mean—my point of view?"

"Don't you care for Lord Lambeth—a little?"

This time Bessie Alden was displeased; she slowly got up from the table, turning her face away from her sister. "You will oblige me by not talking so," she said.

Mrs. Westgate sat watching her for some moments as she moved slowly about the room and went and stood at the window. "I will write to him this afternoon," she said at last.

"Do as you please!" Bessie answered; and presently she turned round. "I am not afraid to say that I like Lord Lambeth. I like him very much."

"He is not clever," Mrs. Westgate declared.

"Well, there have been clever people whom I have disliked," said Bessie Alden; "so that I suppose I may like a stupid one. Besides, Lord Lambeth is not stupid."

"Not so stupid as he looks!" exclaimed her sister, smiling.

"If I were in love with Lord Lambeth, as you said just now, it would be bad policy on your part to abuse him."

"My dear child, don't give me lessons in policy!" cried Mrs. Westgate. "The policy I mean to follow is very deep."

The young girl began to walk about the room again; then she stopped before her sister. "I have never heard in the course of five minutes," she said, "so many hints and innuendoes. I wish you would tell me in plain English what you mean."

"I mean that you may be much annoyed."

"That is still only a hint," said Bessie.

Her sister looked at her, hesitating an instant. "It will

be said of you that you have come after Lord Lambeth—that you followed him."

Bessie Alden threw back her pretty head like a startled hind, and a look flashed into her face that made Mrs. Westgate rise from her chair. "Who says such things as that?" she demanded.

"People here."

"I don't believe it," said Bessie.

"You have a very convenient faculty of doubt. But my policy will be, as I say, very deep. I shall leave you to find out this kind of thing for yourself."

Bessie fixed her eyes upon her sister, and Mrs. Westgate thought for a moment there were tears in them. "Do they talk that way here?" she asked.

"You will see. I shall leave you alone."

"Don't leave me alone," said Bessie Alden. "Take me away."

"No; I want to see what you make of it," her sister continued.

"I don't understand."

"You will understand after Lord Lambeth has come," said Mrs. Westgate with a little laugh.

The two ladies had arranged that on this afternoon Willie Woodley should go with them to Hyde Park, where Bessie Alden expected to derive much entertainment from sitting on a little green chair, under the great trees, beside Rotten Row. The want of a suitable escort had hitherto rendered this pleasure inaccessible; but no escort now, for such an expedition, could have been more suitable than their devoted young countryman, whose mission in life, it might almost be said, was to find chairs for ladies, and who appeared on the stroke of half-past five with a white camellia in his buttonhole.

"I have written to Lord Lambeth, my dear," said Mrs. Westgate to her sister, on coming into the room where Bessie Alden, drawing on her long gray gloves, was entertaining their visitor.

Bessie said nothing, but Willie Woodley exclaimed that his lordship was in town; he had seen his name in the *Morning Post.*

"Do you read the *Morning Post?*" asked Mrs. Westgate.

"Oh, yes; it's great fun," Willie Woodley affirmed.

"I want so to see it," said Bessie; "there is so much about it in Thackeray."

"I will send it to you every morning," said Willie Woodley.

He found them what Bessie Alden thought excellent places, under the great trees, beside the famous avenue whose humors had been made familiar to the young girl's childhood by the pictures in *Punch*. The day was bright and warm, and the crowd of riders and spectators, and the great procession of carriages, were proportionately dense and brilliant. The scene bore the stamp of the London Season at its height, and Bessie Alden found more entertainment in it than she was able to express to her companions. She sat silent, under her parasol, and her imagination, according to its wont, let itself loose into the great changing assemblage of striking and suggestive figures. They stirred up a host of old impressions and preconceptions, and she found herself fitting a history to this person and a theory to that, and making a place for them all in her little private museum of types. But if she said little, her sister on one side and Willie Woodley on the other expressed themselves in lively alternation.

"Look at that green dress with blue flounces," said Mrs. Westgate. "*Quelle toilette!*"

"That's the Marquis of Blackborough," said the young man—"the one in the white coat. I heard him speak the other night in the House of Lords; it was something about ramrods; he called them 'wamwods.' He's an awful swell."

"Did you ever see anything like the way they are pinned back?" Mrs. Westgate resumed. "They never know where to stop."

"They do nothing but stop," said Willie Woodley. "It prevents them from walking. Here comes a great celebrity—Lady Beatrice Bellevue. She's awfully fast; see what little steps she takes."

"Well, my dear," Mrs. Westgate pursued, "I hope you are getting some ideas for your *couturière?*"

"I am getting plenty of ideas," said Bessie, "but I don't know that my *couturière* would appreciate them."

Willie Woodley presently perceived a friend on horseback, who drove up beside the barrier of the Row and beckoned to him. He went forward, and the crowd of pedestrians closed about him, so that for some ten minutes he was hidden from sight. At last he reappeared, bringing a gentleman with him—a gentleman whom Bessie at first supposed to be his friend dismounted. But at a second glance she found herself looking at Lord Lambeth, who was shaking hands with her sister.

"I found him over there," said Willie Woodley, "and I told him you were here."

And then Lord Lambeth, touching his hat a little, shook hands with Bessie. "Fancy your being here!" he said. He was blushing and smiling; he looked very handsome, and he had a kind of splendor that he had not had in America. Bessie Alden's imagination, as we know, was just then in exercise; so that the tall young Englishman, as he stood there looking down at her, had the benefit of it. "He is handsomer and more splendid than anything I have ever seen," she said to herself. And then she remembered that he was a marquis, and she thought he looked like a marquis.

"I say, you know," he cried, "you ought to have let a man know you were here!"

"I wrote to you an hour ago," said Mrs. Westgate.

"Doesn't all the world know it?" asked Bessie, smiling.

"I assure you I didn't know it!" cried Lord Lambeth. "Upon my honor I hadn't heard of it. Ask Woodley now; had I, Woodley?"

"Well, I think you are rather a humbug," said Willie Woodley.

"You don't believe that—do you, Miss Alden?" asked his lordship. "You don't believe I'm a humbug, eh?"

"No," said Bessie, "I don't."

"You are too tall to stand up, Lord Lambeth," Mrs. Westgate observed. "You are only tolerable when you sit down. Be so good as to get a chair."

He found a chair and placed it sidewise, close to the two ladies. "If I hadn't met Woodley I should never have found you," he went on. "Should I, Woodley?"

"Well, I guess not," said the young American.

"Not even with my letter?" asked Mrs. Westgate.

"Ah, well, I haven't got your letter yet; I suppose I shall get it this evening. It was awfully kind of you to write."

"So I said to Bessie," observed Mrs. Westgate.

"Did she say so, Miss Alden?" Lord Lambeth inquired. "I daresay you have been here a month."

"We have been here three," said Mrs. Westgate.

"Have you been here three months?" the young man asked again of Bessie.

"It seems a long time," Bessie answered.

"I say, after that you had better not call me a humbug!" cried Lord Lambeth. "I have only been in town three weeks; but you must have been hiding away; I haven't seen you anywhere."

"Where should you have seen us—where should we have gone?" asked Mrs. Westgate.

"You should have gone to Hurlingham," said Willie Woodley.

"No; let Lord Lambeth tell us," Mrs. Westgate insisted.

"There are plenty of places to go to," said Lord Lambeth; "each one stupider than the other. I mean people's houses; they send you cards."

"No one has sent us cards," said Bessie.

"We are very quiet," her sister declared. "We are here as travelers."

"We have been to Madame Tussaud's," Bessie pursued.

"Oh, I say!" cried Lord Lambeth.

"We thought we should find your image there," said Mrs. Westgate—"yours and Mr. Beaumont's."

"In the Chamber of Horrors?" laughed the young man.

"It did duty very well for a party," said Mrs. Westgate. "All the women were *décolletés*, and many of the figures looked as if they could speak if they tried."

"Upon my word," Lord Lambeth rejoined, "you see people at London parties that look as if they couldn't speak if they tried."

"Do you think Mr. Woodley could find us Mr. Beaumont?" asked Mrs. Westgate.

Lord Lambeth stared and looked round him. "I daresay he could. Beaumont often comes here. Don't you think you could find him, Woodley? Make a dive into the crowd."

"Thank you; I have had enough diving," said Willie Woodley. "I will wait till Mr. Beaumont comes to the surface."

"I will bring him to see you," said Lord Lambeth; "where are you staying?"

"You will find the address in my letter—Jones's Hotel."

"Oh, one of those places just out of Piccadilly? Beastly hole, isn't it?" Lord Lambeth inquired.

"I believe it's the best hotel in London," said Mrs. Westgate.

"But they give you awful rubbish to eat, don't they?" his lordship went on.

"Yes," said Mrs. Westgate.

"I always feel so sorry for the people that come up to town and go to live in those places," continued the young man. "They eat nothing but filth."

"Oh, I say!" cried Willie Woodley.

"Well, how do you like London, Miss Alden?" Lord Lambeth asked, unperturbed by this ejaculation.

"I think it's grand," said Bessie Alden.

"My sister likes it, in spite of the 'filth'!" Mrs. Westgate exclaimed.

"I hope you are going to stay a long time."

"As long as I can," said Bessie.

"And where is Mr. Westgate?" asked Lord Lambeth of this gentleman's wife.

"He's where he always is—in that tiresome New York."

"He must be tremendously clever," said the young man.

"I suppose he is," said Mrs. Westgate.

Lord Lambeth sat for nearly an hour with his American friends; but it is not our purpose to relate their conversation in full. He addressed a great many remarks to Bessie Alden, and finally turned toward her altogether, while Willie Woodley entertained Mrs. Westgate. Bessie herself said very little; she was on her guard, thinking of what her sister had said to her at lunch. Little by little, however, she interested herself in Lord Lambeth again, as she had done at Newport; only it seemed to her that here he might become more interesting. He would be an unconscious part of the antiquity, the impressiveness, the picturesqueness, of England; and poor Bessie Alden, like many a Yankee maiden, was terribly at the mercy of picturesqueness.

"I have often wished I were at Newport again," said the young man. "Those days I spent at your sister's were awfully jolly."

"We enjoyed them very much; I hope your father is better."

"Oh, dear, yes. When I got to England, he was out grouse shooting. It was what you call in America a gigantic fraud. My mother had got nervous. My three weeks at Newport seemed like a happy dream."

"America certainly is very different from England," said Bessie.

"I hope you like England better, eh?" Lord Lambeth rejoined almost persuasively.

"No Englishman can ask that seriously of a person of another country."

Her companion looked at her for a moment. "You mean it's a matter of course?"

"If I were English," said Bessie, "it would certainly seem to me a matter of course that everyone should be a good patriot."

"Oh, dear, yes, patriotism is everything," said Lord Lambeth, not quite following, but very contented. "Now, what are you going to do here?"

"On Thursday I am going to the Tower."

"The Tower?"

"The Tower of London. Did you never hear of it?"

"Oh, yes, I have been there," said Lord Lambeth. "I was taken there by my governess when I was six years old. It's a rum idea, your going there."

"Do give me a few more rum ideas," said Bessie. "I want to see everything of that sort. I am going to Hampton Court, and to Windsor, and to the Dulwich Gallery."

Lord Lambeth seemed greatly amused. "I wonder you don't go to the Rosherville Gardens."

"Are they interesting?" asked Bessie.

"Oh, wonderful."

"Are they very old? That's all I care for," said Bessie.

"They are tremendously old; they are all falling to ruins."

"I think there is nothing so charming as an old ruinous garden," said the young girl. "We must certainly go there."

Lord Lambeth broke out into merriment. "I say, Woodley," he cried, "here's Miss Alden wants to go to the Rosherville Gardens!"

Willie Woodley looked a little blank; he was caught in the fact of ignorance of an apparently conspicuous feature of London life. But in a moment he turned it off. "Very well," he said, "I'll write for a permit."

Lord Lambeth's exhilaration increased. "Gad, I believe you Americans would go anywhere!" he cried.

"We wish to go to Parliament," said Bessie. "That's one of the first things."

"Oh, it would bore you to death!" cried the young man.

"We wish to hear you speak."

"I never speak—except to young ladies," said Lord Lambeth, smiling.

Bessie Alden looked at him a while, smiling, too, in the shadow of her parasol. "You are very strange," she murmured. "I don't think I approve of you."

"Ah, now, don't be severe, Miss Alden," said Lord Lambeth, smiling still more. "Please don't be severe. I want you to like me—awfully."

"To like you awfully? You must not laugh at me, then, when I make mistakes. I consider it my right—as a freeborn American—to make as many mistakes as I choose."

"Upon my word, I didn't laugh at you," said Lord Lambeth.

"And not only that," Bessie went on; "but I hold that all my mistakes shall be set down to my credit. You must think the better of me for them."

"I can't think better of you than I do," the young man declared.

Bessie Alden looked at him a moment again. "You certainly speak very well to young ladies. But why don't you address the House?—isn't that what they call it?"

"Because I have nothing to say," said Lord Lambeth.

"Haven't you a great position?" asked Bessie Alden.

He looked a moment at the back of his glove. "I'll set

that down," he said, "as one of your mistakes—to your credit." And as if he disliked talking about his position, he changed the subject. "I wish you would let me go with you to the Tower, and to Hampton Court, and to all those other places."

"We shall be most happy," said Bessie.

"And of course I shall be delighted to show you the House of Lords—some day that suits you. There are a lot of things I want to do for you. I want to make you have a good time. And I should like very much to present some of my friends to you, if it wouldn't bore you. Then it would be awfully kind of you to come down to Branches."

"We are much obliged to you, Lord Lambeth," said Bessie. "What is Branches?"

"It's a house in the country. I think you might like it."

Willie Woodley and Mrs. Westgate at this moment were sitting in silence, and the young man's ear caught these last words of Lord Lambeth's. "He's inviting Miss Bessie to one of his castles," he murmured to his companion.

Mrs. Westgate, foreseeing what she mentally called "complications," immediately got up; and the two ladies, taking leave of Lord Lambeth, returned, under Mr. Woodley's conduct, to Jones's Hotel.

Lord Lambeth came to see them on the morrow, bringing Percy Beaumont with him—the latter having instantly declared his intention of neglecting none of the usual offices of civility. This declaration, however, when his kinsman informed him of the advent of their American friends, had been preceded by another remark.

"Here they are, then, and you are in for it."

"What am I in for?" demanded Lord Lambeth.

"I will let your mother give it a name. With all respect to whom," added Percy Beaumont, "I must decline on this occasion to do any more police duty. Her Grace must look after you yourself."

"I will give her a chance," said her Grace's son, a trifle grimly. "I shall make her go and see them."

"She won't do it, my boy."

"We'll see if she doesn't," said Lord Lambeth.

But if Percy Beaumont took a somber view of the arrival of the two ladies at Jones's Hotel, he was sufficiently a man of the world to offer them a smiling countenance. He fell into animated conversation—conversation, at least, that was animated on her side—with Mrs. Westgate, while his companion made himself agreeable to the younger lady. Mrs. Westgate began confessing and protesting, declaring and expounding.

"I must say London is a great deal brighter and prettier just now than it was when I was here last—in the month of November. There is evidently a great deal going on, and you seem to have a good many flowers. I have no doubt it is very charming for all you people, and that you amuse yourselves immensely. It is very good of you to let Bessie and me come and sit and look at you. I suppose you will think I am very satirical, but I must confess that that's the feeling I have in London."

"I am afraid I don't quite understand to what feeling you allude," said Percy Beaumont.

"The feeling that it's all very well for you English people. Everything is beautifully arranged for you."

"It seems to me it is very well for some Americans, sometimes," rejoined Beaumont.

"For some of them, yes—if they like to be patronized. But I must say I don't like to be patronized. I may be very eccentric, and undisciplined, and outrageous, but I confess I never was fond of patronage. I like to associate with people on the same terms as I do in my own country; that's a peculiar taste that I have. But here people seem to expect something else—Heaven knows what! I am afraid you will think I am very ungrateful, for I certainly have received a great deal of attention. The last time I was here, a lady sent me a message that I was at liberty to come and see her."

"Dear me! I hope you didn't go," observed Percy Beaumont.

"You are deliciously naïve, I must say that for you!" Mrs. Westgate exclaimed. "It must be a great advantage to you here in London. I suppose that if I myself had a little more naïveté, I should enjoy it more. I should be content to sit on a chair in the park, and see the people pass, and be told that this is the Duchess of Suffolk, and that is the Lord Chamberlain, and that I must be thankful for the privilege of beholding them. I daresay it is very wicked and critical of me to ask for anything else. But I was always critical, and I freely confess to the sin of being fastidious. I am told there is some remarkably superior second-rate society provided here for strangers. *Merci!* I don't want any superior second-rate society. I want the society that I have been accustomed to."

"I hope you don't call Lambeth and me second rate," Beaumont interposed.

"Oh, I am accustomed to you," said Mrs. Westgate. "Do you know that you English sometimes make the most wonderful speeches? The first time I came to London I went out to dine—as I told you, I have received a great deal of attention. After dinner, in the drawing room, I had some conversation with an old lady; I assure you I had. I forget what we talked about, but she presently said, in allusion to something we were discussing, 'Oh, you know, the aristocracy do so-and-so; but in one's own class of life it is very different.' In one's own class of life! What is a poor unprotected American woman to do in a country where she is liable to have that sort of thing said to her?"

"You seem to get hold of some very queer old ladies; I compliment you on your acquaintance!" Percy Beaumont exclaimed. "If you are trying to bring me to admit that London is an odious place, you'll not succeed. I'm extremely fond of it, and I think it the jolliest place in the world."

"*Pour vous autres*. I never said the contrary," Mrs. Westgate retorted. I make use of this expression, because both interlocutors had begun to raise their voices. Percy Beaumont naturally did not like to hear his country abused, and Mrs. Westgate, no less naturally, did not like a stubborn debater.

"Hallo!" said Lord Lambeth; "what are they up to now?" And he came away from the window, where he had been standing with Bessie Alden.

"I quite agree with a very clever countrywoman of mine," Mrs. Westgate continued with charming ardor, though with imperfect relevancy. She smiled at the two gentlemen for a moment with terrible brightness, as if to toss at their feet—upon their native heath—the gauntlet of defiance. "For me, there are only two social positions worth speaking of—that of an American lady and that of the Emperor of Russia."

"And what do you do with the American gentlemen?" asked Lord Lambeth.

"She leaves them in America!" said Percy Beaumont.

On the departure of their visitors, Bessie Alden told her sister that Lord Lambeth would come the next day, to go with them to the Tower, and that he had kindly offered to bring his "trap" and drive them thither. Mrs. Westgate listened in silence to this communication, and for some time afterward she said nothing. But at last, "If you had not requested me the other day not to mention it," she began, "there is something I should venture to ask you." Bessie frowned a little; her dark blue eyes were more dark than blue. But her sister went on. "As it is, I will take the risk. You are not in love with Lord Lambeth: I believe it, perfectly. Very good. But is there, by chance, any danger of your becoming so? It's a very simple question; don't take offense. I have a particular reason," said Mrs. Westgate, "for wanting to know."

Bessie Alden for some moments said nothing; she only looked displeased. "No; there is no danger," she answered at last, curtly.

"Then I should like to frighten them," declared Mrs. Westgate, clasping her jeweled hands.

"To frighten whom?"

"All these people; Lord Lambeth's family and friends."

"How should you frighten them?" asked the young girl.

"It wouldn't be I—it would be you. It would frighten them to think that you should absorb his lordship's young affections."

Bessie Alden, with her clear eyes still overshadowed by her dark brows, continued to interrogate. "Why should that frighten them?"

Mrs. Westgate poised her answer with a smile before delivering it. "Because they think you are not good enough. You are a charming girl, beautiful and amiable, intelligent and clever, and as bien-élevée as it is possible to be; but you are not a fit match for Lord Lambeth."

Bessie Alden was decidedly disgusted. "Where do you

get such extraordinary ideas?" she asked. "You have said some such strange things lately. My dear Kitty, where do you collect them?"

Kitty was evidently enamored of her idea. "Yes, it would put them on pins and needles, and it wouldn't hurt you. Mr. Beaumont is already most uneasy; I could soon see that."

The young girl meditated a moment. "Do you mean that they spy upon him—that they interfere with him?"

"I don't know what power they have to interfere, but I know that a British mama may worry her son's life out."

It has been intimated that, as regards certain disagreeable things, Bessie Alden had a fund of skepticism. She abstained on the present occasion from expressing disbelief, for she wished not to irritate her sister. But she said to herself that Kitty had been misinformed—that this was a traveler's tale. Though she was a girl of a lively imagination, there could in the nature of things be, to her sense, no reality in the idea of her belonging to a vulgar category. What she said aloud was, "I must say that in that case I am very sorry for Lord Lambeth."

Mrs. Westgate, more and more exhilarated by her scheme, was smiling at her again. "If I could only believe it was safe!" she exclaimed. "When you begin to pity him, I, on my side, am afraid."

"Afraid of what?"

"Of your pitying him too much."

Bessie Alden turned away impatiently; but at the end of a minute she turned back. "What if I should pity him too much?" she asked.

Mrs. Westgate hereupon turned away, but after a moment's reflection she also faced her sister again. "It would come, after all, to the same thing," she said.

Lord Lambeth came the next day with his trap, and the two ladies, attended by Willie Woodley, placed themselves under his guidance, and were conveyed eastward, through some of the duskier portions of the metropolis, to the great turreted donjon which overlooks the London shipping. They all descended from their vehicle and entered the famous inclosure; and they secured the services of a venerable beefeater, who, though there

were many other claimants for legendary information,
made a fine exclusive party of them and marched them
through courts and corridors, through armories and
prisons. He delivered his usual peripatetic discourse,
and they stopped and stared, and peeped and stooped,
according to the official admonitions. Bessie Alden
asked the old man in the crimson doublet a great many
questions; she thought it a most fascinating place. Lord
Lambeth was in high good humor; he was constantly
laughing; he enjoyed what he would have called the lark.
Willie Woodley kept looking at the ceilings and tapping
the walls with the knuckle of a pearl-gray glove; and Mrs.
Westgate, asking at frequent intervals to be allowed to
sit down and wait till they came back, was as frequently
informed that they would never come back. To a great
many of Bessie's questions—chiefly on collateral points
of English history—the ancient warder was naturally unable to reply; whereupon she always appealed to Lord
Lambeth. But his lordship was very ignorant. He declared that he knew nothing about that sort of thing, and
he seemed greatly diverted at being treated as an authority.

"You can't expect everyone to know as much as you,"
he said.

"I should expect you to know a great deal more," declared Bessie Alden.

"Women always know more than men about names
and dates and that sort of thing," Lord Lambeth rejoined. "There was Lady Jane Grey we have just been
hearing about, who went in for Latin and Greek and all
the learning of her age."

"*You* have no right to be ignorant, at all events,"
said Bessie.

"Why haven't I as good a right as anyone else?"

"Because you have lived in the midst of all these
things."

"What things do you mean? Axes, and blocks, and
thumbscrews?"

"All these historical things. You belong to a historical
family."

"Bessie is really too historical," said Mrs. Westgate,
catching a word of this dialogue.

"Yes, you are too historical," said Lord Lambeth laughing, but thankful for a formula. "Upon my honor, you are too historical!"

He went with the ladies a couple of days later to Hampton Court, Willie Woodley being also of the party. The afternoon was charming, the famous horse chestnuts were in blossom, and Lord Lambeth, who quite entered into the spirit of the cockney excursionist, declared that it was a jolly old place. Bessie Alden was in ecstasies; she went about murmuring and exclaiming.

"It's too lovely," said the young girl; "it's too enchanting; it's too exactly what it ought to be!"

At Hampton Court the little flocks of visitors are not provided with an official bellwether, but are left to browse at discretion upon the local antiquities. It happened in this manner that, in default of another informant, Bessie Alden, who on doubtful questions was able to suggest a great many alternatives, found herself again applying for intellectual assistance to Lord Lambeth. But he again assured her that he was utterly helpless in such matters—that his education had been sadly neglected.

"And I am sorry it makes you unhappy," he added in a moment.

"You are very disappointing, Lord Lambeth," she said.

"Ah, now don't say that," he cried. "That's the worst thing you could possibly say."

"No," she rejoined, "it is not so bad as to say that I had expected nothing of you."

"I don't know. Give me a notion of the sort of thing you expected."

"Well," said Bessie Alden, "that you would be more what I should like to be—what I should try to be—in your place."

"Ah, my place!" exclaimed Lord Lambeth. "You are always talking about my place!"

The young girl looked at him; he thought she colored a little; and for a moment she made no rejoinder.

"Does it strike you that I am always talking about your place?" she asked.

"I am sure you do it a great honor," he said, fearing he had been uncivil.

"I have often thought about it," she went on after a moment. "I have often thought about your being a hereditary legislator. A hereditary legislator ought to know a great many things."

"Not if he doesn't legislate."

"But you do legislate; it's absurd your saying you don't. You are very much looked up to here—I am assured of that."

"I don't know that I ever noticed it."

"It is because you are used to it, then. You ought to fill the place."

"How do you mean to fill it?" asked Lord Lambeth.

"You ought to be very clever and brilliant, and to know almost everything."

Lord Lambeth looked at her a moment. "Shall I tell you something?" he asked. "A young man in my position, as you call it——"

"I didn't invent the term," interposed Bessie Alden. "I have seen it in a great many books."

"Hang it! you are always at your books. A fellow in my position, then, does very well whatever he does. That's about what I mean to say."

"Well, if your own people are content with you," said Bessie Alden, laughing, "it is not for me to complain. But I shall always think that, properly, you should have been a great mind—a great character."

"Ah, that's very theoretic," Lord Lambeth declared. "Depend upon it, that's a Yankee prejudice."

"Happy the country," said Bessie Alden, "where even people's prejudices are so elevated!"

"Well, after all," observed Lord Lambeth, "I don't know that I am such a fool as you are trying to make me out."

"I said nothing so rude as that; but I must repeat that you are disappointing."

"My dear Miss Alden," exclaimed the young man, "I am the best fellow in the world!"

"Ah, if it were not for that!" said Bessie Alden with a smile.

Mrs. Westgate had a good many more friends in London than she pretended, and before long she had renewed acquaintance with most of them. Their hospitality was extreme, so that, one thing leading to another, she began, as the phrase is, to go out. Bessie Alden, in this way, saw something of what she found it a great satisfaction to call to herself English society. She went to balls and danced, she went to dinners and talked, she went to concerts and listened (at concerts Bessie always listened), she went to exhibitions and wondered. Her enjoyment was keen and her curiosity insatiable, and, grateful in general for all her opportunities, she especially prized the privilege of meeting certain celebrated persons—authors and artists, philosophers and statesmen—of whose renown she had been a humble and distant beholder, and who now, as a part of the habitual furniture of London drawing rooms, struck her as stars fallen from the firmament and become palpable—revealing also sometimes, on contact, qualities not to have been predicted of sidereal bodies. Bessie, who knew so many of her contemporaries by reputation, had a good many personal disappointments; but, on the other hand, she had innumerable satisfactions and enthusiasms, and she communicated the emotions of either class to a dear friend, of her own sex, in Boston, with whom she was in voluminous correspondence. Some of her reflections, indeed, she attempted to impart to Lord Lambeth, who came almost every day to Jones's Hotel, and whom Mrs. Westgate admitted to be really devoted. Captain Littledale, it appeared, had gone to India; and of several others of Mrs. Westgate's ex-pensioners— gentlemen who, as she said, had made, in New York, a clubhouse of her drawing room—no tidings were to be obtained; but Lord Lambeth was certainly attentive enough to make up for the accidental absences, the short memories, all the other irregularities of everyone else. He drove them in the park, he took them to visit private collections of pictures, and, having a house of his own, invited them to dinner. Mrs. Westgate, following the fashion of many of her compatriots, caused herself and her sister to be presented at the English court by her diplomatic representative—for it was in this manner that she alluded to the American minister to England, inquiring what on earth he was put there for, if not to make the proper arrangements for one's going to a Drawing Room.

Lord Lambeth declared that he hated Drawing Rooms, but he participated in the ceremony on the day on which the two ladies at Jones's Hotel repaired to Buckingham Palace in a remarkable coach which his lordship had sent to fetch them. He had on a gorgeous uniform, and Bessie Alden was particularly struck with his appearance—especially when on her asking him, rather foolishly as she felt, if he were a loyal subject, he replied that he was a loyal subject to _her_. This declaration was emphasized by his dancing with her at a royal ball to which the two ladies afterward went, and was not impaired by the fact that she thought he danced very ill. He seemed to her wonderfully kind; she asked herself, with growing vivacity, why he should be so kind. It was his disposition—that seemed the natural answer. She had told her sister that she liked him very much, and now that she liked him more she wondered why. She liked him for his disposition; to this question as well that seemed the natural answer. When once the impressions of London life began to crowd thickly upon her, she completely forgot her sister's warning about the cynicism of public opinion. It had given her great pain at the moment, but there was no particular reason why she should remember it; it corresponded too little with any sensible reality; and it was disagreeable to Bessie to remember disagreeable things. So she was not haunted with the sense of a vulgar imputation. She was not in love with Lord Lambeth—she assured herself of that. It will immediately be observed that when such assurances become necessary the state of a young lady's affections is already ambiguous; and, indeed, Bessie Alden made no attempt to dissimulate—to herself, of course—a certain tenderness that she felt for the young nobleman. She said to herself that she liked the type to which he belonged—the simple, candid, manly, healthy English temperament. She spoke to herself of him as women speak of young men they like—alluded to his bravery (which she had never in the least seen tested), to his honesty and gentlemanliness, and was not silent upon the subject of his good looks. She was perfectly conscious, moreover, that she liked to think of his more adventitious merits; that her imagination was excited and gratified by the sight of a handsome young man endowed with such large opportunities —opportunities she hardly knew for what, but, as she supposed, for doing great things—for setting an example, for exerting an influence, for conferring happiness, for encouraging the arts. She had a kind of ideal of conduct for a young man who should find himself in this magnificent position, and she tried to adapt it to Lord Lambeth's deportment, as you might attempt to fit a silhouette in cut paper upon a shadow projected upon a wall. But Bessie Alden's silhouette refused to coincide with his lordship's image, and this want of harmony sometimes vexed her more than she thought reasonable. When he was absent it was, of course, less striking; then he seemed to her a sufficiently graceful combination of high responsibilities and amiable qualities. But when he sat there within sight, laughing and talking with his customary good humor and simplicity, she measured it more accurately, and she felt acutely that if Lord Lambeth's position was heroic, there was but little of the hero in the young man himself. Then her imagination wandered away from him—very far away; for it was an incontestable fact that at such moments he seemed distinctly dull. I am afraid that while Bessie's imagination was thus invidiously roaming, she cannot have been herself a very lively companion; but it may well have been that these occasional fits of indifference seemed to Lord Lambeth a part of the young girl's personal charm. It had been a part of this charm from the first that he felt that she judged him and measured him more freely and irresponsibly—more at her ease and her leisure, as it were —than several young ladies with whom he had been on the whole about as intimate. To feel this, and yet to feel that she also liked him, was very agreeable to Lord Lambeth. He fancied he had compassed that gratification so desirable to young men of title and fortune—being liked for himself. It is true that a cynical counselor might have whispered to him, "Liked for yourself? Yes; but not so very much!" He had, at any rate, the constant hope of being liked more.

It may seem, perhaps, a trifle singular—but it is

nevertheless true—that Bessie Alden, when he struck her as dull, devoted some time, on grounds of conscience, to trying to like him more. I say on grounds of conscience because she felt that he had been extremely "nice" to her sister, and because she reflected that it was no more than fair that she should think as well of him as he thought of her. This effort was possibly sometimes not so successful as it might have been, for the result of it was occasionally a vague irritation, which expressed itself in hostile criticism of several British institutions. Bessie Alden went to some entertainments at which she met Lord Lambeth; but she went to others at which his lordship was neither actually nor potentially present; and it was chiefly on these latter occasions that she encountered those literary and artistic celebrities of whom mention has been made. After a while she reduced the matter to a principle. If Lord Lambeth should appear anywhere, it was a symbol that there would be no poets and philosophers; and in consequence—for it was almost a strict consequence—she used to enumerate to the young man these objects of her admiration.

"You seem to be awfully fond of those sort of people," said Lord Lambeth one day, as if the idea had just occurred to him.

"They are the people in England I am most curious to see," Bessie Alden replied.

"I suppose that's because you have read so much," said Lord Lambeth gallantly.

"I have not read so much. It is because we think so much of them at home."

"Oh, I see," observed the young nobleman. "In Boston."

"Not only in Boston; everywhere," said Bessie. "We hold them in great honor; they go to the best dinner parties."

"I daresay you are right. I can't say I know many of them."

"It's a pity you don't," Bessie Alden declared. "It would do you good."

"I daresay it would," said Lord Lambeth very humbly. "But I must say I don't like the looks of some of them."

"Neither do I—of some of them. But there are all kinds, and many of them are charming."

"I have talked with two or three of them," the young man went on, "and I thought they had a kind of fawning manner."

"Why should they fawn?" Bessie Alden demanded.

"I'm sure I don't know. Why, indeed?"

"Perhaps you only thought so," said Bessie.

"Well, of course," rejoined her companion, "that's a kind of thing that can't be proved."

"In America they don't fawn," said Bessie.

"Ah, well, then, they must be better company."

Bessie was silent a moment. "That is one of the things I don't like about England," she said; "your keeping the distinguished people apart."

"How do you mean apart?"

"Why, letting them come only to certain places. You never see them."

Lord Lambeth looked at her a moment. "What people do you mean?"

"The eminent people—the authors and artists—the clever people."

"Oh, there are other eminent people besides those," said Lord Lambeth.

"Well, you certainly keep them apart," repeated the young girl.

"And there are other clever people," added Lord Lambeth simply.

Bessie Alden looked at him, and she gave a light laugh. "Not many," she said.

On another occasion—just after a dinner party—she told him that there was something else in England she did not like.

"Oh, I say!" he cried, "haven't you abused us enough?"

"I have never abused you at all," said Bessie; "but I don't like your *precedence*."

"It isn't my precedence!" Lord Lambeth declared, laughing.

"Yes, it is yours—just exactly yours; and I think it's odious," said Bessie.

"I never saw such a young lady for discussing things!

Has someone had the impudence to go before you?"
asked his lordship.

"It is not the going before me that I object to," said
Bessie; "it is their thinking that they have a right to do
it—*a right that I recognize.*"

"I never saw such a young lady as you are for not
'recognizing.' I have no doubt the thing is *beastly,* but
it saves a lot of trouble."

"It makes a lot of trouble. It's horrid," said Bessie.

"But how would you have the first people go?" asked
Lord Lambeth. "They can't go last."

"Whom do you mean by the first people?"

"Ah, if you mean to question first principles!" said
Lord Lambeth.

"If those are your first principles, no wonder some of
your arrangements are horrid," observed Bessie Alden
with a very pretty ferocity. "I am a young girl, so of
course I go last; but imagine what Kitty must feel on
being informed that she is not at liberty to budge until
certain other ladies have passed out."

"Oh, I say, she is not 'informed!'" cried Lord Lambeth. "No one would do such a thing as that."

"She is made to feel it," the young girl insisted—"as
if they were afraid she would make a rush for the door.
No; you have a lovely country," said Bessie Alden, "but
your precedence is horrid."

"I certainly shouldn't think your sister would like it,"
rejoined Lord Lambeth with even exaggerated gravity.
But Bessie Alden could induce him to enter no formal
protest against this repulsive custom, which he seemed
to think an extreme convenience.

Percy Beaumont all this time had been a very much
less frequent visitor at Jones's Hotel than his noble kinsman; he had, in fact, called but twice upon the two
American ladies. Lord Lambeth, who often saw him, reproached him with his neglect and declared that, although
Mrs. Westgate had said nothing about it, he was sure that
she was secretly wounded by it. "She suffers too much
to speak," said Lord Lambeth.

"That's all gammon," said Percy Beaumont; "there's a
limit to what people can suffer!" And, though sending
no apologies to Jones's Hotel, he undertook in a manner

to explain his absence. "You are always there," he said, "and that's reason enough for my not going."

"I don't see why. There is enough for both of us."

"I don't care to be a witness of your—your reckless passion," said Percy Beaumont.

Lord Lambeth looked at him with a cold eye and for a moment said nothing. "It's not so obvious as you might suppose," he rejoined dryly, "considering what a demonstrative beggar I am."

"I don't want to know anything about it—nothing whatever," said Beaumont. "Your mother asks me everytime she sees me whether I believe you are really lost—and Lady Pimlico does the same. I prefer to be able to answer that I know nothing about it—that I never go there. I stay away for consistency's sake. As I said the other day, they must look after you themselves."

"You are devilish considerate," said Lord Lambeth. "They never question me."

"They are afraid of you. They are afraid of irritating you and making you worse. So they go to work very cautiously, and, somewhere or other, they get their information. They know a great deal about you. They know that you have been with those ladies to the dome of St. Paul's and—where was the other place?—to the Thames Tunnel."

"If all their knowledge is as accurate as that, it must be very valuable," said Lord Lambeth.

"Well, at any rate, they know that you have been visiting the 'sights of the metropolis.' They think—very naturally, as it seems to me—that when you take to visiting the sights of the metropolis with a little American girl, there is serious cause for alarm." Lord Lambeth responded to this intimation by scornful laughter, and his companion continued, after a pause: "I said just now I didn't want to know anything about the affair; but I will confess that I am curious to learn whether you propose to marry Miss Bessie Alden."

On this point Lord Lambeth gave his interlocutor no immediate satisfaction; he was musing, with a frown. "By Jove," he said, "they go rather too far. They shall find me dangerous—I promise them."

Percy Beaumont began to laugh. "You don't redeem

your promises. You said the other day you would make your mother call."

Lord Lambeth continued to meditate. "I asked her to call," he said simply.

"And she declined?"

"Yes; but she shall do it yet."

"Upon my word," said Percy Beaumont, "if she gets much more frightened I believe she will." Lord Lambeth looked at him, and he went on. "She will go to the girl herself."

"How do you mean she will go to her?"

"She will beg her off, or she will bribe her. She will take strong measures."

Lord Lambeth turned away in silence, and his companion watched him take twenty steps and then slowly return. "I have invited Mrs. Westgate and Miss Alden to Branches," he said, "and this evening I shall name a day."

"And shall you invite your mother and your sisters to meet them?"

"Explicitly!"

"That will set the duchess off," said Percy Beaumont. "I suspect she will come."

"She may do as she pleases."

Beaumont looked at Lord Lambeth. "You do really propose to marry the little sister, then?"

"I like the way you talk about it!" cried the young man. "She won't gobble me down; don't be afraid."

"She won't leave you on your knees," said Percy Beaumont. "What is the inducement?"

"You talk about proposing: wait till I *have* proposed," Lord Lambeth went on.

"That's right, my dear fellow; think about it," said Percy Beaumont.

"She's a charming girl," pursued his lordship.

"Of course she's a charming girl. I don't know a girl more charming, intrinsically. But there are other charming girls nearer home."

"I like her spirit," observed Lord Lambeth, almost as if he were trying to torment his cousin.

"What's the peculiarity of her spirit?"

"She's not afraid, and she says things out, and she

thinks herself as good as anyone. She is the only girl I have ever seen that was not dying to marry me."

"How do you know that, if you haven't asked her?"

"I don't know how; but I know it."

"I am sure she asked me questions enough about your property and your titles," said Beaumont.

"She has asked me questions, too; no end of them," Lord Lambeth admitted. "But she asked for information, don't you know."

"Information? Aye, I'll warrant she wanted it. Depend upon it that she is dying to marry you just as much and just as little as all the rest of them."

"I shouldn't like her to refuse me—I shouldn't like that."

"If the thing would be so disagreeable, then, both to you and to her, in Heaven's name leave it alone," said Percy Beaumont.

Mrs. Westgate, on her side, had plenty to say to her sister about the rarity of Mr. Beaumont's visits and the nonappearance of the Duchess of Bayswater. She professed, however, to derive more satisfaction from this latter circumstance than she could have done from the most lavish attentions on the part of this great lady. "It is most marked," she said—"most marked. It is a delicious proof that we have made them miserable. The day we dined with Lord Lambeth I was really sorry for the poor fellow." It will have been gathered that the entertainment offered by Lord Lambeth to his American friends had not been graced by the presence of his anxious mother. He had invited several choice spirits to meet them; but the ladies of his immediate family were to Mrs. Westgate's sense—a sense possibly morbidly acute —conspicuous by their absence.

"I don't want to express myself in a manner that you dislike," said Bessie Alden; "but I don't know why you should have so many theories about Lord Lambeth's poor mother. You know a great many young men in New York without knowing their mothers."

Mrs. Westgate looked at her sister and then turned away. "My dear Bessie, you are superb!" she said.

"One thing is certain," the young girl continued. "If I

believed I were a cause of annoyance—however un-
witting—to Lord Lambeth's family, I should insist——"

"Insist upon my leaving England," said Mrs. Westgate.

"No, not that. I want to go to the National Gallery
again; I want to see Stratford-on-Avon and Canterbury
Cathedral. But I should insist upon his coming to see us
no more."

"That would be very modest and very pretty of you;
but you wouldn't do it now."

"Why do you say 'now'?" asked Bessie Alden. "Have I
ceased to be modest?"

"You care for him too much. A month ago, when
you said you didn't, I believe it was quite true. But at
present, my dear child," said Mrs. Westgate, "you
wouldn't find it quite so simple a matter never to see
Lord Lambeth again. I have seen it coming on."

"You are mistaken," said Bessie. "You don't understand."

"My dear child, don't be perverse," rejoined her sister.

"I know him better, certainly, if you mean that," said
Bessie. "And I like him very much. But I don't like him
enough to make trouble for him with his family. However, I don't believe in that."

"I like the way you say 'however,'" Mrs. Westgate exclaimed. "Come; you would not marry him?"

"Oh, no," said the young girl.

Mrs. Westgate for a moment seemed vexed. "Why
not, pray?" she demanded.

"Because I don't care to," said Bessie Alden.

The morning after Lord Lambeth had had, with Percy
Beaumont, that exchange of ideas which has just been
narrated, the ladies at Jones's Hotel received from his
lordship a written invitation to pay their projected visit
to Branches Castle on the following Tuesday. "I think
I have made up a very pleasant party," the young nobleman said. "Several people whom you know, and my
mother and sisters, who have so long been regrettably
prevented from making your acquaintance." Bessie Alden
lost no time in calling her sister's attention to the injustice she had done the Duchess of Bayswater, whose hos-
tility was now proved to be a vain illusion.

"Wait till you see if she comes," said Mrs. Westgate.

"And if she is to meet us at her son's house the obligation was all the greater for her to call upon us."

Bessie had not to wait long, and it appeared that Lord Lambeth's mother now accepted Mrs. Westgate's view of her duties. On the morrow, early in the afternoon, two cards were brought to the apartment of the American ladies—one of them bearing the name of the Duchess of Bayswater and the other that of the Countess of Pimlico. Mrs. Westgate glanced at the clock. "It is not yet four," she said; "they have come early; they wish to see us. We will receive them." And she gave orders that her visitors should be admitted. A few moments later they were introduced, and there was a solemn exchange of amenities. The duchess was a large lady, with a fine fresh color; the Countess of Pimlico was very pretty and elegant.

The duchess looked about her as she sat down—looked not especially at Mrs. Westgate. "I daresay my son has told you that I have been wanting to come and see you," she observed.

"You are very kind," said Mrs. Westgate, vaguely—her conscience not allowing her to assent to this proposition—and, indeed, not permitting her to enunciate her own with any appreciable emphasis.

"He says you were so kind to him in America," said the duchess.

"We are very glad," Mrs. Westgate replied, "to have been able to make him a little more—a little less—a little more comfortable."

"I think he stayed at your house," remarked the Duchess of Bayswater, looking at Bessie Alden.

"A very short time," said Mrs. Westgate.

"Oh!" said the duchess; and she continued to look at Bessie, who was engaged in conversation with her daughter.

"Do you like London?" Lady Pimlico had asked of Bessie, after looking at her a good deal—at her face and her hands, her dress and her hair.

"Very much indeed," said Bessie.

"Do you like this hotel?"

"It is very comfortable," said Bessie.

"Do you like stopping at hotels?" inquired Lady Pimlico after a pause.

"I am very fond of traveling," Bessie answered, "and I suppose hotels are a necessary part of it. But they are not the part I am fondest of."

"Oh, I hate traveling," said the Countess of Pimlico and transferred her attention to Mrs. Westgate.

"My son tells me you are going to Branches," the duchess presently resumed.

"Lord Lambeth has been so good as to ask us," said Mrs. Westgate, who perceived that her visitor had now begun to look at her, and who had her customary happy consciousness of a distinguished appearance. The only mitigation of her felicity on this point was that, having inspected her visitor's own costume, she said to herself, "She won't know how well I am dressed!"

"He has asked me to go, but I am not sure I shall be able," murmured the duchess.

"He had offered us the p—the prospect of meeting you," said Mrs. Westgate.

"I hate the country at this season," responded the duchess.

Mrs. Westgate gave a little shrug. "I think it is pleasanter than London."

But the duchess's eyes were absent again; she was looking very fixedly at Bessie. In a moment she slowly rose, walked to a chair that stood empty at the young girl's right hand, and silently seated herself. As she was a majestic, voluminous woman, this little transaction had, inevitably, an air of somewhat impressive intention. It diffused a certain awkwardness, which Lady Pimlico, as a sympathetic daughter, perhaps desired to rectify in turning to Mrs. Westgate.

"I daresay you go out a great deal," she observed.

"No, very little. We are strangers, and we didn't come here for society."

"I see," said Lady Pimlico. "It's rather nice in town just now."

"It's charming," said Mrs. Westgate. "But we only go to see a few people—whom we like."

"Of course one can't like everyone," said Lady Pimlico.

"It depends upon one's society," Mrs. Westgate rejoined.

The Duchess meanwhile had addressed herself to Bessie. "My son tells me the young ladies in America are so clever."

"I am glad they made so good an impression on him," said Bessie, smiling.

The Duchess was not smiling; her large fresh face was very tranquil. "He is very susceptible," she said. "He thinks everyone clever, and sometimes they are."

"Sometimes," Bessie assented, smiling still.

The duchess looked at her a little and then went on; "Lambeth is very susceptible, but he is very volatile, too."

"Volatile?" asked Bessie.

"He is very inconstant. It won't do to depend on him."

"Ah," said Bessie, "I don't recognize that description. We have depended on him greatly—my sister and I— and he has never disappointed us."

"He will disappoint you yet," said the duchess.

Bessie gave a little laugh, as if she were amused at the duchess's persistency. "I suppose it will depend on what we expect of him."

"The less you expect, the better," Lord Lambeth's mother declared.

"Well," said Bessie, "we expect nothing unreasonable."

The duchess for a moment was silent, though she appeared to have more to say. "Lambeth says he has seen so much of you," she presently began.

"He has been to see us very often; he has been very kind," said Bessie Alden.

"I daresay you are used to that. I am told there is a great deal of that in America."

"A great deal of kindness?" the young girl inquired, smiling.

"Is that what you call it? I know you have different expressions."

"We certainly don't always understand each other," said Mrs. Westgate, the termination of whose interview with Lady Pimlico allowed her to give her attention to their elder visitor.

"I am speaking of the young men calling so much upon the young ladies," the duchess explained.

"But surely in England," said Mrs. Westgate, "the young ladies don't call upon the young men?"

"Some of them do—almost!" Lady Pimlico declared. "When the young men are a great *parti*."

"Bessie, you must make a note of that," said Mrs. Westgate. "My sister," she added, "is a model traveler. She writes down all the curious facts she hears in a little book she keeps for the purpose."

The duchess was a little flushed; she looked all about the room, while her daughter turned to Bessie. "My brother told us you were wonderfully clever," said Lady Pimlico.

"He should have said my sister," Bessie answered—"when she says such things as that."

"Shall you be long at Branches?" the duchess asked, abruptly, of the young girl.

"Lord Lambeth has asked us for three days," said Bessie.

"I shall go," the duchess declared, "and my daughter, too."

"That will be charming!" Bessie rejoined.

"Delightful!" murmured Mrs. Westgate.

"I shall expect to see a great deal of you," the duchess continued. "When I go to Branches I monopolize my son's guests."

"They must be most happy," said Mrs. Westgate very graciously.

"I want immensely to see it—to see the castle," said Bessie to the duchess. "I have never seen one—in England, at least; and you know we have none in America."

"Ah, you are fond of castles?" inquired her Grace.

"Immensely!" replied the young girl. "It has been the dream of my life to live in one."

The duchess looked at her a moment, as if she hardly knew how to take this assurance, which, from her Grace's point of view, was either very artless or very audacious. "Well," she said, rising, "I will show you Branches myself." And upon this the two great ladies took their departure.

"What did they mean by it?" asked Mrs. Westgate, when they were gone.

"They meant to be polite," said Bessie, "because we are going to meet them."

"It is too late to be polite," Mrs. Westgate replied almost grimly. "They meant to overawe us by their fine manners and their grandeur, and to make you *lâcher prise*."

"*Lâcher prise?* What strange things you say!" murmured Bessie Alden.

"They meant to snub us, so that we shouldn't dare to go to Branches," Mrs. Westgate continued.

"On the contrary," said Bessie, "the duchess offered to show me the place herself."

"Yes, you may depend upon it she won't let you out of her sight. She will show you the place from morning till night."

"You have a theory for everything," said Bessie.

"And you apparently have none for anything."

"I saw no attempt to 'overawe' us," said the young girl. "Their manners were not fine."

"They were not even good!" Mrs. Westgate declared.

Bessie was silent a while, but in a few moments she observed that she had a very good theory. "They came to look at me," she said, as if this had been a very ingenious hypothesis. Mrs. Westgate did it justice; she greeted it with a smile and pronounced it most brilliant, while, in reality, she felt that the young girl's skepticism, or her charity, or, as she had sometimes called it appropriately, her idealism, was proof against irony. Bessie, however, remained meditative all the rest of that day and well on into the morrow.

On the morrow, before lunch, Mrs. Westgate had occasion to go out for an hour, and left her sister writing a letter. When she came back she met Lord Lambeth at the door of the hotel, coming away. She thought he looked slightly embarrassed; he was certainly very grave. "I am sorry to have missed you. Won't you come back?" she asked.

"No," said the young man, "I can't. I have seen your sister. I can never come back." Then he looked at her a moment and took her hand. "Goodbye, Mrs. Westgate," he said. "You have been very kind to me." And with

what she thought a strange, sad look in his handsome
young face, he turned away.

She went in, and she found Bessie still writing her
letter; that is, Mrs. Westgate perceived she was sitting at
the table with the pen in her hand and not writing. "Lord
Lambeth has been here," said the elder lady at last.

Then Bessie got up and showed her a pale, serious
face. She bent this face upon her sister for some time,
confessing silently and a little pleading. "I told him," she
said at last, "that we could not go to Branches."

Mrs. Westgate displayed just a spark of irritation.
"He might have waited," she said with a smile, "till one
had seen the castle." Later, an hour afterward, she said,
"Dear Bessie, I wish you might have accepted him."

"I couldn't," said Bessie gently.

"He is an excellent fellow," said Mrs. Westgate.

"I couldn't," Bessie repeated.

"If it is only," her sister added, "because those women
will think that they succeeded—that they paralyzed us!"

Bessie Alden turned away; but presently she added,
"They were interesting; I should have liked to see them
again."

"So should I!" cried Mrs. Westgate significantly.

"And I should have liked to see the castle," said
Bessie. "But now we must leave England," she added.

Her sister looked at her. "You will not wait to go to the
National Gallery?"

"Not now."

"Nor to Canterbury Cathedral?"

Bessie reflected a moment. "We can stop there on our
way to Paris," she said.

Lord Lambeth did not tell Percy Beaumont that the con-
tingency he was not prepared at all to like had occurred;
but Percy Beaumont, on hearing that the two ladies had
left London, wondered with some intensity what had
happened; wondered, that is, until the Duchess of Bayswater came a little to his assistance. The two ladies went
to Paris, and Mrs. Westgate beguiled the journey to that
city by repeating several times—"That's what I regret;
they will think they petrified us." But Bessie Alden seemed
to regret nothing.

DAISY MILLER: A STUDY

IN TWO PARTS

❧

PART I

At the little town of Vevey, in Switzerland, there is a particularly comfortable hotel. There are, indeed, many hotels, for the entertainment of tourists is the business of the place, which, as many travelers will remember, is seated upon the edge of a remarkably blue lake—a lake that it behooves every tourist to visit. The shore of the lake presents an unbroken array of establishments of this order, of every category, from the "grand hotel" of the newest fashion, with a chalk-white front, a hundred balconies, and a dozen flags flying from its roof, to the little Swiss pension of an elder day, with its name inscribed in German-looking lettering upon a pink or yellow wall and an awkward summerhouse in the angle of the garden. One of the hotels at Vevey, however, is famous, even classical, being distinguished from many of its upstart neighbors by an air both of luxury and of maturity. In this region, in the month of June, American travelers are extremely numerous; it may be said, indeed, that Vevey assumes at this period some of the characteristics of an American watering place. There are sights and sounds which evoke a vision, an echo, of Newport and Saratoga. There is a flitting hither and thither of "stylish" young girls, a rustling of muslin flounces, a rattle of dance music in the morning hours, a sound of high-pitched voices at all times. You receive an impression of these things at the excellent inn of the "Trois Couronnes" and are transported in fancy to the Ocean House or to Congress Hall. But at the "Trois Couronnes," it must be added, there are other features that are much at variance with these suggestions: neat German waiters, who look like secretaries of legation; Russian princesses sitting in the garden; little Polish boys walking about, held by the hand, with their governors; a view of the sunny crest of the Dent du Midi and the picturesque towers of the Castle of Chillon.

I hardly know whether it was the analogies or the differences that were uppermost in the mind of a young American, who, two or three years ago, sat in the garden of the "Trois Couronnes," looking about him, rather idly, at some of the graceful objects I have mentioned. It was a beautiful summer morning, and in whatever fashion the young American looked at things, they must have seemed to him charming. He had come from Geneva the day before by the little steamer, to see his aunt, who was staying at the hotel—Geneva having been for a long time his place of residence. But his aunt had a headache—his aunt had almost always a headache—and now she was shut up in her room, smelling camphor, so that he was at liberty to wander about. He was some seven-and-twenty years of age; when his friends spoke of him, they usually said that he was at Geneva "studying." When his enemies spoke of him, they said—but, after all, he had no enemies; he was an extremely amiable fellow, and universally liked. What I should say is, simply, that when certain persons spoke of him they affirmed that the reason of his spending so much time at Geneva was that he was extremely devoted to a lady who lived there—a foreign lady—a person older than himself. Very few Americans —indeed, I think none—had ever seen this lady, about whom there were some singular stories. But Winterbourne had an old attachment for the little metropolis of Calvinism; he had been put to school there as a boy, and he had afterward gone to college there—circumstances which had led to his forming a great many youthful friendships. Many of these he had kept, and they were a source of great satisfaction to him.

After knocking at his aunt's door and learning that she was indisposed, he had taken a walk about the town, and then he had come in to his breakfast. He had now finished his breakfast; but he was drinking a small cup of coffee, which had been served to him on a little table in the garden by one of the waiters who looked like an attaché. At last he finished his coffee and lit a cigarette. Presently a small boy came walking along the path—an urchin of nine or ten. The child, who was diminutive for his years, had an aged expression of countenance, a pale complexion, and sharp little features. He was dressed in knickerbockers, with red stockings, which displayed his poor little spindle-shanks; he also wore a brilliant red cravat. He carried in his hand a long alpenstock, the sharp point of which he thrust into everything that he approached—the flowerbeds, the garden benches, the trains of the ladies' dresses. In front of Winterbourne he paused, looking at him with a pair of bright, penetrating little eyes.

"Will you give me a lump of sugar?" he asked in a sharp, hard little voice—a voice immature and yet, somehow, not young.

Winterbourne glanced at the small table near him, on which his coffee service rested, and saw that several morsels of sugar remained. "Yes, you may take one," he answered; "but I don't think sugar is good for little boys."

This little boy stepped forward and carefully selected three of the coveted fragments, two of which he buried in the pocket of his knickerbockers, depositing the other as promptly in another place. He poked his alpenstock, lance-fashion, into Winterbourne's bench and tried to crack the lump of sugar with his teeth.

"Oh, blazes; it's har-r-d!" he exclaimed, pronouncing the adjective in a peculiar manner.

Winterbourne had immediately perceived that he might have the honor of claiming him as a fellow countryman. "Take care you don't hurt your teeth," he said, paternally.

"I haven't got any teeth to hurt. They have all come out. I have only got seven teeth. My mother counted them last night, and one came out right afterward. She said she'd slap me if any more came out. I can't help it. It's this old Europe. It's the climate that makes them come out. In America they didn't come out. It's these hotels."

Winterbourne was much amused. "If you eat three lumps of sugar, your mother will certainly slap you," he said.

"She's got to give me some candy, then," rejoined his

young interlocutor. "I can't get any candy here—any American candy. American candy's the best candy."

"And are American little boys the best little boys?" asked Winterbourne.

"I don't know. I'm an American boy," said the child.

"I see you are one of the best!" laughed Winterbourne.

"Are you an American man?" pursued this vivacious infant. And then, on Winterbourne's affirmative reply—"American men are the best," he declared.

His companion thanked him for the compliment, and the child, who had now got astride of his alpenstock, stood looking about him, while he attacked a second lump of sugar. Winterbourne wondered if he himself had been like this in his infancy, for he had been brought to Europe at about this age.

"Here comes my sister!" cried the child in a moment. "She's an American girl."

Winterbourne looked along the path and saw a beautiful young lady advancing. "American girls are the best girls," he said cheerfully to his young companion.

"My sister ain't the best!" the child declared. "She's always blowing at me."

"I imagine that is your fault, not hers," said Winterbourne. The young lady meanwhile had drawn near. She was dressed in white muslin, with a hundred frills and flounces, and knots of pale-colored ribbon. She was bareheaded, but she balanced in her hand a large parasol, with a deep border of embroidery; and she was strikingly, admirably pretty. "How pretty they are!" thought Winterbourne, straightening himself in his seat, as if he were prepared to rise.

The young lady paused in front of his bench, near the parapet of the garden, which overlooked the lake. The little boy had now converted his alpenstock into a vaulting pole, by the aid of which he was springing about in the gravel and kicking it up not a little.

"Randolph," said the young lady, "what *are* you doing?"

"I'm going up the Alps," replied Randolph. "This is the way!" And he gave another little jump, scattering the pebbles about Winterbourne's ears.

"That's the way they come down," said Winterbourne.

"He's an American man!" cried Randolph, in his little hard voice.

The young lady gave no heed to this announcement, but looked straight at her brother. "Well, I guess you had better be quiet," she simply observed.

It seemed to Winterbourne that he had been in a manner presented. He got up and stepped slowly toward the young girl, throwing away his cigarette. "This little boy and I have made acquaintance," he said, with great civility. In Geneva, as he had been perfectly aware, a young man was not at liberty to speak to a young unmarried lady except under certain rarely occurring conditions; but here at Vevey, what conditions could be better than these?—a pretty American girl coming and standing in front of you in a garden. This pretty American girl, however, on hearing Winterbourne's observation, simply glanced at him; she then turned her head and looked over the parapet, at the lake and the opposite mountains. He wondered whether he had gone too far, but he decided that he must advance farther, rather than retreat. While he was thinking of something else to say, the young lady turned to the little boy again.

"I should like to know where you got that pole," she said.

"I bought it," responded Randolph.

"You don't mean to say you're going to take it to Italy?"

"Yes, I am going to take it to Italy," the child declared.

The young girl glanced over the front of her dress and smoothed out a knot or two of ribbon. Then she rested her eyes upon the prospect again. "Well, I guess you had better leave it somewhere," she said after a moment.

"Are you going to Italy?" Winterbourne inquired in a tone of great respect.

The young lady glanced at him again. "Yes, sir," she replied. And she said nothing more.

"Are you—a—going over the Simplon?" Winterbourne pursued, a little embarrassed.

"I don't know," she said. "I suppose it's some mountain. Randolph, what mountain are we going over?"

"Going where?" the child demanded.

"To Italy," Winterbourne explained.

"I don't know," said Randolph. "I don't want to go to Italy. I want to go to America."

"Oh, Italy is a beautiful place!" rejoined the young man.

"Can you get candy there?" Randolph loudly inquired.

"I hope not," said his sister. "I guess you have had enough candy, and mother thinks so too."

"I haven't had any for ever so long—for a hundred weeks!" cried the boy, still jumping about.

The young lady inspected her flounces and smoothed her ribbons again; and Winterbourne presently risked an observation upon the beauty of the view. He was ceasing to be embarrassed, for he had begun to perceive that she was not in the least embarrassed herself. There had not been the slightest alteration in her charming complexion; she was evidently neither offended nor flattered. If she looked another way when he spoke to her, and seemed not particularly to hear him, this was simply her habit, her manner. Yet, as he talked a little more and pointed out some of the objects of interest in the view, with which she appeared quite unacquainted, she gradually gave him more of the benefit of her glance; and then he saw that this glance was perfectly direct and unshrinking. It was not, however, what would have been called an immodest glance, for the young girl's eyes were singularly honest and fresh. They were wonderfully pretty eyes; and, indeed, Winterbourne had not seen for a long time anything prettier than his fair countrywoman's various features— her complexion, her nose, her ears, her teeth. He had a great relish for feminine beauty; he was addicted to observing and analyzing it; and as regards this young lady's face he made several observations. It was not at all insipid, but it was not exactly expressive; and though it was eminently delicate, Winterbourne mentally accused it—very forgivingly—of a want of finish. He thought it very possible that Master Randolph's sister was a coquette; he was sure she had a spirit of her own; but in her bright, sweet, superficial little visage there was no mockery, no irony. Before long it became obvious that she was much disposed toward conversation. She told him that they were going to Rome for the winter—she and her mother and Randolph. She asked him if he was a "real American"; she shouldn't have taken him for one; he seemed more like a German—this was said after a little hesitation—especially when he spoke. Winterbourne, laughing, answered that he had met Germans who spoke like Americans, but that he had not, so far as he remembered, met an American who spoke like a German. Then he asked her if she should not be more comfortable in sitting upon the bench which he had just quitted. She answered that she liked standing up and walking about; but she presently sat down. She told him she was from New York State—"if you know where that is." Winterbourne learned more about her by catching hold of her small, slippery brother and making him stand a few minutes by his side.

"Tell me your name, my boy," he said.

"Randolph C. Miller," said the boy sharply. "And I'll tell you her name"; and he leveled his alpenstock at his sister.

"You had better wait till you are asked!" said this young lady calmly.

"I should like very much to know your name," said Winterbourne.

"Her name is Daisy Miller!" cried the child. "But that isn't her real name; that isn't her name on her cards."

"It's a pity you haven't got one of my cards!" said Miss Miller.

"Her real name is Annie P. Miller," the boy went on.

"Ask him *his* name," said his sister, indicating Winterbourne.

But on this point Randolph seemed perfectly indifferent; he continued to supply information with regard to his own family. "My father's name is Ezra B. Miller," he announced. "My father ain't in Europe; my father's in a better place than Europe."

Winterbourne imagined for a moment that this was the manner in which the child had been taught to intimate that Mr. Miller had been removed to the sphere of celestial reward. But Randolph immediately added, "My father's in Schenectady. He's got a big business. My father's rich, you bet!"

"Well!" ejaculated Miss Miller, lowering her parasol

and looking at the embroidered border. Winterbourne presently released the child, who departed, dragging his alpenstock along the path. "He doesn't like Europe," said the young girl. "He wants to go back."

"To Schenectady, you mean?"

"Yes; he wants to go right home. He hasn't got any boys here. There is one boy here, but he always goes round with a teacher; they won't let him play."

"And your brother hasn't any teacher?" Winterbourne inquired.

"Mother thought of getting him one, to travel round with us. There was a lady told her of a very good teacher; an American lady—perhaps you know her—Mrs. Sanders. I think she came from Boston. She told her of this teacher, and we thought of getting him to travel round with us. But Randolph said he didn't want a teacher traveling round with us. He said he wouldn't have lessons when he was in the cars. And we *are* in the cars about half the time. There was an English lady we met in the cars—I think her name was Miss Featherstone; perhaps you know her. She wanted to know why I didn't give Randolph lessons—give him 'instruction,' she called it. I guess he could give me more instruction than I could give him. He's very smart."

"Yes," said Winterbourne; "he seems very smart."

"Mother's going to get a teacher for him as soon as we get to Italy. Can you get good teachers in Italy?"

"Very good, I should think," said Winterbourne.

"Or else she's going to find some school. He ought to learn some more. He's only nine. He's going to college." And in this way Miss Miller continued to converse upon the affairs of her family and upon other topics. She sat there with her extremely pretty hands, ornamented with very brilliant rings, folded in her lap, and with her pretty eyes now resting upon those of Winterbourne, now wandering over the garden, the people who passed by, and the beautiful view. She talked to Winterbourne as if she had known him a long time. He found it very pleasant. It was many years since he had heard a young girl talk so much. It might have been said of this unknown young lady, who had come and sat down beside him upon a bench, that she chattered. She was very quiet; she sat in a charming, tranquil attitude; but her lips and her eyes were constantly moving. She had a soft, slender, agreeable voice, and her tone was decidedly sociable. She gave Winterbourne a history of her movements and intentions and those of her mother and brother, in Europe, and enumerated, in particular, the various hotels at which they had stopped. "That English lady in the cars," she said—"Miss Featherstone—asked me if we didn't all live in hotels in America. I told her I had never been in so many hotels in my life as since I came to Europe. I have never seen so many—it's nothing but hotels." But Miss Miller did not make this remark with a querulous accent; she appeared to be in the best humor with everything. She declared that the hotels were very good, when once you got used to their ways, and that Europe was perfectly sweet. She was not disappointed—not a bit. Perhaps it was because she had heard so much about it before. She had ever so many intimate friends that had been there ever so many times. And then she had had ever so many dresses and things from Paris. Whenever she put on a Paris dress she felt as if she were in Europe.

"It was a kind of a wishing cap," said Winterbourne.

"Yes," said Miss Miller without examining this analogy; "it always made me wish I was here. But I needn't have done that for dresses. I am sure they send all the pretty ones to America; you see the most frightful things here. The only thing I don't like," she proceeded, "is the society. There isn't any society; or, if there is, I don't know where it keeps itself. Do you? I suppose there is some society somewhere, but I haven't seen anything of it. I'm very fond of society, and I have always had a great deal of it. I don't mean only in Schenectady, but in New York. I used to go to New York every winter. In New York I had lots of society. Last winter I had seventeen dinners given me; and three of them were by gentlemen," added Daisy Miller. "I have more friends in New York than in Schenectady—more gentleman friends; and more young lady friends too," she resumed in a moment. She paused again for an instant; she was looking at Winterbourne with all her prettiness in her lively eyes and in her light, slightly monotonous smile. "I have always had," she said, "a great deal of gentlemen's society."

Poor Winterbourne was amused, perplexed, and decidedly charmed. He had never yet heard a young girl express herself in just this fashion; never, at least, save in cases where to say such things seemed a kind of demonstrative evidence of a certain laxity of deportment. And yet was he to accuse Miss Daisy Miller of actual or potential *inconduite*, as they said at Geneva? He felt that he had lived at Geneva so long that he had lost a good deal; he had become dishabituated to the American tone. Never, indeed, since he had grown old enough to appreciate things, had he encountered a young American girl of so pronounced a type as this. Certainly she was very charming, but how deucedly sociable! Was she simply a pretty girl from New York State? Were they all like that, the pretty girls who had a good deal of gentlemen's society? Or was she also a designing, an audacious, an unscrupulous young person? Winterbourne had lost his instinct in this matter, and his reason could not help him. Miss Daisy Miller looked extremely innocent. Some people had told him that, after all, American girls were exceedingly innocent; and others had told him that, after all, they were not. He was inclined to think Miss Daisy Miller was a flirt—a pretty American flirt. He had never, as yet, had any relations with young ladies of this category. He had known, here in Europe, two or three women—persons older than Miss Daisy Miller, and provided, for respectability's sake, with husbands—who were great coquettes—dangerous, terrible women, with whom one's relations were liable to take a serious turn. But this young girl was not a coquette in that sense; she was very unsophisticated; she was only a pretty American flirt. Winterbourne was almost grateful for having found the formula that applied to Miss Daisy Miller. He leaned back in his seat; he remarked to himself that she had the most charming nose he had ever seen; he wondered what were the regular conditions and limitations of one's intercourse with a pretty American flirt. It presently became apparent that he was on the way to learn.

"Have you been to that old castle?" asked the young

girl, pointing with her parasol to the far-gleaming walls of the Château de Chillon.

"Yes, formerly, more than once," said Winterbourne. "You too, I suppose, have seen it?"

"No; we haven't been there. I want to go there dreadfully. Of course I mean to go there. I wouldn't go away from here without having seen that old castle."

"It's a very pretty excursion," said Winterbourne, "and very easy to make. You can drive, you know, or you can go by the little steamer."

"You can go in the cars," said Miss Miller.

"Yes; you can go in the cars," Winterbourne assented.

"Our courier says they take you right up to the castle," the young girl continued. "We were going last week, but my mother gave out. She suffers dreadfully from dyspepsia. She said she couldn't go. Randolph wouldn't go either; he says he doesn't think much of old castles. But I guess we'll go this week, if we can get Randolph."

"Your brother is not interested in ancient monuments?" Winterbourne inquired, smiling.

"He says he don't care much about old castles. He's only nine. He wants to stay at the hotel. Mother's afraid to leave him alone, and the courier won't stay with him; so we haven't been to many places. But it will be too bad if we don't go up there." And Miss Miller pointed again at the Château de Chillon.

"I should think it might be arranged," said Winterbourne. "Couldn't you get some one to stay for the afternoon with Randolph?"

Miss Miller looked at him a moment, and then, very placidly, "I wish *you* would stay with him!" she said.

Winterbourne hesitated a moment. "I should much rather go to Chillon with you."

"With me?" asked the young girl with the same placidity.

She didn't rise, blushing, as a young girl at Geneva would have done; and yet Winterbourne, conscious that he had been very bold, thought it possible she was offended. "With your mother," he answered very respectfully.

But it seemed that both his audacity and his respect

were lost upon Miss Daisy Miller. "I guess my mother won't go, after all," she said. "She don't like to ride round in the afternoon. But did you really mean what you said just now—that you would like to go up there?"

"Most earnestly," Winterbourne declared.

"Then we may arrange it. If mother will stay with Randolph, I guess Eugenio will."

"Eugenio?" the young man inquired.

"Eugenio's our courier. He doesn't like to stay with Randolph; he's the most fastidious man I ever saw. But he's a splendid courier. I guess he'll stay at home with Randolph if mother does, and then we can go to the castle."

Winterbourne reflected for an instant as lucidly as possible—"we" could only mean Miss Daisy Miller and himself. This program seemed almost too agreeable for credence; he felt as if he ought to kiss the young lady's hand. Possibly he would have done so and quite spoiled the project, but at this moment another person, presumably Eugenio, appeared. A tall, handsome man, with superb whiskers, wearing a velvet morning coat and a brilliant watch chain, approached Miss Miller, looking sharply at her companion. "Oh, Eugenio!" said Miss Miller with the friendliest accent.

Eugenio had looked at Winterbourne from head to foot; he now bowed gravely to the young lady. "I have the honor to inform mademoiselle that luncheon is upon the table."

Miss Miller slowly rose. "See here, Eugenio!" she said; "I'm going to that old castle, anyway."

"To the Château de Chillon, mademoiselle?" the courier inquired. "Mademoiselle has made arrangements?" he added in a tone which struck Winterbourne as very impertinent.

Eugenio's tone apparently threw, even to Miss Miller's own apprehension, a slightly ironical light upon the young girl's situation. She turned to Winterbourne, blushing a little—a very little. "You won't back out?" she said.

"I shall not be happy till we go!" he protested.

"And you are staying in this hotel?" she went on. "And you are really an American?"

The courier stood looking at Winterbourne offensively. The young man, at least, thought his manner of looking an offense to Miss Miller; it conveyed an imputation that she "picked up" acquaintances. "I shall have the honor of presenting to you a person who will tell you all about me," he said, smiling and referring to his aunt.

"Oh, well, we'll go some day," said Miss Miller. And she gave him a smile and turned away. She put up her parasol and walked back to the inn beside Eugenio. Winterbourne stood looking after her; and as she moved away, drawing her muslin furbelows over the gravel, said to himself that she had the *tournure* of a princess.

He had, however, engaged to do more than proved feasible, in promising to present his aunt, Mrs. Costello, to Miss Daisy Miller. As soon as the former lady had got better of her headache, he waited upon her in her apartment; and, after the proper inquiries in regard to her health, he asked her if she had observed in the hotel an American family—a mamma, a daughter, and a little boy.

"And a courier?" said Mrs. Costello. "Oh yes, I have observed them. Seen them—heard them—and kept out of their way." Mrs. Costello was a widow with a fortune; a person of much distinction, who frequently intimated that, if she were not so dreadfully liable to sick headaches, she would probably have left a deeper impress upon her time. She had a long, pale face, a high nose, and a great deal of very striking white hair, which she wore in large puffs and *rouleaux* over the top of her head. She had two sons married in New York and another who was now in Europe. This young man was amusing himself at Hamburg, and, though he was on his travels, was rarely perceived to visit any particular city at the moment selected by his mother for her own appearance there. Her nephew, who had come up to Vevey expressly to see her, was therefore more attentive than those who, as she said, were nearer to her. He had imbibed at Geneva the idea that one must always be attentive to one's aunt. Mrs. Costello had not seen him for many years, and she was greatly pleased with him, manifesting her approbation by initiating him into many of the secrets of that social sway which, as she gave him to understand, she exerted in the American capital. She admitted that she was very exclusive; but, if he were acquainted with New York, he would see that one had to be. And her picture of the minutely hierarchical constitution of the society of that city, which she presented to him in many different lights, was, to Winterbourne's imagination, almost oppressively striking.

He immediately perceived, from her tone, that Miss Daisy Miller's place in the social scale was low. "I am afraid you don't approve of them," he said.

"They are very common," Mrs. Costello declared. "They are the sort of Americans that one does one's duty by not—not accepting."

"Ah, you don't accept them?" said the young man.

"I can't, my dear Frederick. I would if I could, but I can't."

"The young girl is very pretty," said Winterbourne in a moment.

"Of course she's pretty. But she is very common."

"I see what you mean, of course," said Winterbourne after another pause.

"She has that charming look that they all have," his aunt resumed. "I can't think where they pick it up; and she dresses in perfection—no, you don't know how well she dresses. I can't think where they get their taste."

"But, my dear aunt, she is not, after all, a Comanche savage."

"She is a young lady," said Mrs. Costello, "who has an intimacy with her mamma's courier."

"An intimacy with the courier?" the young man demanded.

"Oh, the mother is just as bad! They treat the courier like a familiar friend—like a gentleman. I shouldn't wonder if he dines with them. Very likely they have never seen a man with such good manners, such fine clothes, so like a gentleman. He probably corresponds to the young lady's idea of a count. He sits with them in the garden in the evening. I think he smokes."

Winterbourne listened with interest to these disclosures; they helped him to make up his mind about Miss Daisy. Evidently she was rather wild. "Well," he said, "I am not a courier, and yet she was very charming to me."

"You had better have said at first," said Mrs. Costello with dignity, "that you had made her acquaintance."

"We simply met in the garden, and we talked a bit."

"*Tout bonnement!* And pray what did you say?"

"I said I should take the liberty of introducing her to my admirable aunt."

"I am much obliged to you."

"It was to guarantee my respectability," said Winterbourne.

"And pray who is to guarantee hers?"

"Ah, you are cruel!" said the young man. "She's a very nice young girl."

"You don't say that as if you believed it," Mrs. Costello observed.

"She is completely uncultivated," Winterbourne went on. "But she is wonderfully pretty, and, in short, she is very nice. To prove that I believe it, I am going to take her to the Château de Chillon."

"You two are going off there together? I should say it proved just the contrary. How long had you known her, may I ask, when this interesting project was formed? You haven't been twenty-four hours in the house."

"I have known her half an hour!" said Winterbourne, smiling.

"Dear me!" cried Mrs. Costello. "What a dreadful girl!"

Her nephew was silent for some moments. "You really think, then," he began earnestly, and with a desire for trustworthy information—"you really think that——" But he paused again.

"Think what, sir?" said his aunt.

"That she is the sort of young lady who expects a man, sooner or later, to carry her off?"

"I haven't the least idea what such young ladies expect a man to do. But I really think that you had better not meddle with little American girls that are uncultivated, as you call them. You have lived too long out of the country. You will be sure to make some great mistake. You are too innocent."

"My dear aunt, I am not so innocent," said Winterbourne, smiling and curling his mustache.

"You are guilty too, then!"

Winterbourne continued to curl his mustache meditatively. "You won't let the poor girl know you then?" he asked at last.

"Is it literally true that she is going to the Château de Chillon with you?"

"I think that she fully intends it."

"Then, my dear Frederick," said Mrs. Costello, "I must decline the honor of her acquaintance. I am an old woman, but I am not too old, thank Heaven, to be shocked!"

"But don't they all do these things—the young girls in America?" Winterbourne inquired.

Mrs. Costello stared a moment. "I should like to see my granddaughters do them!" she declared grimly.

This seemed to throw some light upon the matter, for Winterbourne remembered to have heard that his pretty cousins in New York were "tremendous flirts." If, therefore, Miss Daisy Miller exceeded the liberal margin allowed to these young ladies, it was probable that anything might be expected of her. Winterbourne was impatient to see her again, and he was vexed with himself that, by instinct, he should not appreciate her justly.

Though he was impatient to see her, he hardly knew what he should say to her about his aunt's refusal to become acquainted with her; but he discovered, promptly enough, that with Miss Daisy Miller there was no great need of walking on tiptoe. He found her that evening in the garden, wandering about in the warm starlight like an indolent sylph, and swinging to and fro the largest fan he had ever beheld. It was ten o'clock. He had dined with his aunt, had been sitting with her since dinner, and had just taken leave of her till the morrow. Miss Daisy Miller seemed very glad to see him; she declared it was the longest evening she had ever passed.

"Have you been all alone?" he asked.

"I have been walking round with mother. But mother gets tired walking round," she answered.

"Has she gone to bed?"

"No; she doesn't like to go to bed," said the young girl. "She doesn't sleep—not three hours. She says she doesn't know how she lives. She's dreadfully nervous. I guess she sleeps more than she thinks. She's gone somewhere after Randolph; she wants to try to get him to go to bed. He doesn't like to go to bed."

"Let us hope she will persuade him," observed Winterbourne.

"She will talk to him all she can; but he doesn't like her to talk to him," said Miss Daisy, opening her fan. "She's going to try to get Eugenio to talk to him. But he isn't afraid of Eugenio. Eugenio's a splendid courier, but he can't make much impression on Randolph! I don't believe he'll go to bed before eleven." It appeared that Randolph's vigil was in fact triumphantly prolonged, for Winterbourne strolled about with the young girl for some time without meeting her mother. "I have been looking round for that lady you want to introduce me to," his companion resumed. "She's your aunt." Then, on Winterbourne's admitting the fact and expressing some curiosity as to how she had learned it, she said she had heard all about Mrs. Costello from the chambermaid. She was very quiet and very *comme il faut;* she wore white puffs; she spoke to no one, and she never dined at the table d'hôte. Every two days she had a headache. "I think that's a lovely description, headache and all!" said Miss Daisy, chattering along in her thin, gay voice. "I want to know her ever so much. I know just what *your* aunt would be; I know I should like her. She would be very exclusive. I like a lady to be exclusive; I'm dying to be exclusive myself. Well, we *are* exclusive, mother and I. We don't speak to everyone—or they don't speak to us. I suppose it's about the same thing. Anyway, I shall be ever so glad to know your aunt."

Winterbourne was embarrassed. "She would be most happy," he said; "but I am afraid those headaches will interfere."

The young girl looked at him through the dusk. "But I suppose she doesn't have a headache every day," she said sympathetically.

Winterbourne was silent a moment. "She tells me she does," he answered at last, not knowing what to say.

Miss Daisy Miller stopped and stood looking at him. Her prettiness was still visible in the darkness; she was opening and closing her enormous fan. "She doesn't

want to know me!" she said suddenly. "Why don't you
say so? You needn't be afraid. I'm not afraid!" And
she gave a little laugh.

Winterbourne fancied there was a tremor in her voice;
he was touched, shocked, mortified by it. "My dear
young lady," he protested, "she knows no one. It's her
wretched health."

The young girl walked on a few steps, laughing still.
"You needn't be afraid," she repeated. "Why should
she want to know me?" Then she paused again; she was
close to the parapet of the garden, and in front of her
was the starlit lake. There was a vague sheen upon its
surface, and in the distance were dimly seen mountain
forms. Daisy Miller looked out upon the mysterious
prospect and then she gave another little laugh. "Gracious! she *is* exclusive!" she said. Winterbourne wondered
whether she was seriously wounded, and for a moment
almost wished that her sense of injury might be such as
to make it becoming in him to attempt to reassure and
comfort her. He had a pleasant sense that she would
be very approachable for consolatory purposes. He felt
then, for the instant, quite ready to sacrifice his aunt, con-
versationally; to admit that she was a proud, rude
woman, and to declare that they needn't mind her. But
before he had time to commit himself to this perilous
mixture of gallantry and impiety, the young lady, re-
suming her walk, gave an exclamation in quite another
tone. "Well, here's Mother! I guess she hasn't got Randolph to go to bed." The figure of a lady appeared, at a
distance, very indistinct in the darkness, and advancing
with a slow and wavering movement. Suddenly it
seemed to pause.

"Are you sure it is your mother? Can you distinguish
her in this thick dusk?" Winterbourne asked.

"Well!" cried Miss Daisy Miller with a laugh; "I guess
I know my own mother. And when she has got on my
shawl, too! She is always wearing my things."

The lady in question, ceasing to advance, hovered
vaguely about the spot at which she had checked her
steps.

"I am afraid your mother doesn't see you," said Winterbourne. "Or perhaps," he added, thinking, with Miss

Miller, the joke permissible—"perhaps she feels guilty about your shawl."

"Oh, it's a fearful old thing!" the young girl replied serenely. "I told her she could wear it. She won't come here because she sees you."

"Ah, then," said Winterbourne, "I had better leave you.

"Oh, no; come on!" urged Miss Daisy Miller.

"I'm afraid your mother doesn't approve of my walking with you."

Miss Miller gave him a serious glance. "It isn't for me; it's for you—that is, it's for *her*. Well, I don't know who it's for! But mother doesn't like any of my gentlemen friends. She's right down timid. She always makes a fuss if I introduce a gentleman. But I *do* introduce them—almost always. If I didn't introduce my gentlemen friends to Mother," the young girl added in her little soft, flat monotone, "I shouldn't think I was natural."

"To introduce me," said Winterbourne, "you must know my name." And he proceeded to pronounce it.

"Oh, dear, I can't say all that!" said his companion with a laugh. But by this time they had come up to Mrs. Miller, who, as they drew near, walked to the parapet of the garden and leaned upon it, looking intently at the lake and turning her back to them. "Mother!" said the young girl in a tone of decision. Upon this the elder lady turned round. "Mr. Winterbourne," said Miss Daisy Miller, introducing the young man very frankly and prettily. "Common," she was, as Mrs. Costello had pronounced her; yet it was a wonder to Winterbourne that, with her commonness, she had a singularly delicate grace.

Her mother was a small, spare, light person, with a wandering eye, a very exiguous nose, and a large forehead, decorated with a certain amount of thin, much frizzled hair. Like her daughter, Mrs. Miller was dressed with extreme elegance; she had enormous diamonds in her ears. So far as Winterbourne could observe, she gave him no greeting—she certainly was not looking at him. Daisy was near her, pulling her shawl straight. "What are you doing, poking round here?" this young lady inquired, but by no means with that harshness of accent which her choice of words may imply.

"I don't know," said her mother, turning toward the lake again.

"I shouldn't think you'd want that shawl!" Daisy exclaimed.

"Well, I do!" her mother answered with a little laugh.

"Did you get Randolph to go to bed?" asked the young girl.

"No; I couldn't induce him," said Mrs. Miller very gently. "He wants to talk to the waiter. He likes to talk to that waiter."

"I was telling Mr. Winterbourne," the young girl went on; and to the young man's ear her tone might have indicated that she had been uttering his name all her life.

"Oh, yes!" said Winterbourne; "I have the pleasure of knowing your son."

Randolph's mamma was silent; she turned her attention to the lake. But at last she spoke. "Well, I don't see how he lives!"

"Anyhow, it isn't so bad as it was at Dover," said Daisy Miller.

"And what occurred at Dover?" Winterbourne asked.

"He wouldn't go to bed at all. I guess he sat up all night in the public parlor. He wasn't in bed at twelve o'clock: I know that."

"It was half-past twelve," declared Mrs. Miller with mild emphasis.

"Does he sleep much during the day?" Winterbourne demanded.

"I guess he doesn't sleep much," Daisy rejoined.

"I wish he would!" said her mother. "It seems as if he couldn't."

"I think he's real tiresome," Daisy pursued.

Then, for some moments, there was silence. "Well, Daisy Miller," said the elder lady, presently, "I shouldn't think you'd want to talk against your own brother!"

"Well, he *is* tiresome, Mother," said Daisy, quite without the asperity of a retort.

"He's only nine," urged Mrs. Miller.

"Well, he wouldn't go to that castle," said the young girl. "I'm going there with Mr. Winterbourne."

To this announcement, very placidly made, Daisy's mamma offered no response. Winterbourne took for granted that she deeply disapproved of the projected excursion; but he said to himself that she was a simple, easily managed person, and that a few deferential protestations would take the edge from her displeasure. "Yes," he began; "your daughter has kindly allowed me the honor of being her guide."

Mrs. Miller's wandering eyes attached themselves, with a sort of appealing air, to Daisy, who, however, strolled a few steps farther, gently humming to herself. "I presume you will go in the cars," said her mother.

"Yes, or in the boat," said Winterbourne.

"Well, of course, I don't know," Mrs. Miller rejoined. "I have never been to that castle."

"It is a pity you shouldn't go," said Winterbourne, beginning to feel reassured as to her opposition. And yet he was quite prepared to find that, as a matter of course, she meant to accompany her daughter.

"We've been thinking ever so much about going," she pursued; "but it seems as if we couldn't. Of course Daisy —she wants to go round. But there's a lady here—I don't know her name—she says she shouldn't think we'd want to go to see castles *here;* she should think we'd want to wait till we got to Italy. It seems as if there would be so many there," continued Mrs. Miller with an air of increasing confidence. "Of course we only want to see the principal ones. We visited several in England," she presently added.

"Ah yes! in England there are beautiful castles," said Winterbourne. "But Chillon, here, is very well worth seeing."

"Well, if Daisy feels up to it—" said Mrs. Miller, in a tone impregnated with a sense of the magnitude of the enterprise. "It seems as if there was nothing she wouldn't undertake."

"Oh, I think she'll enjoy it!" Winterbourne declared. And he desired more and more to make it a certainty that he was to have the privilege of a tête-à-tête with the young lady, who was still strolling along in front of them, softly vocalizing. "You are not disposed, madam," he inquired, "to undertake it yourself?"

Daisy's mother looked at him an instant askance, and then walked forward in silence. Then—"I guess she had better go alone," she said simply. Winterbourne observed to himself that this was a very different type of maternity from that of the vigilant matrons who massed themselves in the forefront of social intercourse in the dark old city at the other end of the lake. But his meditations were interrupted by hearing his name very distinctly pronounced by Mrs. Miller's unprotected daughter.

"Mr. Winterbourne!" murmured Daisy.

"Mademoiselle!" said the young man.

"Don't you want to take me out in a boat?"

"At present?" he asked.

"Of course!" said Daisy.

"Well, Annie Miller!" exclaimed her mother.

"I beg you, madam, to let her go," said Winterbourne ardently; for he had never yet enjoyed the sensation of guiding through the summer starlight a skiff freighted with a fresh and beautiful young girl.

"I shouldn't think she'd want to," said her mother. "I should think she'd rather go indoors."

"I'm sure Mr. Winterbourne wants to take me," Daisy declared. "He's so awfully devoted!"

"I will row you over to Chillon in the starlight."

"I don't believe it!" said Daisy.

"Well!" ejaculated the elder lady again.

"You haven't spoken to me for half an hour," her daughter went on.

"I have been having some very pleasant conversation with your mother," said Winterbourne.

"Well, I want you to take me out in a boat!" Daisy repeated. They had all stopped, and she had turned round and was looking at Winterbourne. Her face wore a charming smile, her pretty eyes were gleaming, she was swinging her great fan about. No; it's impossible to be prettier than that, thought Winterbourne.

"There are half a dozen boats moored at that landing place," he said, pointing to certain steps which descended from the garden to the lake. "If you will do me the honor to accept my arm, we will go and select one of them."

Daisy stood there smiling; she threw back her head and gave a little, light laugh. "I like a gentleman to be formal!" she declared.

"I assure you it's a formal offer."

"I was bound I would make you say something," Daisy went on.

"You see, it's not very difficult," said Winterbourne. "But I am afraid you are chaffing me."

"I think not, sir," remarked Mrs. Miller very gently.

"Do, then, let me give you a row," he said to the young girl.

"It's quite lovely, the way you say that!" cried Daisy.

"It will be still more lovely to do it."

"Yes, it would be lovely!" said Daisy. But she made no movement to accompany him; she only stood there laughing.

"I should think you had better find out what time it is," interposed her mother.

"It is eleven o'clock, madam," said a voice, with a foreign accent, out of the neighboring darkness; and Winterbourne, turning, perceived the florid personage who was in attendance upon the two ladies. He had apparently just approached.

"Oh, Eugenio," said Daisy, "I am going out in a boat!"

Eugenio bowed. "At eleven o'clock, mademoiselle?"

"I am going with Mr. Winterbourne—this very minute."

"Do tell her she can't," said Mrs. Miller to the courier.

"I think you had better not go out in a boat, mademoiselle," Eugenio declared.

Winterbourne wished to Heaven this pretty girl were not so familiar with her courier; but he said nothing.

"I suppose you don't think it's proper!" Daisy exclaimed. "Eugenio doesn't think anything's proper."

"I am at your service," said Winterbourne.

"Does mademoiselle propose to go alone?" asked Eugenio of Mrs. Miller.

"Oh, no; with this gentleman!" answered Daisy's mamma.

The courier looked for a moment at Winterbourne—the latter thought he was smiling—and then, solemnly, with a bow, "As mademoiselle pleases!" he said.

"Oh, I hoped you would make a fuss!" said Daisy. "I don't care to go now."

"I myself shall make a fuss if you don't go," said Winterbourne.

"That's all I want—a little fuss!" And the young girl began to laugh again.

"Mr. Randolph has gone to bed!" the courier announced frigidly.

"Oh, Daisy; now we can go!" said Mrs. Miller.

Daisy turned away from Winterbourne, looking at him, smiling and fanning herself. "Good night," she said; "I hope you are disappointed, or disgusted, or something!"

He looked at her, taking the hand she offered him. "I am puzzled," he answered.

"Well, I hope it won't keep you awake!" she said very smartly; and, under the escort of the privileged Eugenio, the two ladies passed toward the house.

Winterbourne stood looking after them; he was indeed puzzled. He lingered beside the lake for a quarter of an hour, turning over the mystery of the young girl's sudden familiarities and caprices. But the only very definite conclusion he came to was that he should enjoy deucedly "going off" with her somewhere.

Two days afterward he went off with her to the Castle of Chillon. He waited for her in the large hall of the hotel, where the couriers, the servants, the foreign tourists, were lounging about and staring. It was not the place he should have chosen, but she had appointed it. She came tripping downstairs, buttoning her long gloves, squeezing her folded parasol against her pretty figure, dressed in the perfection of a soberly elegant traveling costume. Winterbourne was a man of imagination and, as our ancestors used to say, sensibility; as he looked at her dress and, on the great staircase, her little rapid, confiding step, he felt as if there were something romantic going forward. He could have believed he was going to elope with her. He passed out with her among all the idle people that were assembled there; they were all looking at her very hard; she had begun to chatter as soon as she joined him. Winterbourne's preference had been that they should be conveyed to Chillon in a carriage; but she expressed a lively wish to go in the little steamer; she declared that she had a passion for steamboats. There was always such a lovely breeze upon the water, and you saw such lots of people. The sail was not long, but Winterbourne's companion found time to say a great many things. To the young man himself their little excursion was so much of an escapade—an adventure—that, even allowing for her habitual sense of freedom, he had some expectation of seeing her regard it in the same way. But it must be confessed that, in this particular, he was disappointed. Daisy Miller was extremely animated, she was in charming spirits; but she was apparently not at all excited; she was not fluttered; she avoided neither his eyes nor those of anyone else; she blushed neither when she looked at him nor when she felt that people were looking at her. People continued to look at her a great deal, and Winterbourne took much satisfaction in his pretty companion's distinguished air. He had been a little afraid that she would talk loud, laugh overmuch, and even, perhaps, desire to move about the boat a good deal. But he quite forgot his fears; he sat smiling, with his eyes upon her face, while, without moving from her place, she delivered herself of a great number of original reflections. It was the most charming garrulity he had ever heard. He had assented to the idea that she was "common"; but was she so, after all, or was he simply getting used to her commonness? Her conversation was chiefly of what metaphysicians term the objective cast, but every now and then it took a subjective turn.

"What on *earth* are you so grave about?" she suddenly demanded, fixing her agreeable eyes upon Winterbourne's.

"Am I grave?" he asked. "I had an idea I was grinning from ear to ear."

"You look as if you were taking me to a funeral. If that's a grin, your ears are very near together."

"Should you like me to dance a hornpipe on the deck?"

"Pray do, and I'll carry round your hat. It will pay the expenses of our journey."

"I never was better pleased in my life," murmured Winterbourne.

She looked at him a moment and then burst into a little

laugh. "I like to make you say those things! You're a queer mixture!"

In the castle, after they had landed, the subjective element decidedly prevailed. Daisy tripped about the vaulted chambers, rustled her skirts in the corkscrew staircases, flirted back with a pretty little cry and a shudder from the edge of the *oubliettes*, and turned a singularly well-shaped ear to everything that Winterbourne told her about the place. But he saw that she cared very little for feudal antiquities and that the dusky traditions of Chillon made but a slight impression upon her. They had the good fortune to have been able to walk about without other companionship than that of the custodian; and Winterbourne arranged with this functionary that they should not be hurried—that they should linger and pause wherever they chose. The custodian interpreted the bargain generously—Winterbourne, on his side, had been generous—and ended by leaving them quite to themselves. Miss Miller's observations were not remarkable for logical consistency; for anything she wanted to say she was sure to find a pretext. She found a great many pretexts in the rugged embrasures of Chillon for asking Winterbourne sudden questions about himself—his family, his previous history, his tastes, his habits, his intentions—and for supplying information upon corresponding points in her own personality. Of her own tastes, habits, and intentions Miss Miller was prepared to give the most definite, and indeed the most favorable account.

"Well, I hope you know enough!" she said to her companion, after he had told her the history of the unhappy Bonivard. "I never saw a man that knew so much!" The history of Bonivard had evidently, as they say, gone into one ear and out of the other. But Daisy went on to say that she wished Winterbourne would travel with them and "go round" with them; they might know something, in that case. "Don't you want to come and teach Randolph?" she asked. Winterbourne said that nothing could possibly please him so much, but that he had unfortunately other occupations. "Other occupations? I don't believe it!" said Miss Daisy. "What do you mean? You are not in business." The young man ad-

mitted that he was not in business; but he had engage-
ments which, even within a day or two, would force
him to go back to Geneva. "Oh, bother!" she said; "I
don't believe it!" and she began to talk about something
else. But a few moments later, when he was pointing out
to her the pretty design of an antique fireplace, she
broke out irrelevantly, "You don't mean to say you are
going back to Geneva?"

"It is a melancholy fact that I shall have to return to
Geneva tomorrow."

"Well, Mr. Winterbourne," said Daisy, "I think you're
horrid!"

"Oh, don't say such dreadful things!" said Winterbourne—"just at the last!"

"The last!" cried the young girl; "I call it the first. I
have half a mind to leave you here and go straight back
to the hotel alone." And for the next ten minutes she did
nothing but call him horrid. Poor Winterbourne was fairly bewildered; no young lady had as yet done him the
honor to be so agitated by the announcement of his
movements. His companion, after this, ceased to pay
any attention to the curiosities of Chillon or the beauties
of the lake; she opened fire upon the mysterious charmer
in Geneva whom she appeared to have instantly taken it
for granted that he was hurrying back to see. How did
Miss Daisy Miller know that there was a charmer in
Geneva? Winterbourne, who denied the existence of such
a person, was quite unable to discover, and he was divided between amazement at the rapidity of her induc-
tion and amusement at the frankness of her *persiflage*.
She seemed to him, in all this, an extraordinary mixture
of innocence and crudity. "Does she never allow you
more than three days at a time?" asked Daisy ironically.
"Doesn't she give you a vacation in summer? There's no
one so hard worked but they can get leave to go off
somewhere at this season. I suppose, if you stay another day, she'll come after you in the boat. Do wait
over till Friday, and I will go down to the landing to see
her arrive!" Winterbourne began to think he had been
wrong to feel disappointed in the temper in which the
young lady had embarked. If he had missed the personal
accent, the personal accent was now making its appear-

ance. It sounded very distinctly, at last, in her telling him she would stop "teasing" him if he would promise her solemnly to come down to Rome in the winter.

"That's not a difficult promise to make," said Winterbourne. "My aunt has taken an apartment in Rome for the winter and has already asked me to come and see her."

"I don't want you to come for your aunt," said Daisy; "I want you to come for me." And this was the only allusion that the young man was ever to hear her make to his invidious kinswoman. He declared that, at any rate, he would certainly come. After this Daisy stopped teasing. Winterbourne took a carriage, and they drove back to Vevey in the dusk; the young girl was very quiet.

In the evening Winterbourne mentioned to Mrs. Costello that he had spent the afternoon at Chillon with Miss Daisy Miller.

"The Americans—of the courier?" asked this lady.

"Ah, happily," said Winterbourne, "the courier stayed at home."

"She went with you all alone?"

"All alone."

Mrs. Costello sniffed a little at her smelling bottle. "And that," she exclaimed, "is the young person whom you wanted me to know!"

PART II

Winterbourne, who had returned to Geneva the day after his excursion to Chillon, went to Rome toward the end of January. His aunt had been established there for several weeks, and he had received a couple of letters from her. "Those people you were so devoted to last summer at Vevey have turned up here, courier and all," she wrote. "They seem to have made several acquaintances, but the courier continues to be the most intime.

The young lady, however, is also very intimate with some third-rate Italians, with whom she rackets about in a way that makes much talk. Bring me that pretty novel of Cherbuliez's—*Paule Méré*—and don't come later than the 23rd."

In the natural course of events, Winterbourne, on arriving in Rome, would presently have ascertained Mrs. Miller's address at the American banker's and have gone to pay his compliments to Miss Daisy. "After what happened at Vevey, I think I may certainly call upon them," he said to Mrs. Costello.

"If, after what happens—at Vevey and everywhere—you desire to keep up the acquaintance, you are very welcome. Of course a man may know everyone. Men are welcome to the privilege!"

"Pray what is it that happens—here, for instance?" Winterbourne demanded.

"The girl goes about alone with her foreigners. As to what happens further, you must apply elsewhere for information. She has picked up half a dozen of the regular Roman fortune hunters, and she takes them about to people's houses. When she comes to a party she brings with her a gentleman with a good deal of manner and a wonderful mustache."

"And where is the mother?"

"I haven't the least idea. They are very dreadful people."

Winterbourne meditated a moment. "They are very ignorant—very innocent only. Depend upon it they are not bad."

"They are hopelessly vulgar," said Mrs. Costello. "Whether or no being hopelessly vulgar is being 'bad' is a question for the metaphysicians. They are bad enough to dislike, at any rate; and for this short life that is quite enough."

The news that Daisy Miller was surrounded by half a dozen wonderful mustaches checked Winterbourne's impulse to go straightway to see her. He had, perhaps, not definitely flattered himself that he had made an ineffaceable impression upon her heart, but he was annoyed at hearing of a state of affairs so little in harmony with an image that had lately flitted in and out of his own meditations; the image of a very pretty girl looking out of an old Roman window and asking herself urgently when Mr. Winterbourne would arrive. If, however, he determined to wait a little before reminding Miss Miller of his claims to her consideration, he went very soon to call upon two or three other friends. One of these friends was an American lady who had spent several winters at Geneva, where she had placed her children at school. She was a very accomplished woman, and she lived in the Via Gregoriana. Winterbourne found her in a little crimson drawing room on a third floor; the room was filled with southern sunshine. He had not been there ten minutes when the servant came in, announcing "Madame Mila!" This announcement was presently followed by the entrance of little Randolph Miller, who stopped in the middle of the room and stood staring at Winterbourne. An instant later his pretty sister crossed the threshold; and then, after a considerable interval, Mrs. Miller slowly advanced.

"I know you!" said Randolph.

"I'm sure you know a great many things," exclaimed Winterbourne, taking him by the hand. "How is your education coming on?"

Daisy was exchanging greetings very prettily with her hostess, but when she heard Winterbourne's voice she quickly turned her head. "Well, I declare!" she said.

"I told you I should come, you know," Winterbourne rejoined, smiling.

"Well, I didn't believe it," said Miss Daisy.

"I am much obliged to you," laughed the young man.

"You might have come to see me!" said Daisy.

"I arrived only yesterday."

"I don't believe that!" the young girl declared.

Winterbourne turned with a protesting smile to her mother, but this lady evaded his glance, and, seating herself, fixed her eyes upon her son. "We've got a bigger place than this," said Randolph. "It's all gold on the walls."

Mrs. Miller turned uneasily in her chair. "I told you if I were to bring you, you would say something!" she murmured.

"I told you!" Randolph exclaimed. "I tell you, sir!" he

added jocosely, giving Winterbourne a thump on the knee. "It is bigger, too!"

Daisy had entered upon a lively conversation with her hostess; Winterbourne judged it becoming to address a few words to her mother. "I hope you have been well since we parted at Vevey," he said.

Mrs. Miller now certainly looked at him—at his chin. "Not very well, sir," she answered.

"She's got the dyspepsia," said Randolph. "I've got it too. Father's got it. I've got it most!"

This announcement, instead of embarrassing Mrs. Miller, seemed to relieve her. "I suffer from the liver," she said. "I think it's this climate; it's less bracing than Schenectady, especially in the winter season. I don't know whether you know we reside at Schenectady. I was saying to Daisy that I certainly hadn't found any one like Dr. Davis, and I didn't believe I should. Oh, at Schenectady he stands first; they think everything of him. He has so much to do, and yet there was nothing he wouldn't do for me. He said he never saw anything like my dyspepsia, but he was bound to cure it. I'm sure there was nothing he wouldn't try. He was just going to try something new when we came off. Mr. Miller wanted Daisy to see Europe for herself. But I wrote to Mr. Miller that it seems as if I couldn't get on without Dr. Davis. At Schenectady he stands at the very top; and there's a great deal of sickness there, too. It affects my sleep."

Winterbourne had a good deal of pathological gossip with Dr. Davis's patient, during which Daisy chattered unremittingly to her own companion. The young man asked Mrs. Miller how she was pleased with Rome. "Well, I must say I am disappointed," she answered. "We had heard so much about it; I suppose we had heard too much. But we couldn't help that. We had been led to expect something different."

"Ah, wait a little, and you will become very fond of it," said Winterbourne.

"I hate it worse and worse every day!" cried Randolph.

"You are like the infant Hannibal," said Winterborne.

"No, I ain't!" Randolph declared at a venture.

"You are not much like an infant," said his mother.

"But we have seen places," she resumed, "that I should put a long way before Rome." And in reply to Winterbourne's interrogation, "There's Zürich," she concluded, "I think Zürich is lovely; and we hadn't heard half so much about it."

"The best place we've seen is the City of Richmond!" said Randolph.

"He means the ship," his mother explained. "We crossed in that ship. Randolph had a good time on the *City of Richmond*."

"It's the best place I've seen," the child repeated. "Only it was turned the wrong way."

"Well, we've got to turn the right way some time," said Mrs. Miller with a little laugh. Winterbourne expressed the hope that her daughter at least found some gratification in Rome, and she declared that Daisy was quite carried away. "It's on account of the society—the society's splendid. She goes round everywhere; she has made a great number of acquaintances. Of course she goes round more than I do. I must say they have been very sociable; they have taken her right in. And then she knows a great many gentlemen. Oh, she thinks there's nothing like Rome. Of course, it's a great deal pleasanter for a young lady if she knows plenty of gentlemen."

By this time Daisy had turned her attention again to Winterbourne. "I've been telling Mrs. Walker how mean you were!" the young girl announced.

"And what is the evidence you have offered?" asked Winterbourne, rather annoyed at Miss Miller's want of appreciation of the zeal of an admirer who on his way down to Rome had stopped neither at Bologna nor at Florence, simply because of a certain sentimental impatience. He remembered that a cynical compatriot had once told him that American women—the pretty ones, and this gave a largeness to the axiom—were at once the most exacting in the world and the least endowed with a sense of indebtedness.

"Why, you were awfully mean at Vevey," said Daisy. "You wouldn't do anything. You wouldn't stay there when I asked you."

"My dearest young lady," cried Winterbourne, with

eloquence, "have I come all the way to Rome to encounter your reproaches?"

"Just hear him say that!" said Daisy to her hostess, giving a twist to a bow on this lady's dress. "Did you ever hear anything so quaint?"

"So quaint, my dear?" murmured Mrs. Walker in the tone of a partisan of Winterbourne.

"Well, I don't know," said Daisy, fingering Mrs. Walker's ribbons. "Mrs. Walker, I want to tell you something."

"Mother-r," interposed Randolph, with his rough ends to his words, "I tell you you've got to go. Eugenio'll raise —something!"

"I'm not afraid of Eugenio," said Daisy with a toss of her head. "Look here, Mrs. Walker," she went on, "you know I'm coming to your party."

"I am delighted to hear it."

"I've got a lovely dress!"

"I am very sure of that."

"But I want to ask a favor—permission to bring a friend."

"I shall be happy to see any of your friends," said Mrs. Walker, turning with a smile to Mrs. Miller.

"Oh, they are not my friends," answered Daisy's mamma, smiling shyly in her own fashion. "I never spoke to them."

"It's an intimate friend of mine—Mr. Giovanelli," said Daisy without a tremor in her clear little voice or a shadow on her brilliant little face.

Mrs. Walker was silent a moment; she gave a rapid glance at Winterbourne. "I shall be glad to see Mr. Giovanelli," she then said.

"He's an Italian," Daisy pursued with the prettiest serenity. "He's a great friend of mine; he's the handsomest man in the world—except Mr. Winterbourne! He knows plenty of Italians, but he wants to know some Americans. He thinks ever so much of Americans. He's tremendously clever. He's perfectly lovely!"

It was settled that this brilliant personage should be brought to Mrs. Walker's party, and then Mrs. Miller prepared to take her leave. "I guess we'll go back to the hotel," she said.

"You may go back to the hotel, Mother, but I'm going to take a walk," said Daisy.

"She's going to walk with Mr. Giovanelli," Randolph proclaimed.

"I am going to the Pincio," said Daisy, smiling.

"Alone, my dear—at this hour?" Mrs. Walker asked. The afternoon was drawing to a close—it was the hour for the throng of carriages and of contemplative pedestrians. "I don't think it's safe, my dear," said Mrs. Walker.

"Neither do I," subjoined Mrs. Miller. "You'll get the fever, as sure as you live. Remember what Dr. Davis told you!"

"Give her some medicine before she goes," said Randolph.

The company had risen to its feet; Daisy, still showing her pretty teeth, bent over and kissed her hostess. "Mrs. Walker, you are too perfect," she said. "I'm not going alone; I am going to meet a friend."

"Your friend won't keep you from getting the fever," Mrs. Miller observed.

"Is it Mr. Giovanelli?" asked the hostess.

Winterbourne was watching the young girl; at this question his attention quickened. She stood there, smiling and smoothing her bonnet ribbons; she glanced at Winterbourne. Then, while she glanced and smiled, she answered, without a shade of hesitation, "Mr. Giovanelli—the beautiful Giovanelli."

"My dear young friend," said Mrs. Walker, taking her hand pleadingly, "don't walk off to the Pincio at this hour to meet a beautiful Italian."

"Well, he speaks English," said Mrs. Miller.

"Gracious me!" Daisy exclaimed, "I don't want to do anything improper. There's an easy way to settle it." She continued to glance at Winterbourne. "The Pincio is only a hundred yards distant; and if Mr. Winterbourne were as polite as he pretends, he would offer to walk with me!"

Winterbourne's politeness hastened to affirm itself, and the young girl gave him gracious leave to accompany her. They passed downstairs before her mother, and at the door Winterbourne perceived Mrs. Miller's carriage drawn up, with the ornamental courier whose acquaintance he had made at Vevey seated within. "Goodbye, Eugenio!"

cried Daisy; "I'm going to take a walk." The distance
from the Via Gregoriana to the beautiful garden at the
other end of the Pincian Hill is, in fact, rapidly traversed.
As the day was splendid, however, and the concourse of
vehicles, walkers, and loungers numerous, the young Americans found their progress much delayed. This fact was
highly agreeable to Winterbourne, in spite of his consciousness of his singular situation. The slow-moving, idly gazing
Roman crowd bestowed much attention upon the extremely pretty young foreign lady who was passing through it
upon his arm; and he wondered what on earth had been
in Daisy's mind when she proposed to expose herself,
unattended, to its appreciation. His own mission, to her
sense, apparently, was to consign her to the hands of
Mr. Giovanelli; but Winterbourne, at once annoyed and
gratified, resolved that he would do no such thing.

"Why haven't you been to see me?" asked Daisy. "You
can't get out of that."

"I have had the honor of telling you that I have only
just stepped out of the train."

"You must have stayed in the train a good while after
it stopped!" cried the young girl with her little laugh.
"I suppose you were asleep. You have had time to go to
see Mrs. Walker."

"I knew Mrs. Walker—" Winterbourne began to explain.

"I know where you knew her. You knew her at Geneva.
She told me so. Well, you knew me at Vevey. That's just
as good. So you ought to have come." She asked him no
other question than this; she began to prattle about her
own affairs. "We've got splendid rooms at the hotel;
Eugenio says they're the best rooms in Rome. We are
going to stay all winter, if we don't die of the fever; and
I guess we'll stay then. It's a great deal nicer than I
thought; I thought it would be fearfully quiet; I was sure
it would be awfully poky. I was sure we should be going
round all the time with one of those dreadful old men
that explain about the pictures and things. But we only
had about a week of that, and now I'm enjoying myself. I
know ever so many people, and they are all so charming. The society's extremely select. There are all kinds
—English, and Germans, and Italians. I think I like the

English best. I like their style of conversation. But there
are some lovely Americans. I never saw anything so hospitable. There's something or other every day. There's
not much dancing; but I must say I never thought
dancing was everything. I was always fond of conversation. I guess I shall have plenty at Mrs. Walker's, her
rooms are so small." When they had passed the gate of
the Pincian Gardens, Miss Miller began to wonder where
Mr. Giovanelli might be. "We had better go straight to
that place in front," she said, "where you look at the
view."

"I certainly shall not help you to find him." Winterbourne declared.

"Then I shall find him without you," said Miss Daisy.

"You certainly won't leave me!" cried Winterbourne.

She burst into her little laugh. "Are you afraid you'll get
lost—or run over? But there's Giovanelli, leaning against
that tree. He's staring at the women in the carriages:
did you ever see anything so cool?"

Winterbourne perceived at some distance a little man
standing with folded arms nursing his cane. He had a
handsome face, an artfully poised hat, a glass in one eye,
and a nosegay in his buttonhole. Winterbourne looked at
him a moment and then said, "Do you mean to speak to
that man?"

"Do I mean to speak to him? Why, you don't suppose
I mean to communicate by signs?"

"Pray understand, then," said Winterbourne, "that
I intend to remain with you."

Daisy stopped and looked at him, without a sign of
troubled consciousness in her face, with nothing but the
presence of her charming eyes and her happy dimples.
"Well, she's a cool one!" thought the young man.

"I don't like the way you say that," said Daisy. "It's
too imperious."

"I beg your pardon if I say it wrong. The main point
is to give you an idea of my meaning."

The young girl looked at him more gravely, but with
eyes that were prettier than ever. "I have never allowed
a gentleman to dictate to me, or to interfere with anything I do."

"I think you have made a mistake," said Winterbourne.

"You should sometimes listen to a gentleman—the right one."

Daisy began to laugh again. "I do nothing but listen to gentlemen!" she exclaimed. "Tell me if Mr. Giovanelli is the right one?"

The gentleman with the nosegay in his bosom had now perceived our two friends, and was approaching the young girl with obsequious rapidity. He bowed to Winterbourne as well as to the latter's companion; he had a brilliant smile, an intelligent eye; Winterbourne thought him not a bad-looking fellow. But he nevertheless said to Daisy, "No, he's not the right one."

Daisy evidently had a natural talent for performing introductions; she mentioned the name of each of her companions to the other. She strolled along with one of them on each side of her; Mr. Giovanelli, who spoke English very cleverly—Winterbourne afterward learned that he had practiced the idiom upon a great many American heiresses—addressed her a great deal of very polite nonsense; he was extremely urbane, and the young American, who said nothing, reflected upon that profundity of Italian cleverness which enables people to appear more gracious in proportion as they are more acutely disappointed. Giovanelli, of course, had counted upon something more intimate; he had not bargained for a party of three. But he kept his temper in a manner which suggested far-stretching intentions. Winterbourne flattered himself that he had taken his measure. "He is not a gentleman," said the young American; "he is only a clever imitation of one. He is a music master, or a penny-a-liner, or a third-rate artist. D—n his good looks!" Mr. Giovanelli had certainly a very pretty face; but Winterbourne felt a superior indignation at his own lovely fellow countrywoman's not knowing the difference between a spurious gentleman and a real one. Giovanelli chattered and jested and made himself wonderfully agreeable. It was true that, if he was an imitation, the imitation was brilliant. "Nevertheless," Winterbourne said to himself, "a nice girl ought to know!" And then he came back to the question whether this was, in fact, a nice girl. Would a nice girl, even allowing for her being a little American flirt, make a rendezvous with a presumably low-lived foreigner? The rendezvous in this case, indeed, had been in broad daylight and in the most crowded corner of Rome, but was it not impossible to regard the choice of these circumstances as a proof of extreme cynicism? Singular though it may seem, Winterbourne was vexed that the young girl, in joining her *amoroso*, should not appear more impatient of his own company, and he was vexed because of his inclination. It was impossible to regard her as a perfectly well-conducted young lady; she was wanting in a certain indispensable delicacy. It would therefore simplify matters greatly to be able to treat her as the object of one of those sentiments which are called by romancers "lawless passions." That she should seem to wish to get rid of him would help him to think more lightly of her, and to be able to think more lightly of her would make her much less perplexing. But Daisy, on this occasion, continued to present herself as an inscrutable combination of audacity and innocence.

She had been walking some quarter of an hour, attended by her two cavaliers, and responding in a tone of very childish gaiety, as it seemed to Winterbourne, to the pretty speeches of Mr. Giovanelli, when a carriage that had detached itself from the revolving train drew up beside the path. At the same moment Winterbourne perceived that his friend Mrs. Walker—the lady whose house he had lately left—was seated in the vehicle and was beckoning to him. Leaving Miss Miller's side, he hastened to obey her summons. Mrs. Walker was flushed; she wore an excited air. "It is really too dreadful," she said. "That girl must not do this sort of thing. She must not walk here with you two men. Fifty people have noticed her."

Winterbourne raised his eyebrows. "I think it's a pity to make too much fuss about it."

"It's a pity to let the girl ruin herself!"

"She is very innocent," said Winterbourne.

"She's very crazy!" cried Mrs. Walker. "Did you ever see anything so imbecile as her mother? After you had all left me just now, I could not sit still for thinking of it. It seemed too pitiful, not even to attempt to save her. I ordered the carriage and put on my bonnet, and came here as quickly as possible. Thank Heaven I have found you!"

"What do you propose to do with us?" asked Winterbourne, smiling.

"To ask her to get in, to drive her about here for half an hour, so that the world may see she is not running absolutely wild, and then to take her safely home."

"I don't think it's a very happy thought," said Winterbourne; "but you can try."

Mrs. Walker tried. The young man went in pursuit of Miss Miller, who had simply nodded and smiled at his interlocutor in the carriage and had gone her way with her companion. Daisy, on learning that Mrs. Walker wished to speak to her, retraced her steps with a perfect good grace and with Mr. Giovanelli at her side. She declared that she was delighted to have a chance to present this gentleman to Mrs. Walker. She immediately achieved the introduction, and declared that she had never in her life seen anything so lovely as Mrs. Walker's carriage rug.

"I am glad you admire it," said this lady, smiling sweetly. "Will you get in and let me put it over you?"

"Oh, no, thank you," said Daisy. "I shall admire it much more as I see you driving round with it."

"Do get in and drive with me!" said Mrs. Walker.

"That would be charming, but it's so enchanting just as I am!" and Daisy gave a brilliant glance at the gentlemen on either side of her.

"It may be enchanting, dear child, but it is not the custom here," urged Mrs. Walker, leaning forward in her victoria, with her hands devoutly clasped.

"Well, it ought to be, then!" said Daisy. "If I didn't walk I should expire."

"You should walk with your mother, dear," cried the lady from Geneva, losing patience.

"With my mother dear!" exclaimed the young girl. Winterbourne saw that she scented interference. "My mother never walked ten steps in her life. And then, you know," she added with a laugh, "I am more than five years old."

"You are old enough to be more reasonable. You are old enough, dear Miss Miller, to be talked about."

Daisy looked at Mrs. Walker, smiling intensely. "Talked about? What do you mean?"

"Come into my carriage, and I will tell you."

Daisy turned her quickened glance again from one of the gentlemen beside her to the other. Mr. Giovanelli was bowing to and fro, rubbing down his gloves and laughing very agreeably; Winterbourne thought it a most unpleasant scene. "I don't think I want to know what you mean," said Daisy presently. "I don't think I should like it."

Winterbourne wished that Mrs. Walker would tuck in her carriage rug and drive away, but this lady did not enjoy being defied, as she afterward told him. "Should you prefer being thought a very reckless girl?" she demanded.

"Gracious!" exclaimed Daisy. She looked again at Mr. Giovanelli, then she turned to Winterbourne. There was a little pink flush in her cheek; she was tremendously pretty. "Does Mr. Winterbourne think," she asked slowly, smiling, throwing back her head, and glancing at him from head to foot, "that, to save my reputation, I ought to get into the carriage?"

Winterbourne colored; for an instant he hesitated greatly. It seemed so strange to hear her speak that way of her "reputation." But he himself, in fact, must speak in accordance with gallantry. The finest gallantry, here, was simply to tell her the truth; and the truth, for Winterbourne, as the few indications I have been able to give have made him known to the reader, was that Daisy Miller should take Mrs. Walker's advice. He looked at her exquisite prettiness, and then he said, very gently, "I think you should get into the carriage."

Daisy gave a violent laugh. "I never heard anything so stiff! If this is improper, Mrs. Walker," she pursued, "then I am all improper, and you must give me up. Goodbye; I hope you'll have a lovely ride!" and, with Mr. Giovanelli, who made a triumphantly obsequious salute, she turned away.

Mrs. Walker sat looking after her, and there were tears in Mrs. Walker's eyes. "Get in here, sir," she said to Winterbourne, indicating the place beside her. The young man answered that he felt bound to accompany Miss

Miller, whereupon Mrs. Walker declared that if he refused her this favor she would never speak to him again. She was evidently in earnest. Winterbourne overtook Daisy and her companion, and, offering the young girl his hand, told her that Mrs. Walker had made an imperious claim upon his society. He expected that in answer she would say something rather free, something to commit herself still further to that "recklessness" from which Mrs. Walker had so charitably endeavored to dissuade her. But she only shook his hand, hardly looking at him, while Mr. Giovanelli bade him farewell with a too emphatic flourish of the hat.

Winterbourne was not in the best possible humor as he took his seat in Mrs. Walker's victoria. "That was not clever of you," he said candidly, while the vehicle mingled again with the throng of carriages.

"In such a case," his companion answered, "I don't wish to be clever; I wish to be *earnest!*"

"Well, your earnestness has only offended her and put her off."

"It has happened very well," said Mrs. Walker. "If she is so perfectly determined to compromise herself, the sooner one knows it the better; one can act accordingly."

"I suspect she meant no harm," Winterbourne rejoined.

"So I thought a month ago. But she has been going too far."

"What has she been doing?"

"Everything that is not done here. Flirting with any man she could pick up; sitting in corners with mysterious Italians; dancing all the evening with the same partners; receiving visits at eleven o'clock at night. Her mother goes away when visitors come."

"But her brother," said Winterbourne, laughing, "sits up till midnight."

"He must be edified by what he sees. I'm told that at their hotel everyone is talking about her, and that a smile goes round among all the servants when a gentleman comes and asks for Miss Miller."

"The servants be hanged!" said Winterbourne angrily. "The poor girl's only fault," he presently added, "is that she is very uncultivated."

"She is naturally indelicate," Mrs. Walker declared.

"Take that example this morning. How long had you known her at Vevey?"

"A couple of days."

"Fancy, then, her making it a personal matter that you should have left the place!"

Winterbourne was silent for some moments; then he said, "I suspect, Mrs. Walker, that you and I have lived too long at Geneva!" And he added a request that she should inform him with what particular design she had made him enter her carriage.

"I wished to beg you to cease your relations with Miss Miller—not to flirt with her—to give her no further opportunity to expose herself—to let her alone, in short."

"I'm afraid I can't do that," said Winterbourne. "I like her extremely."

"All the more reason that you shouldn't help her to make a scandal."

"There shall be nothing scandalous in my attentions to her."

"There certainly will be in the way she takes them. But I have said what I had on my conscience," Mrs. Walker pursued. "If you wish to rejoin the young lady I will put you down. Here, by the way, you have a chance."

The carriage was traversing that part of the Pincian Garden that overhangs the wall of Rome and overlooks the beautiful Villa Borghese. It is bordered by a large parapet, near which there are several seats. One of the seats at a distance was occupied by a gentleman and a lady, toward whom Mrs. Walker gave a toss of her head. At the same moment these persons rose and walked toward the parapet. Winterbourne had asked the coachman to stop; he now descended from the carriage. His companion looked at him a moment in silence; then, while he raised his hat, she drove majestically away. Winterbourne stood there; he had turned his eyes toward Daisy and her cavalier. They evidently saw no one; they were too deeply occupied with each other. When they reached the low garden wall, they stood a moment looking off at the great flat-topped pine clusters of the Villa Borghese; then Giovanelli seated himself, familiarly, upon the broad ledge of the wall. The western sun in the opposite sky sent out a brilliant shaft through a couple of cloud bars, whereupon Daisy's companion took her parasol out of her hands and opened it. She came a little nearer, and he held the parasol over her; then, still holding it, he let it rest upon her shoulder, so that both of their heads were hidden from Winterbourne. This young man lingered a moment, then he began to walk. But he walked—not toward the couple with the parasol; toward the residence of his aunt, Mrs. Costello.

He flattered himself on the following day that there was no smiling among the servants when he, at least, asked for Mrs. Miller at her hotel. This lady and her daughter, however, were not at home; and on the next day after, repeating his visit, Winterbourne again had the misfortune not to find them. Mrs. Walker's party took place on the evening of the third day, and, in spite of the frigidity of his last interview with the hostess, Winterbourne was among the guests. Mrs. Walker was one of those American ladies who, while residing abroad, make a point, in their own phrase, of studying European society, and she had on this occasion collected several specimens of her diversely born fellow mortals to serve, as it were, as textbooks. When Winterbourne arrived, Daisy Miller was not there, but in a few moments he saw her mother come in alone, very shyly and ruefully. Mrs. Miller's hair above her exposed-looking temples was more frizzled than ever. As she approached Mrs. Walker, Winterbourne also drew near.

"You see, I've come all alone," said poor Mrs. Miller. "I'm so frightened; I don't know what to do. It's the first time I've ever been to a party alone, especially in this country. I wanted to bring Randolph or Eugenio, or someone, but Daisy just pushed me off by myself. I ain't used to going round alone."

"And does not your daughter intend to favor us with her society?" demanded Mrs. Walker impressively.

"Well, Daisy's all dressed," said Mrs. Miller with that accent of the dispassionate, if not of the philosophic, historian with which she always recorded the current incidents of her daughter's career. "She got dressed on purpose before dinner. But she's got a friend of hers there; that gentleman—the Italian—that she wanted to bring. They've got going at the piano; it seems as if they couldn't leave off. Mr. Giovanelli sings splendidly. But I guess they'll come before very long," concluded Mrs. Miller hopefully.

"I'm sorry she should come in that way," said Mrs. Walker.

"Well, I told her that there was no use in her getting dressed before dinner if she was going to wait three hours," responded Daisy's mamma. "I didn't see the use of her putting on such a dress as that to sit round with Mr. Giovanelli."

"This is most horrible!" said Mrs. Walker, turning away and addressing herself to Winterbourne. *"Elle s'affiche.* It's her revenge for my having ventured to remonstrate with her. When she comes, I shall not speak to her."

Daisy came after eleven o'clock; but she was not, on such an occasion, a young lady to wait to be spoken to. She rustled forward in radiant loveliness, smiling and chattering, carrying a large bouquet, and attended by Mr. Giovanelli. Everyone stopped talking and turned and looked at her. She came straight to Mrs. Walker. "I'm afraid you thought I never was coming, so I sent mother off to tell you. I wanted to make Mr. Giovanelli practice some things before he came; you know he sings beautifully, and I want you to ask him to sing. This is Mr. Giovanelli; you know I introduced him to you; he's got the most lovely voice, and he knows the most charming set of songs. I made him go over them this evening on purpose; we had the greatest time at the hotel." Of all this Daisy delivered herself with the sweetest, brightest audibleness, looking now at her hostess and now round the room, while she gave a series of little pats, round her shoulders, to the edges of her dress. "Is there anyone I know?" she asked.

"I think every one knows you!" said Mrs. Walker pregnantly, and she gave a very cursory greeting to Mr. Giovanelli. This gentleman bore himself gallantly. He smiled and bowed and showed his white teeth; he curled his mustaches and rolled his eyes and performed all the proper functions of a handsome Italian at an evening party. He sang very prettily half a dozen songs, though Mrs. Walker afterward declared that she had been quite unable to find out who asked him. It was apparently not Daisy who had given him his orders. Daisy sat at a distance from the piano, and though she had publicly, as it were, professed a high admiration for his singing, talked, not inaudibly, while it was going on.

"It's a pity these rooms are so small; we can't dance," she said to Winterbourne, as if she had seen him five minutes before.

"I am not sorry we can't dance," Winterbourne answered; "I don't dance."

"Of course you don't dance; you're too stiff," said Miss Daisy. "I hope you enjoyed your drive with Mrs. Walker!"

"No, I didn't enjoy it; I preferred walking with you."

"We paired off: that was much better," said Daisy. "But did you ever hear anything so cool as Mrs. Walker's wanting me to get into her carriage and drop poor Mr. Giovanelli, and under the pretext that it was proper? People have different ideas! It would have been most unkind; he had been talking about that walk for ten days."

"He should not have talked about it at all," said Winterbourne; "he would never have proposed to a young lady of this country to walk about the streets with him."

"About the streets?" cried Daisy with her pretty stare. "Where, then, would he have proposed to her to walk? The Pincio is not the streets, either; and I, thank goodness, am not a young lady of this country. The young ladies of this country have a dreadfully poky time of it, so far as I can learn; I don't see why I should change my habits for *them.*"

"I am afraid your habits are those of a flirt," said Winterbourne gravely.

"Of course they are," she cried, giving him her little smiling stare again. "I'm a fearful, frightful flirt! Did you ever hear of a nice girl that was not? But I suppose you will tell me now that I am not a nice girl."

"You're a very nice girl; but I wish you would flirt with me, and me only," said Winterbourne.

"Ah! thank you—thank you very much; you are the last man I should think of flirting with. As I have had the pleasure of informing you, you are too stiff."

"You say that too often," said Winterbourne.

Daisy gave a delighted laugh. "If I could have the sweet hope of making you angry, I should say it again."

"Don't do that; when I am angry I'm stiffer than ever. But if you won't flirt with me, do cease, at least, to flirt with your friend at the piano; they don't understand that sort of thing here."

"I thought they understood nothing else!" exclaimed Daisy.

"Not in young unmarried women."

"It seems to me much more proper in young unmarried women than in old married ones," Daisy declared.

"Well," said Winterbourne, "when you deal with natives you must go by the custom of the place. Flirting is a purely American custom; it doesn't exist here. So when you show yourself in public with Mr. Giovanelli, and without your mother——"

"Gracious! poor Mother!" interposed Daisy.

"Though you may be flirting, Mr. Giovanelli is not; he means something else."

"He isn't preaching, at any rate," said Daisy with vivacity. "And if you want very much to know, we are neither of us flirting; we are too good friends for that: we are very intimate friends."

"Ah!" rejoined Winterbourne, "if you are in love with each other, it is another affair."

She had allowed him up to this point to talk so frankly that he had no expectation of shocking her by this ejaculation; but she immediately got up, blushing visibly, and leaving him to exclaim mentally that little American flirts were the queerest creatures in the world. "Mr. Giovanelli, at least," she said, giving her interlocutor a single glance, "never says such very disagreeable things to me."

Winterbourne was bewildered; he stood, staring. Mr. Giovanelli had finished singing. He left the piano and came over to Daisy. "Won't you come into the other room and have some tea?" he asked, bending before her with his ornamental smile.

Daisy turned to Winterbourne, beginning to smile again. He was still more perplexed, for this inconsequent smile made nothing clear, though it seemed to prove, indeed, that she had a sweetness and softness that reverted instinctively to the pardon of offenses. "It has never occurred to Mr. Winterbourne to offer me any tea," she said with her little tormenting manner.

"I have offered you advice," Winterbourne rejoined.

"I prefer weak tea!" cried Daisy, and she went off with the brilliant Giovanelli. She sat with him in the adjoining room, in the embrasure of the window, for the rest of the evening. There was an interesting performance at the piano, but neither of these young people gave heed to it. When Daisy came to take leave of Mrs. Walker, this lady conscientiously repaired the weakness of which she had been guilty at the moment of the young girl's arrival. She turned her back straight upon Miss Miller and left her to depart with what grace she might. Winterbourne was standing near the door; he saw it all. Daisy turned very pale and looked at her mother, but Mrs. Miller was humbly unconscious of any violation of the usual social forms. She appeared, indeed, to have felt an incongruous impulse to draw attention to her own striking observance of them. "Good night, Mrs. Walker," she said; "we've had a beautiful evening. You see, if I let Daisy come to parties without me, I don't want her to go away without me." Daisy turned away, looking with a pale, grave face at the circle near the door; Winterbourne saw that, for the first moment, she was too much shocked and puzzled even for indignation. He on his side was greatly touched.

"That was very cruel," he said to Mrs. Walker.

"She never enters my drawing room again!" replied his hostess.

Since Winterbourne was not to meet her in Mrs. Walker's drawing room, he went as often as possible to Mrs. Miller's hotel. The ladies were rarely at home, but when he found them, the devoted Giovanelli was always present. Very often the brilliant little Roman was in the drawing room with Daisy alone, Mrs. Miller being apparently constantly of the opinion that discretion is the better part of surveillance. Winterbourne noted, at first with surprise, that Daisy on these occasions was never embarrassed or annoyed by his own entrance; but he very presently began to feel that she had no more surprises for him; the unexpected in her behavior was the only thing to expect. She showed no displeasure at her tête-à-tête with Giovanelli being interrupted; she could chatter as freshly and freely with two gentlemen as with one; there was always, in her conversation, the same odd mixture of audacity and puerility. Winterbourne remarked to himself that if she was seriously interested in Giovanelli, it was very singular that she should not take more trouble to preserve the sanctity of their interviews; and he liked her the more for her innocent-looking indifference and her apparently inexhaustible good humor. He could hardly have said why, but she seemed to him a girl who would never be jealous. At the risk of exciting a somewhat derisive smile on the reader's part, I may affirm that with regard to the women who had hitherto interested him, it very often seemed to Winterbourne among the possibilities that, given certain contingencies, he should be afraid—literally afraid—of these ladies; he had a pleasant sense that he should never be afraid of Daisy Miller. It must be added that this sentiment was not altogether flattering to Daisy; it was part of his conviction, or rather of his apprehension, that she would prove a very light young person.

But she was evidently very much interested in Giovanelli. She looked at him whenever he spoke; she was perpetually telling him to do this and to do that; she was constantly "chaffing" and abusing him. She appeared completely to have forgotten that Winterbourne had said anything to displease her at Mrs. Walker's little party. One Sunday afternoon, having gone to St. Peter's with his aunt, Winterbourne perceived Daisy strolling about the great church in company with the inevitable Giovanelli. Presently he pointed out the young girl and her cavalier to Mrs. Costello. This lady looked at them a moment through her eyeglass, and then she said:

"That's what makes you so pensive in these days, eh?"

"I had not the least idea I was pensive," said the young man.

"You are very much preoccupied; you are thinking of something."

"And what is it," he asked, "that you accuse me of thinking of?"

"Of that young lady's—Miss Baker's, Miss Chandler's—

what's her name?—Miss Miller's intrigue with that little barber's block."

"Do you call it an intrigue," Winterbourne asked—"an affair that goes on with such peculiar publicity?"

"That's their folly," said Mrs. Costello; "it's not their merit."

"No," rejoined Winterbourne, with something of that pensiveness to which his aunt had alluded. "I don't believe that there is anything to be called an intrigue."

"I have heard a dozen people speak of it; they say she is quite carried away by him."

"They are certainly very intimate," said Winterbourne.

Mrs. Costello inspected the young couple again with her optical instrument. "He is very handsome. One easily sees how it is. She thinks him the most elegant man in the world, the finest gentleman. She has never seen anything like him; he is better, even, than the courier. It was the courier probably who introduced him; and if he succeeds in marrying the young lady, the courier will come in for a magnificent commission."

"I don't believe she thinks of marrying him," said Winterbourne, "and I don't believe he hopes to marry her."

"You may be very sure she thinks of nothing. She goes on from day to day, from hour to hour, as they did in the Golden Age. I can imagine nothing more vulgar. And at the same time," added Mrs. Costello, "depend upon it that she may tell you any moment that she is 'engaged.'"

"I think that is more than Giovanelli expects," said Winterbourne.

"Who is Giovanelli?"

"The little Italian. I have asked questions about him and learned something. He is apparently a perfectly respectable little man. I believe he is, in a small way, a *cavaliere avvocato*. But he doesn't move in what are called the first circles. I think it is really not absolutely impossible that the courier introduced him. He is evidently immensely charmed with Miss Miller. If she thinks him the finest gentleman in the world, he, on his side, has never found himself in personal contact with such splendor, such opulence, such expensiveness as this young lady's. And then she must seem to him wonderfully pretty and interesting. I rather doubt that he dreams of marrying her. That must appear to him too impossible a piece of luck. He has nothing but his handsome face to offer, and there is a substantial Mr. Miller in that mysterious land of dollars. Giovanelli knows that he hasn't a title to offer. If he were only a count or a *marchese!* He must wonder at his luck, at the way they have taken him up."

"He accounts for it by his handsome face and thinks Miss Miller a young lady *qui se passe ses fantaisies!*" said Mrs. Costello.

"It is very true," Winterbourne pursued, "that Daisy and her mamma have not yet risen to that stage of—what shall I call it?—of culture at which the idea of catching a count or a *marchese* begins. I believe that they are intellectually incapable of that conception."

"Ah! but the *avvocato* can't believe it," said Mrs. Costello.

Of the observation excited by Daisy's "intrigue," Winterbourne gathered that day at St. Peter's sufficient evidence. A dozen of the American colonists in Rome came to talk with Mrs. Costello, who sat on a little portable stool at the base of one of the great pilasters. The vesper service was going forward in splendid chants and organ tones in the adjacent choir, and meanwhile, between Mrs. Costello and her friends, there was a great deal said about poor little Miss Miller's going really "too far." Winterbourne was not pleased with what he heard, but when, coming out upon the great steps of the church, he saw Daisy, who had emerged before him, get into an open cab with her accomplice and roll away through the cynical streets of Rome, he could not deny to himself that she was going very far indeed. He felt very sorry for her—not exactly that he believed that she had completely lost her head, but because it was painful to hear so much that was pretty, and undefended, and natural assigned to a vulgar place among the categories of disorder. He made an attempt after this to give a hint to Mrs. Miller. He met one day in the Corso a friend, a tourist like himself, who had just come out of the Doria Palace, where he had been walking through the beautiful gallery. His friend talked for a moment about the superb portrait of Innocent X by Velasquez which hangs in one of the cabinets of the palace, and then said, "And in the same cabinet, by the way, I had the pleasure of contemplating a picture of a different kind—that pretty American girl whom you pointed out to me last week." In answer to Winterbourne's inquiries, his friend narrated that the pretty American girl—prettier than ever—was seated with a companion in the secluded nook in which the great papal portrait was enshrined.

"Who was her companion?" asked Winterbourne.

"A little Italian with a bouquet in his buttonhole. The girl is delightfully pretty, but I thought I understood from you the other day that she was a young lady *du meilleur monde.*"

"So she is!" answered Winterbourne; and having assured himself that his informant had seen Daisy and her companion but five minutes before, he jumped into a cab and went to call on Mrs. Miller. She was at home; but she apologized to him for receiving him in Daisy's absence.

"She's gone out somewhere with Mr. Giovanelli," said Mrs. Miller. "She's always going round with Mr. Giovanelli."

"I have noticed that they are very intimate," Winterbourne observed.

"Oh, it seems as if they couldn't live without each other!" said Mrs. Miller. "Well, he's a real gentleman, anyhow. I keep telling Daisy she's engaged!"

"And what does Daisy say?"

"Oh, she says she isn't engaged. But she might as well be!" this impartial parent resumed; "she goes on as if she was. But I've made Mr. Giovanelli promise to tell me, if *she* doesn't. I should want to write to Mr. Miller about it—shouldn't you?"

Winterbourne replied that he certainly should; and the state of mind of Daisy's mamma struck him as so unprecedented in the annals of parental vigilance that he gave up as utterly irrelevant the attempt to place her upon her guard.

After this Daisy was never at home, and Winterbourne ceased to meet her at the houses of their common acquaintance, because, as he perceived, these shrewd people had quite made up their minds that she was going too far. They ceased to invite her; and they intimated that they desired to express to observant Europeans the great truth that, though Miss Daisy Miller was a young American lady, her behavior was not representative—was regarded by her compatriots as abnormal. Winterbourne wondered how she felt about all the cold shoulders that were turned toward her, and sometimes it annoyed him to suspect that she did not feel at all. He said to himself that she was too light and childish, too uncultivated and unreasoning, too provincial, to have reflected upon her ostracism, or even to have perceived it. Then at other moments he believed that she carried about in her elegant and irresponsible little organism a defiant, passionate, perfectly observant consciousness of the impression she produced. He asked himself whether Daisy's defiance came from the consciousness of innocence, or from her being, essentially, a young person of the reckless class. It must be admitted that holding one's self to a belief in Daisy's "innocence" came to seem to Winterbourne more and more a matter of fine-spun gallantry. As I have already had occasion to relate, he was angry at finding himself reduced to chopping logic about this young lady; he was vexed at his want of instinctive certitude as to how far her eccentricities were generic, national, and how far they were personal. From either view of them he had somehow missed her, and now it was too late. She was "carried away" by Mr. Giovanelli.

A few days after his brief interview with her mother, he encountered her in that beautiful abode of flowering desolation known as the Palace of the Caesars. The early Roman spring had filled the air with bloom and perfume, and the rugged surface of the Palatine was muffled with tender verdure. Daisy was strolling along the top of one of those great mounds of ruin that are embanked with mossy marble and paved with monumental inscriptions. It seemed to him that Rome had never been so lovely as just then. He stood, looking off at the enchanting harmony of line and color that remotely encircles the city, inhaling the softly humid odors, and feeling the freshness of the year and the antiquity of the place reaffirm themselves in mysterious interfusion. It seemed to him also that Daisy had never looked so pretty, but this had been an observation of his whenever he met her. Giovanelli was at her side, and Giovanelli, too, wore an aspect of even unwonted brilliancy.

"Well," said Daisy, "I should think you would be lonesome!"

"Lonesome?" asked Winterbourne.

"You are always going round by yourself. Can't you get anyone to walk with you?"

"I am not so fortunate," said Winterbourne, "as your companion."

Giovanelli, from the first, had treated Winterbourne with distinguished politeness. He listened with a deferential air to his remarks; he laughed punctiliously at his pleasantries; he seemed disposed to testify to his belief that Winterbourne was a superior young man. He carried himself in no degree like a jealous wooer; he had obviously a great deal of tact; he had no objection to your expecting a little humility of him. It even seemed to Winterbourne at times that Giovanelli would find a certain mental relief in being able to have a private understanding with him—to say to him, as an intelligent man, that, bless you, *he* knew how extraordinary was this young lady, and didn't flatter himself with delusive—or at least *too* delusive—hopes of matrimony and dollars. On this occasion he strolled away from his companion to pluck a sprig of almond blossom, which he carefully arranged in his buttonhole.

"I know why you say that," said Daisy, watching Giovanelli. "Because you think I go round too much with *him*." And she nodded at her attendant.

"Every one thinks so—if you care to know," said Winterbourne.

"Of course I care to know!" Daisy exclaimed seriously. "But I don't believe it. They are only pretending to be shocked. They don't really care a straw what I do. Besides, I don't go round so much."

"I think you will find they do care. They will show it disagreeably."

Daisy looked at him a moment. "How disagreeably?"

"Haven't you noticed anything?" Winterbourne asked.

"I have noticed you. But I noticed you were as stiff as an umbrella the first time I saw you."

"You will find I am not so stiff as several others," said Winterbourne, smiling.

"How shall I find it?"

"By going to see the others."

"What will they do to me?"

"They will give you the cold shoulder. Do you know what that means?"

Daisy was looking at him intently; she began to color. "Do you mean as Mrs. Walker did the other night?"

"Exactly!" said Winterbourne.

She looked away at Giovanelli, who was decorating himself with his almond blossom. Then looking back at Winterbourne, "I shouldn't think you would let people be so unkind!" she said.

"How can I help it?" he asked.

"I should think you would say something."

"I do say something"; and he paused a moment. "I say that your mother tells me that she believes you are engaged."

"Well, she does," said Daisy very simply.

Winterbourne began to laugh. "And docs Randolph believe it?" he asked.

"I guess Randolph doesn't believe anything," said Daisy. Randolph's skepticism excited Winterbourne to further hilarity, and he observed that Giovanelli was coming back to them. Daisy, observing it too, addressed herself again to her countryman. "Since you have mentioned it," she said, "I *am* engaged." * * * Winterbourne looked at her; he had stopped laughing. "You don't believe!" she added.

He was silent a moment; and then, "Yes, I believe it," he said.

"Oh, no, you don't!" she answered. "Well, then—I am not!"

The young girl and her cicerone were on their way to the gate of the enclosure, so that Winterbourne, who had but lately entered, presently took leave of them. A week afterward he went to dine at a beautiful villa on the Caelian Hill, and, on arriving, dismissed his hired vehicle. The evening was charming, and he promised himself the satisfaction of walking home beneath the Arch of Constantine and past the vaguely lighted monuments of the Forum. There was a waning moon in the sky, and her radiance was not brilliant, but she was veiled in a thin cloud curtain which seemed to diffuse and equalize it. When, on his return from the villa (it was eleven o'clock), Winterbourne approached the dusky circle of the Colosseum, it recurred to him, as a lover of the picturesque, that the interior, in the pale moonshine, would be well worth a glance. He turned aside and walked to one of the empty arches, near which, as he observed, an open carriage—one of the little Roman streetcabs—was stationed. Then he passed in, among the cavernous shadows of the great structure, and emerged upon the clear and silent arena. The place had never seemed to him more impressive. One-half of the gigantic circus was in deep shade, the other was sleeping in the luminous dusk. As he stood there he began to murmur Byron's famous lines, out of "Manfred," but before he had finished his quotation he remembered that if nocturnal meditations in the Colosseum are recommended by the poets, they are deprecated by the doctors. The historic atmosphere was there, certainly; but the historic atmosphere, scientifically considered, was no better than a villainous miasma. Winterbourne walked to the middle of the arena, to take a more general glance, intending thereafter to make a hasty retreat. The great cross in the center was covered with shadow; it was only as he drew near it that he made it out distinctly. Then he saw that two persons were stationed upon the low steps which formed its base. One of these was a woman, seated; her companion was standing in front of her.

Presently the sound of the woman's voice came to him distinctly in the warm night air. "Well, he looks at us as one of the old lions or tigers may have looked at the Christian martyrs!" These were the words he heard, in the familiar accent of Miss Daisy Miller.

"Let us hope he is not very hungry," responded the ingenious Giovanelli. "He will have to take me first; you will serve for dessert!"

Winterbourne stopped, with a sort of horror, and, it must be added, with a sort of relief. It was as if a sudden

illumination had been flashed upon the ambiguity of
Daisy's behavior, and the riddle had become easy to read.
She was a young lady whom a gentleman need no longer
be in pains to respect. He stood there, looking at her—
looking at her companion and not reflecting that though
he saw them vaguely, he himself must have been more
brightly visible. He felt angry with himself that he had
bothered so much about the right way of regarding Miss
Daisy Miller. Then, as he was going to advance again,
he checked himself, not from the fear that he was doing
her injustice, but from a sense of the danger of appearing unbecomingly exhilarated by this sudden revulsion
from cautious criticism. He turned away toward the entrance of the place, but, as he did so, he heard Daisy
speak again.

"Why, it was Mr. Winterbourne! He saw me, and he
cuts me!"

What a clever little reprobate she was, and how smartly she played at injured innocence! But he wouldn't cut
her. Winterbourne came forward again and went toward
the great cross. Daisy had got up; Giovanelli lifted his
hat. Winterbourne had now begun to think simply of the
craziness, from a sanitary point of view, of a delicate
young girl lounging away the evening in this nest of
malaria. What if she *were* a clever little reprobate? That
was no reason for her dying of the *perniciosa*. "How long
have you been here?" he asked almost brutally.

Daisy, lovely in the flattering moonlight, looked at
him a moment. Then—"All the evening," she answered,
gently.... "I never saw anything so pretty."

"I am afraid," said Winterbourne, "that you will not
think Roman fever very pretty. This is the way people
catch it. I wonder," he added, turning to Giovanelli,
"that you, a native Roman, should countenance such a
terrible indiscretion."

"Ah," said the handsome native, "for myself I am not
afraid."

"Neither am I—for you! I am speaking for this young
lady."

Giovanelli lifted his well-shaped eyebrows and showed
his brilliant teeth. But he took Winterbourne's rebuke

with docility. "I told the signorina it was a grave indiscretion, but when was the signorina ever prudent?"

"I never was sick, and I don't mean to be!" the signorina declared. "I don't look like much, but I'm healthy! I was bound to see the Colosseum by moonlight; I shouldn't have wanted to go home without that; and we have had the most beautiful time, haven't we, Mr. Giovanelli? If there has been any danger, Eugenio can give me some pills. He has got some splendid pills."

"I should advise you," said Winterbourne, "to drive home as fast as possible and take one!"

"What you say is very wise," Giovanelli rejoined. "I will go and make sure the carriage is at hand." And he went forward rapidly.

Daisy followed with Winterbourne. He kept looking at her; she seemed not in the least embarrassed. Winterbourne said nothing; Daisy chattered about the beauty of the place. "Well, I *have* seen the Colosseum by moonlight!" she exclaimed. "That's one good thing." Then, noticing Winterbourne's silence, she asked him why he didn't speak. He made no answer; he only began to laugh. They passed under one of the dark archways; Giovanelli was in front with the carriage. Here Daisy stopped a moment, looking at the young American. "*Did* you believe I was engaged, the other day?" she asked.

"It doesn't matter what I believed the other day," said Winterbourne, still laughing.

"Well, what do you believe now?"

"I believe that it makes very little difference whether you are engaged or not!"

He felt the young girl's pretty eyes fixed upon him through the thick gloom of the archway; she was apparently going to answer. But Giovanelli hurried her forward. "Quick! quick!" he said; "if we get in by midnight we are quite safe."

Daisy took her seat in the carriage,. and the fortunate Italian placed himself beside her. "Don't forget Eugenio's pills!" said Winterbourne as he lifted his hat.

"I don't care," said Daisy in a little strange tone, "whether I have Roman fever or not!" Upon this the cab driver cracked his whip, and they rolled away over the desultory patches of the antique pavement.

Winterbourne, to do him justice, as it were, mentioned to no one that he had encountered Miss Miller, at midnight, in the Colosseum with a gentleman; but nevertheless, a couple of days later, the fact of her having been there under these circumstances was known to every member of the little American circle, and commented accordingly. Winterbourne reflected that they had of course known it at the hotel, and that, after Daisy's return, there had been an exchange of remarks between the porter and the cab driver. But the young man was conscious, at the same moment, that it had ceased to be a matter of serious regret to him that the little American flirt should be "talked about" by low-minded menials. These people, a day or two later, had serious information to give: the little American flirt was alarmingly ill. Winterbourne, when the rumor came to him, immediately went to the hotel for more news. He found that two or three charitable friends had preceded him, and that they were being entertained in Mrs. Miller's salon by Randolph.

"It's going round at night," said Randolph—"that's what made her sick. She's always going round at night. I shouldn't think she'd want to, it's so plaguy dark. You can't see anything here at night, except when there's a moon. In America there's always a moon!" Mrs. Miller was invisible; she was now, at least, giving her daughter the advantage of her society. It was evident that Daisy was dangerously ill.

Winterbourne went often to ask for news of her, and once he saw Mrs. Miller, who, though deeply alarmed, was, rather to his surprise, perfectly composed, and, as it appeared, a most efficient and judicious nurse. She talked a good deal about Dr. Davis, but Winterbourne paid her the compliment of saying to himself that she was not, after all, such a monstrous goose. "Daisy spoke of you the other day," she said to him. "Half the time she doesn't know what she's saying, but that time I think she did. She gave me a message she told me to tell you. She told me to tell you that she never was engaged to that handsome Italian. I am sure I am very glad; Mr. Giovanelli hasn't been near us since she was taken ill. I thought he was so much of a gentleman; but

I don't call that very polite! A lady told me that he was afraid I was angry with him for taking Daisy round at night. Well, so I am, but I suppose he knows I'm a lady. I would scorn to scold him. Anyway, she says she's not engaged. I don't know why she wanted you to know, but she said to me three times, 'Mind you tell Mr. Winterbourne.' And then she told me to ask if you remembered the time you went to that castle in Switzerland. But I said I wouldn't give any such messages as that. Only, if she is not engaged, I'm sure I'm glad to know it."

But, as Winterbourne had said, it mattered very little. A week after this, the poor girl died; it had been a terrible case of the fever. Daisy's grave was in the little Protestant cemetery, in an angle of the wall of imperial Rome, beneath the cypresses and the thick spring flowers. Winterbourne stood there beside it, with a number of other mourners, a number larger than the scandal excited by the young lady's career would have led you to expect. Near him stood Giovanelli, who came nearer still before Winterbourne turned away. Giovanelli was very pale: on this occasion he had no flower in his buttonhole; he seemed to wish to say something. At last he said, "She was the most beautiful young lady I ever saw, and the most amiable"; and then he added in a moment, "and she was the most innocent."

Winterbourne looked at him and presently repeated his words, "And the most innocent?"

"The most innocent!"

Winterbourne felt sore and angry. "Why the devil," he asked, "did you take her to that fatal place?"

Mr. Giovanelli's urbanity was apparently imperturbable. He looked on the ground a moment, and then he said, "For myself I had no fear; and she wanted to go."

"That was no reason!" Winterbourne declared.

The subtle Roman again dropped his eyes. "If she had lived, I should have got nothing. She would never have married me, I am sure."

"She would never have married you?"

"For a moment I hoped so. But no. I am sure."

Winterbourne listened to him: he stood staring at the raw protuberance among the April daisies. When he

turned away again, Mr. Giovanelli, with his light, slow
step, had retired.

Winterbourne almost immediately left Rome; but the
following summer he again met his aunt, Mrs. Costello
at Vevey. Mrs. Costello was fond of Vevey. In the interval Winterbourne had often thought of Daisy Miller and
her mystifying manners. One day he spoke of her to his
aunt—said it was on his conscience that he had done her
injustice.

"I am sure I don't know," said Mrs. Costello. "How
did your injustice affect her?"

"She sent me a message before her death which I
didn't understand at the time; but I have understood it
since. She would have appreciated one's esteem."

"Is that a modest way," asked Mrs. Costello, "of saying that she would have reciprocated one's affection?"

Winterbourne offered no answer to this question; but
he presently said, "You were right in that remark that
you made last summer. I was booked to make a mistake.
I have lived too long in foreign parts."

Nevertheless, he went back to live at Geneva, whence
there continue to come the most contradictory accounts
of his motives of sojourn: a report that he is "studying"
hard—an intimation that he is much interested in a very
clever foreign lady.

THE ASPERN PAPERS

❧

I

I had taken Mrs. Prest into my confidence; in truth without her I should have made but little advance, for the fruitful idea in the whole business dropped from her friendly lips. It was she who invented the short cut, who severed the Gordian knot. It is not supposed to be the nature of women to rise as a general thing to the largest and most liberal view—I mean of a practical scheme; but it has struck me that they sometimes throw off a bold conception—such as a man would not have risen to—with singular serenity. "Simply ask them to take you in on the footing of a lodger?"—I don't think that unaided I should have risen to that. I was beating about the bush, trying to be ingenious, wondering by what combination of arts I might become an acquaintance, when she offered this happy suggestion that the way to become an acquaintance was first to become an inmate. Her actual knowledge of the Misses Bordereau was scarcely larger than mine, and indeed I had brought with me from England some definite facts which were new to her. Their name had been mixed up ages before with one of the greatest names of the century, and they lived now in Venice in obscurity, on very small means, unvisited, unapproachable, in a dilapidated old palace on an out-of-the-way canal: this was the substance of my friend's impression of them. She herself had been established in Venice for fifteen years and had done a great deal of good there; but the circle of her benevolence did not include the two shy, mysterious and, as it was somehow

supposed, scarcely respectable Americans (they were believed to have lost in their long exile all national quality,
besides having had, as their name implied, some French
strain in their origin), who asked no favors and desired
no attention. In the early years of her residence she had
made an attempt to see them, but this had been successful only as regards the little one, as Mrs. Prest called
the niece; though in reality as I afterward learned she
was considerably the bigger of the two. She had heard
Miss Bordereau was ill and had a suspicion that she was
in want; and she had gone to the house to offer assistance, so that if there were suffering (and American suffering), she should at least not have it on her conscience. The "little one" received her in the great cold,
tarnished Venetian *sala*, the central hall of the house,
paved with marble and roofed with dim crossbeams, and
did not even ask her to sit down. This was not encouraging for me, who wished to sit so fast, and I remarked as
much to Mrs. Prest. She however replied with profundity,
"Ah, but there's all the difference: I went to confer a
favor and you will go to ask one. If they are proud you
will be on the right side." And she offered to show me
their house to begin with—to row me thither in her
gondola. I let her know that I had already been to look
at it half a dozen times; but I accepted her invitation,
for it charmed me to hover about the place. I had made
my way to it the day after my arrival in Venice (it had
been described to me in advance by the friend in England to whom I owed definite information as to their
possession of the papers), and I had besieged it with
my eyes while I considered my plan of campaign. Jeffrey
Aspern had never been in it that I knew of; but some
note of his voice seemed to abide there by a roundabout
implication, a faint reverberation.

Mrs. Prest knew nothing about the papers, but she
was interested in my curiosity, as she was always interested in the joys and sorrows of her friends. As we
went, however, in her gondola, gliding there under the
sociable hood with the bright Venetian picture framed on
either side by the movable window, I could see that she
was amused by my infatuation, the way my interest in
the papers had become a fixed idea. "One would think

you expected to find in them the answer to the riddle of the universe," she said; and I denied the impeachment only by replying that if I had to choose between that precious solution and a bundle of Jeffrey Aspern's letters I knew indeed which would appear to me the greater boon. She pretended to make light of his genius, and I took no pains to defend him. One doesn't defend one's god: one's god is in himself a defense. Besides, today, after his long comparative obscuration, he hangs high in the heaven of our literature, for all the world to see; he is a part of the light by which we walk. The most I said was that he was no doubt not a woman's poet: to which she rejoined aptly enough that he had been at least Miss Bordereau's. The strange thing had been for me to discover in England that she was still alive: it was as if I had been told Mrs. Siddons was, or Queen Caroline, or the famous Lady Hamilton, for it seemed to me that she belonged to a generation as extinct. "Why, she must be tremendously old—at least a hundred," I had said; but on coming to consider dates I saw that it was not strictly necessary that she should have exceeded by very much the common span. Nonetheless she was very far advanced in life, and her relations with Jeffrey Aspern had occurred in her early womanhood. "That is her excuse," said Mrs. Prest, half-sententiously and yet also somewhat as if she were ashamed of making a speech so little in the real tone of Venice. As if a woman needed an excuse for having loved the divine poet! He had been not only one of the most brilliant minds of his day (and in those years, when the century was young, there were, as everyone knows, many), but one of the most genial men and one of the handsomest.

The niece, according to Mrs. Prest, was not so old, and she risked the conjecture that she was only a grandniece. This was possible; I had nothing but my share in the very limited knowledge of my English fellow worshipper John Cumnor, who had never seen the couple. The world, as I say, had recognized Jeffrey Aspern, but Cumnor and I had recognized him most. The multitude, today, flocked to his temple, but of that temple he and I regarded ourselves as the ministers. We held, justly, as I think, that we had done more for his memory than

anyone else, and we had done it by opening lights into
his life. He had nothing to fear from us because he had
nothing to fear from the truth, which alone at such a
distance of time we could be interested in establishing.
His early death had been the only dark spot in his life,
unless the papers in Miss Bordereau's hands should perversely bring out others. There had been an impression
about 1825 that he had "treated her badly," just as there
had been an impression that he had "served," as the
London populace says, several other ladies in the same
way. Each of these cases Cumnor and I had been able
to investigate, and we had never failed to acquit him
conscientiously of shabby behavior. I judged him perhaps more indulgently than my friend; certainly, at any
rate, it appeared to me that no man could have walked
straighter in the given circumstances. These were almost
always awkward. Half the women of his time, to speak
liberally, had flung themselves at his head, and out of
this pernicious fashion many complications, some of them
grave, had not failed to arise. He was not a woman's
poet, as I had said to Mrs. Prest, in the modern phase
of his reputation; but the situation had been different
when the man's own voice was mingled with his song.
That voice, by every testimony, was one of the sweetest
ever heard. "Orpheus and the Maenads!" was the exclamation that rose to my lips when I first turned over
his correspondence. Almost all the Maenads were unreasonable, and many of them insupportable; it struck me in
short that he was kinder, more considerate than, in his
place (if I could imagine myself in such a place!) I
should have been.

It was certainly strange beyond all strangeness, and I
shall not take up space with attempting to explain it,
that whereas in all these other lines of research we had
to deal with phantoms and dust, the mere echoes of
echoes, the one living source of information that had
lingered on into our time had been unheeded by us.
Every one of Aspern's contemporaries had, according
to our belief, passed away; we had not been able to
look into a single pair of eyes into which his had looked
or to feel a transmitted contact in any aged hand that his
had touched. Most dead of all did poor Miss Borde-

reau appear, and yet she alone had survived. We exhausted in the course of months our wonder that we had not found her out sooner, and the substance of our explanation was that she had kept so quiet. The poor lady on the whole had had reason for doing so. But it was a revelation to us that it was possible to keep so quiet as that in the latter half of the nineteenth century—the age of newspapers and telegrams and photographs and interviewers. And she had taken no great trouble about it either: she had not hidden herself away in an undiscoverable hole; she had boldly settled down in a city of exhibition. The only secret of her safety that we could perceive was that Venice contained so many curiosities that were greater than she. And then accident had somehow favored her, as was shown for example in the fact that Mrs. Prest had never happened to mention her to me, though I had spent three weeks in Venice—under her nose, as it were—five years before. Mrs. Prest had not mentioned this much to anyone; she appeared almost to have forgotten she was there. Of course she had not the responsibilities of an editor. It was no explanation of the old woman's having eluded us to say that she lived abroad, for our researches had again and again taken us (not only by correspondence but by personal inquiry) to France, to Germany, to Italy, in which countries, not counting his important stay in England, so many of the too few years of Aspern's career were spent. We were glad to think at least that in all our publishings (some people consider I believe that we have overdone them), we had only touched in passing and in the most discreet manner on Miss Bordereau's connection. Oddly enough, even if we had had the material (and we often wondered what had become of it), it would have been the most difficult episode to handle.

The gondola stopped, the old palace was there; it was a house of the class which in Venice carries even in extreme dilapidation the dignified name. "How charming! It's gray and pink!" my companion exclaimed; and that is the most comprehensive description of it. It was not particularly old, only two or three centuries; and it had an air not so much of decay as of quiet discouragement, as if it had rather missed its career. But its wide

front, with a stone balcony from end to end of the
piano nobile or most important floor, was architectural
enough, with the aid of various pilasters and arches; and
the stucco with which in the intervals it had long ago
been endued was rosy in the April afternoon. It overlooked a clean, melancholy, unfrequented canal, which
had a narrow *riva* or convenient footway on either side.
"I don't know why—there are no brick gables," said
Mrs. Prest, "but this corner has seemed to me before
more Dutch than Italian, more like Amsterdam than
like Venice. It's perversely clean, for reasons of its own;
and though you can pass on foot scarcely anyone ever
thinks of doing so. It has the air of a Protestant Sunday.
Perhaps the people are afraid of the Misses Bordereau.
I daresay they have the reputation of witches."

I forget what answer I made to this—I was given
up to two other reflections. The first of these was that
if the old lady lived in such a big, imposing house she
could not be in any sort of misery and therefore would
not be tempted by a chance to let a couple of rooms. I
expressed this idea to Mrs. Prest, who gave me a very
logical reply. "If she didn't live in a big house how
could it be a question of her having rooms to spare? If
she were not amply lodged herself you would lack ground
to approach her. Besides, a big house here, and especially
in this *quartier perdu*, proves nothing at all: it is perfectly compatible with a state of penury. Dilapidated old
palazzi, if you will go out of the way for them, are to be
had for five shillings a year. And as for the people who
live in them—no, until you have explored Venice socially
as much as I have you can form no idea of their domestic
desolation. They live on nothing, for they have nothing
to live on." The other idea that had come into my head
was connected with a high blank wall which appeared to
confine an expanse of ground on one side of the house.
Blank I call it, but it was figured over with the patches
that please a painter, repaired breaches, crumblings of
plaster, extrusions of brick that had turned pink with
time; and a few thin trees, with the poles of certain
rickety trellises, were visible over the top. The place was
a garden, and apparently it belonged to the house. It

suddenly occurred to me that if it did belong to the house I had my pretext.

I sat looking out on all this with Mrs. Prest (it was covered with the golden glow of Venice) from the shade of our *felze*, and she asked me if I would go in then, while she waited for me, or come back another time. At first I could not decide—it was doubtless very weak of me. I wanted still to think I *might* get a footing, and I was afraid to meet failure, for it would leave me, as I remarked to my companion, without another arrow for my bow. "Why not another?" she inquired as I sat there hesitating and thinking it over; and she wished to know why even now and before taking the trouble of becoming an inmate (which might be wretchedly uncomfortable after all, even if it succeeded), I had not the resource of simply offering them a sum of money down. In that way I might obtain the documents without bad nights.

"Dearest lady," I exclaimed, "excuse the impatience of my tone when I suggest that you must have forgotten the very fact (surely I communicated it to you) which pushed me to throw myself upon your ingenuity. The old woman won't have the documents spoken of; they are personal, delicate, intimate, and she hasn't modern notions, God bless her! If I should sound that note first I should certainly spoil the game. I can arrive at the papers only by putting her off her guard, and I can put her off her guard only by ingratiating diplomatic practices. Hypocrisy, duplicity are my only chance. I am sorry for it, but for Jeffrey Aspern's sake I would do worse still. First I must take tea with her; then tackle the main job." And I told over what had happened to John Cumnor when he wrote to her. No notice whatever had been taken of his first letter, and the second had been answered very sharply, in six lines, by the niece. "Miss Bordereau requested her to say that she could not imagine what he meant by troubling them. They had none of Mr. Aspern's papers, and if they had should never think of showing them to anyone on any account whatever. She didn't know what he was talking about and begged he would let her alone." I certainly did not want to be met that way.

"Well," said Mrs. Prest after a moment, provokingly,

"perhaps after all they haven't any of his things. If they deny it flat how are you sure?"

"John Cumnor is sure, and it would take me long to tell you how his conviction, or his very strong presumption—strong enough to stand against the old lady's not unnatural fib—has built itself up. Besides, he makes much of the internal evidence of the niece's letter."

"The internal evidence?"

"Her calling him 'Mr. Aspern.'"

"I don't see what that proves."

"It proves familiarity, and familiarity implies the possession of mementoes, or relics. I can't tell you how that 'Mr.' touches me—how it bridges over the gulf of time and brings our hero near to me—nor what an edge it gives to my desire to see Juliana. You don't say, 'Mr.' Shakespeare."

"Would I, any more, if I had a box full of his letters?"

"Yes, if he had been your lover and someone wanted them!" And I added that John Cumnor was so convinced, and so all the more convinced by Miss Bordereau's tone, that he would have come himself to Venice on the business were it not that for him there was the obstacle that it would be difficult to disprove his identity with the person who had written to them, which the old ladies would be sure to suspect in spite of dissimulation and a change of name. If they were to ask him point-blank if he were not their correspondent it would be too awkward for him to lie; whereas I was fortunately not tied in that way. I was a fresh hand and could say no without lying.

"But you will have to change your name," said Mrs. Prest. "Juliana lives out of the world as much as it is possible to live, but none the less she has probably heard of Mr. Aspern's editors; she perhaps possesses what you have published."

"I have thought of that," I returned; and I drew out of my pocketbook a visiting card, neatly engraved with a name that was not my own.

"You are very extravagant; you might have written it," said my companion.

"This looks more genuine."

"Certainly, you are prepared to go far! But it will be

awkward about your letters; they won't come to you in that mask."

"My banker will take them in, and I will go every day to fetch them. It will give me a little walk."

"Shall you only depend upon that?" asked Mrs. Prest. "Aren't you coming to see me?"

"Oh, you will have left Venice, for the hot months, long before there are any results. I am prepared to roast all summer—as well as hereafter, perhaps you'll say! Meanwhile, John Cumnor will bombard me with letters addressed, in my feigned name, to the care of the *padrona*."

"She will recognize his hand," my companion suggested.

"On the envelope he can disguise it."

"Well, you're a precious pair! Doesn't it occur to you that even if you are able to say you are not Mr. Cumnor in person they may still suspect you of being his emissary?"

"Certainly, and I see only one way to parry that."

"And what may that be?"

I hesitated a moment. "To make love to the niece."

"Ah," cried Mrs. Prest, "wait till you see her!"

II

"I must work the garden—I must work the garden," I said to myself, five minutes later, as I waited, upstairs, in the long, dusky *sala*, where the bare scagliola floor gleamed vaguely in a chink of the closed shutters. The place was impressive but it looked cold and cautious. Mrs. Prest had floated away, giving me a rendezvous at the end of half an hour by some neighboring water steps; and I had been let into the house, after pulling the rusty bell wire, by a little red-headed, white-faced maidservant, who was very young and not ugly and wore clicking pattens and a shawl in the fashion of a hood. She had not contented herself with opening the door from above by the usual arrangement of a creaking pulley, though she had looked down at me first from an upper window, dropping the inevitable challenge which in Italy precedes the hospitable act. As a general thing I was irritated by this survival of medieval manners, though as I liked the old I suppose I ought to have liked it; but I was so determined to be genial that I took my false card out of my pocket and held it up to her, smiling as if it were a magic token. It had the effect of one indeed, for it brought her, as I say, all the way down. I begged her to hand it to her mistress, having first written on it in Italian the words, "Could you very kindly see a gentleman, an American, for a moment?" The little maid was not hostile, and I reflected that even that was perhaps something gained. She colored, she smiled and looked both frightened and pleased. I could see that my arrival was a great affair, that visits were rare in that house, and that she was a person who would have liked a sociable place. When she pushed forward the heavy door behind me I felt that I had a foot in the citadel. She pattered across the damp, stony lower hall and I followed her up the high staircase—stonier still, as it seemed—without an invitation. I think she had meant I should wait for her below, but such was not my idea, and I took up my station in the *sala*. She flitted, at the far end of it, into impenetrable regions, and I looked at the place with my heart beating as I had known it to do in the dentist's parlor. It was gloomy and stately, but it owed its character almost entirely to its noble shape and to the fine architectural doors —as high as the doors of houses—which, leading into the various rooms, repeated themselves on either side at intervals. They were surmounted with old faded painted escutcheons, and here and there, in the spaces between them, brown pictures, which I perceived to be bad, in battered frames, were suspended. With the exception of several straw-bottomed chairs with their backs to the wall, the grand obscure vista contained nothing else to minister to effect. It was evidently never used save as a passage, and little even as that. I may add that by the time the door opened again through which the maidservant had escaped, my eyes had grown used to the want of light.

I had not meant by my private ejaculation that I must myself cultivate the soil of the tangled enclosure which lay beneath the windows, but the lady who came toward me from the distance over the hard, shining floor might have supposed as much from the way in which, as I went rapidly to meet her, I exclaimed, taking care to speak Italian: "The garden, the garden—do me the pleasure to tell me if it's yours!"

She stopped short, looking at me with wonder; and then, "Nothing here is mine," she answered in English, coldly and sadly.

"Oh, you are English; how delightful!" I remarked, ingenuously. "But surely the garden belongs to the house?"

"Yes, but the house doesn't belong to me." She was a long, lean, pale person, habited apparently in a dull-colored dressing gown, and she spoke with a kind of mild literalness. She did not ask me to sit down, any more than years before (if she were the niece) she had asked Mrs. Prest, and we stood face to face in the empty pompous hall.

"Well then, would you kindly tell me to whom I must address myself? I'm afraid you'll think me odiously intrusive, but you know I *must* have a garden—upon my honor I must!"

Her face was not young, but it was simple; it was not fresh, but it was mild. She had large eyes which were not bright, and a great deal of hair which was not "dressed," and long fine hands which were—possibly—not clean. She clasped these members almost convulsively as, with a confused, alarmed look, she broke out, "Oh, don't take it away from us; we like it ourselves!"

"You have the use of it then?"

"Oh, yes. If it wasn't for that!" And she gave a shy, melancholy smile.

"Isn't it a luxury, precisely? That's why, intending to be in Venice some weeks, possibly all summer, and having some literary work, some reading and writing to do, so that I must be quiet, and yet if possible a great deal in the open air—that's why I have felt that a garden is really indispensable. I appeal to your own experience," I went on, smiling. "Now can't I look at yours?"

"I don't know, I don't understand," the poor woman murmured, planted there and letting her embarrassed eyes wander all over my strangeness.

"I mean only from one of those windows—such grand ones as you have here—if you will let me open the shutters." And I walked toward the back of the house. When I had advanced halfway I stopped and waited, as if I took it for granted she would accompany me. I had been of necessity very abrupt, but I strove at the same time to give her the impression of extreme courtesy. "I have been looking at furnished rooms all over the place, and it seems impossible to find any with a garden attached. Naturally in a place like Venice gardens are rare. It's absurd if you like, for a man, but I can't live without flowers."

"There are none to speak of down there." She came nearer to me, as if, though she mistrusted me, I had drawn her by an invisible thread. I went on again, and she continued as she followed me: "We have a few, but they are very common. It costs too much to cultivate them; one has to have a man."

"Why shouldn't I be the man?" I asked. "I'll work without wages; or rather I'll put in a gardener. You shall have the sweetest flowers in Venice."

She protested at this, with a queer little sigh which might also have been a gush of rapture at the picture I presented. Then she observed, "We don't know you—we don't know you."

"You know me as much as I know you; that is much more, because you know my name. And if you are English I am almost a countryman."

"We are not English," said my companion, watching me helplessly while I threw open the shutters of one of the divisions of the wide high window.

"You speak the language so beautifully: might I ask what you are?" Seen from above the garden was certainly shabby; but I perceived at a glance that it had great capabilities. She made no rejoinder, she was so lost in staring at me, and I exclaimed, "You don't mean to say you are also by chance American?"

"I don't know; we used to be."

"Used to be? Surely you haven't changed?"

"It's so many years ago—we are nothing."

"So many years that you have been living here? Well, I don't wonder at that; it's a grand old house. I suppose you all use the garden," I went on, "but I assure you I shouldn't be in your way. I would be very quiet and stay in one corner."

"We all use it?" she repeated after me, vaguely, not coming close to the window but looking at my shoes. She appeared to think me capable of throwing her out.

"I mean all your family, as many as you are."

"There is only one other; she is very old—she never goes down."

"Only one other, in all this great house!" I feigned to be not only amazed but almost scandalized. "Dear lady, you must have space then to spare!"

"To spare?" she repeated, in the same dazed way.

"Why, you surely don't live (two quiet women—I see you are quiet, at any rate) in fifty rooms!" Then with a burst of hope and cheer I demanded: "Couldn't you let me two or three? That would set me up!"

I had now struck the note that translated my purpose, and I need not reproduce the whole of the tune I played. I ended by making my interlocutress believe that I was an honorable person, though of course I did not even attempt to persuade her that I was not an eccentric one. I repeated that I had studies to pursue; that I wanted quiet; that I delighted in a garden and had vainly sought one up and down the city; that I would undertake that before another month was over the dear old house should be smothered in flowers. I think it was the flowers that won my suit, for I afterward found that Miss Tita (for such the name of this high tremulous spinster proved somewhat incongruously to be) had an insatiable appetite for them. When I speak of my suit as won I mean that before I left her she had promised that she would refer the question to her aunt. I inquired who her aunt might be and she answered, "Why, Miss Bordereau!" with an air of surprise, as if I might have been expected to know. There were contradictions like this in Tita Bordereau which, as I observed later, contributed to

make her an odd and affecting person. It was the study
of the two ladies to live so that the world should not
touch them, and yet they had never altogether accepted
the idea that it never heard of them. In Tita at any rate
a grateful susceptibility to human contact had not died out,
and contact of a limited order there would be if I should
come to live in the house.

"We have never done anything of the sort; we have
never had a lodger or any kind of inmate." So much as
this she made a point of saying to me. "We are very
poor, we live very badly. The rooms are very bare—that
you might take; they have nothing in them. I don't know
how you would sleep, how you would eat."

"With your permission, I could easily put in a bed and
a few tables and chairs. *C'est la moindre des choses* and
the affair of an hour or two. I know a little man from
whom I can hire what I should want for a few months,
for a trifle, and my gondolier can bring the things round
in his boat. Of course in this great house you must have
a second kitchen, and my servant, who is a wonderfully
handy fellow" (this personage was an evocation of the
moment), "can easily cook me a chop there. My tastes
and habits are of the simplest; I live on flowers!" And
then I ventured to add that if they were very poor it was
all the more reason they should let their rooms. They
were bad economists—I had never heard of such a waste
of material.

I saw in a moment that the good lady had never before been spoken to in that way, with a kind of humorous firmness which did not exclude sympathy but was on
the contrary founded on it. She might easily have told me
that my sympathy was impertinent, but this by good fortune did not occur to her. I left her with the understanding that she would consider the matter with her
aunt and that I might come back the next day for their
decision.

"The aunt will refuse; she will think the whole proceeding very *louche!*" Mrs. Prest declared shortly after this,
when I had resumed my place in her gondola. She had
put the idea into my head and now (so little are women
to be counted on) she appeared to take a despondent
view of it. Her pessimism provoked me and I pretended

to have the best hopes; I went so far as to say that I had a distinct presentiment that I should succeed. Upon this Mrs. Prest broke out, "Oh, I see what's in your head! You fancy you have made such an impression in a quarter of an hour that she is dying for you to come and can be depended upon to bring the old one round. If you do get in you'll count it as a triumph."

I did count it as a triumph, but only for the editor (in the last analysis), not for the man, who had not the tradition of personal conquest. When I went back on the morrow the little maidservant conducted me straight through the long *sala* (it opened there as before in perfect perspective and was lighter now, which I thought a good omen) into the apartment from which the recipient of my former visit had emerged on that occasion. It was a large shabby parlor, with a fine old painted ceiling and a strange figure sitting alone at one of the windows. They come back to me now almost with the palpitation they caused, the successive feelings that accompanied my consciousness that as the door of the room closed behind me I was really face to face with the Juliana of some of Aspern's most exquisite and most renowned lyrics. I grew used to her afterward, though never completely; but as she sat there before me my heart beat as fast as if the miracle of resurrection had taken place for my benefit. Her presence seemed somehow to contain his, and I felt nearer to him at that first moment of seeing her than I ever had been before or ever have been since. Yes, I remember my emotions in their order, even including a curious little tremor that took me when I saw that the niece was not there. With her, the day before, I had become sufficiently familiar, but it almost exceeded my courage (much as I had longed for the event) to be left alone with such a terrible relic as the aunt. She was too strange, too literally resurgent. Then came a check, with the perception that we were not really face to face, inasmuch as she had over her eyes a horrible green shade which, for her, served almost as a mask. I believed for the instant that she had put it on expressly, so that from underneath it she might scrutinize me without being scrutinized herself. At the same time it increased the presumption that there was a ghastly death's-head lurk-

ing behind it. The divine Juliana as a grinning skull—the
vision hung there until it passed. Then it came to me
that she *was* tremendously old—so old that death might
take her at any moment, before I had time to get what
I wanted from her. The next thought was a correction
to that; it lighted up the situation. She would die next
week, she would die tomorrow—then I could seize her
papers. Meanwhile she sat there neither moving nor
speaking. She was very small and shrunken, bent forward,
with her hands in her lap. She was dressed in black, and
her head was wrapped in a piece of old black lace which
showed no hair.

My emotion keeping me silent she spoke first, and
the remark she made was exactly the most unexpected.

III

"Our house is very far from the center, but the little
canal is very *comme il faut*."

"It's the sweetest corner of Venice and I can imagine
nothing more charming," I hastened to reply. The old
lady's voice was very thin and weak, but it had an agreeable, cultivated murmur, and there was wonder in the
thought that that individual note had been in Jeffrey
Aspern's ear.

"Please to sit down there. I hear very well," she said
quietly, as if perhaps I had been shouting at her; and
the chair she pointed to was at a certain distance. I
took possession of it, telling her that I was perfectly
aware that I had intruded, that I had not been properly
introduced and could only throw myself upon her indul-
gence. Perhaps the other lady, the one I had had the
honor of seeing the day before, would have explained
to her about the garden. That was literally what had given
me courage to take a step so unconventional. I had fallen
in love at sight with the whole place (she herself probably was so used to it that she did not know the im-

pression it was capable of making on a stranger), and I had felt it was really a case to risk something. Was her own kindness in receiving me a sign that I was not wholly out in my calculation? It would render me extremely happy to think so. I could give her my word of honor that I was a most respectable, inoffensive person and that as an inmate they would be barely conscious of my existence. I would conform to any regulations, any restrictions if they would only let me enjoy the garden. Moreover I should be delighted to give her references, guarantees; they would be of the very best, both in Venice and in England as well as in America.

She listened to me in perfect stillness and I felt that she was looking at me with great attention, though I could see only the lower part of her bleached and shriveled face. Independently of the refining process of old age it had a delicacy which once must have been great. She had been very fair, she had had a wonderful complexion. She was silent a little after I had ceased speaking; then she inquired, "If you are so fond of a garden why don't you go to *terra firma,* where there are so many far better than this?"

"Oh, it's the combination!" I answered, smiling; and then, with rather a flight of fancy, "It's the idea of a garden in the middle of the sea."

"It's not in the middle of the sea; you can't see the water."

I stared a moment, wondering whether she wished to convict me of fraud. "Can't see the water? Why, dear madam, I can come up to the very gate in my boat."

She appeared inconsequent, for she said vaguely in reply to this, "Yes, if you have got a boat. I haven't any; it's many years since I have been in one of the gondolas." She uttered these words as if the gondolas were a curious faraway craft which she knew only by hearsay.

"Let me assure you of the pleasure with which I would put mine at your service!" I exclaimed. I had scarcely said this, however, before I became aware that the speech was in questionable taste and might also do me the injury of making me appear too eager, too possessed of a hidden motive. But the old woman remained impenetrable and her attitude bothered me by suggesting that she had a fuller vision of me than I had of her. She gave me no thanks for my somewhat extravagant offer but remarked that the lady I had seen the day before was her niece; she would presently come in. She had asked her to stay away a little on purpose, because she herself wished to see me at first alone. She relapsed into silence, and I asked myself why she had judged this necessary and what was coming yet; also whether I might venture on some judicious remark in praise of her companion. I went so far as to say that I should be delighted to see her again: she had been so very courteous to me, considering how odd she must have thought me—a declaration which drew from Miss Bordereau another of her whimsical speeches.

"She has very good manners; I bred her up myself!" I was on the point of saying that that accounted for the easy grace of the niece, but I arrested myself in time, and the next moment the old woman went on: "I don't care who you may be—I don't want to know; it signifies very little today." This had all the air of being a formula of dismissal, as if her next words would be that I might take myself off now that she had had the amusement of looking on the face of such a monster of indiscretion. Therefore I was all the more surprised when she added, with her soft, venerable quaver, "You may have as many rooms as you like—if you will pay a good deal of money."

I hesitated but for a single instant, long enough to ask myself what she meant in particular by this condition. First it struck me that she must have really a large sum in her mind; then I reasoned quickly that her idea of a large sum would probably not correspond to my own. My deliberation, I think, was not so visible as to diminish the promptitude with which I replied, "I will pay with pleasure and of course in advance whatever you may think is proper to ask me."

"Well then, a thousand francs a month," she rejoined instantly, while her baffling green shade continued to cover her attitude.

The figure, as they say, was startling and my logic had been at fault. The sum she had mentioned was, by the Venetian measure of such matters, exceedingly large; there was many an old palace in an out-of-the-way corner that I might on such terms have enjoyed by the year. But so far as my small means allowed I was prepared to spend money, and my decision was quickly taken. I would pay her with a smiling face what she asked, but in that case I would give myself the compensation of extracting the papers from her for nothing. Moreover if she had asked five times as much I should have risen to the occasion; so odious would it have appeared to me to stand chaffering with Aspern's Juliana. It was queer enough to have a question of money with her at all. I assured her that her views perfectly met my own and that on the morrow I should have the pleasure of putting three months' rent into her hand. She received this announcement with serenity and with no apparent sense that after all it would be becoming of her to say that I ought to see the rooms first. This did not occur to her and indeed her serenity was mainly what I wanted. Our little bargain was just concluded when the door opened and the younger lady appeared on the threshold. As soon as Miss Bordereau saw her niece she cried out almost gaily, "He will give three thousand—three thousand tomorrow!"

Miss Tita stood still, with her patient eyes turning from one of us to the other; then she inquired, scarcely above her breath, "Do you mean francs?"

"Did you mean francs or dollars?" the old woman asked of me at this.

"I think francs were what you said," I answered, smiling.

"That is very good," said Miss Tita, as if she had become conscious that her own question might have looked overreaching.

"What do *you* know? You are ignorant," Miss Bordereau remarked; not with acerbity but with a strange, soft coldness.

"Yes, of money—certainly of money!" Miss Tita hastened to exclaim.

"I am sure you have your own branches of knowledge," I took the liberty of saying, genially. There was something painful to me, somehow, in the turn the conversation had taken, in the discussion of the rent.

"She had a very good education when she was young.

I looked into that myself," said Miss Bordereau. Then she added, "But she has learned nothing since."

"I have always been with you," Miss Tita rejoined very mildly, and evidently with no intention of making an epigram.

"Yes, but for that!" her aunt declared with more satirical force. She evidently meant that but for this her niece would never have got on at all; the point of the observation however being lost on Miss Tita, though she blushed at hearing her history revealed to a stranger. Miss Bordereau went on, addressing herself to me: "And what time will you come tomorrow with the money?"

"The sooner the better. If it suits you I will come at noon."

"I am always here but I have my hours," said the old woman, as if her convenience were not to be taken for granted.

"You mean the times when you receive?"

"I never receive. But I will see you at noon, when you come with the money."

"Very good, I shall be punctual"; and I added, "May I shake hands with you, on our contract?" I thought there ought to be some little form, it would make me really feel easier, for I foresaw that there would be no other. Besides, though Miss Bordereau could not today be called personally attractive and there was something even in her wasted antiquity that bade one stand at one's distance, I felt an irresistible desire to hold in my own for a moment the hand that Jeffrey Aspern had pressed.

For a minute she made no answer, and I saw that my proposal failed to meet with her approbation. She indulged in no movement of withdrawal, which I half-expected; she only said coldly, "I belong to a time when that was not the custom."

I felt rather snubbed but I exclaimed good humoredly to Miss Tita, "Oh, you will do as well!" I shook hands with her while she replied, with a small flutter, "Yes, yes, to show it's all arranged!"

"Shall you bring the money in gold?" Miss Bordereau demanded, as I was turning to the door.

I looked at her a moment. "Aren't you a little afraid, after all, of keeping such a sum as that in the house?"

It was not that I was annoyed at her avidity but I was really struck with the disparity between such a treasure and such scanty means of guarding it.

"Whom should I be afraid of if I am not afraid of you?" she asked with her shrunken grimness.

"Ah well," said I, laughing, "I shall be in point of fact a protector and I will bring gold if you prefer."

"Thank you," the old woman returned with dignity and with an inclination of her head which evidently signified that I might depart. I passed out of the room, reflecting that it would not be easy to circumvent her. As I stood in the *sala* again I saw that Miss Tita had followed me, and I supposed that as her aunt had neglected to suggest that I should take a look at my quarters it was her purpose to repair the omission. But she made no such suggestion; she only stood there with a dim, though not a languid smile, and with an effect of irresponsible, incompetent youth which was almost comically at variance with the faded facts of her person. She was not infirm, like her aunt, but she struck me as still more helpless, because her inefficiency was spiritual, which was not the case with Miss Bordereau's. I waited to see if she would offer to show me the rest of the house, but I did not precipitate the question, inasmuch as my plan was from this moment to spend as much of my time as possible in her society. I only observed at the end of a minute:

"I have had better fortune than I hoped. It was very kind of her to see me. Perhaps you said a good word for me."

"It was the idea of the money," said Miss Tita.

"And did you suggest that?"

"I told her that you would perhaps give a good deal."

"What made you think that?"

"I told her I thought you were rich."

"And what put that idea into your head?"

"I don't know; the way you talked."

"Dear me, I must talk differently now," I declared. "I'm sorry to say it's not the case."

"Well," said Miss Tita, "I think that in Venice the *forestieri*, in general, often give a great deal for something that after all isn't much." She appeared to make this remark with a comforting intention, to wish to remind me that if I had been extravagant I was not really foolishly singular. We walked together along the *sala,* and as I took its magnificent measure I said to her that I was afraid it would not form a part of my *quartiere.* Were my rooms by chance to be among those that opened into it? "Not if you go above, on the second floor," she answered with a little startled air, as if she had rather taken for granted I would know my proper place.

"And I infer that that's where your aunt would like me to be."

"She said your apartments ought to be very distinct."

"That certainly would be best." And I listened with respect while she told me that up above I was free to take whatever I liked; that there was another staircase, but only from the floor on which we stood, and that to pass from it to the garden-story or to come up to my lodging I should have in effect to cross the great hall. This was an immense point gained; I foresaw that it would constitute my whole leverage in my relations with the two ladies. When I asked Miss Tita how I was to manage at present to find my way up she replied with an access of that sociable shyness which constantly marked her manner.

"Perhaps you can't. I don't see—unless I should go with you." She evidently had not thought of this before.

We ascended to the upper floor and visited a long succession of empty rooms. The best of them looked over the garden; some of the others had a view of the blue lagoon, above the opposite rough-tiled housetops. They were all dusty and even a little disfigured with long neglect, but I saw that by spending a few hundred francs I should be able to convert three or four of them into a convenient habitation. My experiment was turning out costly, yet now that I had all but taken possession I ceased to allow this to trouble me. I mentioned to my companion a few of the things that I should put in, but she replied rather more precipitately than usual that I might do exactly what I liked; she seemed to wish to notify me that the Misses Bordereau would take no overt interest in my proceedings. I guessed that her aunt had instructed her to adopt this tone, and I may as well say now that I came afterward to distinguish perfectly (as I believed) between the speeches she made on her own responsibility and those the old lady imposed upon her. She took no notice of the unswept condition of the rooms and indulged in no explanations nor apologies. I said to myself that this was a sign that Juliana and her niece (disenchanting idea!) were untidy persons, with a low Italian standard; but I afterward recognized that a lodger who had forced an entrance had no *locus standi* as a critic. We looked out of a good many windows, for there was nothing within the rooms to look at, and still I wanted to linger. I asked her what several different objects in the prospect might be, but in no case did she appear to know. She was evidently not familiar with the view—it was as if she had not looked at it for years—and I presently saw that she was too preoccupied with something else to pretend to care for it. Suddenly she said—the remark was not suggested:

"I don't know whether it will make any difference to you, but the money is for me."

"The money?"

"The money you are going to bring."

"Why, you'll make me wish to stay here two or three years." I spoke as benevolently as possible, though it had begun to act on my nerves that with these women so associated with Aspern the pecuniary question should constantly come back.

"That would be very good for me," she replied, smiling.

"You put me on my honor!"

She looked as if she failed to understand this, but went on: "She wants me to have more. She thinks she is going to die."

"Ah, not soon, I hope!" I exclaimed with genuine feeling. I had perfectly considered the possibility that she would destroy her papers on the day she should feel her end really approach. I believed that she would cling to them till then, and I think I had an idea that she read Aspern's letters over every night or at least pressed them to her withered lips. I would have given a good deal to have a glimpse of the latter spectacle. I asked

Miss Tita if the old lady were seriously ill, and she
replied that she was only very tired—she had lived so
very, very long. That was what she said herself—she
wanted to die for a change. Besides, all her friends
were dead long ago; either they ought to have remained
or she ought to have gone. That was another thing her
aunt often said—she was not at all content.

"But people don't die when they like, do they?" Miss
Tita inquired. I took the liberty of asking why, if there
was actually enough money to maintain both of them,
there would not be more than enough in case of her
being left alone. She considered this difficult problem
a moment and then she said, "Oh, well, you know, she
takes care of me. She thinks that when I'm alone I
shall be a great fool, I shall not know how to manage."

"I should have supposed rather that you took care of
her. I'm afraid she is very proud."

"Why, have you discovered that already?" Miss Tita
cried with the glimmer of an illumination in her face.

"I was shut up with her there for a considerable
time, and she struck me, she interested me extremely.
It didn't take me long to make my discovery. She won't
have much to say to me while I'm here."

"No, I don't think she will," my companion averred.

"Do you suppose she has some suspicion of me?"

Miss Tita's honest eyes gave me no sign that I had
touched a mark. "I shouldn't think so—letting you in
after all so easily."

"Oh, so easily! she has covered her risk. But where
is it that one could take an advantage of her?"

"I oughtn't to tell you if I knew, ought I?" And Miss
Tita added, before I had time to reply to this, smiling
dolefully, "Do you think we have any weak points?"

"That's exactly what I'm asking. You would only have
to mention them for me to respect them religiously."

She looked at me, at this, with that air of timid but
candid and even gratified curiosity with which she had
confronted me from the first; and then she said, "There
is nothing to tell. We are terribly quiet. I don't know how
the days pass. We have no life."

"I wish I might think that I should bring you a little."

"Oh, we know what we want," she went on. "It's all right."

There were various things I desired to ask her: how in the world they did live; whether they had any friends or visitors, any relations in America or in other countries. But I judged such an inquiry would be premature; I must leave it to a later chance. "Well, don't *you* be proud," I contented myself with saying. "Don't hide from me altogether."

"Oh, I must stay with my aunt," she returned, without looking at me. And at the same moment, abruptly, without any ceremony of parting, she quitted me and disappeared, leaving me to make my own way downstairs. I remained a while longer, wandering about the bright desert (the sun was pouring in) of the old house, thinking the situation over on the spot. Not even the pattering little *serva* came to look after me, and I reflected that after all this treatment showed confidence.

IV

Perhaps it did, but all the same, six weeks later, toward the middle of June, the moment when Mrs. Prest undertook her annual migration, I had made no measureable advance. I was obliged to confess to her that I had no results to speak of. My first step had been unexpectedly rapid, but there was no appearance that it would be followed by a second. I was a thousand miles from taking tea with my hostesses—that privilege of which, as I reminded Mrs. Prest, we both had had a vision. She reproached me with wanting boldness, and I answered that even to be bold you must have an opportunity: you may push on through a breach but you can't batter down a dead wall. She answered that the breach I had already made was big enough to admit an army and accused me of wasting precious hours in whimpering in her salon when I ought to have been carrying on the struggle in the field. It is true that I went to see her very often, on the theory that it would console me (I freely expressed my discouragement) for my want of success on my own premises. But I began to perceive that it did not console me to be perpetually chaffed for my scruples, especially when I was really so vigilant; and I was rather glad when my derisive friend closed her house for the summer. She had expected to gather amusement from the drama of my intercourse with the Misses Bordereau, and she was disappointed that the intercourse, and consequently the drama, had not come off. "They'll lead you on to your ruin," she said before she left Venice. "They'll get all your money without showing you a scrap." I think I settled down to my business with more concentration after she had gone away.

It was a fact that up to that time I had not, save on a single brief occasion, had even a moment's contact with my queer hostesses. The exception had occurred when I carried them according to my promise the terrible three thousand francs. Then I found Miss Tita waiting for me in the hall, and she took the money from my hand so that I did not see her aunt. The old lady had promised to receive me, but she apparently thought nothing of breaking that vow. The money was contained in a bag of chamois leather, of respectable dimensions, which my banker had given me, and Miss Tita had to make a big fist to receive it. This she did with extreme solemnity, though I tried to treat the affair a little as a joke. It was in no jocular strain, yet it was with simplicity, that she inquired, weighing the money in her two palms: "Don't you think it's too much?" To which I replied that that would depend upon the amount of pleasure I should get for it. Hereupon she turned away from me quickly, as she had done the day before, murmuring in a tone different from any she had used hitherto: "Oh, pleasure, pleasure—there's no pleasure in this house!"

After this, for a long time, I never saw her, and I wondered that the common chances of the day should not have helped us to meet. It could only be evident that she was immensely on her guard against them; and in addition to this the house was so big that for each other we were lost in it. I used to look out for her hopefully as I crossed the sala in my comings and goings, but I was not rewarded with a glimpse of the tail of her dress. It was as if she never peeped out of her aunt's apartment. I used to wonder what she did there week after week and year after year. I had never encountered such a violent *parti pris* of seclusion; it was more than keeping quiet— it was like hunted creatures feigning death. The two ladies appeared to have no visitors whatever and no sort of contact with the world. I judged at least that people could not have come to the house and that Miss Tita could not have gone out without my having some observation of it. I did what I disliked myself for doing (reflecting that it was only once in a way): I questioned my servant about their habits and let him divine that I should be interested in any information he could pick up. But he picked up amazingly little for a knowing Venetian: it must be added that where there is a perpetual fast there are very few crumbs on the floor. His cleverness in other ways was sufficient, if it was not quite all that I had attributed to him on the occasion of my first interview with Miss Tita. He had helped my gondolier to bring me round a boatload of furniture; and when these articles had been carried to the top of the palace and distributed according to our associated wisdom he organized my household with such promptitude as was consistent with the fact that it was composed exclusively of himself. He made me in short as comfortable as I could be with my indifferent prospects. I should have been glad if he had fallen in love with Miss Bordereau's maid or, failing this, had taken her in aversion; either event might have brought about some kind of catastrophe, and a catastrophe might have led to some parley. It was my idea that she would have been sociable, and I myself on various occasions saw her flit to and fro on domestic errands, so that I was sure she was accessible. But I tasted of no gossip from that fountain, and I afterward learned that Pasquale's affections were fixed upon an object that made him heedless of other women. This was a young lady with a powdered face, a yellow cotton gown, and much leisure, who used often to come to see him. She practiced, at her convenience, the art of a stringer of beads (these ornaments are made in Venice, in profusion; she had her pocket full of them, and I used to find them on the floor of my apartment), and kept an eye on the maiden in the house. It was not for me of course to make the domestics tattle, and I never said a word to Miss Bordereau's cook.

It seemed to me a proof of the old lady's determination to have nothing to do with me that she should never have sent me a receipt for my three months' rent. For some days I looked out for it and then, when I had given it up, I wasted a good deal of time in wondering what her reason had been for neglecting so indispensable and familiar a form. At first I was tempted to send her a reminder, after which I relinquished the idea (against my judgment as to what was right in the particular case), on the general ground of wishing to keep quiet. If Miss Bordereau suspected me of ulterior aims she would suspect me less if I should be businesslike, and yet I consented not to be so. It was possible she intended her omission as an impertinence, a visible irony, to show how she could overreach people who attempted to overreach her. On that hypothesis it was well to let her see that one did not notice her little tricks. The real reading of the matter, I afterward perceived, was simply the poor old woman's desire to emphasize the fact that I was in the enjoyment of a favor as rigidly limited as it had been liberally bestowed. She had given me part of her house, and now she would not give me even a morsel of paper with her name on it. Let me say that even at first this did not make me too miserable, for the whole episode was essentially delightful to me. I foresaw that I should have a summer after my own literary heart and the sense of holding my opportunity was much greater than the sense of losing it. There could be no Venetian business without patience, and since I adored the place I was much more in the spirit of it for having laid in a large provision. That spirit kept me perpetual company and seemed to look out at me from the revived immortal face—in which all his genius shone—of the great poet who was my prompter. I had invoked him and he had come; he hovered before me half the time; it was as if his bright ghost had returned to earth to tell me that he regarded the affair as his own no less

than mine and that we should see it fraternally, cheerfully to a conclusion. It was as if he had said, "Poor dear,
be easy with her; she has some natural prejudices; only
give her time. Strange as it may appear to you she was
very attractive in 1820. Meanwhile are we not in Venice
together, and what better place is there for the meeting
of dear friends? See how it glows with the advancing
summer; how the sky and the sea and the rosy air and
the marble of the palaces all shimmer and melt together."
My eccentric private errand became a part of the general romance and the general glory—I felt even a mystic
companionship, a moral fraternity with all those who in
the past had been in the service of art. They had worked
for beauty, for a devotion; and what else was I doing?
That element was in everything that Jeffrey Aspern had
written, and I was only bringing it to the light.

I lingered in the *sala* when I went to and fro; I used
to watch—as long as I thought decent—the door that led
to Miss Bordereau's part of the house. A person observing me might have supposed I was trying to cast a spell
upon it or attempting some odd experiment in hypnotism.
But I was only praying it would open or thinking what
treasure probably lurked behind it. I hold it singular, as
I look back, that I should never have doubted for a moment that the sacred relics were there; never have failed
to feel a certain joy at being under the same roof with
them. After all they were under my hand—they had not
escaped me yet; and they made my life continuous, in a
fashion, with the illustrious life they had touched at the
other end. I lost myself in this satisfaction to the point of
assuming—in my quiet extravagance—that poor Miss Tita
also went back, went back, as I used to phrase it. She
did indeed, the gentle spinster, but not quite so far as
Jeffrey Aspern, who was simply hearsay to her, quite as
he was to me. Only she had lived for years with Juliana,
she had seen and handled the papers and (even though
she was stupid) some esoteric knowledge had rubbed
off on her. That was what the old woman represented
—esoteric knowledge; and this was the idea with which
my editorial heart used to thrill. It literally beat faster
often, of an evening, when I had been out, as I stopped
with my candle in the re-echoing hall on my way up to

bed. It was as if at such a moment as that, in the stillness, after the long contradiction of the day, Miss
Bordereau's secrets were in the air, the wonder of her
survival more palpable. These were the acute impressions. I had them in another form, with more of a certain
sort of reciprocity, during the hours that I sat in the
garden looking up over the top of my book at the closed
windows of my hostess. In these windows no sign of
life ever appeared; it was as if, for fear of my catching a
glimpse of them, the two ladies passed their days in
the dark. But this only proved to me that they had
something to conceal; which was what I had wished to
demonstrate. Their motionless shutters became as expressive as eyes consciously closed, and I took comfort
in thinking that at all events though invisible themselves
they saw me between the lashes.

I made a point of spending as much time as possible
in the garden, to justify the picture I had originally given
of my horticultural passion. And I not only spent time,
but (hang it! as I said) I spent money. As soon as I had
got my rooms arranged and could give the proper thought
to the matter I surveyed the place with a clever expert
and made terms for having it put in order. I was sorry to
do this, for personally I liked it better as it was, with its
weeds and its wild, rough tangle, its sweet, characteristic
Venetian shabbiness. I had to be consistent, to keep my
promise that I would smother the house in flowers. Moreover I formed this graceful project that by flowers I
would make my way—I would succeed by big nosegays. I
would batter the old women with lilies—I would bombard their citadel with roses. Their door would have to
yield to the pressure when a mountain of carnations
should be piled up against it. The place in truth had been
brutally neglected. The Venetian capacity for dawdling
is of the largest, and for a good many days unlimited
litter was all my gardener had to show for his ministra-
tions. There was a great digging of holes and carting
about of earth, and after a while I grew so impatient
that I had thoughts of sending for my bouquets to the
nearest stand. But I reflected that the ladies would see
through the chinks of their shutters that they must have
been bought and might make up their minds from this that

I was a humbug. So I composed myself and finally, though
the delay was long, perceived some appearances of
bloom. This encouraged me, and I waited serenely
enough till they multiplied. Meanwhile the real summer
days arrived and began to pass, and as I look back upon
them they seem to me almost the happiest of my life.
I took more and more care to be in the garden whenever it was not too hot. I had an arbor arranged and a
low table and an armchair put into it; and I carried out
books and portfolios (I had always some business of
writing in hand), and worked and waited and mused and
hoped, while the golden hours elapsed and the plants
drank in the light and the inscrutable old palace turned
pale and then, as the day waned, began to flush in it and
my papers rustled in the wandering breeze of the
Adriatic.

Considering how little satisfaction I got from it at first
it is remarkable that I should not have grown more
tired of wondering what mystic rites of ennui the Misses
Bordereau celebrated in their darkened rooms; whether
this had always been the tenor of their life and how in
previous years they had escaped elbowing their neighbors.
It was clear that they must have had other habits and
other circumstances; that they must once have been
young or at least middle-aged. There was no end to the
questions it was possible to ask about them and no end
to the answers it was not possible to frame. I had known
many of my country-people in Europe and was familiar
with the strange ways they were liable to take up there;
but the Misses Bordereau formed altogether a new type
of the American absentee. Indeed it was plain that the
American name had ceased to have any application to
them—I had seen this in the ten minutes I spent in the
old woman's room. You could never have said whence
they came, from the appearance of either of them;
wherever it was they had long ago dropped the local accent and fashion. There was nothing in them that one
recognized, and putting the question of speech aside they
might have been Norwegians or Spaniards. Miss Bordereau,
after all, had been in Europe nearly three-quarters of a
century; it appeared by some verses addressed to her by
Aspern on the occasion of his own second absence from

America—verses of which Cumnor and I had after infinite conjecture established solidly enough the date— that she was even then, as a girl of twenty, on the foreign side of the sea. There was an implication in the poem (I hope not just for the phrase) that he had come back for her sake. We had no real light upon her circumstances at that moment, any more than we had upon her origin, which we believed to be of the sort usually spoken of as modest. Cumnor had a theory that she had been a governess in some family in which the poet visited and that, in consequence of her position, there was from the first something unavowed, or rather something positively clandestine, in their relations. I on the other hand had hatched a little romance according to which she was the daughter of an artist, a painter or a sculptor, who had left the western world when the century was fresh, to study in the ancient schools. It was essential to my hypothesis that this amiable man should have lost his wife, should have been poor and unsuccessful and should have had a second daughter, of a disposition quite different from Juliana's. It was also indispensable that he should have been accompanied to Europe by these young ladies and should have established himself there for the remainder of a struggling, saddened life. There was a further implication that Miss Bordereau had had in her youth a perverse and adventurous, albeit a generous and fascinating character, and that she had passed through some singular vicissitudes. By what passions had she been ravaged, by what sufferings had she been blanched, what store of memories had she laid away for the monotonous future?

I asked myself these things as I sat spinning theories about her in my arbor and the bees droned in the flowers. It was incontestable that, whether for right or for wrong, most readers of certain of Aspern's poems (poems not as ambiguous as the sonnets—scarcely more divine, I think—of Shakespeare) had taken for granted that Juliana had not always adhered to the steep footway of renunciation. There hovered about her name a perfume of reckless passion, an intimation that she had not been exactly as the respectable young person in general. Was this a sign that her singer had betrayed her, had given

her away, as we say nowadays, to posterity? Certain it
is that it would have been difficult to put one's finger on
the passage in which her fair fame suffered an imputation. Moreover was not any fame fair enough that was
so sure of duration and was associated with works immortal through their beauty? It was a part of my idea
that the young lady had had a foreign lover (and an un-
edifying tragical rupture) before her meeting with Jeffrey
Aspern. She had lived with her father and sister in a
queer old-fashioned, expatriated, artistic Bohemia, in the
days when the aesthetic was only the academic and the
painters who knew the best models for a *contadina* and
pifferaro wore peaked hats and long hair. It was a society
less furnished than the coteries of today (in its ignorance
of the wonderful chances, the opportunities of the early
bird, with which its path was strewn), with tatters of old
stuff and fragments of old crockery; so that Miss
Bordereau appeared not to have picked up or have in-
herited many objects of importance. There was no enviable bric-a-brac, with its provoking legend of cheapness,
in the room in which I had seen her. Such a fact as that
suggested bareness, but nonetheless it worked happily
into the sentimental interest I had always taken in the
early movements of my countrymen as visitors to Europe. When Americans went abroad in 1820 there was
something romantic, almost heroic in it, as compared
with the perpetual ferryings of the present hour, when
photography and other conveniences have annihilated
surprise. Miss Bordereau sailed with her family on a tossing brig, in the days of long voyages and sharp differences; she had her emotions on the top of yellow
diligences, passed the night at inns where she dreamed
of travelers' tales, and was struck, on reaching the
Eternal City, with the elegance of Roman pearls and
scarfs. There was something touching to me in all that,
and my imagination frequently went back to the period.
If Miss Bordereau carried it there of course Jeffrey
Aspern at other times had done so a great deal more. It
was a much more important fact, if one were looking at
his genius critically, that he had lived in the days before
the general transfusion. It had happened to me to regret
that he had known Europe at all; I should have liked to

see what he would have written without that experience,
by which he had incontestably been enriched. But as his
fate had ordered otherwise I went with him—I tried to
judge how the Old World would have struck him. It
was not only there, however, that I watched him; the
relations he had entertained with the new had even a
livelier interest. His own country after all had had most
of his life, and his muse, as they said at that time, was
essentially American. That was originally what I had
loved him for: that at a period when our native land
was nude and crude and provincial, when the famous
"atmosphere" it is supposed to lack was not even missed,
when literature was lonely there and art and form almost impossible, he had found means to live and write
like one of the first; to be free and general and not at all
afraid; to feel, understand, and express everything.

V

I was seldom at home in the evening, for when I attempted to occupy myself in my apartments the lamplight brought in a swarm of noxious insects, and it was
too hot for closed windows. Accordingly I spent the late
hours either on the water (the moonlight of Venice is
famous), or in the splendid square which serves as a
vast forecourt to the strange old basilica of Saint Mark.
I sat in front of Florian's café, eating ices, listening to
music, talking with acquaintances: the traveler will remember how the immense cluster of tables and little
chairs stretches like a promontory into the smooth lake
of the Piazza. The whole place, of a summer's evening,
under the stars and with all the lamps, all the voices and
light footsteps on marble (the only sounds of the arcades
that enclose it), is like an open-air saloon dedicated to
cooling drinks and to a still finer degustation—that of
the exquisite impressions received during the day. When
I did not prefer to keep mine to myself there was always

a stray tourist, disencumbered of his Baedeker, to discuss them with, or some domesticated painter rejoicing in the return of the season of strong effects. The wonderful church, with its low domes and bristling embroideries, the mystery of its mosaic and sculpture, looking ghostly in the tempered gloom, and the sea breeze passed between the twin columns of the Piazzetta, the lintels of a door no longer guarded, as gently as if a rich curtain were swaying there. I used sometimes on these occasions to think of the Misses Bordereau and of the pity of their being shut up in apartments which in the Venetian July even Venetian vastness did not prevent from being stuffy. Their life seemed miles away from the life of the Piazza, and no doubt it was really too late to make the austere Juliana change her habits. But poor Miss Tita would have enjoyed one of Florian's ices, I was sure; sometimes I even had thoughts of carrying one home to her. Fortunately my patience bore fruit, and I was not obliged to do anything so ridiculous.

One evening about the middle of July I came in earlier than usual—I forget what chance had led to this—and instead of going up to my quarters made my way into the garden. The temperature was very high; it was such a night as one would gladly have spent in the open air, and I was in no hurry to go to bed. I had floated home in my gondola, listening to the slow splash of the oar in the narrow dark canals, and now the only thought that solicited me was the vague reflection that it would be pleasant to recline at one's length in the fragrant darkness on a garden bench. The odor of the canal was doubtless at the bottom of that aspiration and the breath of the garden, as I entered it, gave consistency to my purpose. It was delicious—just such an air as must have trembled with Romeo's vows when he stood among the flowers and raised his arms to his mistress's balcony. I looked at the windows of the palace to see if by chance the example of Verona (Verona being not far off) had been followed; but everything was dim, as usual, and everything was still. Juliana, on summer nights in her youth, might have murmured down from open windows at Jeffrey Aspern, but Miss Tita was not a poet's mistress any more than I was a poet. This however did not pre-

vent my gratification from being great as I became aware
on reaching the end of the garden that Miss Tita was
seated in my little bower. At first I only made out an indistinct figure, not in the least counting on such an overture from one of my hostesses; it even occurred to me
that some sentimental maidservant had stolen in to keep
a tryst with her sweetheart. I was going to turn away, not
to frighten her, when the figure rose to its height and I
recognized Miss Bordereau's niece. I must do myself the
justice to say that I did not wish to frighten her either,
and much as I had longed for some such accident I
should have been capable of retreating. It was as if I had
laid a trap for her by coming home earlier than usual
and adding to that eccentricity by creeping into the garden. As she rose she spoke to me, and then I reflected
that perhaps, secure in my almost inveterate absence,
it was her nightly practice to take a lonely airing. There
was no trap, in truth, because I had had no suspicion.
At first I took for granted that the words she uttered expressed discomfiture at my arrival; but as she repeated
them—I had not caught them clearly—I had the surprise
of hearing her say, "Oh, dear, I'm so very glad you've
come!" She and her aunt had in common the property of
unexpected speeches. She came out of the arbor almost
as if she were going to throw herself into my arms.

I hasten to add that she did nothing of the kind; she
did not even shake hands with me. It was a gratification
to her to see me and presently she told me why—because she was nervous when she was out-of-doors at
night alone. The plants and bushes looked so strange in
the dark, and there were all sorts of queer sounds—she
could not tell what they were—like the noises of animals.
She stood close to me, looking about her with an air of
greater security but without any demonstration of interest
in me as an individual. Then I guessed that nocturnal
prowlings were not in the least her habit, and I was also
reminded (I had been struck with the circumstance in
talking with her before I took possession) that it was
impossible to overestimate her simplicity.

"You speak as if you were lost in the backwoods,"
I said, laughing. "How you manage to keep out of this
charming place when you have only three steps to take

to get into it is more than I have yet been able to discover. You hide away mighty well so long as I am on the premises, I know; but I had a hope that you peeped out a little at other times. You and your poor aunt are worse off than Carmelite nuns in their cells. Should you mind telling me how you exist without air, without exercise, without any sort of human contact? I don't see how you carry on the common business of life."

She looked at me as if I were talking some strange tongue, and her answer was so little of an answer that I was considerably irritated. "We go to bed very early—earlier than you would believe." I was on the point of saying that this only deepened the mystery when she gave me some relief by adding, "Before you came we were not so private. But I never have been out at night."

"Never in these fragrant alleys, blooming here under your nose?"

"Ah," said Miss Tita, "they were never nice till now!" There was an unmistakable reference in this and a flattering comparison, so that it seemed to me I had gained a small advantage. As it would help me to follow it up to establish a sort of grievance I asked her why, since she thought my garden nice, she had never thanked me in any way for the flowers I had been sending up in such quantities for the previous three weeks. I had not been discouraged—there had been, as she would have observed, a daily armful; but I had been brought up in the common forms and a word of recognition now and then would have touched me in the right place.

"Why I didn't know they were for me!"

"They were for both of you. Why should I make a difference?"

Miss Tita reflected as if she might be thinking of a reason for that, but she failed to produce one. Instead of this she asked abruptly, "Why in the world do you want to know us?"

"I ought after all to make a difference," I replied. "That question is your aunt's; it isn't yours. You wouldn't ask it if you hadn't been put up to it."

"She didn't tell me to ask you," Miss Tita replied without confusion; she was the oddest mixture of the shrinking and the direct.

"Well, she has often wondered about it herself and expressed her wonder to you. She has insisted on it, so that she has put the idea into your head that I am insufferably pushing. Upon my word I think I have been very discreet. And how completely your aunt must have lost every tradition of sociability, to see anything out of the way in the idea that respectable intelligent people, living as we do under the same roof, should occasionally exchange a remark! What could be more natural? We are of the same country, and we have at least some of the same tastes, since, like you, I am intensely fond of Venice."

My interlocutress appeared incapable of grasping more than one clause in any proposition, and she declared quickly, eagerly, as if she were answering my whole speech: "I am not in the least fond of Venice. I should like to go far away!"

"Has she always kept you back so?" I went on, to show her that I could be as irrelevant as herself.

"She told me to come out tonight; she has told me very often," said Miss Tita. "It is I who wouldn't come. I don't like to leave her."

"Is she too weak, is she failing?" I demanded, with more emotion, I think, than I intended to show. I judged this by the way her eyes rested upon me in the darkness. It embarrassed me a little, and to turn the matter off I continued genially: "Do let us sit down together comfortably somewhere, and you will tell me all about her."

Miss Tita made no resistance to this. We found a bench less secluded, less confidential, as it were, than the one in the arbor; and we were still sitting there when I heard midnight ring out from those clear bells of Venice which vibrate with a solemnity of their own over the lagoon and hold the air so much more than the chimes of other places. We were together more than an hour, and our interview gave, as it struck me, a great lift to my undertaking. Miss Tita accepted the situation without a protest; she had avoided me for three months, yet now she treated me almost as if these three months had made me an old friend. If I had chosen I might have inferred from this that though she had avoided me she had given a good deal of consideration to doing so. She paid no at-

tention to the flight of time—never worried at my keeping her so long away from her aunt. She talked freely,
answering questions and asking them and not even taking
advantage of certain longish pauses with which they inevitably alternated to say she thought she had better go
in. It was almost as if she were waiting for something—
something I might say to her—and intended to give me
my opportunity. I was the more struck by this as she
told me that her aunt had been less well for a good many
days and in a way that was rather new. She was weaker;
at moments it seemed as if she had no strength at all;
yet more than ever before she wished to be left alone.
That was why she had told her to come out—not even to
remain in her own room, which was alongside; she said
her niece irritated her, made her nervous. She sat still for
hours together, as if she were asleep; she had always done
that, musing and dozing; but at such times formerly she
gave at intervals some small sign of life, of interest, liking
her companion to be near her with her work. Miss Tita
confided to me that at present her aunt was so motionless
that she sometimes feared she was dead; moreover she
took hardly any food—one couldn't see what she lived
on. The great thing was that she still on most days got
up; the serious job was to dress her, to wheel her out
of her bedroom. She clung to as many of her old habits
as possible and she had always, little company as they
had received for years, made a point of sitting in the
parlor.

I scarcely knew what to think of all this—of Miss
Tita's sudden conversion to sociability and of the strange
circumstance that the more the old lady appeared to decline toward her end the less she should desire to be
looked after. The story did not hang together, and I even
asked myself whether it were not a trap laid for me, the
result of a design to make me show my hand. I could not
have told why my companions (as they could only by
courtesy be called) should have this purpose—why they
should try to trip up so lucrative a lodger. At any rate I
kept on my guard, so that Miss Tita should not have
occasion again to ask me if I had an *arrière-pensée*.
Poor woman, before we parted for the night my mind was
at rest as to *her* capacity for entertaining one.

She told me more about their affairs than I had hoped;
there was no need to be prying, for it evidently drew her
out simply to feel that I listened, that I cared. She
ceased wondering why I cared, and at last, as she spoke of
the brilliant life they had led years before, she almost
chattered. It was Miss Tita who judged it brilliant; she said
that when they first came to live in Venice, years and
years before (I saw that her mind was essentially vague
about dates and the order in which events had occurred),
there was scarcely a week that they had not some visitor
or did not make some delightful *passeggio* in the city. They
had seen all the curiosities; they had even been to the Lido
in a boat (she spoke as if I might think there was a way
on foot); they had had a collation there, brought in three
baskets and spread out on the grass. I asked her what
people they had known and she said, Oh! very nice ones
—the Cavaliere Bombicci and the Contessa Altemura,
with whom they had had a great friendship. Also English people—the Churtons and the Goldies and Mrs.
Stock-Stock, whom they had loved dearly; she was dead
and gone, poor dear. That was the case with most of
their pleasant circle (this expression was Miss Tita's
own), though a few were left, which was a wonder considering how they had neglected them. She mentioned
the names of two or three Venetian old women; of a
certain doctor, very clever, who was so kind—he came
as a friend, he had really given up practice; of the *avvocato* Pochintesta, who wrote beautiful poems and had
addressed one to her aunt. These people came to see
them without fail every year, usually at the *capo d'anno,*
and of old her aunt used to make them some little present—her aunt and she together: small things that she,
Miss Tita, made herself, like paper lampshades or mats
for the decanters of wine at dinner or those woolen things
that in cold weather were worn on the wrists. The last
few years there had not been many presents; she could
not think what to make, and her aunt had lost her interest and never suggested. But the people came all the
same; if the Venetians liked you once they liked you forever.

There was something affecting in the good faith of
this sketch of former social glories; the picnic at the Lido

had remained vivid through the ages, and poor Miss Tita evidently was of the impression that she had had a brilliant youth. She had in fact had a glimpse of the Venetian world in its gossiping, home-keeping, parsimonious, professional walks; for I observed for the first time that she had acquired by contact something of the trick of the familiar, soft-sounding, almost infantile speech of the place. I judged that she had imbibed this invertebrate dialect from the natural way the names of things and people—mostly purely local—rose to her lips. If she knew little of what they represented she knew still less of anything else. Her aunt had drawn in—her failing interest in the table mats and lampshades was a sign of that —and she had not been able to mingle in society or to entertain it alone; so that the matter of her reminiscences struck one as an old world altogether. If she had not been so decent her references would have seemed to carry one back to the queer rococo Venice of Casanova. I found myself falling into the error of thinking of her too as one of Jeffrey Aspern's contemporaries; this came from her having so little in common with my own. It was possible, I said to myself, that she had not even heard of him; it might very well be that Juliana had not cared to lift even for her the veil that covered the temple of her youth. In this case she perhaps would not know of the existence of the papers, and I welcomed that presumption—it made me feel more safe with her—until I remembered that we had believed the letter of disavowal received by Cumnor to be in the handwriting of the niece. If it had been dictated to her she had of course to know what it was about; yet after all the effect of it was to repudiate the idea of any connection with the poet. I held it probable at all events that Miss Tita had not read a word of his poetry. Moreover if, with her companion, she had always escaped the interviewer there was little occasion for her having got it into her head that people were "after" the letters. People had not been after them, inasmuch as they had not heard of them; and Cumnor's fruitless feeler would have been a solitary accident.

When midnight sounded Miss Tita got up; but she stopped at the door of the house only after she had wandered two or three times with me round the garden.

"When shall I see you again?" I asked before she went in; to which she replied with promptness that she should like to come out the next night. She added however that she should not come—she was so far from doing everything she liked.

"You might do a few things that *I* like," I said with a sigh.

"Oh, you—I don't believe you!" she murmured at this, looking at me with her simple solemnity.

"Why don't you believe me?"

"Because I don't understand you."

"That is just the sort of occasion to have faith." I could not say more, though I should have liked to, as I saw that I only mystified her; for I had no wish to have it on my conscience that I might pass for having made love to her. Nothing less should I have seemed to do had I continued to beg a lady to "believe in me" in an Italian garden on a midsummer night. There was some merit in my scruples, for Miss Tita lingered and lingered: I perceived that she felt that she should not really soon come down again and wished therefore to protract the present. She insisted too on making the talk between us personal to ourselves; and altogether her behavior was such as would have been possible only to a completely innocent woman.

"I shall like the flowers better now that I know they are also meant for me."

"How could you have doubted it? If you will tell me the kind you like best I will send a double lot of them."

"Oh, I like them all best!" Then she went on, familiarly: "Shall you study—shall you read and write—when you go up to your rooms?"

"I don't do that at night, at this season. The lamplight brings in the animals."

"You might have known that when you came."

"I did know it!"

"And in winter do you work at night?"

"I read a good deal, but I don't often write." She listened as if these details had a rare interest, and suddenly a temptation quite at variance with the prudence I had been teaching myself associated itself with her plain, mild face. Ah yes, she was safe and I could make her safer!

It seemed to me from one moment to another that I could not wait longer—that I really must take a sounding. So I went on: "In general before I go to sleep—very often in bed (it's a bad habit, but I confess to it), I read some great poet. In nine cases out of ten it's a volume of Jeffrey Aspern."

I watched her well as I pronounced that name but I saw nothing wonderful. Why should I indeed—was not Jeffrey Aspern the property of the human race?

"Oh, we read him—we *have* read him," she quietly replied.

"He is my poet of poets—I know him almost by heart."

For an instant Miss Tita hesitated; then her sociability was too much for her.

"Oh, by heart—that's nothing!" she murmured, smiling. "My aunt used to know him—to know him"—she paused an instant and I wondered what she was going to say—"to know him as a visitor."

"As a visitor?" I repeated, staring.

"He used to call on her and take her out."

I continued to stare. "My dear lady, he died a hundred years ago!"

"Well," she said mirthfully, "my aunt is a hundred and fifty."

"Mercy on us!" I exclaimed; "why didn't you tell me before? I should like so to ask her about him."

"She wouldn't care for that—she wouldn't tell you," Miss Tita replied.

"I don't care what she cares for! She *must* tell me—it's not a chance to be lost."

"Oh, you should have come twenty years ago: then she still talked about him."

"And what did she say?" I asked eagerly.

"I don't know—that he liked her immensely."

"And she—didn't she like him?"

"She said he was a god." Miss Tita gave me this information flatly, without expression; her tone might have made it a piece of trivial gossip. But it stirred me deeply as she dropped the words into the summer night; it seemed such a direct testimony.

"Fancy, fancy!" I murmured. And then, "Tell me this,

please—has she got a portrait of him? They are distressingly rare."

"A portrait? I don't know," said Miss Tita; and now there was discomfiture in her face. "Well, good night!" she added; and she turned into the house.

I accompanied her into the wide, dusky, stone-paved passage which on the ground floor corresponded with our grand *sala*. It opened at one end into the garden, at the other upon the canal, and was lighted now only by the small lamp that was always left for me to take up as I went to bed. An extinguished candle which Miss Tita apparently had brought down with her stood on the same table with it. "Good night, good night!" I replied, keeping beside her as she went to get her light. "Surely you would know, shouldn't you, if she had one?"

"If she had what?" the poor lady asked, looking at me queerly over the flame of her candle.

"A portrait of the god. I don't know what I wouldn't give to see it."

"I don't know what she has got. She keeps her things locked up." And Miss Tita went away, toward the staircase, with the sense evidently that she had said too much.

I let her go—I wished not to frighten her—and I contented myself with remarking that Miss Bordereau would not have locked up such a glorious possession as that—a thing a person would be proud of and hang up in a prominent place on the parlor wall. Therefore of course she had not any portrait. Miss Tita made no direct answer to this and, candle in hand, with her back to me, ascended two or three stairs. Then she stopped short and turned round, looking at me across the dusky space.

"Do you write—do you write?" There was a shake in her voice—she could scarcely bring out what she wanted to ask.

"Do I write? Oh, don't speak of my writing on the same day with Aspern's!"

"Do you write about *him*—do you pry into his life?"

"Ah, that's your aunt's question; it can't be yours!" I said, in a tone of slightly wounded sensibility.

"All the more reason then that you should answer it. Do you, please?"

I thought I had allowed for the falsehoods I should have to tell; but I found that in fact when it came to the point I had not. Besides, now that I had an opening there was a kind of relief in being frank. Lastly (it was perhaps fanciful, even fatuous), I guessed that Miss Tita personally would not in the last resort be less my friend. So after a moment's hesitation I answered, "Yes, I have written about him and I am looking for more material. In heaven's name have you got any?"

"*Santo Dio!*" she exclaimed, without heeding my question; and she hurried upstairs and out of sight. I might count upon her in the last resort, but for the present she was visibly alarmed. The proof of it was that she began to hide again, so that for a fortnight I never beheld her. I found my patience ebbing and after four or five days of this I told the gardener to stop the flowers.

VI

One afternoon, as I came down from my quarters to go out, I found Miss Tita in the *sala*: it was our first encounter on that ground since I had come to the house. She put on no air of being there by accident; there was an ignorance of such arts in her angular, diffident directness. That I might be quite sure she was waiting for me she informed me of the fact and told me that Miss Bordereau wished to see me: she would take me into the room at that moment if I had time. If I had been late for a love tryst I would have stayed for this, and I quickly signified that I should be delighted to wait upon the old lady. "She wants to talk with you—to know you," Miss Tita said, smiling as if she herself appreciated that idea; and she led me to the door of her aunt's apartment. I stopped her a moment before she had opened it, looking at her with some curiosity. I told her that this was a great satisfaction to me and a great honor; but all the same I should like to ask what had made Miss Bordereau change so suddenly. It was only the other day that she wouldn't suffer me near her. Miss Tita was not embarrassed by my question; she had as many little unexpected serenities as if she told fibs, but the odd part of them was that they had on the contrary their source in her truthfulness. "Oh, my aunt changes," she answered; "it's so terribly dull—I suppose she's tired."

"But you told me that she wanted more and more to be alone."

Poor Miss Tita colored, as if she found me over-insistent. "Well, if you don't believe she wants to see you—I haven't invented it! I think people often are capricious when they are very old."

"That's perfectly true. I only wanted to be clear as to whether you have repeated to her what I told you the other night."

"What you told me?"

"About Jeffrey Aspern—that I am looking for materials."

"If I had told her do you think she would have sent for you?"

"That's exactly what I want to know. If she wants to keep him to herself she might have sent for me to tell me so."

"She won't speak of him," said Miss Tita. Then as she opened the door she added in a lower tone, "I have told her nothing."

The old woman was sitting in the same place in which I had seen her last, in the same position, with the same mystifying bandage over her eyes. Her welcome was to turn her almost invisible face to me and show me that while she sat silent she saw me clearly. I made no motion to shake hands with her; I felt too well on this occasion that that was out of place forever. It had been sufficiently enjoined upon me that she was too sacred for that sort of reciprocity—too venerable to touch. There was something so grim in her aspect (it was partly the accident of her green shade), as I stood there to be measured, that I ceased on the spot to feel any doubt as to her knowing my secret, though I did not in the least suspect that Miss Tita had not just spoken the truth. She had not betrayed me, but the old woman's brooding instinct had served her; she had turned me over and over in the long, still hours, and she had guessed. The worst of it was that she looked terribly like an old woman who at a pinch would burn her papers. Miss Tita pushed a chair forward, saying to me, "This will be a good place for you to sit." As I took possession of it I asked after Miss Bordereau's health; expressed the hope that in spite of the very hot weather it was satisfactory. She replied that it was good enough—good enough; that it was a great thing to be alive.

"Oh, as to that, it depends upon what you compare it with!" I exclaimed, laughing.

"I don't compare—I don't compare. If I did that I should have given everything up long ago."

I liked to think that this was a subtle allusion to the rapture she had known in the society of Jeffrey Aspern—though it was true that such an allusion would have accorded ill with the wish I imputed to her to keep him buried in her soul. What it accorded with was my constant conviction that no human being had ever had a more delightful social gift than his, and what it seemed to convey was that nothing in the world was worth speaking of if one pretended to speak of that. But one did not! Miss Tita sat down beside her aunt, looking as if she had reason to believe some very remarkable conversation would come off between us.

"It's about the beautiful flowers," said the old lady; "you sent us so many—I ought to have thanked you for them before. But I don't write letters and I receive only at long intervals."

She had not thanked me while the flowers continued to come, but she departed from her custom so far as to send for me as soon as she began to fear that they would not come any more. I noted this; I remembered what an acquisitive propensity she had shown when it was a question of extracting gold from me, and I privately rejoiced at the happy thought I had had in suspending my tribute. She had missed it and she was willing to make a concession to bring it back. At the first sign of this concession I could only go to meet her. "I am afraid you have not had many, of late, but they shall begin again immediately—tomorrow, tonight."

"Oh, do send us some tonight!" Miss Tita cried, as if it were an immense circumstance.

"What else should you do with them? It isn't a manly taste to make a bower of your room," the old woman remarked.

"I don't make a bower of my room, but I am exceedingly fond of growing flowers, of watching their ways. There is nothing unmanly in that: it has been the amusement of philosophers, of statesmen in retirement; even I think of great captains."

"I suppose you know you can sell them—those you don't use," Miss Bordereau went on. "I daresay they wouldn't give you much for them; still, you could make a bargain."

"Oh, I have never made a bargain, as you ought to know. My gardener disposes of them and I ask no questions."

"I would ask a few, I can promise you!" said Miss Bordereau; and it was the first time I had heard her laugh. I could not get used to the idea that this vision of pecuniary profit was what drew out the divine Juliana most.

"Come into the garden yourself and pick them; come as often as you like; come every day. They are all for you," I pursued, addressing Miss Tita and carrying off this veracious statement by treating it as an innocent joke. "I can't imagine why she doesn't come down," I added, for Miss Bordereau's benefit.

"You must make her come; you must come up and fetch her," said the old woman, to my stupefaction. "That odd thing you have made in the corner would be a capital place for her to sit."

The allusion to my arbor was irreverent; it confirmed the impression I had already received that there was a flicker of impertinence in Miss Bordereau's talk, a strange mocking lambency which must have been a part of her adventurous youth and which had outlived passions and faculties. Nonetheless I asked, "Wouldn't it be possible for you to come down there yourself? Wouldn't it do you good to sit there in the shade, in the sweet air?"

"Oh, sir, when I move out of this it won't be to sit in the air, and I'm afraid that any that may be stirring around me won't be particularly sweet! It will be a very dark shade indeed. But that won't be just yet," Miss Bordereau continued cannily, as if to correct any hopes that this courageous allusion to the last receptacle of her mortality might lead me to entertain. "I have sat here many a day and I have had enough of arbors in my time. But I'm not afraid to wait till I'm called."

Miss Tita had expected some interesting talk, but perhaps she found it less genial on her aunt's side (considering that I had been sent for with a civil intention) than she had hoped. As if to give the conversation a turn that would put our companion in a light more favorable she said to me, "Didn't I tell you the other night that she had sent me out? You see that I can do what I like!"

"Do you pity her—do you teach her to pity herself?" Miss Bordereau demanded before I had time to answer this appeal. "She has a much easier life than I had when I was her age."

"You must remember that it has been quite open to me to think you rather inhuman."

"Inhuman? That's what the poets used to call the women a hundred years ago. Don't try that; you won't do as well as they!" Juliana declared. "There is no more poetry in the world—that I know of at least. But I won't bandy words with you," she pursued, and I well remember the old-fashioned, artificial sound she gave to the speech. "You have made me talk, talk! It isn't good for me at all." I got up at this and told her I would take no more of her time; but she detained me to ask, "Do you remember, the day I saw you about the rooms, that you offered us the use of your gondola?" And when I assented, promptly, struck again with her disposition to make a "good thing" of being there and wondering what she now had in her eye, she broke out, "Why don't you take that girl out in it and show her the place?"

"Oh, dear Aunt, what do you want to do with me?"

cried the "girl" with a piteous quaver. "I know all about the place!"

"Well then, go with him as a cicerone!" said Miss Bordereau with an effect of something like cruelty in her implacable power of retort—an incongruous suggestion that she was a sarcastic, profane, cynical old woman. "Haven't we heard that there have been all sorts of changes in all these years? You ought to see them and at your age (I don't mean because you're so young) you ought to take the chances that come. You're old enough, my dear, and this gentleman won't hurt you. He will show you the famous sunsets, if they still go on—*do* they go on? The sun set for me so long ago. But that's not a reason. Besides, I shall never miss you; you think you are too important. Take her to the Piazza; it used to be very pretty," Miss Bordereau continued, addressing herself to me. "What have they done with the funny old church? I hope it hasn't tumbled down. Let her look at the shops; she may take some money, she may buy what she likes."

Poor Miss Tita had got up, discountenanced and helpless, and as we stood there before her aunt it would certainly have seemed to a spectator of the scene that the old woman was amusing herself at our expense. Miss Tita protested, in a confusion of exclamations and murmurs; but I lost no time in saying that if she would do me the honor to accept the hospitality of my boat I would engage that she should not be bored. Or if she did not want so much of my company the boat itself, with the gondolier, was at her service; he was a capital oar and she might have every confidence. Miss Tita, without definitely answering this speech, looked away from me, out of the window, as if she were going to cry; and I remarked that once we had Miss Bordereau's approval we could easily come to an understanding. We would take an hour, whichever she liked, one of the very next days. As I made my obeisance to the old lady I asked her if she would kindly permit me to see her again.

For a moment she said nothing; then she inquired, "Is it very necessary to your happiness?"

"It diverts me more than I can say."

"You are wonderfully civil. Don't you know it almost kills *me?*"

"How can I believe that when I see you more animated, more brilliant than when I came in?"

"That is very true, Aunt," said Miss Tita. "I think it does you good."

"Isn't it touching, the solicitude we each have that the other shall enjoy herself?" sneered Miss Bordereau. "If you think me brilliant today you don't know what you are talking about; you have never seen an agreeable woman. Don't try to pay me a compliment; I have been spoiled," she went on. "My door is shut, but you may sometimes knock."

With this she dismissed me, and I left the room. The latch closed behind me, but Miss Tita, contrary to my hope, had remained within. I passed slowly across the hall and before taking my way downstairs I waited a little. My hope was answered; after a minute Miss Tita followed me. "That's a delightful idea about the Piazza," I said. "When will you go—tonight, tomorrow?"

She had been disconcerted, as I have mentioned, but I had already perceived and I was to observe again that when Miss Tita was embarrassed she did not (as most women would have done) turn away from you and try to escape, but came closer, as it were, with a deprecating, clinging appeal to be spared, to be protected. Her attitude was perpetually a sort of prayer for assistance, for explanation; and yet no woman in the world could have been less of a comedian. From the moment you were kind to her she depended on you absolutely; her self-consciousness dropped from her and she took the greatest intimacy, the innocent intimacy which was the only thing she could conceive, for granted. She told me she did not know what had got into her aunt; she had changed so quickly, she had got some idea. I replied that she must find out what the idea was and then let me know; we would go and have an ice together at Florian's, and she should tell me while we listened to the band.

"Oh, it will take me a long time to find out!" she said, rather ruefully; and she could promise me this satisfaction neither for that night nor for the next. I was patient now, however, for I felt that I had only to wait; and in fact at the end of the week, one lovely evening after dinner, she stepped into my gondola, to which in honor of the occasion I had attached a second oar.

We swept in the course of five minutes into the Grand Canal; whereupon she uttered a murmur of ecstasy as fresh as if she had been a tourist just arrived. She had forgotten how splendid the great waterway looked on a clear, hot summer evening, and how the sense of floating between marble palaces and reflected lights disposed the mind to sympathetic talk. We floated long and far, and though Miss Tita gave no high-pitched voice to her satisfaction I felt that she surrendered herself. She was more than pleased, she was transported; the whole thing was an immense liberation. The gondola moved with slow strokes, to give her time to enjoy it, and she listened to the plash of the oars, which grew louder and more musically liquid as we passed into narrow canals, as if it were a revelation of Venice. When I asked her how long it was since she had been in a boat she answered, "Oh, I don't know; a long time—not since my aunt began to be ill." This was not the only example she gave me of her extreme vagueness about the previous years and the line which marked off the period when Miss Bordereau flourished. I was not at liberty to keep her out too long, but we took a considerable *giro* before going to the Piazza. I asked her no questions, keeping the conversation on purpose away from her domestic situation and the things I wanted to know; I poured treasures of information about Venice into her ears, described Florence and Rome, discoursed to her on the charms and advantages of travel. She reclined, receptive, on the deep leather cushions, turned her eyes conscientiously to everything I pointed out to her, and never mentioned to me till sometime afterward that she might be supposed to know Florence better than I, as she had lived there for years with Miss Bordereau. At last she asked, with the shy impatience of a child, "Are we not really going to the Piazza? That's what I want to see!" I immediately gave the order that we should go straight; and then we sat silent with the expectation of arrival. As some time still passed, however, she said suddenly, of her own movement, "I have found out what is the matter with my aunt: she is afraid you will go!"

"What has put that into her head?"

"She has had an idea you have not been happy. That is why she is different now."

"You mean she wants to make me happier?"

"Well, she wants you not to go; she wants you to stay."

"I suppose you mean on account of the rent," I remarked candidly.

Miss Tita's candor showed itself a match for my own. "Yes, you know; so that I shall have more."

"How much does she want you to have?" I asked, laughing. "She ought to fix the sum, so that I may stay till it's made up."

"Oh, that wouldn't please me," said Miss Tita. "It would be unheard of, your taking that trouble."

"But suppose I should have my own reasons for staying in Venice?"

"Then it would be better for you to stay in some other house."

"And what would your aunt say to that?"

"She wouldn't like it at all. But I should think you would do well to give up your reasons and go away altogether."

"Dear Miss Tita," I said, "it's not so easy to give them up!"

She made no immediate answer to this, but after a moment she broke out: "I think I know what your reasons are!"

"I daresay, because the other night I almost told you how I wish you would help me to make them good."

"I can't do that without being false to my aunt."

"What do you mean, being false to her?"

"Why, she would never consent to what you want. She has been asked, she has been written to. It made her fearfully angry."

"Then she *has* got papers of value?" I demanded quickly.

"Oh, she has got everything!" sighed Miss Tita with a curious weariness, a sudden lapse into gloom.

These words caused all my pulses to throb, for I

regarded them as precious evidence. For some minutes I was too agitated to speak, and in the interval the gondola approached the Piazzetta. After we had disembarked I asked my companion whether she would rather walk round the square or go and sit at the door of the café; to which she replied that she would do whichever I liked best—I must only remember again how little time she had. I assured her there was plenty to do both, and we made the circuit of the long arcades. Her spirits revived at the sight of the bright shop windows, and she lingered and stopped, admiring or disapproving of their contents, asking me what I thought of things, theorizing about prices. My attention wandered from her; her words of a while before, "Oh, she has got everything!" echoed so in my consciousness. We sat down at last in the crowded circle at Florian's, finding an unoccupied table among those that were ranged in the square. It was a splendid night and all the world was out-of-doors; Miss Tita could not have wished the elements more auspicious for her return to society. I saw that she enjoyed it even more than she told; she was agitated with the multitude of her impressions. She had forgotten what an attractive thing the world is, and it was coming over her that somehow she had for the best years of her life been cheated of it. This did not make her angry; but as she looked all over the charming scene her face had, in spite of its smile of appreciation, the flush of a sort of wounded surprise. She became silent, as if she were thinking with a secret sadness of opportunities, forever lost, which ought to have been easy; and this gave me a chance to say to her, "Did you mean a while ago that your aunt has a plan of keeping me on by admitting me occasionally to her presence?"

"She thinks it will make a difference with you if you sometimes see her. She wants you so much to stay that she is willing to make that concession."

"And what good does she consider that I think it will do me to see her?"

"I don't know; she thinks it's interesting," said Miss Tita simply. "You told her you found it so."

"So I did; but everyone doesn't think so."

"No, of course not, or more people would try."

"Well, if she is capable of making that reflection she is capable also of making this further one," I went on: "that I must have a particular reason for not doing as others do, in spite of the interest she offers—for not leaving her alone." Miss Tita looked as if she failed to grasp this rather complicated proposition; so I continued, "If you have not told her what I said to you the other night may she not at least have guessed it?"

"I don't know; she is very suspicious."

"But she has not been made so by indiscreet curiosity, by persecution?"

"No, no; it isn't that," said Miss Tita, turning on me a somewhat troubled face. "I don't know how to say it: it's on account of something—ages ago, before I was born—in her life."

"Something? What sort of thing?" I asked as if I myself could have no idea.

"Oh, she has never told me," Miss Tita answered; and I was sure she was speaking the truth.

Her extreme limpidity was almost provoking, and I felt for the moment that she would have been more satisfactory if she had been less ingenuous. "Do you suppose it's something to which Jeffrey Aspern's letters and papers—I mean the things in her possession—have reference?"

"I daresay it is!" my companion exclaimed as if this were a very happy suggestion. "I have never looked at any of those things."

"None of them? Then how do you know what they are?"

"I don't," said Miss Tita placidly. "I have never had them in my hands. But I have seen them when she has had them out."

"Does she have them out often?"

"Not now, but she used to. She is very fond of them."

"In spite of their being compromising?"

"Compromising?" Miss Tita repeated as if she was ignorant of the meaning of the word. I felt almost as one who corrupts the innocence of youth.

"I mean their containing painful memories."

"Oh, I don't think they are painful."

"You mean you don't think they affect her reputation?"

At this a singular look came into the face of Miss Bordereau's niece—a kind of confession of helplessness, an appeal to me to deal fairly, generously with her. I had brought her to the Piazza, placed her among charming influences, paid her an attention she appreciated, and now I seemed to let her perceive that all this had been a bribe—a bribe to make her turn in some way against her aunt. She was of a yielding nature and capable of doing almost anything to please a person who was kind to her; but the greatest kindness of all would be not to presume too much on this. It was strange enough, as I afterward thought, that she had not the least air of resenting my want of consideration for her aunt's character, which would have been in the worst possible taste if anything less vital (from my point of view) had been at stake. I don't think she really measured it. "Do you mean that she did something bad?" she asked in a moment.

"Heaven forbid I should say so, and it's none of my business. Besides, if she did," I added, laughing, "it was in other ages, in another world. But why should she not destroy her papers?"

"Oh, she loves them too much."

"Even now, when she may be near her end?"

"Perhaps when she's sure of that she will."

"Well, Miss Tita," I said, "it's just what I should like you to prevent."

"How can I prevent it?"

"Couldn't you get them away from her?"

"And give them to you?"

This put the case very crudely, though I am sure there was no irony in her intention. "Oh, I mean that you might let me see them and look them over. It isn't for myself; there is no personal avidity in my desire. It is simply that they would be of such immense interest to the public, such immeasurable importance as a contribution to Jeffrey Aspern's history."

She listened to me in her usual manner, as if my speech were full of reference to things she had never heard of, and I felt particularly like the reporter of a newspaper who forces his way into a house of mourning. This was especially the case when after a moment she said. "There was a gentleman who some time ago wrote to her in very much those words. He also wanted her papers."

"And did she answer him?" I asked, rather ashamed of myself for not having her rectitude.

"Only when he had written two or three times. He made her very angry."

"And what did she say?"

"She said he was a devil," Miss Tita replied simply.

"She used that expression in her letter?"

"Oh, no; she said it to me. She made me write to him."

"And what did you say?"

"I told him there were no papers at all."

"Ah, poor gentleman!" I exclaimed.

"I knew there were, but I wrote what she bade me."

"Of course you had to do that. But I hope I shall not pass for a devil."

"It will depend upon what you ask me to do for you," said Miss Tita, smiling.

"Oh, if there is a chance of *your* thinking so my affair is in a bad way! I shan't ask you to steal for me, nor even to fib—for you can't fib, unless on paper. But the principal thing is this—to prevent her from destroying the papers."

"Why, I have no control of her," said Miss Tita. "It's she who controls me."

"But she doesn't control her own arms and legs, does she? The way she would naturally destroy her letters would be to burn them. Now she can't burn them without fire, and she can't get fire unless you give it to her."

"I have always done everything she has asked," my companion rejoined. "Besides, there's Olimpia."

I was on the point of saying that Olimpia was probably corruptible, but I thought it best not to sound that note. So I simply inquired if that faithful domestic could not be managed.

"Everyone can be managed by my aunt," said Miss Tita. And then she observed that her holiday was over; she must go home.

I laid my hand on her arm, across the table, to stay her a moment. "What I want of you is a general promise to help me."

"Oh, how can I—how can I?" she asked, wondering and troubled. She was half-surprised, half-frightened at my wishing to make her play an active part.

"This is the main thing: to watch her carefully and warn me in time, before she commits that horrible sacrilege."

"I can't watch her when she makes me go out."

"That's very true."

"And when you do, too."

"Mercy on us; do you think she will have done anything tonight?"

"I don't know; she is very cunning."

"Are you trying to frighten me?" I asked.

I felt this inquiry sufficiently answered when my companion murmured in a musing, almost envious way, "Oh, but she loves them—she loves them!"

This reflection, repeated with such emphasis, gave me great comfort; but to obtain more of that balm I said, "If she shouldn't intend to destroy the objects we speak of before her death she will probably have made some disposition by will."

"By will?"

"Hasn't she made a will for your benefit?"

"Why, she has so little to leave. That's why she likes money," said Miss Tita.

"Might I ask, since we are really talking things over, what you and she live on?"

"On some money that comes from America, from a lawyer. He sends it every quarter. It isn't much!"

"And won't she have disposed of that?"

My companion hesitated—I saw she was blushing. "I believe it's mine," she said; and the look and tone which accompanied these words betrayed so the absence of the habit of thinking of herself that I almost thought her charming. The next instant she added, "But she had a lawyer once, ever so long ago. And some people came and signed something."

"They were probably witnesses. And you were not asked to sign? Well then," I argued rapidly and hopefully, "it is because you are the legatee; she has left all her documents to you!"

"If she has it's with very strict conditions," Miss Tita responded, rising quickly, while the movement gave the words a little character of decision. They seemed to imply that the bequest would be accompanied with a command that the articles bequeathed should remain concealed from every inquisitive eye and that I was very much mistaken if I thought she was the person to depart from an injunction so solemn.

"Oh, of course you will have to abide by the terms," I said; and she uttered nothing to mitigate the severity of this conclusion. Nonetheless, later, just before we disembarked at her own door, on our return, which had taken place almost in silence, she said to me abruptly, "I will do what I can to help you." I was grateful for this— it was very well so far as it went; but it did not keep me from remembering that night in a worried waking hour that I now had her word for it to reinforce my own impression that the old woman was very cunning.

VII

The fear of what this side of her character might have led her to do made me nervous for days afterward. I waited for an intimation from Miss Tita; I almost figured to myself that it was her duty to keep me informed, to let me know definitely whether or no Miss Bordereau had sacrificed her treasures. But as she gave no sign I lost patience and determined to judge so far as was possible with my own senses. I sent late one afternoon to ask if I might pay the ladies a visit, and my servant came back with surprising news. Miss Bordereau could be approached without the least difficulty; she had been moved out into the *sala* and was sitting by the window that overlooked the garden. I descended and found this picture correct; the old lady had been wheeled forth into

the world and had a certain air, which came mainly perhaps from some brighter element in her dress, of being
prepared again to have converse with it. It had not yet,
however, begun to flock about her; she was perfectly
alone and, though the door leading to her own quarters
stood open, I had at first no glimpse of Miss Tita. The
window at which she sat had the afternoon shade and,
one of the shutters having been pushed back, she could
see the pleasant garden, where the summer sun had by
this time dried up too many of the plants—she could
see the yellow light and the long shadows.

"Have you come to tell me that you will take the
rooms for six months more?" she asked as I approached
her, startling me by something coarse in her cupidity almost as much as if she had not already given me a specimen of it. Juliana's desire to make our acquaintance
lucrative had been, as I have sufficiently indicated, a false
note in my image of the woman who had inspired a great
poet with immortal lines; but I may say here definitely
that I recognized after all that it behooved me to make
a large allowance for her. It was I who had kindled the
unholy flame; it was I who had put into her head that she
had the means of making money. She appeared never to
have thought of that; she had been living wastefully for
years, in a house five times too big for her, on a footing
that I could explain only by the presumption that, excessive as it was, the space she enjoyed cost her next to
nothing and that small as were her revenues they left
her, for Venice, an appreciable margin. I had descended
on her one day and taught her to calculate, and my almost extravagant comedy on the subject of the garden
had presented me irresistibly in the light of a victim. Like
all persons who achieve the miracle of changing their
point of view when they are old she had been intensely
converted; she had seized my hint with a desperate,
tremulous clutch.

I invited myself to go and get one of the chairs that
stood, at a distance, against the wall (she had given herself no concern as to whether I should sit or stand);
and while I placed it near her I began, gaily, "Oh, dear
madam, what an imagination you have, what an intellectual sweep! I am a poor devil of a man of letters who

lives from day to day. How can I take palaces by the year? My existence is precarious. I don't know whether six months hence I shall have bread to put in my mouth. I have treated myself for once; it has been an immense luxury. But when it comes to going on——!"

"Are your rooms too dear? if they are you can have more for the same money," Juliana responded. "We can arrange, we can *combinare*, as they say here."

"Well yes, since you ask me, they are too dear," I said. "Evidently you suppose me richer than I am."

She looked at me in her barricaded way. "If you write books don't you sell them?"

"Do you mean don't people buy them? A little— not so much as I could wish. Writing books, unless one be a great genius—and even then!—is the last road to fortune. I think there is no more money to be made by literature."

"Perhaps you don't choose good subjects. What do you write about?" Miss Bordereau inquired.

"About the books of other people. I'm a critic, an historian, in a small way." I wondered what she was coming to.

"And what other people, now?"

"Oh, better ones than myself: the great writers mainly —the great philosophers and poets of the past; those who are dead and gone and can't speak for themselves."

"And what do you say about them?"

"I say they sometimes attached themselves to very clever women!" I answered, laughing. I spoke with great deliberation, but as my words fell upon the air they struck me as imprudent. However, I risked them and I was not sorry, for perhaps after all the old woman would be will ing to treat. It seemed to be tolerably obvious that she knew my secret: why therefore drag the matter out? But she did not take what I had said as a confession; she only asked:

"Do you think it's right to rake up the past?"

"I don't know that I know what you mean by raking it up; but how can we get at it unless we dig a little? The present has such a rough way of treading it down."

"Oh, I like the past, but I don't like critics," the old woman declared with her fine tranquillity.

"Neither do I, but I like their discoveries."

"Aren't they mostly lies?"

"The lies are what they sometimes discover," I said, smiling at the quiet impertinence of this. "They often lay bare the truth."

"The truth is God's, it isn't man's; we had better leave it alone. Who can judge of it—who can say?"

"We are terribly in the dark, I know," I admitted; "but if we give up trying what becomes of all the fine things? What becomes of the work I just mentioned, that of the great philosophers and poets? It is all vain words if there is nothing to measure it by."

"You talk as if you were a tailor," said Miss Bordereau whimsically; and then she added quickly, in a different manner, "This house is very fine; the proportions are magnificent. Today I wanted to look at this place again. I made them bring me out here. When your man came, just now, to learn if I would see you, I was on the point of sending for you, to ask if you didn't mean to go on. I wanted to judge what I'm letting you have. This *sala* is very grand," she pursued, like an auctioneer, moving a little, as I guessed, her invisible eyes. "I don't believe you often have lived in such a house, eh?"

"I can't often afford to!" I said.

"Well then, how much will you give for six months?"

I was on the point of exclaiming—and the air of excruciation in my face would have denoted a moral fact—"Don't, Juliana; for *his* sake, don't!" But I controlled myself and asked less passionately: "Why should I remain so long as that?"

"I thought you liked it," said Miss Bordereau with her shriveled dignity.

"So I thought I should."

For a moment she said nothing more, and I left my own words to suggest to her what they might. I half-expected her to say, coldly enough, that if I had been disappointed we need not continue the discussion, and this in spite of the fact that I believed her now to have in her mind (however it had come there) what would have told her that my disappointment was natural. But to my extreme surprise she ended by observing: "If you don't think we have treated you well enough perhaps we can discover some way of treating you better." This speech was somehow so incongruous that it made me laugh again, and I excused myself by saying that she talked as if I were a sulky boy, pouting in the corner, to be "brought round." I had not a grain of complaint to make; and could anything have exceeded Miss Tita's graciousness in accompanying me a few nights before to the Piazza? At this the old woman went on: "Well, you brought it on yourself!" And then in a different tone, "She is a very nice girl." I assented cordially to this proposition, and she expressed the hope that I did so not merely to be obliging, but that I really liked her. Meanwhile I wondered still more what Miss Bordereau was coming to. "Except for me, today," she said, "she has not a relation in the world." Did she by describing her niece as amiable and unencumbered wish to represent her as a *parti?*

It was perfectly true that I could not afford to go on with my rooms at a fancy price and that I had already devoted to my undertaking almost all the hard cash I had set apart for it. My patience and my time were by no means exhausted, but I should be able to draw upon them only on a more usual Venetian basis. I was willing to pay the venerable woman with whom my pecuniary dealings were such a discord twice as much as any other *padrona di casa* would have asked, but I was not willing to pay her twenty times as much. I told her so plainly, and my plainness appeared to have some success, for she exclaimed, "Very good; you have done what I asked —you have made an offer!"

"Yes, but not for half a year. Only by the month."

"Oh, I must think of that then." She seemed disappointed that I would not tie myself to a period, and I guessed that she wished both to secure me and to discourage me; to say severely, "Do you dream that you can get off with less than six months? Do you dream that even by the end of that time you will be appreciably nearer your victory?" What was more in my mind was that she had a fancy to play me the trick of making me engage myself when in fact she had annihilated the papers. There was a moment when my suspense on this point was so acute that I all but broke out with the question, and what kept it back was but a kind of instinctive recoil (lest it should be a mistake), from the last violence of self-exposure. She was such a subtle old witch that one could never tell where one stood with her. You may imagine whether it cleared up the puzzle when, just after she had said she would think of my proposal and without any formal transition, she drew out of her pocket with an embarrassed hand a small object wrapped in crumpled white paper. She held it there a moment and then she asked, "Do you know much about curiosities?"

"About curiosities?"

"About antiquities, the old gimcracks that people pay so much for today. Do you know the kind of price they bring?"

I thought I saw what was coming, but I said ingenuously, "Do you want to buy something?"

"No, I want to sell. What would an amateur give me for that?" She unfolded the white paper and made a motion for me to take from her a small oval portrait. I possessed myself of it with a hand of which I could only hope that she did not perceive the tremor, and she added, "I would part with it only for a good price."

At the first glance I recognized Jeffrey Aspern, and I was well aware that I flushed with the act. As she was watching me however I had the consistency to exclaim, "What a striking face! Do tell me who it is."

"It's an old friend of mine, a very distinguished man in his day. He gave it to me himself, but I'm afraid to mention his name, lest you never should have heard of him, critic and historian as you are. I know the world goes fast and one generation forgets another. He was all the fashion when I was young."

She was perhaps amazed at my assurance, but I was surprised at hers; at her having the energy, in her state of health and at her time of life, to wish to sport with me that way simply for her private entertainment—the humor to test me and practice on me. This, at least, was the interpretation that I put upon her production of the portrait, for I could not believe that she really desired to sell it or cared for any information I might give her. What she wished was to dangle it before my eyes and put a prohibitive price on it. "The face comes back to me, it torments me," I said, turning the object this way and that and looking at it very critically. It was a careful but not a supreme work of art, larger than the ordinary miniature and representing a young man with a remarkably handsome face, in a high-collared green coat and a buff waistcoat. I judged the picture to have a valuable quality of resemblance and to have been painted when the model was about twenty-five years old. There are, as all the world knows, three other portraits of the poet in existence, but none of them is of so early a date as this elegant production. "I have never seen the original but I have seen other likenesses," I went on. "You expressed doubt of this generation having heard of the gentleman, but he strikes me for all the world as a celebrity. Now who is he? I can't put my finger on him—I can't give him a label. Wasn't he a writer? Surely he's a poet." I was determined that it should be she, not I, who should first pronounce Jeffrey Aspern's name.

My resolution was taken in ignorance of Miss Bordereau's extremely resolute character, and her lips never formed in my hearing the syllables that meant so much for her. She neglected to answer my question but raised her hand to take back the picture, with a gesture which though ineffectual was in a high degree peremptory. "It's only a person who should know for himself that would give me my price," she said with a certain dryness.

"Oh, then, you have a price?" I did not restore the precious thing; not from any vindictive purpose but because I instinctively clung to it. We looked at each other hard while I retained it.

"I know the least I would take. What it occurred to me to ask you about is the most I shall be able to get."

She made a movement, drawing herself together as if, in a spasm of dread at having lost her treasure, she were going to attempt the immense effort of rising to snatch it from me. I instantly placed it in her hand again, saying as I did so, "I should like to have it myself, but with your ideas I could never afford it."

She turned the small oval plate over in her lap, with its face down, and I thought I saw her catch her breath a little, as if she had had a strain or an escape. This however did not prevent her saying in a moment, "You would buy a likeness of a person you don't know, by an artist who has no reputation?"

"The artist may have no reputation, but that thing is wonderfully well painted," I replied, to give myself a reason.

"It's lucky you thought of saying that, because the painter was my father."

"That makes the picture indeed precious!" I exclaimed, laughing; and I may add that a part of my laughter came from my satisfaction in finding that I had been right in my theory of Miss Bordereau's origin. Aspern had of course met the young lady when he went to her father's studio as a sitter. I observed to Miss Bordereau that if she would entrust me with her property for twenty-four hours I should be happy to take advice upon it; but she made no answer to this save to slip it in silence into her pocket. This convinced me still more that she had no sincere intention of selling it during her lifetime, though she may have desired to satisfy herself as to the sum her niece, should she leave it to her, might expect eventually to obtain for it. "Well, at any rate I hope you will not offer it without giving me notice," I said as she remained irresponsive. "Remember that I am a possible purchaser."

"I should want your money first!" she returned with unexpected rudeness; and then, as if she bethought herself that I had just cause to complain of such an insinuation and wished to turn the matter off, asked abruptly what I talked about with her niece when I went out with her that way in the evening.

"You speak as if we had set up the habit," I replied. "Certainly I should be very glad if it were to become a habit. But in that case I should feel a still greater scruple at betraying a lady's confidence."

"Her confidence? Has she got confidence?"

"Here she is—she can tell you herself," I said; for Miss Tita now appeared on the threshold of the old woman's parlor. "Have you got confidence, Miss Tita? Your aunt wants very much to know."

"Not in her, not in her!" the younger lady declared, shaking her head with a dolefulness that was neither jocular nor affected. "I don't know what to do with her; she has fits of horrid imprudence. She is so easily tired— and yet she has begun to roam—to drag herself about the house." And she stood looking down at her im- memorial companion with a sort of helpless wonder, as if all their years of familiarity had not made her per- versities, on occasion, any more easy to follow.

"I know what I'm about. I'm not losing my mind. I daresay you would like to think so," said Miss Bor- dereau with a cynical little sigh.

"I don't suppose you came out here yourself. Miss Tita must have had to lend you a hand," I interposed with a pacifying intention.

"Oh, she insisted that we should push her; and when she insists!" said Miss Tita in the same tone of appre- hension; as if there were no knowing what service that she disapproved of her aunt might force her next to render.

"I have always got most things done I wanted, thank God! The people I have lived with have humored me," the old woman continued, speaking out of the gray ashes of her vanity.

"I suppose you mean that they have obeyed you."

"Well, whatever it is, when they like you."

"It's just because I like you that I want to resist," said Miss Tita with a nervous laugh.

"Oh, I suspect you'll bring Miss Bordereau upstairs next to pay me a visit," I went on; to which the old lady replied:

"Oh, no; I can keep an eye on you from here!"

"You are very tired; you will certainly be ill tonight!" cried Miss Tita.

"Nonsense, my dear; I feel better at this moment than I have done for a month. Tomorrow I shall come out again. I want to be where I can see this clever gentle- man."

"Shouldn't you perhaps see me better in your sitting room?" I inquired.

"Don't you mean shouldn't you have a better chance at me?" she returned, fixing me a moment with her green shade.

"Ah, I haven't that anywhere! I look at you but I don't see you."

"You excite her dreadfully—and that is not good," said Miss Tita, giving me a reproachful, appealing look.

"I want to watch you—I want to watch you!" the old lady went on.

"Well then, let us spend as much of our time together as possible—I don't care where—and that will give you every facility."

"Oh, I've seen you enough for today. I'm satisfied. Now I'll go home." Miss Tita laid her hands on the back of her aunt's chair and began to push, but I begged her to let me take her place. "Oh, yes, you may move me this way—you shan't in any other!" Miss Bordereau exclaimed as she felt herself propelled firmly and easily over the smooth, hard floor. Before we reached the door of her own apartment she commanded me to stop, and she took a long, last look up and down the noble *sala*. "Oh, it's a magnificent house!" she murmured; after which I pushed her forward. When we had entered the parlor Miss Tita told me that she should now be able to manage, and at the same moment the little red-haired *donna* came to meet her mistress. Miss Tita's idea was evidently to get her aunt immediately back to bed. I confess that in spite of this urgency I was guilty of the indiscretion of lingering; it held me there to think that I was nearer the documents I coveted—that they were probably put away somewhere in the faded, unsociable room. The place had indeed a bareness which did not suggest hidden treasures; there were no dusky nooks nor curtained corners, no massive cabinets nor chests with iron bands. Moreover it was possible, it was perhaps even probable that the old lady had consigned her relics to her bedroom, to some battered box that was shoved under the bed, to the drawer of some lame dressing table, where they would be in the range of vision by the dim night lamp. Nonetheless I scrutinized every article of furniture, every conceivable cover for a hoard, and noticed that there were half a dozen things with drawers, and in particular a tall old secretary, with brass ornaments of the style of the Empire—a receptacle somewhat rickety but still capable of keeping a great many secrets.

I don't know why this article fascinated me so, inasmuch as I certainly had no definite purpose of breaking into it; but I stared at it so hard that Miss Tita noticed me and changed color. Her doing this made me think I was right and that wherever they might have been before the Aspern papers at that moment languished behind the peevish little lock of the secretary. It was hard to remove my eyes from the dull mahogany front when I reflected that a simple panel divided me from the goal of my hopes; but I remembered my prudence and with an effort took leave of Miss Bordereau. To make the effort graceful I said to her that I should certainly bring her an opinion about the little picture.

"The little picture?" Miss Tita asked, surprised.

"What do *you* know about it, my dear?" the old woman demanded. "You needn't mind. I have fixed my price."

"And what may that be?"

"A thousand pounds."

"Oh Lord!" cried poor Miss Tita irrepressibly.

"Is that what she talks to you about?" said Miss Bordereau.

"Imagine your aunt's wanting to know!" I had to separate from Miss Tita with only those words, though I should have liked immensely to add, "For heaven's sake meet me tonight in the garden!"

VIII

As it turned out the precaution had not been needed, for three hours later, just as I had finished my dinner, Miss Bordereau's niece appeared, unannounced, in the open doorway of the room in which my simple repasts were served. I remember well that I felt no surprise at seeing her, which is not a proof that I did not believe in her timidity. It was immense, but in a case in which there was a particular reason for boldness it never would have prevented her from running up to my rooms. I saw that she was now quite full of a particular reason; it threw her forward—made her seize me, as I rose to meet her, by the arm.

"My aunt is very ill; I think she is dying!"

"Never in the world," I answered bitterly. "Don't you be afraid!"

"Do go for a doctor—do, do! Olimpia is gone for the one we always have, but she doesn't come back; I don't know what has happened to her. I told her that if he was not at home she was to follow him where he had gone; but apparently she is following him all over Venice. I don't know what to do—she looks so as if she were sinking."

"May I see her, may I judge?" I asked. "Of course I shall be delighted to bring someone; but hadn't we better send my man instead, so that I may stay with you?"

Miss Tita assented to this and I dispatched my servant for the best doctor in the neighborhood. I hurried downstairs with her, and on the way she told me that an hour after I quitted them in the afternoon Miss Bordereau had had an attack of "oppression," a terrible difficulty in breathing. This had subsided but had left her so exhausted that she did not come up: she seemed all gone. I repeated that she was not gone, that she would not go yet; whereupon Miss Tita gave me a sharper sidelong glance than she had ever directed at me and said, "Really, what do you mean? I suppose you don't accuse her of making believe!" I forget what reply I made to this, but I grant that in my heart I thought the old woman capable of any weird maneuver. Miss Tita wanted to know what I had done to her; her aunt had told her that I had made her so angry. I declared I had done nothing—I had been exceedingly careful; to which my companion rejoined that Miss Bordereau had assured her she had had a scene with me—a scene that had upset her. I answered with some resentment that it was a scene of her own making—that I couldn't think what she was angry with me for unless for not seeing my way to give a thousand pounds for the portrait of Jeffrey Aspern. "And did she show you that? Oh, gracious—oh, deary me!" groaned Miss Tita, who appeared to feel that the situation was passing out of her control and that the elements of her fate were thickening around her. I said that I would give anything to possess it, yet that I had not a thousand pounds; but I stopped when we came to the door of Miss Bordereau's room. I had an immense curiosity to pass it, but I thought it my duty to represent to Miss Tita that if I made the invalid angry she ought perhaps to be spared the sight of me. "The sight of you? Do you think she can see?" my companion demanded almost with indignation. I did think so but forebore to say it, and I softly followed my conductress.

I remember that what I said to her as I stood for a moment beside the old woman's bed was, "Does she never show you her eyes then? Have you never seen them?" Miss Bordereau had been divested of her green shade, but (it was not my fortune to behold Juliana in her nightcap) the upper half of her face was covered by the fall of a piece of dingy lacelike muslin, a sort of extemporized hood which, wound round her head, descended to the end of her nose, leaving nothing visible but her white withered cheeks and puckered mouth, closed tightly and, as it were, consciously. Miss Tita gave me a glance of surprise, evidently not seeing a reason for my impatience. "You mean that she always wears something? She does it to preserve them."

"Because they are so fine?"

"Oh, today, today!" And Miss Tita shook her head, speaking very low. "But they used to be magnificent!"

"Yes indeed, we have Aspern's word for that." And as I looked again at the old woman's wrappings I could imagine that she had not wished to allow people a reason to say that the great poet had overdone it. But I did not waste my time in considering Miss Bordereau, in whom the appearance of respiration was so slight as to suggest that no human attention could ever help her more. I turned my eyes all over the room, rummaging with them the closets, the chests of drawers, the tables. Miss Tita met them quickly and read, I think, what was in them; but she did not answer it, turning away restlessly, anxiously, so that I felt rebuked, with reason, for a preoccupation that was almost profane in the presence of our dying companion. All the same I took another look, endeavoring to pick out mentally the place to try first, for a person who should wish to put his hand on Miss Bordereau's papers directly after her death. The room was a dire confusion; it looked like the room of an old actress. There were clothes hanging over chairs, odd-looking, shabby bundles here and there, and various pasteboard boxes piled together, battered, bulging, and discolored, which might have been fifty years old. Miss Tita after a moment noticed the direction of my eyes again and, as if she guessed how I judged the air of the place (forgetting I had no business to judge it at all), said, perhaps to defend herself from the imputation of complicity in such untidiness:

"She likes it this way; we can't move things. There are old bandboxes she has had most of her life." Then she added, half taking pity on my real thought, "Those things were *there*." And she pointed to a small, low trunk which stood under a sofa where there was just room for it. It appeared to be a queer, superannuated coffer, of painted wood, with elaborate handles and shriveled straps and with the color (it had last been endued with a coat of light green) much rubbed off. It evidently had traveled with Juliana in the olden time— in the days of her adventures, which it had shared. It would have made a strange figure arriving at a modern hotel.

"*Were* there—they aren't now?" I asked, startled by Miss Tita's implication.

She was going to answer, but at that moment the doctor came in—the doctor whom the little maid had been sent to fetch and whom she had at last overtaken. My servant, going on his own errand, had met her with her companion in tow, and in the sociable Venetian spirit, retracing his steps with them, had also come up to the threshold of Miss Bordereau's room, where I saw him peeping over the doctor's shoulder. I motioned him away the more instantly that the sight of his prying face reminded me that I myself had almost as little to do there—an admonition confirmed by the sharp way the little doctor looked at me, appearing to take me for a rival who had the field before him. He was a short, fat, brisk gentleman who wore the tall hat of his profession and seemed to look at everything but his patient. He looked particularly at me, as if it struck him that I should be better for a dose, so that I bowed to him and left him with the women, going down to smoke a cigar in the garden. I was nervous; I could not go further; I could not leave the place. I don't know exactly what I thought might happen, but it seemed to me important to be there. I wandered about in the alleys—the warm night had come on—smoking cigar after cigar and looking at the light in Miss Bordereau's windows. They were open now, I could see; the situation was different. Sometimes the light moved, but not quickly; it did not suggest the hurry of a crisis. Was the old woman dying, or was she already dead? Had the doctor said that there was nothing to be done at her tremendous age but to let her quietly pass away; or had he simply announced with a look a little more conventional that the end of the end had come? Were the other two women moving about to perform the offices that follow in such a case? It made me uneasy not to be nearer, as if I thought the doctor himself might carry away the papers with him. I bit my cigar hard as it came over me again that perhaps there were now no papers to carry!

I wandered about for an hour—for an hour and a half. I looked out for Miss Tita at one of the windows, having a vague idea that she might come there to give me some sign. Would she not see the red tip of my cigar moving about in the dark and feel that I wanted eminently to know what the doctor had said? I am afraid it is a proof my anxieties had made me gross that I should have taken in some degree for granted that at such an hour, in the midst of the greatest change that could take place in her life, they were uppermost also in poor Miss Tita's mind. My servant came down and spoke to me; he knew nothing save that the doctor had gone after a visit of half an hour. If he had stayed half an hour then Miss Bordereau was still alive: it could not have taken so much time as that to enunciate the contrary. I sent the man out of the house; there were moments when the sense of his curiosity annoyed me, and this was one of them. *He* had been watching my cigar tip from an upper window, if Miss Tita had not; he could not know what I was after and I could not tell him, though I was conscious he had fantastic private theories about me which he thought fine and which I, had I known them, should have thought offensive.

I went upstairs at last but I ascended no higher than the *sala*. The door of Miss Bordereau's apartment was open, showing from the parlor the dimness of a poor candle. I went toward it with a light tread, and at the same moment Miss Tita appeared and stood looking at me as I approached. "She's better—she's better," she said, even before I had asked. "The doctor has given her something; she woke up, came back to life while he was there. He says there is no immediate danger."

"No immediate danger? Surely he thinks her condition strange!"

"Yes, because she had been excited. That affects her dreadfully."

"It will do so again then, because she excites herself. She did so this afternoon."

"Yes; she mustn't come out any more," said Miss Tita, with one of her lapses into a deeper placidity.

"What is the use of making such a remark as that if you begin to rattle her about again the first time she bids you?"

"I won't—I won't do it any more."

"You must learn to resist her," I went on.

"Oh, yes, I shall; I shall do so better if you tell me it's right."

"You mustn't do it for me; you must do it for yourself. It all comes back to you, if you are frightened."

"Well, I am not frightened now," said Miss Tita cheerfully. "She is very quiet."

"Is she conscious again—does she speak?"

"No, she doesn't speak, but she takes my hand. She holds it fast."

"Yes," I rejoined, "I can see what force she still has by the way she grabbed that picture this afternoon. But if she holds you fast how comes it that you are here?"

Miss Tita hesitated a moment; though her face was in deep shadow (she had her back to the light in the parlor and I had put down my own candle far off, near the door of the *sala*), I thought I saw her smile ingenuously. "I came on purpose—I heard your step."

"Why, I came on tiptoe, as inaudibly as possible."

"Well, I heard you," said Miss Tita.

"And is your aunt alone now?"

"Oh, no; Olimpia is sitting there."

On my side I hesitated. "Shall we then step in there?" And I nodded at the parlor; I wanted more and more to be on the spot.

"We can't talk there—she will hear us."

I was on the point of replying that in that case we would sit silent, but I was too conscious that this would not do, as there was something I desired immensely to ask her. So I proposed that we should walk a little in the *sala,* keeping more at the other end, where we should not disturb the old lady. Miss Tita assented unconditionally; the doctor was coming again, she said, and she would be there to meet him at the door. We strolled through the fine superfluous hall, where on the marble floor—particularly as at first we said nothing—our footsteps were more audible than I had expected. When we reached the other end—the wide window, inveterately closed, connecting with the balcony that overhung the canal—I suggested that we should remain there, as she would see the doctor arrive still better. I opened the window and we passed out on the balcony. The air of the canal seemed even heavier, hotter than that of the *sala.* The place was hushed and void; the quiet neighborhood had gone to sleep. A lamp, here and there, over the narrow black water, glimmered in double; the voice of a man going homeward singing, with his jacket on his shoulder and his hat on his ear, came to us from a distance. This did not prevent the scene from being very *comme il faut*, as Miss Bordereau had called it the first time I saw her. Presently a gondola passed along the canal with its slow rhythmical plash, and as we listened we watched it in silence. It did not stop, it did not carry the doctor; and after it had gone on I said to Miss Tita:

"And where are they now—the things that were in the trunk?"

"In the trunk?"

"That green box you pointed out to me in her room. You said her papers had been there; you seemed to imply that she had transferred them."

"Oh, yes; they are not in the trunk," said Miss Tita.

"May I ask if you have looked?"

"Yes, I have looked—for you."

"How for me, dear Miss Tita? Do you mean you would have given them to me if you had found them?" I asked, almost trembling.

She delayed to reply and I waited. Suddenly she broke out, "I don't know what I would do—what I wouldn't!"

"Would you look again—somewhere else?"

She had spoken with a strange, unexpected emotion, and she went on in the same tone: "I can't—I can't —while she lies there. It isn't decent."

"No, it isn't decent," I replied gravely. "Let the poor lady rest in peace." And the words, on my lips, were not hypocritical, for I felt reprimanded and shamed.

Miss Tita added in a moment, as if she had guessed this and were sorry for me, but at the same time wished to explain that I did drive her on or at least did insist too much: "I can't deceive her that way. I can't deceive her—perhaps on her deathbed."

"Heaven forbid I should ask you, though I have been guilty myself!"

"You have been guilty?"

"I have sailed under false colors." I felt now as if I must tell her that I had given her an invented name, on account of my fear that her aunt would have heard of me and would refuse to take me in. I explained this and also that I had really been a party to the letter written to them by John Cumnor months before.

She listened with great attention, looking at me with parted lips, and when I had made my confession she said, "Then your real name—what is it?" She repeated it over twice when I had told her, accompanying it with the exclamation "Gracious, gracious!" Then she added, "I like your own best."

"So do I," I said, laughing. "Ouf! it's a relief to get rid of the other."

"So it was a regular plot—a kind of conspiracy?"

"Oh, a conspiracy—we were only two," I replied, leaving out Mrs. Prest of course.

She hesitated; I thought she was perhaps going to say that we had been very base. But she remarked after a moment, in a candid, wondering way, "How much you must want them!"

"Oh, I do, passionately!" I conceded, smiling. And this chance made me go on, forgetting my compunction of a moment before. "How can she possibly have changed their place herself? How can she walk? How can she arrive at that sort of muscular exertion? How can she lift and carry things?"

"Oh, when one wants and when one has so much will!" said Miss Tita, as if she had thought over my question already herself and had simply had no choice but that answer—the idea that in the dead of night, or at some moment when the coast was clear, the old woman had been capable of a miraculous effort.

"Have you questioned Olimpia? Hasn't she helped her—hasn't she done it for her?" I asked; to which Miss Tita replied promptly and positively that their servant had had nothing to do with the matter, though without admitting definitely that she had spoken to her. It was as if she were a little shy, a little ashamed now of letting me see how much she had entered into my uneasiness and had me on her mind. Suddenly she said to me, without any immediate relevance:

"I feel as if you were a new person, now that you have got a new name."

"It isn't a new one; it is a very good old one, thank heaven!"

She looked at me a moment. "I do like it better."

"Oh, if you didn't I would almost go on with the other!"

"Would you really?"

I laughed again, but for all answer to this inquiry I said, "Of course if she can rummage about that way she can perfectly have burnt them."

"You must wait—you must wait," Miss Tita moralized mournfully; and her tone ministered little to my patience, for it seemed after all to accept that wretched

possibility. I would teach myself to wait, I declared
nevertheless; because in the first place I could not do
otherwise and in the second I had her promise, given
me the other night, that she would help me.

"Of course if the papers are gone that's no use," she
said; not as if she wished to recede, but only to be
conscientious.

"Naturally. But if you could only find out!" I
groaned, quivering again.

"I thought you said you would wait."

"Oh, you mean wait even for that?"

"For what then?"

"Oh, nothing," I replied, rather foolishly, being
ashamed to tell her what had been implied in my submission to delay—the idea that she would do more than
merely find out. I know not whether she guessed this;
at all events she appeared to become aware of the necessity for being a little more rigid.

"I didn't promise to deceive, did I? I don't think I
did."

"It doesn't much matter whether you did or not, for
you couldn't!"

I don't think Miss Tita would have contested this
even had she not been diverted by our seeing the doctor's
gondola shoot into the little canal and approach the
house. I noted that he came as fast as if he believed
that Miss Bordereau was still in danger. We looked down
at him while he disembarked and then went back into
the *sala* to meet him. When he came up however I
naturally left Miss Tita to go off with him alone, only
asking her leave to come back later for news.

I went out of the house and took a long walk, as
far as the Piazza, where my restlessness declined to
quit me. I was unable to sit down (it was very late
now but there were people still at the little tables in
front of the cafés); I could only walk round and
round, and I did so half a dozen times. I was uncomfortable, but it gave me a certain pleasure to have told
Miss Tita who I was really was. At last I took my
way home again, slowly getting all but inextricably lost,
as I did whenever I went out in Venice: so that it was
considerably past midnight when I reached my door. The

sala, upstairs, was as dark as usual and my lamp as I crossed it found nothing satisfactory to show me. I was disappointed, for I had notified Miss Tita that I would come back for a report, and I thought she might have left a light there as a sign. The door of the ladies' apartment was closed; which seemed an intimation that my faltering friend had gone to bed, tired of waiting for me. I stood in the middle of the place, considering, hoping she would hear me and perhaps peep out, saying to myself too that she would never go to bed with her aunt in a state so critical; she would sit up and watch —she would be in a chair, in her dressing gown. I went nearer the door; I stopped there and listened. I heard nothing at all and at last I tapped gently. No answer came and after another minute I turned the handle. There was no light in the room; this ought to have prevented me from going in, but it had no such effect. If I have candidly narrated the importunities, the indelicacies, of which my desire to possess myself of Jeffrey Aspern's papers had rendered me capable I need not shrink from confessing this last indiscretion. I think it was the worst thing I did; yet there were extenuating circumstances. I was deeply though doubtless not disinterestedly anxious for more news of the old lady, and Miss Tita had accepted from me, as it were, a rendezvous which it might have been a point of honor with me to keep. It may be said that her leaving the place dark was a positive sign that she released me, and to this I can only reply that I desired not to be released.

The door of Miss Bordereau's room was open and I could see beyond it the faintness of a taper. There was no sound—my footstep caused no one to stir. I came further into the room; I lingered there with my lamp in my hand. I wanted to give Miss Tita a chance to come to me if she were with her aunt, as she must be. I made no noise to call her; I only waited to see if she would not notice my light. She did not, and I explained this (I found afterward I was right) by the idea that she had fallen asleep. If she had fallen asleep her aunt was not on her mind, and my explanation ought to have led me to go out as I had come. I must repeat again that it did not, for I found myself at the same moment

thinking of something else. I had no definite purpose,
no bad intention, but I felt myself held to the spot by
an acute, though absurd, sense of opportunity. For what
I could not have said, inasmuch as it was not in my
mind that I might commit a theft. Even if it had been
I was confronted with the evident fact that Miss Bordereau did not leave her secretary, her cupboard, and
the drawers of her tables gaping. I had no keys, no
tools, and no ambition to smash her furniture. Nonetheless it came to me that I was now, perhaps alone, unmolested, at the hour of temptation and secrecy, nearer
to the tormenting treasure than I had ever been. I held
up my lamp, let the light play on the different objects as
if it could tell me something. Still there came no movement from the other room. If Miss Tita was sleeping
she was sleeping sound. Was she doing so—generous
creature—on purpose to leave me the field? Did she
know I was there and was she just keeping quiet to see
what I would do—what I *could* do? But what could I
do, when it came to that? She herself knew even better
than I how little.

I stopped in front of the secretary, looking at it very
idiotically; for what had it to say to me after all? In
the first place it was locked, and in the second it almost surely contained nothing in which I was interested.
Ten to one the papers had been destroyed; and even if
they had not been destroyed the old woman would not
have put them in such a place as that after removing
them from the green trunk—would not have transferred
them, if she had the idea of their safety on her brain,
from the better hiding place to the worse. The secretary
was more conspicuous, more accessible in a room in
which she could no longer mount guard. It opened with
a key, but there was a little brass handle, like a button,
as well; I saw this as I played my lamp over it. I did
something more than this at that moment: I caught
a glimpse of the possibility that Miss Tita wished me
really to understand. If she did not wish me to understand, if she wished me to keep away, why had she not
locked the door of communication between the sitting
room and the *sala?* That would have been a definite
sign that I was to leave them alone. If I did not leave

them alone she meant me to come for a purpose—a purpose now indicated by the quick, fantastic idea that to oblige me she had unlocked the secretary. She had not left the key, but the lid would probably move if I touched the button. This theory fascinated me, and I bent over very close to judge. I did not propose to do anything, not even—not in the least—to let down the lid; I only wanted to test my theory, to see if the cover *would* move. I touched the button with my hand—a mere touch would tell me; and as I did so (it is embarrassing for me to relate it), I looked over my shoulder. It was a chance, an instinct, for I had not heard anything. I almost let my luminary drop and certainly I stepped back, straightening myself up at what I saw. Miss Bordereau stood there in her nightdress, in the doorway of her room, watching me; her hands were raised, she had lifted the everlasting curtain that covered half her face, and for the first, the last, the only time I beheld her extraordinary eyes. They glared at me, they made me horribly ashamed. I never shall forget her strange little bent white tottering figure, with its lifted head, her attitude, her expression; neither shall I forget the tone in which as I turned, looking at her, she hissed out passionately, furiously:

"Ah, you publishing scoundrel!"

I know not what I stammered, to excuse myself, to explain; but I went toward her, to tell her I meant no harm. She waved me off with her old hands, retreating before me in horror; and the next thing I knew she had fallen back with a quick spasm, as if death had descended on her, into Miss Tita's arms.

IX

I left Venice the next morning, as soon as I learned that the old lady had not succumbed, as I feared at the moment, to the shock I had given her—the shock I may

also say she had given me. How in the world could I
have supposed her capable of getting out of bed by herself? I failed to see Miss Tita before going; I only saw
the *donna*, whom I entrusted with a note for her younger mistress. In this note I mentioned that I should be
absent but for a few days. I went to Treviso, to Bas-
sano, to Castelfranco; I took walks and drives and
looked at musty old churches with ill-lighted pictures
and spent hours seated smoking at the doors of cafés,
where there were flies and yellow curtains, on the shady
side of sleepy little squares. In spite of these pastimes,
which were mechanical and perfunctory, I scantily enjoyed my journey: there was too strong a taste of the
disagreeable in my life. It had been devilish awkward, as
the young men say, to be found by Miss Bordereau
in the dead of night examining the attachment of her
bureau; and it had not been less so to have to believe for
a good many hours afterward that it was highly probable
I had killed her. In writing to Miss Tita I attempted to
minimize these irregularities; but as she gave me no
word of answer I could not know what impression I made
upon her. It rankled in my mind that I had been called
a publishing scoundrel, for certainly I did publish and
certainly I had not been very delicate. There was a moment when I stood convinced that the only way to make
up for this latter fault was to take myself away altogether on the instant; to sacrifice my hopes and relieve the
two poor women forever of the oppression of my intercourse. Then I reflected that I had better try a short
absence first, for I must already have had a sense (unex-
pressed and dim) that in disappearing completely it
would not be merely my own hopes that I should con-
demn to extinction. It would perhaps be sufficient if I
stayed away long enough to give the elder lady time to
think she was rid of me. That she would wish to be rid
of me after this (if I was not rid of her) was now not to
be doubted: that nocturnal scene would have cured her
of the disposition to put up with my company for the
sake of my dollars. I said to myself that after all I could
not abandon Miss Tita, and I continued to say this even
while I observed that she quite failed to comply with my
earnest request (I had given her two or three addresses,

at little towns, *poste restante*) that she would let me know how she was getting on. I would have made my servant write to me but that he was unable to manage a pen. It struck me there was a kind of scorn in Miss Tita's silence (little disdainful as she had ever been), so that I was uncomfortable and sore. I had scruples about going back and yet I had others about not doing so, for I wanted to put myself on a better footing. The end of it was that I did return to Venice on the twelfth day; and as my gondola gently bumped against Miss Bordereau's steps a certain palpitation of suspense told me that I had done myself a violence in holding off so long.

I had faced about so abruptly that I had not telegraphed to my servant. He was therefore not at the station to meet me, but he poked out his head from an upper window when I reached the house. "They have put her into the earth, *la vecchia*," he said to me in the lower hall, while he shouldered my valise; and he grinned and almost winked, as if he knew I should be pleased at the news.

"She's dead!" I exclaimed, giving him a very different look.

"So it appears, since they have buried her."

"It's all over? When was the funeral?"

"The other yesterday. But a funeral you could scarcely call it, signore; it was a dull little passeggio of two gondolas. *Poveretta!*" the man continued, referring apparently to Miss Tita. His conception of funerals was apparently that they were mainly to amuse the living.

I wanted to know about Miss Tita—how she was and where she was—but I asked him no more questions till we had got upstairs. Now that the fact had met me I took a bad view of it, especially of the idea that poor Miss Tita had had to manage by herself after the end. What did she know about arrangements, about the steps to take in such a case? *Poveretta* indeed! I could only hope that the doctor had given her assistance and that she had not been neglected by the old friends of whom she had told me, the little band of the faithful whose fidelity consisted in coming to the house once a year. I elicited from my servant that two old ladies and an old

gentleman had in fact rallied round Miss Tita and had
supported her (they had come for her in a gondola of
their own) during the journey to the cemetery, the little
red-walled island of tombs which lies to the north of the
town, on the way to Murano. It appeared from these
circumstances that the Misses Bordereau were Catholics,
a discovery I had never made, as the old woman could
not go to church and her niece, so far as I perceived,
either did not or went only to early mass in the parish,
before I was stirring. Certainly even the priests respect-
ed their seclusion; I had never caught the whisk of the
curato's skirt. That evening, an hour later, I sent my
servant down with five words written on a card, to ask
Miss Tita if she would see me for a few moments. She
was not in the house, where he had sought her, he told
me when he came back, but in the garden walking about
to refresh herself and gathering flowers. He had found
her there and she would be very happy to see me.

I went down and passed half an hour with poor Miss
Tita. She had always had a look of musty mourning (as
if she were wearing out old robes of sorrow that would
not come to an end), and in this respect there was no
appreciable change in her appearance. But she evidently had been crying, crying a great deal—simply, satisfy-
ingly, refreshingly, with a sort of primitive, retarded
sense of loneliness and violence. But she had none of the
formalism or the self-consciousness of grief, and I was
almost surprised to see her standing there in the first
dusk with her hands full of flowers, smiling at me with
her reddened eyes. Her white face, in the frame of her
mantilla, looked longer, leaner than usual. I had had an
idea that she would be a good deal disgusted with me—
would consider that I ought to have been on the spot to
advise her, to help her; and, though I was sure there
was no rancor in her composition and no great conviction of the importance of her affairs, I had prepared
myself for a difference in her manner, for some little injured look, half-familiar, half-estranged, which should
say to my conscience, "Well, you are a nice person to
have professed things!" But historic truth compels me to
declare that Tita Bordereau's countenance expressed un-
qualified pleasure in seeing her late aunt's lodger. That

touched him extremely, and he thought it simplified his situation until he found it did not. I was as kind to her that evening as I knew how to be, and I walked about the garden with her for half an hour. There was no explanation of any sort between us; I did not ask her why she had not answered my letter. Still less did I repeat what I had said to her in that communication; if she chose to let me suppose that she had forgotten the position in which Miss Bordereau surprised me that night and the effect of the discovery on the old woman I was quite willing to take it that way: I was grateful to her for not treating me as if I had killed her aunt.

We strolled and strolled and really not much passed between us save the recognition of her bereavement, conveyed in my manner and in a visible air that she had of depending on me now, since I let her see that I took an interest in her. Miss Tita had none of the pride that makes a person wish to preserve the look of independence; she did not in the least pretend that she knew at present what would become of her. I forebore to touch particularly on that, however, for I certainly was not prepared to say that I would take charge of her. I was cautious; not ignobly, I think, for I felt that her knowledge of life was so small that in her unsophisticated vision there would be no reason why—since I seemed to pity her—I should not look after her. She told me how her aunt had died, very peacefully at the last, and how everything had been done afterward by the care of her good friends (fortunately, thanks to me, she said, smiling, there was money in the house; and she repeated that when once the Italians like you they are your friends for life); and when we had gone into this she asked me about my *giro*, my impressions, the places I had seen. I told her what I could, making it up partly, I am afraid, as in my depression I had not seen much; and after she had heard me she exclaimed, quite as if she had forgotten her aunt and her sorrow, "Dear, dear, how much I should like to do such things—to take a little journey!" It came over me for the moment that I ought to propose some tour, say I would take her anywhere she liked; and I remarked at any rate that some excursion —to give her a change—might be managed: we would

think of it, talk it over. I said never a word to her about
the Aspern documents; asked no questions as to what
she had ascertained or what had otherwise happened
with regard to them before Miss Bordereau's death. It
was not that I was not on pins and needles to know,
but that I thought it more decent not to betray my anxiety so soon after the catastrophe. I hoped she herself
would say something, but she never glanced that way,
and I thought this natural at the time. Later however,
that night, it occurred to me that her silence was somewhat strange; for if she had talked of my movements, of
anything so detached as the Giorgione at Castelfranco,
she might have alluded to what she could easily remember was in my mind. It was not to be supposed that the
emotion produced by her aunt's death had blotted out
the recollection that I was interested in that lady's relics,
and I fidgeted afterward as it came to me that her reticence might very possibly mean simply that nothing had
been found. We separated in the garden (it was she who
said she must go in); now that she was alone in the
rooms I felt that (judged, at any rate, by Venetian
ideas) I was on rather a different footing in regard to
visiting her there. As I shook hands with her for good-
night I asked her if she had any general plan—had
thought over what she had better do. "Oh, yes, oh, yes,
but I haven't settled anything yet," she replied quite
cheerfully. Was her cheerfulness explained by the impression that I would settle for her?

I was glad the next morning that we had neglected
practical questions, for this gave me a pretext for seeing
her again immediately. There was a very practical question to be touched upon. I owed it to her to let her
know formally that of course I did not expect her to
keep me on as a lodger, and also to show some interest
in her own tenure, what she might have on her hands
in the way of a lease. But I was not destined, as it happened, to converse with her for more than an instant on
either of these points. I sent her no message; I simply
went down to the *sala* and walked to and fro there. I
knew she would come out; she would very soon discover
I was there. Somehow I preferred not to be shut up with
her; gardens and big halls seemed better places to talk.

It was a splendid morning, with something in the air that told of the waning of the long Venetian summer; a freshness from the sea which stirred the flowers in the garden and made a pleasant draught in the house, less shuttered and darkened now than when the old woman was alive. It was the beginning of autumn, of the end of the golden months. With this it was the end of my experiment—or would be in the course of half an hour, when I should really have learned that the papers had been reduced to ashes. After that there would be nothing left for me but to go to the station; for seriously (and as it struck me in the morning light) I could not linger there to act as guardian to a piece of middle-aged female helplessness. If she had not saved the papers wherein should I be indebted to her? I think I winced a little as I asked myself how much, if she *had* saved them, I should have to recognize and, as it were, to reward such a courtesy. Might not that circumstance after all saddle me with a guardianship? If this idea did not make me more uncomfortable as I walked up and down it was because I was convinced I had nothing to look to. If the old woman had not destroyed everything before she pounced upon me in the parlor she had done so afterward.

It took Miss Tita rather longer than I had expected to guess that I was there; but when at last she came out she looked at me without surprise. I said to her that I had been waiting for her, and she asked why I had not let her know. I was glad the next day that I had checked myself before remarking that I had wished to see if a friendly intuition would not tell her: it became a satisfaction to me that I had not indulged in that rather tender joke. What I did say was virtually the truth—that I was too nervous, since I expected her now to settle my fate.

"Your fate?" said Miss Tita, giving me a queer look; and as she spoke I noticed a rare change in her. She was different from what she had been the evening before—less natural, less quiet. She had been crying the day before and she was not crying now, and yet she struck me as less confident. It was as if something had happened to her during the night, or at least as if she had thought of something that troubled her—something in particular that affected her relations with me, made them more embarrassing and complicated. Had she simply perceived that her aunt's not being there now altered my position?

"I mean about our papers. *Are* there any? You must know now."

"Yes, there are a great many; more than I supposed." I was struck with the way her voice trembled as she told me this.

"Do you mean that you have got them in there—and that I may see them?"

"I don't think you can see them," said Miss Tita with an extraordinary expression of entreaty in her eyes, as if the dearest hope she had in the world now was that I would not take them from her. But how could she expect me to make such a sacrifice as that after all that had passed between us? What had I come back to Venice for but to see them, to take them? My delight at learning they were still in existence was such that if the poor woman had gone down on her knees to beseech me never to mention them again I would have treated the proceeding as a bad joke. "I have got them but I can't show them," she added.

"Not even to me? Ah, Miss Tita!" I groaned, with a voice of infinite remonstrance and reproach.

She colored, and the tears came back to her eyes; I saw that it cost her a kind of anguish to take such a stand but that a dreadful sense of duty had descended upon her. It made me quite sick to find myself confronted with that particular obstacle; all the more that it appeared to me I had been extremely encouraged to leave it out of account. I almost considered that Miss Tita had assured me that if she had no greater hindrance than that——! "You don't mean to say you made her a deathbed promise? It was precisely against your doing anything of that sort that I thought I was safe. Oh, I would rather she had burned the papers outright than that!"

"No, it isn't a promise," said Miss Tita.

"Pray what is it then?"

She hesitated and then she said, "She tried to burn them, but I prevented it. She had hid them in her bed."

"In her bed?"

"Between the mattresses. That's where she put them when she took them out of the trunk. I can't understand how she did it, because Olimpia didn't help her. She tells me so, and I believe her. My aunt only told her afterward, so that she shouldn't touch the bed—anything but the sheets. So it was badly made," added Miss Tita simply.

"I should think so! And how did she try to burn them?"

"She didn't try much; she was too weak, those last days. But she told me—she charged me. Oh, it was terrible! She couldn't speak after that night; she could only make signs."

"And what did you do?"

"I took them away. I locked them up."

"In the secretary?

"Yes, in the secretary," said Miss Tita, reddening again.

"Did you tell her you would burn them?"

"No, I didn't—on purpose."

"On purpose to gratify me?"

"Yes, only for that."

"And what good will you have done me if after all you won't show them?"

"Oh, none; I know that—I know that."

"And did she believe you had destroyed them?"

"I don't know what she believed at the last. I couldn't tell—she was too far gone."

"Then if there was no promise and no assurance I can't see what ties you."

"Oh, she hated it so—she hated it so! She was so jealous. But here's the portrait—you may have that," Miss Tita announced, taking the little picture, wrapped up in the same manner in which her aunt had wrapped it, out of her pocket.

"I may have it—do you mean you give it to me?" I questioned, staring, as it passed into my hand.

"Oh, yes."

"But it's worth money—a large sum."

"Well!" said Miss Tita, still with her strange look.

I did not know what to make of it, for it could scarce-

ly mean that she wanted to bargain like her aunt. She
spoke as if she wished to make me a present. "I can't
take it from you as a gift," I said, "and yet I can't afford to pay you for it according to the ideas Miss Bordereau had of its value. She rated it at a thousand
pounds."

"Couldn't we sell it?" asked Miss Tita.

"God forbid! I prefer the picture to the money."

"Well then keep it."

"You are very generous."

"So are you."

"I don't know why you should think so," I replied;
and this was a truthful speech, for the singular creature
appeared to have some very fine reference in her mind,
which I did not in the least seize.

"Well, you have made a great difference for me," said
Miss Tita.

I looked at Jeffrey Aspern's face in the little picture,
partly in order not to look at that of my interlocutress,
which had begun to trouble me, even to frighten me a
little—it was so self-conscious, so unnatural. I made no
answer to this last declaration; I only privately consulted
Jeffrey Aspern's delightful eyes with my own (they were
so young and brilliant, and yet so wise, so full of vision);
I asked him what on earth was the matter with Miss
Tita. He seemed to smile at me with friendly mockery,
as if he were amused at my case. I had got into a pickle
for him—as if he needed it! He was unsatisfactory, for
the only moment since I had known him. Nevertheless,
now that I held the little picture in my hand I felt that it
would be a precious possession. "Is this a bribe to make
me give up the papers?" I demanded in a moment, perversely. "Much as I value it, if I were to be obliged to
choose, the papers are what I should prefer. Ah, but
ever so much!"

"How can you choose—how can you choose?" Miss
Tita asked, slowly, lamentably.

"I see! Of course there is nothing to be said, if you
regard the interdiction that rests upon you as quite insurmountable. In this case it must seem to you that to
part with them would be an impiety of the worst kind,
a simple sacrilege!"

Miss Tita shook her head, full of her dolefulness. "You would understand if you had known her. I'm afraid," she quavered suddenly—"I'm afraid! She was terrible when she was angry."

"Yes, I saw something of that, that night. She was terrible. Then I saw her eyes. Lord, they were fine!"

"I see them—they stare at me in the dark!" said Miss Tita.

"You are nervous, with all you have been through."

"Oh, yes, very—very!"

"You mustn't mind; that will pass away," I said, kindly. Then I added, resignedly, for it really seemed to me that I must accept the situation, "Well, so it is, and it can't be helped. I must renounce." Miss Tita, at this, looking at me, gave a low, soft moan, and I went on: "I only wish to heaven she had destroyed them; then there would be nothing more to say. And I can't understand why, with her ideas, she didn't."

"Oh, she lived on them!" said Miss Tita.

"You can imagine whether that makes me want less to see them," I answered, smiling. "But don't let me stand here as if I had it in my soul to tempt you to do anything base. Naturally you will understand if I give up my rooms. I leave Venice immediately." And I took up my hat, which I had placed on a chair. We were still there rather awkwardly, on our feet, in the middle of the *sala*. She had left the door of the apartments open behind her but she had not led me that way.

A kind of spasm came into her face as she saw me take my hat. "Immediately—do you mean today?" The tone of the words was tragical—they were a cry of desolation.

"Oh, no; not so long as I can be of the least service to you."

"Well, just a day or two more—just two or three days," she panted. Then controlling herself, she added in another manner, "She wanted to say something to me—the last day—something very particular, but she couldn't."

"Something very particular?"

"Something more about the papers."

"And did you guess—have you any idea?"

"No, I have thought—but I don't know. I have thought all kinds of things."

"And for instance?"

"Well, that if you were a relation it would be different."

"If I were a relation?"

"If you were not a stranger. Then it would be the same for you as for me. Anything that is mine—would be yours, and you could do what you like. I couldn't prevent you—and you would have no responsibility."

She brought out this droll explanation with a little nervous rush, as if she were speaking words she had got by heart. They gave me an impression of subtlety and at first I failed to follow. But after a moment her face helped me to see further, and then a light came into my mind. It was embarrassing, and I bent my head over Jeffrey Aspern's portrait. What an odd expression was in his face! "Get out of it as you can, my dear fellow!" I put the picture into the pocket of my coat and said to Miss Tita, "Yes, I'll sell it for you. I shan't get a thousand pounds by any means, but I shall get something good."

She looked at me with tears in her eyes, but she seemed to try to smile as she remarked, "We can divide the money."

"No, no, it shall be all yours." Then I went on, "I think I know what your poor aunt wanted to say. She wanted to give directions that her papers should be buried with her."

Miss Tita appeared to consider this suggestion for a moment; after which she declared, with striking decision, "Oh no, she wouldn't have thought that safe!"

"It seems to me nothing could be safer."

"She had an idea that when people want to publish they are capable——" And she paused, blushing.

"Of violating a tomb? Mercy on us, what must she have thought of me!"

"She was not just, she was not generous!" Miss Tita cried with sudden passion.

The light that had come into my mind a moment before increased. "Ah, don't say that, for we *are* a dreadful race." Then I pursued, "If she left a will, that may give you some idea."

"I have found nothing of the sort—she destroyed it. She was very fond of me," Miss Tita added incongruously. "She wanted me to be happy. And if any person should be kind to me—she wanted to speak of that."

I was almost awestricken at the astuteness with which the good lady found herself inspired, transparent astuteness as it was and sewn, as the phrase is, with white thread. "Depend upon it she didn't want to make any provision that would be agreeable to me."

"No, not to you but to me. She knew I should like it if you could carry out your idea. Not because she cared for you but because she did think of me," Miss Tita went on with her unexpected, persuasive volubility. "You could see them—you could use them." She stopped, seeing that I perceived the sense of that conditional—stopped long enough for me to give some sign which I did not give. She must have been conscious, however, that though my face showed the greatest embarrassment that was ever painted on a human countenance it was not set as a stone, it was also full of compassion. It was a comfort to me a long time afterward to consider that she could not have seen in me the smallest symptom of disrespect. "I don't know what to do; I'm too tormented, I'm too ashamed!" she continued with vehemence. Then turning away from me and burying her face in her hands she burst into a flood of tears. If she did not know what to do it may be imagined whether I did any better. I stood there dumb, watching her while her sobs resounded in the great empty hall. In a moment she was facing me again, with her streaming eyes. "I would give you everything—and she would understand, where she is—she would forgive me!"

"Ah, Miss Tita—ah, Miss Tita," I stammered, for all reply. I did not know what to do, as I say, but at a venture I made a wild, vague movement, in consequence of which I found myself at the door. I remember standing there and saying, "It wouldn't do—it wouldn't do!" pensively, awkwardly, grotesquely, while I looked away to the opposite end of the *sala* as if there were a beautiful view there. The next thing I remember is that I was downstairs and out of the house. My gondola was there and my gondolier, reclining on the cushions, sprang up as soon as he saw me. I jumped in and to his usual *"Dove commanda?"* I replied, in a tone that made him stare, "Anywhere, anywhere; out into the lagoon!"

He rowed me away and I sat there prostrate, groaning softly to myself, with my hat pulled over my face. What in the name of the preposterous did she mean if she did not mean to offer me her hand? That was the price— that was the price! And did she think I wanted it, poor deluded, infatuated, extravagant lady? My gondolier, be- hind me, must have seen my ears red as I wondered, sitting there under the fluttering *tenda*, with my hidden face, noticing nothing as we passed—wondered whether her delusion, her infatuation had been my own reckless work. Did she think I had made love to her, even to get the papers? I had not, I had not; I repeated that over to myself for an hour, for two hours, till I was wearied if not convinced. I don't know where my gondolier took me; we floated aimlessly about on the lagoon, with slow, rare strokes. At last I became conscious that we were near the Lido, far up, on the right hand, as you turn your back to Venice, and I made him put me ashore. I wanted to walk, to move, to shed some of my bewilderment. I crossed the narrow strip and got to the sea beach—I took my way toward Malamocco. But presently I flung myself down again on the warm sand, in the breeze, on the coarse dry grass. It took it out of me to think I had been so much at fault, that I had unwittingly but nonetheless deplorably trifled. But I had not given her cause—distinctly I had not. I had said to Mrs. Prest that I would make love to her; but it had been a joke without consequences and I had never said it to Tita Bor- dereau. I had been as kind as possible, because I really liked her; but since when had that become a crime where a woman of such an age and such an appearance was concerned? I am far from remembering clearly the succession of events and feelings during this long day of confusion, which I spent entirely in wandering about, without going home, until late at night; it only comes back to me that there were moments when I pacified my conscience and others when I lashed it into pain. I did not laugh all day—that I do recollect; the case, however it might have struck others, seemed to me so little amusing. It would have been better perhaps for me to feel the comic side of it. At any rate, whether I had given cause or not it went without saying that I could not pay the price. I could not accept. I could not, for a bundle of tattered papers, marry a ridiculous, pathetic, provincial old woman. It was a proof that she did not think the idea would come to me, her having determined to suggest it herself in that practical, argumentative, heroic way, in which the timidity however had been so much more striking than the boldness that her reasons appeared to come first and her feelings afterward.

As the day went on I grew to wish that I had never heard of Aspern's relics, and I cursed the extravagant curiosity that had put John Cumnor on the scent of them. We had more than enough material without them, and my predicament was the just punishment of that most fatal of human follies, our not having known when to stop. It was very well to say it was no predicament, that the way out was simple, that I had only to leave Venice by the first train in the morning, after writing a note to Miss Tita, to be placed in her hand as soon as I got clear of the house; for it was a strong sign that I was embarrassed that when I tried to make up the note in my mind in advance (I would put it on paper as soon as I got home, before going to bed), I could not think of anything but "How can I thank you for the rare confidence you have placed in me?" That would never do; it sounded exactly as if an acceptance were to follow. Of course I might go away without writing a word, but that would be brutal and my idea was still to exclude brutal solutions. As my confusion cooled I was lost in wonder at the importance I had attached to Miss Bordereau's crumpled scraps; the thought of them became odious to me, and I was as vexed with the old witch for the superstition that had prevented her from destroying them as I was with myself for having already spent more money than I could afford in attempting to control their fate. I forget what I did, where I went after leaving the Lido and at what hour or with what recovery of composure I made my way back to my boat. I only know

that in the afternoon, when the air was aglow with the
sunset, I was standing before the church of Saints John
and Paul and looking up at the small square-jawed face
of Bartolommeo Colleoni, the terrible *condottiere* who
sits so sturdily astride of his huge bronze horse, on the
high pedestal on which Venetian gratitude maintains him.
The statue is incomparable, the finest of all mounted
figures, unless that of Marcus Aurelius, who rides be-
nignant before the Roman Capitol, be finer: but I was
not thinking of that; I only found myself staring at the
triumphant captain as if he had an oracle on his lips.
The western light shines into all his grimness at that
hour and makes it wonderfully personal. But he continued
to look far over my head, at the red immersion of another day—he had seen so many go down into the lagoon
through the centuries—and if he were thinking of battles
and stratagems they were of a different quality from any
I had to tell him of. He could not direct me what to do,
gaze up at him as I might. Was it before this or after
that I wandered about for an hour in the small canals,
to the continued stupefaction of my gondolier, who had
never seen me so restless and yet so void of a purpose
and could extract from me no order but "Go anywhere—
everywhere—all over the place"? He reminded me that
I had not lunched and expressed therefore respectfully
the hope that I would dine earlier. He had had long
periods of leisure during the day, when I had left the
boat and rambled, so that I was not obliged to consider
him, and I told him that that day, for a change, I would
touch no meat. It was an effect of poor Miss Tita's proposal, not altogether auspicious, that I had quite lost my
appetite. I don't know why it happened that on this
occasion I was more than ever struck with that queer
air of sociability, of cousinship and family life, which
makes up half the expression of Venice. Without streets
and vehicles, the uproar of wheels, the brutality of horses,
and with its little winding ways where people crowd together, where voices sound as in the corridors of a house,
where the human step circulates as if it skirted the angles
of furniture and shoes never wear out, the place has
the character of an immense collective apartment, in
which Piazza San Marco is the most ornamented corner

and palaces and churches, for the rest, play the part of great divans of repose, tables of entertainment, expanses of decoration. And somehow the splendid common domicile, familiar, domestic, and resonant, also resembles a theater, with actors clicking over bridges and, in straggling processions, tripping along *fondamentas*. As you sit in your gondola the footways that in certain parts edge the canals assume to the eye the importance of a stage, meeting it at the same angle, and the Venetian figures, moving to and fro against the battered scenery of their little houses of comedy, strike you as members of an endless dramatic troupe.

I went to bed that night very tired, without being able to compose a letter to Miss Tita. Was this failure the reason why I became conscious the next morning as soon as I awoke of a determination to see the poor lady again the first moment she would receive me? That had something to do with it, but what had still more was the fact that during my sleep a very odd revulsion had taken place in my spirit. I found myself aware of this almost as soon as I opened my eyes; it made me jump out of my bed with the movement of a man who remembers that he has left the house door ajar or a candle burning under a shelf. Was I still in time to save my goods? That question was in my heart; for what had now come to pass was that in the unconscious cerebration of sleep I had swung back to a passionate appreciation of Miss Bordereau's papers. They were now more precious than ever, and a kind of ferocity had come into my desire to possess them. The condition Miss Tita had attached to the possession of them no longer appeared an obstacle worth thinking of, and for an hour, that morning, my repentant imagination brushed it aside. It was absurd that I should be able to invent nothing; absurd to renounce so easily and turn away helpless from the idea that the only way to get hold of the papers was to unite myself to her for life. I would not unite myself and yet I would have them. I must add that by the time I sent down to ask if she would see me I had invented no alternative, though to do so I had had all the time that I was dressing. This failure was humiliating, yet what could the alternative be? Miss Tita sent back word that I might

come; and as I descended the stairs and crossed the
sala to her door—this time she received me in her aunt's
forlorn parlor—I hoped she would not think my errand
was to tell her I accepted her hand. She certainly would
have made the day before the reflection that I declined it.

As soon as I came into the room I saw that she had
drawn this inference, but I also saw something which
had not been in my forecast. Poor Miss Tita's sense of
her failure had produced an extraordinary alteration in
her, but I had been too full of my literary concupiscence
to think of that. Now I perceived it; I can scarcely tell
how it startled me. She stood in the middle of the room
with a face of mildness bent upon me, and her look of
forgiveness, of absolution, made her angelic. It beautified
her; she was younger; she was not a ridiculous old
woman. This optical trick gave her a sort of phantas-
magoric brightness, and while I was still the victim of it
I heard a whisper somewhere in the depths of my conscience: "Why not, after all—why not?" It seemed to
me I was ready to pay the price. Still more distinctly
however than the whisper I heard Miss Tita's own voice.
I was so struck with the different effect she made upon
me that at first I was not clearly aware of what she was
saying; then I perceived she had bade me goodbye—she
said something about hoping I should be very happy.

"Goodbye—goodbye?" I repeated with an inflection
interrogative and probably foolish.

I saw she did not feel the interrogation, she only
heard the words; she had strung herself up to accepting
our separation and they fell upon her ear as a proof.
"Are you going today?" she asked. "But it doesn't matter,
for whenever you go I shall not see you again. I don't
want to." And she smiled strangely, with an infinite
gentleness. She had never doubted that I had left her
the day before in horror. How could she, since I had not
come back before night to contradict, even as a simple
form, such an idea? And now she had the force of soul—
Miss Tita with force of soul was a new conception—to
smile at me in her humiliation.

"What shall you do—where shall you go?" I asked.

"Oh, I don't know. I have done the great thing. I have
destroyed the papers."

"Destroyed them?" I faltered.

"Yes; what was I to keep them for? I burned them last night, one by one, in the kitchen."

"One by one?" I repeated, mechanically.

"It took a long time—there were so many." The room seemed to go round me as she said this, and a real darkness for a moment descended upon my eyes. When it passed Miss Tita was there still, but the transfiguration was over and she had changed back to a plain, dingy, elderly person. It was in this character she spoke as she said, "I can't stay with you longer, I can't;" and it was in this character that she turned her back upon me, as I had turned mine upon her twenty-four hours before, and moved to the door of her room. Here she did what I had not done when I quitted her—she paused long enough to give me one look. I have never forgotten it and I sometimes still suffer from it, though it was not resentful. No, there was no resentment, nothing hard or vindictive in poor Miss Tita; for when, later, I sent her in exchange for the portrait of Jeffrey Aspern a larger sum of money than I had hoped to be able to gather for her, writing to her that I had sold the picture, she kept it with thanks; she never sent it back. I wrote to her that I had sold the picture, but I admitted to Mrs. Prest, at the time (I met her in London, in the autumn), that it hangs above my writing table. When I look at it my chagrin at the loss of the letters becomes almost intolerable.

THE ALTAR OF THE DEAD

~

I

He had a mortal dislike, poor Stransom, to lean anniversaries, and he disliked them still more when they made a pretense of a figure. Celebrations and suppressions were equally painful to him, and there was only one of the former that found a place in his life. Again and again he had kept in his own fashion the day of the year on which Mary Antrim died. It would be more to the point perhaps to say that the day kept *him:* it kept him at least, effectually, from doing anything else. It took hold of him year after year with a hand of which time had softened but had never loosened the touch. He waked up to this feast of memory as consciously as he would have waked up to his marriage morn. Marriage had had, of old, but too little to say to the matter: for the girl who was to have been his bride there had been no bridal embrace. She had died of a malignant fever after the wedding day had been fixed, and he had lost, before fairly tasting it, an affection that promised to fill his life to the brim.

Of that benediction, however, it would have been false to say this life could really be emptied: it was still ruled by a pale ghost, it was still ordered by a sovereign presence. He had not been a man of numerous passions, and even in all these years no sense had grown stronger with him than the sense of being bereft. He had needed no priest and no altar to make him forever widowed. He had done many things in the world—he had done almost all things but one: he had never forgotten. He had tried to put into his existence whatever else might take up room in it, but he had never made it anything but a house of which the mistress was eternally absent. She was most absent of all on the recurrent December day that his tenacity set apart. He had no designed observance of it, but his nerves made it all their own. They always drove him forth on a long walk, for the goal of his pilgrimage was far. She had been buried in a London suburb, in a place then almost natural, but which he had seen lose, one after another, every feature of freshness. It was in truth during the moments he stood there that his eyes beheld the place least. They looked at another image, they opened to another light. Was it a credible future? Was it an incredible past? Whatever it was, it was an immense escape from the actual.

It is true that, if there were no other dates than this, there were other memories; and by the time George Stransom was fifty-five such memories had greatly multiplied. There were other ghosts in his life than the ghost of Mary Antrim. He had perhaps not had more losses than most men, but he had counted his losses more; he had not seen death more closely, but he had, in a manner, felt it more deeply. He had formed little by little the habit of numbering his Dead; it had come to him tolerably early in life that there was something one had to do for them. They were there in their simplified, intensified essence, their conscious absence and expressive patience, as personally there as if they had only been stricken dumb. When all sense of them failed, all sound of them ceased, it was as if their purgatory were really still on earth: they asked so little that they got, poor things, even less, and died again, died every day, of the hard usage of life. They had no organized service, no reserved place, no honor, no shelter, no safety. Even ungenerous people provided for the living, but even those who were called most generous did nothing for the others. So, on George Stransom's part, there grew up with the years a determination that he at least would do something—do it, that is, for his own—and perform the great charity without reproach. Every man had his own, and every man had, to meet this charity, the ample resources of the soul.

It was doubtless the voice of Mary Antrim that spoke
for them best; at any rate, as the years went on, he
found himself in regular communion with these alternative associates, with those whom indeed he always
called in his thoughts the Others. He spared them the
moments, he organized the charity. How it grew up he
probably never could have told you, but what came to
pass was that an altar, such as was, after all, within
everybody's compass, lighted with perpetual candles and
dedicated to these secret rites, reared itself in his spiritual spaces. He had wondered of old, in some embarrassment, whether he had a religion; being very sure, and
not a little content, that he had not at all events the
religion some of the people he had known wanted him
to have. Gradually this question was straightened out
for him; it became clear to him that the religion instilled
by his earliest consciousness had been simply the religion of the Dead. It suited his inclination, it satisfied
his spirit, it gave employment to his piety. It answered
his love of great offices, of a solemn and splendid ritual;
for no shrine could be more bedecked and no ceremonial
more stately than those to which his worship was attached. He had no imagination about these things save
that they were accessible to everyone who should ever
feel the need of them. The poorest could build such
temples of the spirit—could make them blaze with candles and smoke with incense, make them flush with pictures and flowers. The cost, in common phrase, of keeping them up fell entirely on the liberal heart.

II

He had this year, on the eve of his anniversary, as it
happened, an emotion not unconnected with that range
of feeling. Walking home at the close of a busy day, he
was arrested in the London street by the particular effect
of a shopfront which lighted the dull brown air with

its mercenary grin, and before which several persons were gathered. It was the window of a jeweler whose diamonds and sapphires seemed to laugh, in flashes like high notes of sound, with the mere joy of knowing how much more they were "worth" than most of the dingy pedestrians staring at them from the other side of the pane. Stransom lingered long enough to suspend, in a vision, a string of pearls about the white neck of Mary Antrim, and then was kept an instant longer by the sound of a voice he knew. Next to him was a mumbling old woman, and beyond the old woman a gentleman with a lady on his arm. It was from him, from Paul Creston, the voice had proceeded; he was talking with the lady of some precious object in the window. Stransom had no sooner recognized him than the old woman turned away; but simultaneously with this increase of opportunity he became aware of a strangeness which stayed him in the very act of laying his hand on his friend's arm. It lasted only a few seconds, but a few seconds were long enough for the flash of a wild question. Was *not* Mrs. Creston dead?—the ambiguity met him there in the short drop of her husband's voice, the drop conjugal, if it ever was, and in the way the two figures leaned to each other. Creston, making a step to look at something else, came nearer, glanced at him, started, and exclaimed—a circumstance the effect of which was at first only to leave Stransom staring— staring back across the months at the different face, the wholly other face the poor man had shown him last, the blurred, ravaged mask bent over the open grave by which they had stood together. Creston was not in mourning now; he detached his arm from his companion's to grasp the hand of the older friend. He colored as well as smiled in the strong light of the shop when Stransom raised a tentative hat to the lady. Stransom had just time to see that she was pretty before he found himself gaping at a fact more portentous. "My dear fellow, let me make you acquainted with my wife."

Creston had blushed and stammered over it, but in half a minute, at the rate we live in polite society, it had practically become, for Stransom, the mere memory of a shock. They stood there and laughed and talked; Stransom had instantly whisked the shock out of the

way, to keep it for private consumption. He felt himself grimacing, he heard himself exaggerating the usual,
but he was conscious that he had turned slightly faint.
That new woman, that hired performer, Mrs. Creston?
Mrs. Creston had been more living for him than any
woman but one. This lady had a face that shone as
publicly as the jeweler's window, and in the happy candor
with which she wore her monstrous character there was
an effect of gross immodesty. The character of Paul
Creston's wife, thus attributed to her, was monstrous
for reasons which Stransom could see that his friend
perfectly knew that he knew. The happy pair had just
arrived from America, and Stransom had not needed to
be told this to divine the nationality of the lady. Somehow
it deepened the foolish air that her husband's confused
cordiality was unable to conceal. Stransom recalled that
he had heard of poor Creston's having, while his
bereavement was still fresh, gone to the United States
for what people in such predicaments call a little change.
He had found the little change; indeed, he had brought
the little change back; it was the little change that stood
there and that, do what he would, he couldn't, while he
showed those high front teeth of his, look like anything
but a conscious ass about. They were going into the
shop, Mrs. Creston said, and she begged Mr. Stransom
to come with them and help to decide. He thanked her,
opening his watch and pleading an engagement for which
he was already late, and they parted while she shrieked
into the fog, "Mind now you come to see me right away!"
Creston had had the delicacy not to suggest that, and
Stransom hoped it hurt him somewhere to hear her
scream it to all the echoes.

He felt quite determined, as he walked away, never
in his life to go near her. She was perhaps a human
being, but Creston oughn't to have shown her without
precautions, oughtn't indeed to have shown her at all.
His precautions should have been those of a forger or
a murderer, and the people at home would never have
mentioned extradition. This was a wife for foreign service
or purely external use; a decent consideration would
have spared her the injury of comparisons. Such were the
first reflections of George Stransom's amazement; but

as he sat alone that night—these were particular hours that he always passed alone—the harshness dropped from them and left only the pity. *He* could spend an evening with Kate Creston, if the man to whom she had given everything couldn't. He had not known her twenty years, and she was the only woman for whom he might perhaps have been unfaithful. She was all cleverness and sympathy and charm; her house had been the very easiest in all the world, and her friendship the very firmest. Without accidents he had loved her, without accidents everyone had loved her; she had made the passions about her as regular as the moon makes the tides. She had been also, of course, far too good for her husband, but he never suspected it, and in nothing had she been more admirable than in the exquisite art with which she tried to keep everyone else (keeping Creston was no trouble) from finding it out. Here was a man to whom she had devoted her life and for whom she had given it up—dying to bring into the world a child of his bed; and she had had only to submit to her fate to have, ere the grass was green on her grave, no more existence for him than a domestic servant he had replaced. The frivolity, the indecency of it made Stransom's eyes fill; and he had that evening a rich, almost happy sense that he alone, in a world without delicacy, had a right to hold up his head. While he smoked, after dinner, he had a book in his lap, but he had no eyes for his page; his eyes, in the swarming void of things, seemed to have caught Kate Creston's, and it was into their sad silences he looked. It was to him her sentient spirit had turned, knowing that it was of her he would think. He thought, for a long time, of how the closed eyes of dead women could still live—how they could open again, in a quiet lamplit room, long after they had looked their last. They had looks that remained, as great poets had quoted lines.

The newspaper lay by his chair—the thing that came in the afternoon, and the servants thought one wanted; without sense for what was in it, he had mechanically unfolded and then dropped it. Before he went to bed he took it up, and this time, at the top of a paragraph, he was caught by five words that made him start. He stood staring, before the fire, at the "Death of Sir Acton Hague,

K.C.B.," the man who, ten years earlier, had been the nearest of his friends, and whose deposition from this eminence had practically left it without an occupant. He had seen him after that catastrophe, but he had not seen him for years. Standing there before the fire, he turned cold as he read what had befallen him. Promoted a short time previous to the governorship of the Westward Islands, Acton Hague had died, in the bleak honor of this exile, of an illness consequent on the bite of a poisonous snake. His career was compressed by the newspaper into a dozen lines, the perusal of which excited on George Stransom's part no warmer feeling than one of relief at the absence of any mention of their quarrel, an incident accidentally tainted at the time, thanks to their joint immersion in large affairs, with a horrible publicity. Public, indeed, was the wrong Stransom had, to his own sense, suffered, the insult he had blankly taken from the only man with whom he had ever been intimate; the friend, almost adored, of his university years, the subject, later, of his passionate loyalty; so public that he had never spoken of it to a human creature, so public that he had completely overlooked it. It had made the difference for him that friendship too was all over, but it had only made just that one. The shock of interests had been private, intensely so; but the action taken by Hague had been in the face of men. Today it all seemed to have occurred merely to the end that George Stransom should think of him as "Hague," and measure exactly how much he himself could feel like a stone. He went cold, suddenly, and horribly cold, to bed.

III

The next day, in the afternoon, in the great gray suburb, he felt that his long walk had tired him. In the dreadful cemetery alone he had been on his feet an hour.

Instinctively, coming back, they had taken him a devious course, and it was a desert in which no circling cabman hovered over possible prey. He paused on a corner and measured the dreariness; then he became aware in the gathered dusk that he was in one of those tracts of London which are less gloomy by night than by day, because, in the former case, of the civil gift of light. By day there was nothing, but by night there were lamps, and George Stransom was in a mood which made lamps good in themselves. It wasn't that they could show him anything; it was only that they could burn clear. To his surprise, however, after a while, they did show him something: the arch of a high doorway approached by a low terrace of steps, in the depth of which—it formed a dim vestibule—the raising of a curtain, at the moment he passed, gave him a glimpse of an avenue of gloom with a glow of tapers at the end. He stopped and looked up, making out that the place was a church. The thought quickly came to him that, since he was tired, he might rest there; so that, after a moment, he had in turn pushed up the leathern curtain and gone in. It was a temple of the old persuasion, and there had evidently been a function—perhaps a service for the dead; the high altar was still a blaze of candles. This was an exhibition he always liked, and he dropped into a seat with relief. More than it had ever yet come home to him it struck him as good that there should be churches.

This one was almost empty, and the other altars were dim; a verger shuffled about, an old woman coughed, but it seemed to Stransom there was hospitality in the thick, sweet air. Was it only the savor of the incense, or was it something larger and more guaranteed? He had at any rate quitted the great gray suburb and come nearer to the warm center. He presently ceased to feel an intruder—he gained at last even a sense of community with the only worshipper in his neighborhood, the somber presence of a woman, in mourning unrelieved, whose back was all he could see of her, and who had sunk deep into prayer at no great distance from him. He wished he could sink, like her, to the very bottom, be as motionless, as rapt in prostration. After a few moments he shifted his seat; it was almost indelicate to be

so aware of her. But Stransom subsequently lost himself
altogether; he floated away on the sea of light. If occasions like this had been more frequent in his life, he
would have been more frequently conscious of the great
original type, set up in a myriad temples, of the unapproachable shrine he had erected in his mind. That shrine
had begun as a reflection of ecclesiastical pomps, but the
echo had ended by growing more distinct than the
sound. The sound now rang out, the type blazed at him
with all its fires and with a mystery of radiance in which
endless meanings could glow. The thing became, as he
sat there, his appropriate altar, and each starry candle
an appropriate vow. He numbered them, he named them,
he grouped them—it was the silent roll call of his Dead.
They made together a brightness vast and intense—a
brightness in which the mere chapel of his thoughts grew
so dim that, as it faded away, he asked himself if he
shouldn't find his real comfort in some material act,
some outward worship.

This idea took possession of him while, at a distance,
the black-robed lady continued prostrate; he was quietly
thrilled with his conception, which at last brought him to
his feet in his sudden excitement of a plan. He wandered
softly about the church, pausing in the different chapels,
which were all, save one, applied to a special devotion.
It was in this one, dark and ungarnished, he stood
longest—the length of time it took him fully to grasp the
conception of gilding it with his bounty. He should snatch
it from no other rites and associate it with nothing profane; he would simply take it as it should be given up to
him and make it a masterpiece of splendor and a mountain of fire. Tended sacredly all the year, with the
sanctifying church around it, it would always be ready
for his offices. There would be difficulties, but from the
first they presented themselves only as difficulties surmounted. Even for a person so little affiliated, the thing
would be a matter of arrangement. He saw it all in advance, and how bright in especial the place would become to him in the intermission of toil and the dusk of
afternoons; how rich in assurance at all times, but especially in the indifferent world. Before withdrawing he
drew nearer again to the spot where he had first sat

down, and in the movement he met the lady whom he had seen praying and who was now on her way to the door. She passed him quickly, and he had only a glimpse of her pale face and her unconscious, almost sightless eyes. For that instant she looked faded and handsome.

This was the origin of the rites more public, yet certainly esoteric, that he at last found himself able to establish. It took a long time, it took a year; and both the process and the result would have been—for any who knew—a vivid picture of his good faith. No one did know, in fact—no one but the bland ecclesiastic whose acquaintance he had promptly sought, whose objections he had softly overridden, whose curiosity and sympathy he had artfully charmed, whose assent to his eccentric munificence he had eventually won, and who had asked for concessions in exchange for indulgences. Stransom had of course at an early stage of his inquiry been referred to the bishop, and the bishop had been delightfully human; the bishop had been almost amused. Success was within sight, at any rate, from the moment the attitude of those whom it concerned became liberal in response to liberality. The altar and the small chapel that enclosed it, consecrated to an ostensible and customary worship, were to be splendidly maintained; all that Stransom reserved to himself was the number of his lights and the free enjoyment of his intention. When the intention had taken complete effect, the enjoyment became even greater than he had ventured to hope. He liked to think of this effect when he was far from it—he liked to convince himself of it yet again when he was near. He was not often, indeed, so near as that a visit to it had not perforce something of the patience of a pilgrimage; but the time he gave to his devotion came to seem to him more a contribution to his other interests than a betrayal of them. Even a loaded life might be easier when one had added a new necessity to it.

How much easier was probably never guessed by those who simply knew that there were hours when he disappeared, and for many of whom there was a vulgar reading of what they used to call his plunges. These plunges were into depths quieter than the deep sea caves; and the habit, at the end of a year or two, had become the

one it would have cost him most to relinquish. Now they
had really, his Dead, something that was indefeasibly
theirs; and he liked to think that they might, in cases, be
the Dead of others, as well as that the Dead of others
might be invoked there under the protection of what he
had done. Whoever bent a knee on the carpet he had
laid down appeared to him to act in the spirit of his intention. Each of his lights had a name for him, and from
time to time a new light was kindled. This was what he
had fundamentally agreed for, that there should always
be room for them all. What those who passed or lingered
saw was simply the most resplendent of the altars, called
suddenly into vivid usefulness, with a quiet elderly man,
for whom it evidently had a fascination, often seated
there in a maze or a doze; but half the satisfaction of the
spot, for this mysterious and fitful worshipper, was that
he found the years of his life there, and the ties, the affections, the struggles, the submissions, the conquests, if
there had been such a record of that adventurous journey
in which the beginnings and the endings of human relations are the lettered milestones. He had in general little
taste for the past as a past of his own history; at other
times and in other places, it mostly seemed to him pitiful
to consider and impossible to repair; but on these occasions he accepted it with something of that positive glad-
ness with which one adjusts one's self to an ache that is
beginning to succumb to treatment. To the treatment of
time the malady of life begins at a given moment to succumb; and these were doubtless the hours at which that
truth most came home to him. The day was written for
him there on which he had first become acquainted with
death, and the successive phases of the acquaintance
were each marked with a flame.

The flames were gathering thick at present, for
Stransom had entered that dark defile of our earthly
descent in which someone dies every day. It was only
yesterday that Kate Creston had flashed out her white
fire; yet already there were younger stars ablaze on the
tips of the tapers. Various persons in whom his interest
had not been intense drew closer to him by entering
this company. He went over it, head by head, till he felt
like the shepherd of a huddled flock, with all a shepherd's

vision of differences imperceptible. He knew his candles apart, up to the color of the flame, and would still have known them had their positions all been changed. To other imaginations they might stand for other things— that they should stand for something to be hushed before was all he desired; but he was intensely conscious of the personal note of each and of the distinguishable way it contributed to the concert. There were hours at which he almost caught himself wishing that certain of his friends would now die, that he might establish with them in this manner a connection more charming than, as it happened, it was possible to enjoy with them in life. In regard to those from whom one was separated by the long curves of the globe such a connection could only be an improvement; it brought them instantly within reach. Of course there were gaps in the constellation, for Stransom knew he could only pretend to act for his own, and it was not every figure passing before his eyes into the great obscure that was entitled to a memorial. There was a strange sanctification in death, but some characters were more sanctified by being forgotten than by being remembered. The greatest blank in the shining page was the memory of Acton Hague, of which he inveterately tried to rid himself. For Acton Hague no flame could ever rise on any altar of his.

IV

Every year, the day he walked back from the great graveyard, he went to church as he had done the day his idea was born. It was on this occasion, as it happened, after a year had passed, that he began to observe his altar to be haunted by a worshipper at least as frequent as himself. Others of the faithful, and in the rest of the church, came and went, appealing sometimes, when they disappeared, to a vague or to a particular recognition; but this unfailing presence was always to be observed when he arrived and still in possession when he departed. He was surprised, the first time, at the promptitude with which it assumed an identity for him—the identity of the lady whom, two years before, on his anniversary, he had seen so intensely bowed, and of whose tragic face he had had so flitting a vision. Given the time that had elapsed, his recollection of her was fresh enough to make him wonder. Of himself she had, of course, no impression, or, rather, she had none at first. The time came when her manner of transacting her business suggested to him that she had gradually guessed his call to be of the same order. She used his altar for her own purpose; he could only hope that, sad and solitary as she always struck him, she used it for her own Dead. There were interruptions, infidelities, all on his part, calls to other associations and duties; but as the months went on he found her whenever he returned, and he ended by taking pleasure in the thought that he had given her almost the contentment he had given himself. They worshipped side by side so often that there were moments when he wished he might be sure, so straight did their prospect stretch away of growing old together in their rites. She was younger than he, but she looked as if her Dead were at least as numerous as his candles. She had no color, no sound, no fault, and another of the things about which he had made up his mind was that she had no fortune. She was always black-robed, as if she had had a succession of sorrows. People were not poor, after all, whom so many losses could overtake; they were positively rich when they had so much to give up. But the air of this devoted and indifferent woman, who always made, in any attitude, a beautiful, accidental line, conveyed somehow to Stransom that she had known more kinds of trouble than one.

He had a great love of music and little time for the joy of it; but occasionally, when workaday noises were muffled by Saturday afternoons, it used to come back to him that there were glories. There were, moreover, friends who reminded him of this, and side by side with whom he found himself sitting out concerts. On one of these winter evenings, in St. James' Hall, he became aware, after he had seated himself, that the lady he had so often seen at church was in the place next him and was evidently alone, as he also this time happened to be. She was at first too absorbed in the consideration of the program to heed him, but when she at last glanced at him he took advantage of the movement to speak to her, greeting her with the remark that he felt as if he already knew her. She smiled as she said: "Oh, yes! I recognize you." Yet in spite of this admission of their long acquaintance, it was the first time he had ever seen her smile. The effect of it was suddenly to contribute more to that acquaintance than all the previous meetings had done. He hadn't "taken in," he said to himself, that she was so pretty. Later that evening (it was while he rolled along in a hansom on his way to dine out) he added that he hadn't taken in that she was so interesting. The next morning, in the midst of his work, he quite suddenly and irrelevantly reflected that his impression of her, beginning so far back, was like a winding river that had at last reached the sea.

His work was indeed blurred a little, all that day, by the sense of what had now passed between them. It wasn't much, but it had just made the difference. They had listened together to Beethoven and Schumann; they had talked in the pauses and at the end, when at the door, to which they moved together, he had asked her if he could help her in the matter of getting away. She had thanked him and put up her umbrella, slipping into the crowd without an allusion to their meeting yet again, and leaving him to remember at leisure that not a word had been exchanged about the place in which they frequently met. This circumstance seemed to him at one moment natural enough and at another perverse. She mightn't in the least have recognized his warrant for speaking to her; and yet; if she hadn't, he would have judged her an underbred woman. It was odd that, when nothing had really ever brought them together, he should have been able successfully to assume that they were in a manner old friends—that this negative quantity was somehow more than they could express. His success, it was true, had been qualified by her quick escape, so that there grew up in him an absurd desire to put it to some better test. Save insofar as some other improbable

accident might assist him, such a test could be only to
meet her afresh at church. Left to himself he would have
gone to church the very next afternoon, just for the
curiosity of seeing if he should find her there. But he was
not left to himself, a fact he discovered quite at the last,
after he had virtually made up his mind to go. The influence that kept him away really revealed to him how
little to himself his Dead ever left him. They reminded
him that he went only for them—for nothing else in the
world.

The force of this reminder kept him away ten days; he
hated to connect the place with anything but his offices,
or to give a glimpse of the curiosity that had been on the
point of moving him. It was absurd to weave a tangle
about a matter so simple as a custom of devotion that
might so easily have been daily or hourly; yet the tangle
got itself woven. He was sorry, he was disappointed; it
was as if a long, happy spell had been broken and he had
lost a familiar security. At the last, however, he asked
himself if he was to stay away forever from the fear of
this muddle about motives. After an interval, neither
longer nor shorter than usual, he re-entered the church
with a clear conviction that he should scarcely heed the
presence or the absence of the lady of the concert. This
indifference didn't prevent his instantly perceiving that
for the only time since he had first seen her she was not
on the spot. He had now no scruple about giving her
time to arrive, but she didn't arrive, and when he went
away still missing her he was quite profanely and con-
sentingly sorry. If her absence made the tangle more
intricate, that was only her fault. By the end of another
year it was very intricate indeed; but by that time he
didn't in the least care, and it was only his cultivated
consciousness that had given him scruples. Three times in
three months he had gone to church without finding her,
and he felt that he had not needed these occasions to
show him that his suspense had quite dropped. Yet it
was, incongruously, not indifference, but a refinement of
delicacy that had kept him from asking the sacristan,
who would of course immediately have recognized his
description of her, whether she had been seen at other
hours. His delicacy had kept him from asking any ques-

tion about her at any time, and it was exactly the same virtue that had left him so free to be decently civil to her at the concert.

This happy advantage now served him anew, enabling him when she finally met his eyes—it was after a fourth trial—to determine without hesitation to wait till she should retire. He joined her in the street as soon as she had done so, and asked her if he might accompany her a certain distance. With her placid permission he went as far as a house in the neighborhood at which she had business; she let him know it was not where she lived. She lived, as she said, in a mere slum, with an old aunt, a person in connection with whom she spoke of the engrossment of humdrum duties and regular occupations. She was not, the mourning niece, in her first youth, and her vanished freshness had left something behind which, for Stransom, represented the proof that it had been tragically sacrificed. Whatever she gave him the assurance of she gave it without references. She might in fact have been a divorced duchess, and she might have been an old maid who taught the harp.

V

They fell at last into the way of walking together almost every time they met, though, for a long time, they never met anywhere save at church. He couldn't ask her to come and see him, and, as if she had not a proper place to receive him, she never invited him. As much as himself she knew the world of London, but from an undiscussed instinct of privacy they haunted the region not mapped on the social chart. On the return she always made him leave her at the same corner. She looked with him, as a pretext for a pause, at the depressed things in suburban shopfronts; and there was never a word he had said to her that she had not beautifully understood. For long ages he never knew her name, any more than she had ever pronounced his own; but it was not their names that mattered, it was only their perfect practice and their common need.

These things made their whole relation so impersonal that they had not the rules or reasons people found in ordinary friendships. They didn't care for the things it was supposed necessary to care for in the intercourse of the world. They ended one day (they never knew which of them expressed it first) by throwing out the idea that they didn't care for each other. Over this idea they grew quite intimate; they rallied to it in a way that marked a fresh start in their confidence. If to feel deeply together about certain things wholly distinct from themselves didn't constitute a safety, where was safety to be looked for? Not lightly nor often, not without occasion nor without emotion, any more than in any other reference by serious people to a mystery of their faith; but when something had happened to warm, as it were, the air for it, they came as near as they could come to calling their Dead by name. They felt it was coming very near to utter their thought at all. The word "they" expressed enough; it limited the mention, it had a dignity of its own, and if, in their talk, you had heard our friends use it, you might have taken them for a pair of pagans of old alluding decently to the domesticated gods. They never knew— at least Stransom never knew—how they had learned to be sure about each other. If it had been with each a question of what the other was there for, the certitude had come in some fine way of its own. Any faith, after all, has the instinct of propagation, and it was as natural as it was beautiful that they should have taken pleasure on the spot in the imagination of a following. If the following was for each but a following of one, it had proved in the event to be sufficient. Her debt, however, of course, was much greater than his, because while she had only given him a worshipper he had given her a magnificent temple. Once she said she pitied him for the length of his list (she had counted his candles almost as often as himself) and this made him wonder what could have been the length of hers. He had wondered before at the coincidence of their losses, especially as from time to time a new candle was set up. On some occasion some accident led him to express this curiosity, and she answered as if she was surprised that he hadn't already understood. "Oh, for me, you know, the more there are the better—there could never be too many. I should like hundreds and hundreds—I should like thousands; I should like a perfect mountain of light."

Then, of course, in a flash, he understood. "Your Dead are only One?"

She hesitated as she had never hesitated. "Only One," she answered, coloring as if now he knew her innermost secret. It really made him feel that he knew less than before, so difficult was it for him to reconstitute a life in which a single experience had reduced all others to nought. His own life, round its central hollow, had been packed close enough. After this she appeared to have regretted her confession, though at the moment she spoke there had been pride in her very embarrassment. She declared to him that his own was the larger, the dearer possession—the portion one would have chosen if one had been able to choose; she assured him she could perfectly imagine some of the echoes with which his silences were peopled. He knew she couldn't; one's relation to what one had loved and hated had been a relation too distinct from the relations of others. But this didn't affect the fact that they were growing old together in their piety. She was a feature of that piety, but even at the ripe stage of acquaintance in which they occasionally arranged to meet at a concert, or to go together to an exhibition, she was not a feature of anything else. The most that happened was that his worship became paramount. Friend by friend dropped away till at last there were more emblems on his altar than houses left him to enter. She was more than any other the friend who remained, but she was unknown to all the rest. Once when she had discovered, as they called it, a new star, she used the expression that the chapel at last was full.

"Oh, no!" Stransom replied, "there is a great thing wanting for that! The chapel will never be full till a candle is set up before which all the others will pale. It will be the tallest candle of all."

Her mild wonder rested on him. "What candle do you mean?"

"I mean, dear lady, my own."

He had learned after a long time that she earned money by her pen, writing under a designation that she never told him in magazines that he never saw. She knew too well what he couldn't read and what she couldn't write, and she taught him to cultivate indifference with a success that did much for their good relations. Her invisible industry was a convenience to him; it helped his contented thought of her, the thought that rested in the dignity of her proud, obscure life, her little remunerated art and her little impenetrable home. Lost, with her obscure relative, in her dim suburban world, she came to the surface for him in distant places. She was really the priestess of his altar, and whenever he quitted England he committed it to her keeping. She proved to him afresh that women have more of the spirit of religion than men; he felt his fidelity pale and faint in comparison with hers. He often said to her that since he had so little time to live he rejoiced in her having so much; so glad was he to think she would guard the temple when he should have ceased. He had a great plan for that, which, of course, he told her, too, a bequest of money to keep it up in undiminished state. Of the administration of this fund he would appoint her superintendent, and, if the spirit should move her, she might kindle a taper even for him.

"And who will kindle one even for me?" she gravely inquired.

VI

She was always in mourning, yet the day he came back from the longest absence he had yet made her appearance immediately told him she had lately had a bereavement. They met on this occasion as she was leaving the church, so that, postponing his own entrance, he instantly offered to turn round and walk away with her. She considered, then she said: "Go in now, but come and see me in an hour." He knew the small vista of her street, closed at the end and as dreary as an empty pocket, where the pairs of shabby little houses, semidetached but indissolubly united, were like married couples on bad terms. Often, however, as he had gone to the beginning, he had never gone beyond. Her aunt was dead—that he immediately guessed, as well as that it made a difference; but when she had for the first time mentioned her number he found himself, on her leaving him, not a little agitated by this sudden liberality. She was not a person with whom, after all, one got on so very fast; it had taken him months and months to learn her name, years and years to learn her address. If she had looked, on this reunion, so much older to him, how in the world did he look to her? She had reached the period of life that he had long since reached, when, after separations, the dreadful clock-face of the friend we meet announces the hour we have tried to forget. He couldn't have said what he expected, as, at the end of his waiting, he turned the corner at which, for years, he had always paused; simply not to pause was a sufficient cause for emotion. It was an event, somehow; and in all their long acquaintance there had never been such a thing. The event grew larger when, five minutes later, in the faint elegance of her little drawing room, she quavered out some greeting which showed the measure she took of it. He had a strange sense of having come for something in particular; strange because, literally, there was nothing particular between them, nothing save that they were at one on their great point, which had long ago become a magnificent matter of course. It was true that, after she had said, "You can always come now, you know," the thing he was there for seemed already to have happened. He asked her if it was the death of her aunt that made the difference; to which she replied: "She never knew I knew you. I wished her not to." The beautiful clearness of her candor—her faded beauty was like a summer twilight—disconnected the words from any image of deceit. They might have struck him as the record of a deep dissimulation; but she had always given him a sense of noble reasons. The vanished aunt was present, as he looked about him, in the small complacencies of the room, the beaded velvet and the fluted moreen; and though, as we know, he had the worship of the dead, he found himself not definitely regretting this lady. If she was not in his long list, however, she was in her niece's short one, and Stransom presently observed to his friend that now, at least, in the place they haunted together, she would have another object of devotion.

"Yes, I shall have another. She was very kind to me. It's that that makes the difference."

He judged, wondering a good deal before he made any motion to leave her, that the difference would somehow be very great and would consist of still other things than her having let him come in. It rather chilled him, for they had been happy together as they were. He extracted from her at any rate an intimation that she should now have larger means, that her aunt's tiny fortune had come to her, so that there was henceforth only one to consume what had formerly been made to suffice for two. This was a joy to Stransom, because it had hitherto been equally impossible for him either to offer her presents or to find contentment in not doing so. It was too ugly to be at her side that way, abounding himself and yet not able to overflow—a demonstration that would have been a signally false note. Even her better situation too seemed only to draw out in a sense the loneliness of her future. It would merely help her to live more and more for their small ceremonial, at a time when he himself had begun wearily to feel that, having set it in motion, he might depart. When they had sat a while in the pale parlor she got up and said: "This isn't *my* room: let us go into mine." They had only to cross the narrow hall, as he found, to pass into quite another air. When she had closed the door of the second room, as she called it, he felt that he had at last real possession of her. The place had the flush of life—it was expressive; its dark red walls were articulate with memories and relics. These were simple things —photographs and watercolors, scraps of writing framed and ghosts of flowers embalmed; but only a moment was needed to show him they had a common meaning.

It was here that she had lived and worked; and she had already told him she would make no change of scene. He saw that the objects about her mainly had reference to certain places and times; but after a minute he distinguished among them a small portrait of a gentleman. At a distance and without their glasses, his eyes were only caught by it enough to feel a vague curiosity. Presently this impulse carried him nearer, and in another moment he was staring at the picture in stupefaction and with the sense that some sound had broken from him. He was further conscious that he showed his companion a white face when he turned round on her with the exclamation: "Acton Hague!"

She gave him back his astonishment. "Did you know him?"

"He was the friend of all my youth—my early manhood. And *you* knew him?"

She colored at this, and for a moment her answer failed; her eyes took in everything in the place, and a strange irony reached her lips as she echoed: "Knew him?"

Then Stransom understood, while the room heaved like the cabin of a ship, that its whole contents cried out with him, that it was a museum in his honor, that all her later years had been addressed to him, and that the shrine he himself had reared had been passionately converted to this use. It was all for Acton Hague that she had kneeled every day at his altar. What need had there been for a consecrated candle when he was present in the whole array? The revelation seemed to smite our friend in the face, and he dropped into a seat and sat silent. He had quickly become aware that she was shocked at the vision of his own shock, but as she sank on the sofa beside him and laid her hand on his arm he perceived almost as soon that she was unable to resent it as much as she would have liked.

He learned in that instant two things: one of them was that even in so long a time she had gathered no knowledge of his great intimacy and his great quarrel; the other was that, in spite of this ignorance, strangely enough, she supplied on the spot a reason for his confusion. "How extraordinary," he presently exclaimed, "that we should never have known!"

She gave a wan smile, which seemed to Stransom stranger even than the fact itself. "I never, never spoke of him."

Stransom looked about the room again. "Why then, if your life had been so full of him?"

"Mayn't I put you that question as well. Hadn't your life also been full of him?"

"Anyone's, everyone's life was who had the wonderful experience of knowing him. I never spoke of him," Stransom added in a moment, "because he did me—years ago—an unforgettable wrong." She was silent, and with the full effect of his presence all about them it almost startled her visitor to hear no protest escape from her. She accepted his words; he turned his eyes to her again to see in what manner she accepted them. It was with rising tears, and an extraordinary sweetness in the movement of putting out her hand to take his own. Nothing more wonderful had ever appeared to Stransom than, in that little chamber of remembrance and homage, to see her convey with such exquisite mildness that, as from Acton Hague, any injury was credible. The clock ticked in the stillness—Hague had probably given it to her—and while he let her hold his hand with a tenderness that was almost an assumption of responsibility for his old pain as well as his new, Stransom after a minute broke out: "Good God, how he must have used *you!*"

She dropped his hand at this, got up, and, moving

across the room, made straight a small picture to which, on examining it, he had given a slight push. Then, turning round on him, with her pale gaiety recovered: "I've forgiven him!" she declared.

"I know what you've done," said Stransom; "I know what you've done for years." For a moment they looked at each other across the room, with their long community of service in their eyes. This short passage made, to Stransom's sense, for the woman before him, an immense, an absolutely naked confession; which was presently, suddenly blushing red and changing her place again, what she appeared to become aware that he perceived in it. He got up. "How you must have loved him!"

"Women are not like men. They can love even where they've suffered."

"Women are wonderful," said Stransom. "But I assure you I've forgiven him, too."

"If I had known of anything so strange, I wouldn't have brought you here."

"So that we might have gone on in our ignorance to the last?"

"What do you call the last?" she asked, smiling still.

At this he could smile back at her. "You'll see—when it comes."

She reflected a moment. "This is better perhaps; but as we were—it was good."

"Did it never happen that he spoke of me?" Stransom inquired.

Considering more intently, she made no answer, and he quickly recognized that he would have been adequately answered by her asking how often he himself had spoken of their terrible friend. Suddenly a brighter light broke in her face, and an excited idea sprang to her lips in the question: "You *have* forgiven him?"

"How, if I hadn't, could I linger here?"

She winced, for an instant, at the deep but unintended irony of this; but even while she did so, she panted quickly: "Then in the lights on your altar?"

"There's never a light for Acton Hague!"

She stared, with a great visible fall. "But if he's one of your Dead?"

"He's one of the world's, if you like—he's one of

yours. But he's not one of mine. Mine are only the Dead who died possessed of me. They're mine in death because they were mine in life."

"*He* was yours in life, then, even if for a while he ceased to be. If you forgave him, you went back to him. Those whom we've once loved——"

"Are those who can hurt us most," Stransom broke in.

"Ah, it's not true—you've *not* forgiven him!" she wailed with a passion that startled him.

He looked at her a moment. "What was it he did to you?"

"Everything!" Then abruptly she put out her hand in farewell. "Goodbye."

He turned as cold as he had turned that night he read of the death of Acton Hague. "You mean that we meet no more?"

"Not as we have met—not *there!*"

He stood aghast at this snap of their great bond, at the renouncement that rang out in the word she so passionately emphasized. "But what's changed—for you?"

She hesitated, in all the vividness of a trouble that, for the first time since he had known her, made her splendidly stern. "How can you understand now when you didn't understand before?"

"I didn't understand before only because I didn't know. Now that I know, I see what I've been living with for years," Stransom went on very gently.

She looked at him with a larger allowance, as if she appreciated his good nature. "How can I, then, with this new knowledge of my own, ask you to continue to live with it?"

"I set up my altar, with its multiplied meanings——" Stransom began; but she quickly interrupted him:

"You set up your altar, and when I wanted one most I found it magnificently ready. I used it, with the gratitude I've always shown you, for I knew from of old that it was dedicated to Death. I told you, long ago, that my Dead were not many. Yours were, but all you had done for them was none too much for *my* worship! You had placed a great light for Each—I gathered them together for One!"

"We had simply different intentions," Stransom replied. "That, as you say, I perfectly knew, and I don't see why your intention shouldn't still sustain you."

"That's because you're generous—you can imagine and think. But the spell is broken."

It seemed to poor Stransom, in spite of his resistance, that it really was, and the prospect stretched gray and void before him. All, however, that he could say was: "I hope you'll try before you give up."

"If I had known you had ever known him, I should have taken for granted he had his candle," she presently rejoined. "What's changed, as you say, is that on making the discovery I find he never has had it. That makes *my* attitude"—she paused a moment, as if thinking how to express it, then said simply—"all wrong."

"Come once again," Stransom pleaded.

"Will you give him his candle?" she asked.

He hesitated, but only because it would sound ungracious; not because he had a doubt of his feeling. "I can't do that!" he declared at last.

"Then goodbye." And she gave him her hand again.

He had got his dismissal; besides which, in the agitation of everything that had opened out to him, he felt the need to recover himself as he could only do in solitude. Yet he lingered—lingered to see if she had no compromise to express, no attenuation to propose. But he only met her great lamenting eyes, in which indeed he read that she was as sorry for him as for anyone else. This made him say: "At least, at any rate, I may see you here."

"Oh, yes! come if you like. But I don't think it will do."

Stransom looked round the room once more; he felt in truth by no means sure it would do. He felt also stricken and more and more cold, and his chill was like an ague in which he had to make an effort not to shake. "I must try on my side, if you can't try on yours," he dolefully rejoined. She came out with him to the hall and into the doorway, and here he put to her the question that seemed to him the one he could least answer from his own wit. "Why have you never let me come before?"

"Because my aunt would have seen you, and I should have had to tell her how I came to know you."

"And what would have been the objection to that?"

"It would have entailed other explanations; there would at any rate have been that danger."

"Surely she knew you went every day to church," Stransom objected.

"She didn't know what I went for."

"Of me then she never even heard?"

"You'll think I was deceitful. But I didn't need to be!"

Stransom was now on the lower doorstep, and his hostess held the door half-closed behind him. Through what remained of the opening he saw her framed face. He made a supreme appeal. "What *did* he do to you?"

"It would have come out—*she* would have told you. That fear, at my heart—that was my reason!" And she closed the door, shutting him out.

VIII

He had ruthlessly abandoned her—that, of course, was what he had done. Stransom made it all out in solitude, at leisure, fitting the unmatched pieces gradually together and dealing one by one with a hundred obscure points. She had known Hague only after her present friend's relations with him had wholly terminated; obviously indeed a good while after; and it was natural enough that of his previous life she should have ascertained only what he had judged good to communicate. There were passages it was quite conceivable that even in moments of the tenderest expansion, he should have withheld. Of many facts in the career of a man so in the eye of the world there was of course a common knowledge; but this lady lived apart from public affairs, and the only period perfectly clear to her would have been the period following the dawn of her own drama. A man, in her place, would have "looked up" the past

—would even have consulted old newspapers. It remained singular indeed that in her long contact with the partner of her retrospect no accident had lighted a train; but there was no arguing about that; the accident had in fact come; it had simply been that security had prevailed. She had taken what Hague had given her, and her blankness in respect of his other connections was only a touch in the picture of that plasticity Stransom had supreme reason to know so great a master could have been trusted to produce.

This picture, for a while, was all that our friend saw; he caught his breath again and again as it came over him that the woman with whom he had had for years so fine a point of contact was a woman whom Acton Hague, of all men in the world, had more or less fashioned. Such as she sat there today, she was ineffaceably stamped with him. Beneficent, blameless as Stransom held her, he couldn't rid himself of the sense that he had been the victim of a fraud. She had imposed upon him hugely, though she had known it as little as he. All this later past came back to him as a time grotesquely misspent. Such at least were his first reflections; after a while he found himself more divided and only, at the end of it, more troubled. He imagined, recalled, reconstituted, figured out for himself the truth she had refused to give him; the effect of which was to make her seem to him only more saturated with her fate. He felt her spirit, in the strange business, to be finer than his own in the very degree in which she might have been, in which she certainly had been, more wronged. A woman, when she was wronged, was always more wronged than a man, and there were conditions when the least she could have got off with was more than the most he could have to endure. He was sure this rare creature wouldn't have got off with the least. He was awestruck at the thought of such a surrender —such a prostration. Molded indeed she had been by powerful hands, to have converted her injury into an exaltation so sublime. The fellow had only had to die for everything that was ugly in him to be washed out in a torrent. It was vain to try to guess what had taken place, but nothing could be clearer than that she had

ended by accusing herself. She absolved him at every
point, she adored her very wounds. The passion by
which he had profited had rushed back after its ebb,
and now the tide of tenderness, arrested forever at flood,
was too deep even to fathom. Stransom sincerely considered that he had forgiven him; but how little he had
achieved the miracle that she had achieved! His forgiveness was silence, but hers was mere unuttered sound.
The light she had demanded for his altar would have
broken his silence with a blare; whereas all the lights
in the church were for her too great a hush.

She had been right about the difference—she had
spoken the truth about the change; Stransom felt before
long that he was perversely but definitely jealous. *His*
tide had ebbed, not flowed; if he had "forgiven" Acton
Hague, that forgiveness was a motive with a broken
spring. The very fact of her appeal for a material sign,
a sign that should make her dead lover equal there
with the others, presented the concession to Stransom
as too handsome for the case. He had never thought
of himself as hard, but an exorbitant article might easily
render him so. He moved round and round this one,
but only in widening circles—the more he looked at it
the less acceptable it appeared. At the same time he
had no illusion about the effect of his refusal; he perfectly saw that it was the beginning of a separation.
He left her alone for many days; but when at last he
called upon her again this conviction acquired a depress-
ing force. In the interval he had kept away from the
church, and he needed no fresh assurance from her to
know she had not entered it. The change was complete
enough; it had broken up her life. Indeed it had broken
up his, for all the fires of his shrine seemed to him
suddenly to have been quenched. A great indifference
fell upon him, the weight of which was in itself a pain;
and he never knew what his devotion had been for him
till, in that shock, it stopped like a dropped watch.
Neither did he know with how large a confidence he
had counted on the final service that had now failed;
the mortal deception was that in this abandonment the
whole future gave way.

These days of her absence proved to him of what

she was capable; all the more that be never dreamed she was vindictive or even resentful. It was not in anger she had forsaken him; it was in absolute submission to hard reality, to crude destiny. This came home to him when he sat with her again in the room in which her late aunt's conversation lingered like the tone of a cracked piano. She tried to make him forget how much they were estranged; but in the very presence of what they had given up it was impossible not to be sorry for her. He had taken from her so much more than she had taken from him. He argued with her again, told her she could now have the altar to herself; but she only shook her head with pleading sadness, begging him not to waste his breath on the impossible, the extinct. Couldn't he see that, in relation to her private need, the rites he had established were practically an elaborate exclusion? She regretted nothing that had happened; it had all been right so long as she didn't know, and it was only that now she knew too much, and that from the moment their eyes were open they would simply have to conform. It had doubtless been happiness enough for them to go on together so long. She was gentle, grateful, resigned; but this was only the form of a deep immutability. He saw that he should never more cross the threshold of the second room, and he felt how much this alone would make a stranger of him and give a conscious stiffness to his visits. He would have hated to plunge again into that well of reminders, but he enjoyed quite as little the vacant alternative.

After he had been with her three or four times it seemed to him that to have come at last into her house had had the horrid effect of diminishing their intimacy. He had known her better, had liked her in greater freedom, when they merely walked together or kneeled together. Now they only pretended; before they had been nobly sincere. They began to try their walks again, but it proved a lame imitation, for these things, from the first, beginning or ending, had been connected with their visits to the church. They had either strolled away as they came out or had gone in to rest on the return. Besides, Stransom now grew weary; he couldn't walk as of old. The omission made everything false; it was a horrible mutilation of their lives. Our friend was frank and monotonous; he made no mystery of his remonstrance and no secret of his predicament. Her response, whatever it was, always came to the same thing —an implied invitation to him to judge, if he spoke of predicaments, of how much comfort she had in hers. For him indeed there was no comfort even in complaint, for every allusion to what had befallen them only made the author of their trouble more present. Acton Hague was between them, that was the essence of the matter; and he was never so much between them as when they were face to face. Stransom, even while he wanted to banish him, had the strangest sense of desiring a satisfaction that could come only from having accepted him. Deeply disconcerted by what he knew, he was still worse tormented by really not knowing. Perfectly aware that it would have been horribly vulgar to abuse his old friend or to tell his companion the story of their quarrel, it yet vexed him that her depth of reserve should give him no opening and should have the effect of a magnanimity greater even than his own.

He challenged himself, denounced himself, asked himself if he were in love with her that he should care so much what adventures she had had. He had never for a moment admitted that he was in love with her; therefore nothing could have surprised him more than to discover that he was jealous. What but jealousy could give a man that sore, contentious wish to have the detail of what would make him suffer? Well enough he knew indeed that he should never have it from the only person who, today, could give it to him. She let him press her with his somber eyes, only smiling at him with an exquisite mercy and breathing equally little the word that would expose her secret and the word that would appear to deny his literal right to bitterness. She told nothing, she judged nothing; she accepted everything but the possibility of her return to the old symbols. Stransom divined that for her, too, they had been vividly individual, had stood for particular hours or particular attributes—particular links in her chain. He made it clear to himself, as he believed, that his difficulty lay in the fact that the very nature of the plea for his faithless friend constituted a prohibition; that it happened to have come from *her* was precisely the vice that attached to it. To the voice of impersonal generosity he felt sure he would have listened; he would have deferred to an advocate who, speaking from abstract justice, knowing of his omission, without having known Hague, should have had the imagination to say: "Oh, remember only the best of him; pity him; provide for him!" To provide for him on the very ground of having discovered another of his turpitudes was not to pity him, but to glorify him. The more Stransom thought, the more he made it out that this relation of Hague's, whatever it was, could only have been a deception finely practiced. Where had it come into the life that all men saw? Why had he never heard of it, if it had had the frankness of an attitude honorable? Stransom knew enough of his other ties, of his obligations and appearances, not to say enough of his general character, to be sure there had been some infamy. In one way or another the poor woman had been coldly sacrificed. That was why, at the last as well as the first, he must still leave him out.

IX

And yet this was no solution, especially after he had talked again to his friend of all it had been his plan that she should finally do for him. He had talked in the other days, and she had responded with a frankness qualified only by a courteous reluctance—a reluctance that touched him—to linger on the question of his death. She had then practically accepted the charge, suffered him to feel that he could depend upon her to be the eventual guardian of his shrine; and it was in the name of what had so passed between them that he appealed to her not to forsake him in his old age. She listened to him now with a sort of shining coldness and all her habitual forbearance to insist on her terms; her

deprecation was even still tenderer, for it expressed the
compassion of her own sense that he was abandoned.
Her terms, however, remained the same, and scarcely
the less audible for not being uttered; although he was
sure that, secretly, even more than he, she felt bereft
of the satisfaction his solemn trust was to have provided for her. They both missed the rich future, but she
missed it most, because, after all, it was to have been
entirely hers; and it was her acceptance of the loss that
gave him the full measure of her preference for the
thought of Acton Hague over any other thought whatever. He had humor enough to laugh rather grimly when
he said to himself: "Why the deuce does she like him
so much more than she likes me?"—the reasons being
really so conceivable. But even his faculty of analysis
left the irritation standing, and this irritation proved
perhaps the greatest misfortune that had ever overtaken
him. There had been nothing yet that made him so much
want to give up. He had of course by this time well
reached the age of renouncement; but it had not hitherto been vivid to him that it was time to give up everything.

Practically, at the end of six months, he had renounced the friendship that was once so charming and
comforting. His privation had two faces, and the face
it had turned to him on the occasion of his last attempts to cultivate that friendship was the one he could
look at least. This was the privation he inflicted; the
other was the privation he bore. The conditions she
never phrased he used to murmur to himself in solitude:
"One more, one more—only just one." Certainly he was
going down; he often felt it when he caught himself,
over his work, staring at vacancy and giving voice to
that inanity. There was proof enough besides in his being
so weak and so ill. His irritation took the form of melancholy, and his melancholy that of the conviction that
his health had quite failed. His altar, moreover, had
ceased to exist; his chapel, in his dreams, was a great
dark cavern. All the lights had gone out—all his Dead
had died again. He couldn't exactly see at first how it
had been in the power of his late companion to ex-
tinguish them, since it was neither for her nor by her

that they had been called into being. Then he understood that it was essentially in his own soul the revival
had taken place, and that in the air of this soul they
were now unable to breathe. The candles might mechanically burn, but each of them had lost its luster. The
church had become a void; it was his presence, her presence, their common presence, that had made the indispensable medium. If anything was wrong everything was
—her silence spoiled the tune.

Then, when three months were gone, he felt so lonely
that he went back; reflecting that as they had been his
best society for years his Dead perhaps wouldn't let
him forsake them without doing something more for him.
They stood there, as he had left them, in their tall radiance, the bright cluster that had already made him, on
occasions when he was willing to compare small things
with great, liken them to a group of sea lights on the
edge of the ocean of life. It was a relief to him, after
a while, as he sat there, to feel that they had still a
virtue. He was more and more easily tired, and he always drove now; the action of his heart was weak, and
gave him none of the reassurance conferred by the action of his fancy. Nonetheless he returned yet again,
returned several times, and finally, during six months,
haunted the place with a renewal of frequency and a
strain of impatience. In winter the church was un-
warmed, and exposure to cold was forbidden him, but
the glow of his shrine was an influence in which he could
almost bask. He sat and wondered to what he had reduced his absent associate, and what she now did with
the hours of her absence. There were other churches,
there were other altars, there were other candles; in
one way or another her piety would still operate; he
couldn't absolutely have deprived her of her rites. So he
argued, but without contentment; for he well enough
knew there was no other such rare semblance of the
mountain of light she had once mentioned to him as the
satisfaction of her need. As this semblance again gradually grew great to him and his pious practice more regular, there was a sharper and sharper pang for him in
the imagination of her darkness; for never so much as
in these weeks had his rites been real, never had his

gathered company seemed so to respond and even to
invite. He lost himself in the large luster, which was
more and more what he had from the first wished it
to be—as dazzling as the vision of heaven in the mind
of a child. He wandered in the fields of light; he passed,
among the tall tapers, from tier to tier, from fire to
fire, from name to name, from the white intensity of one
clear emblem, of one saved soul, to another. It was in
the quiet sense of having saved his souls that his deep,
strange instinct rejoiced. This was no dim theological
rescue, no boon of a contingent world; they were saved
better than faith or works could save them, saved for
the warm world they had shrunk from dying to, for
actuality, for continuity, for the certainty of human remembrance.

By this time he had survived all his friends; the last
straight flame was three years old; there was no one
to add to the list. Over and over he called his roll, and
it appeared to him compact and complete. Where should
he put in another; where, if there were no other objection, would it stand in its place in the rank? He reflected,
with a want of sincerity of which he was quite conscious, that it would be difficult to determine that place.
More and more, besides, face to face with his little
legion, reading over endless histories, handling the
empty shells and playing with the silence—more and
more he could see that he had never introduced an alien.
He had had his great compassions, his indulgences—
there were cases in which they had been immense: but
what had his devotion after all been, if it hadn't been
fundamentally a respect? He was, however, himself surprised at his stiffness; by the end of the winter the
responsibility of it was what was uppermost in his
thoughts. The refrain had grown old to them, the plea
for just one more. There came a day when, for simple
exhaustion, if symmetry should really demand just one
more, he was ready to take symmetry into account.
Symmetry was harmony, and the idea of harmony began
to haunt him; he said to himself that harmony was of
course everything. He took, in fancy, his composition to
pieces, redistributing it into other lines, making other
juxtapositions and contrasts. He shifted this and that

candle; he made the spaces different; he effaced the disfigurement of a possible gap. There were subtle and complex relations, a scheme of cross reference, and moments in which he seemed to catch a glimpse of the void so sensible to the woman who wandered in exile or sat where he had seen her with the portrait of Acton Hague. Finally, in this way, he arrived at a conception of the total, the ideal, which left a clear opportunity for just another figure. "Just one more, to round it off; just one more, just one," continued to hum itself in his head. There was a strange confusion in the thought, for he felt the day to be near when he too should be one of the Others. What, in this case, would the Others matter to him, since they only mattered to the living? Even as one of the Dead, what would his altar matter to him, since his particular dream of keeping it up had melted away? What had harmony to do with the case, if his lights were all to be quenched? What he had hoped for was an instituted thing. He might perpetuate it on some other pretext, but his special meaning would have dropped. This meaning was to have lasted with the life of the one other person who understood it.

In March he had an illness during which he spent a fortnight in bed, and when he revived a little he was told of two things that had happened. One was that a lady, whose name was not known to the servants (she left none), had been three times to ask about him; the other was that in his sleep, and on an occasion when his mind evidently wandered, he was heard to murmur again and again: "Just one more—just one." As soon as he found himself able to go out, and before the doctor in attendance had pronounced him so, he drove to see the lady who had come to ask about him. She was not at home; but this gave him the opportunity, before his strength should fail again, to take his way to the church. He entered the church alone; he had declined, in a happy manner he possessed of being able to decline effectively, the company of his servant or of a nurse. He knew now perfectly what these good people thought; they had discovered his clandestine connection, the magnet that had drawn him for so many years, and doubtless attached a significance of their own to the odd words they had repeated to him. The nameless lady was the clandestine connection—a fact nothing could have made clearer than his indecent haste to rejoin her. He sank on his knees before his altar, and his head fell over on his hands. His weakness, his life's weariness, overtook him. It seemed to him he had come for the great surrender. At first he asked himself how he should get away; then, with the failing belief in the power, the very desire to move gradually left him. He had come, as he always came, to lose himself; the fields of light were still there to stray in; only this time, in straying, he would never come back. He had given himself to his Dead, and it was good; this time his Dead would keep him. He couldn't rise from his knees; he believed he should never rise again; all he could do was to lift his face and fix his eyes upon his lights. They looked unusually, strangely splendid, but the one that always drew him most had an unprecedented luster. It was the central voice of the choir, the glowing heart of the brightness, and on this occasion it seemed to expand, to spread great wings of flame. The whole altar flared—it dazzled and blinded; but the source of the vast radiance burned clearer than the rest; it gathered itself into form, and the form was human beauty and human charity; it was the far-off face of Mary Antrim. She smiled at him from the glory of heaven—she brought the glory down with her to take him. He bowed his head in submission, and at the same moment another wave rolled over him. Was it the quickening of joy to pain? In the midst of his joy, at any rate, he felt his buried face grow hot as with some communicated knowledge that had the force of a reproach. It suddenly made him contrast that very rapture with the bliss he had refused to another. This breath of the passion immortal was all that other had asked; the descent of Mary Antrim opened his spirit with a great compunctious throb for the descent of Acton Hague. It was as if Stransom had read what her eyes said to him.

After a moment he looked round him in a despair which made him feel as if the source of life were ebbing. The church had been empty—he was alone; but he wanted to have something done, to make a last appeal.

This idea gave him strength for an effort; he rose to his feet with a movement that made him turn, supporting himself by the back of a bench. Behind him was a prostrate figure, a figure he had seen before; a woman in deep mourning, bowed in grief or in prayer. He had seen her in other days—the first time he came into the church and he slightly wavered there, looking at her again till she seemed to become aware he had noticed her. She raised her head and met his eyes: the partner of his long worship was there. She looked across at him an instant with a face wondering and scared; he saw that he had given her an alarm. Then quickly rising, she came straight to him with both hands out.

"Then you *could* come? God sent you!" he murmured, with a happy smile.

"You're very ill—you shouldn't be here," she urged in anxious reply.

"God sent me, too, I think. I was ill when I came, but the sight of you does wonders." He held her hands, and they steadied and quickened him. "I've something to tell you."

"Don't tell me!" she tenderly pleaded; "let me tell you. This afternoon, by a miracle, the sweetest of miracles, the sense of our difference left me. I was out —I was near, thinking, wandering alone, when, on the spot, something changed in my heart. It's my confession —there it is. To come back, to come back on the instant—the idea gave me wings. It was as if I suddenly saw something—as if it all became possible. I could come for what you yourself came for: that was enough. So here I am. It's not for my own—that's over. But I'm here for *them*." And breathless, infinitely relieved by her low, precipitate explanation, she looked with eyes that reflected all its splendor at the magnificence of their altar.

"They're here for you," Stransom said, "they're present tonight as they've never been. They speak for you —don't you see?—in a passion of light—they sing out like a choir of angels. Don't you hear what they say?— they offer the very thing you asked of me."

"Don't talk of it—don't think of it; forget it!" She spoke in hushed supplication, and while the apprehension deepened in her eyes she disengaged one of her hands and passed an arm round him, to support him better, to help him to sink into a seat.

He let himself go, resting on her; he dropped upon the bench, and she fell on her knees beside him with his arm on her shoulder. So he remained an instant, staring up at his shrine. "They say there's a gap in the array—they say it's not full, complete. Just one more," he went on, softly—"isn't that what you wanted? Yes, one more, one more."

"Ah, no more—no more!" she wailed as if with a quick, new horror of it, under her breath.

"Yes, one more," he repeated simply; "just one!" And with this his head dropped on her shoulder; she felt that in his weakness he had fainted. But alone with him in the dusky church a great dread was on her of what might still happen, for his face had the whiteness of death.

THE TURN OF THE SCREW

❧

The story had held us, round the fire, sufficiently breathless, but except the obvious remark that it was gruesome, as, on Christmas Eve in an old house, a strange tale should essentially be, I remember no comment uttered till somebody happened to say that it was the only case he had met in which such a visitation had fallen on a child. The case, I may mention, was that of an apparition in just such an old house as had gathered us for the occasion—an appearance, of a dreadful kind, to a little boy sleeping in the room with his mother and waking her up in the terror of it; waking her not to dissipate his dread and soothe him to sleep again, but to encounter also, herself, before she had succeeded in doing so, the same sight that had shaken him. It was this observation that drew from Douglas—not immediately, but later in the evening—a reply that had the interesting consequence to which I call attention. Someone else told a story not particularly effective, which I saw he was not following. This I took for a sign that he had himself something to produce and that we should only have to wait. We waited in fact till two nights later; but that same evening, before we scattered, he brought out what was in his mind.

"I quite agree—in regard to Griffin's ghost, or whatever it was—that its appearing first to the little boy, at so tender an age, adds a particular touch. But it's not the first occurrence of its charming kind that I know to have involved a child. If the child gives the effect another turn of the screw, what do you say to *two* children——?"

"We say, of course," somebody exclaimed, "that they give two turns! Also that we want to hear about them."

I can see Douglas there before the fire, to which he had got up to present his back, looking down at his interlocutor with his hands in his pockets. "Nobody but me, till now, has ever heard. It's quite too horrible." This, naturally, was declared by several voices to give the thing the utmost price, and our friend, with quiet art, prepared his triumph by turning his eyes over the rest of us and going on: "It's beyond everything. Nothing at all that I know touches it."

"For sheer terror?" I remember asking.

He seemed to say it was not so simple as that; to be really at a loss how to qualify it. He passed his hand over his eyes, made a little wincing grimace. "For dreadful—dreadfulness!"

"Oh, how delicious!" cried one of the women.

He took no notice of her; he looked at me, but as if, instead of me, he saw what he spoke of. "For general uncanny ugliness and horror and pain."

"Well then," I said, "just sit right down and begin."

He turned round to the fire, gave a kick to a log, watched it an instant. Then as he faced us again: "I can't begin. I shall have to send to town." There was a unanimous groan at this, and much reproach; after which, in his preoccupied way, he explained. "The story's written. It's in a locked drawer—it has not been out for years. I could write to my man and enclose the key; he could send down the packet as he finds it." It was to me in particular that he appeared to propound this—appeared almost to appeal for aid not to hesitate. He had broken a thickness of ice, the formation of many a winter; had had his reasons for a long silence. The others resented postponement, but it was just his scruples that charmed me. I adjured him to write by the first post and to agree with us for an early hearing; then I asked him if the experience in question had been his own. To this his answer was prompt. "Oh, thank God, no!"

"And is the record yours? You took the thing down?"

"Nothing but the impression. I took that *here*"—he tapped his heart. "I've never lost it."

"Then your manuscript——?"

"Is in old, faded ink, and in the most beautiful hand." He hung fire again. "A woman's. She has been dead these twenty years. She sent me the pages in question before she died." They were all listening now, and of course there was somebody to be arch, or at any rate to draw the inference. But if he put the inference by without a smile it was also without irritation. "She was a most charming person, but she was ten years older than I. She was my sister's governess," he quietly said. "She was the most agreeable woman I've ever known in her position; she would have been worthy of any whatever. It was long ago, and this episode was long before. I was at Trinity, and I found her at home on my coming down the second summer. I was much there that year—it was a beautiful one; and we had, in her off-hours, some strolls and talks in the garden—talks in which she struck me as awfully clever and nice. Oh yes; don't grin: I liked her extremely and am glad to this day to think she liked me, too. If she hadn't she wouldn't have told me. She had never told anyone. It wasn't simply that she said so, but that I knew she hadn't. I was sure; I could see. You'll easily judge why when you hear."

"Because the thing had been such a scare?"

He continued to fix me. "You'll easily judge," he repeated: "*you* will."

I fixed him, too. "I see. She was in love."

He laughed for the first time. "You *are* acute. Yes, she was in love. That is, she had been. That came out—she couldn't tell her story without its coming out. I saw it, and she saw I saw it; but neither of us spoke of it. I remember the time and the place—the corner of the lawn, the shade of the great beeches and the long, hot summer afternoon. It wasn't a scene for a shudder; but oh——!" He quitted the fire and dropped back into his chair.

"You'll receive the packet Thursday morning?" I inquired.

"Probably not till the second post."

"Well then; after dinner——"

"You'll all meet me here?" He looked us round again. "Isn't anybody going?" It was almost the tone of hope.

"Everybody will stay!"

"I will—and I will!" cried the ladies whose departure had been fixed. Mrs. Griffin, however, expressed the need for a little more light. "Who was it she was in love with?"

"The story will tell," I took upon myself to reply.

"Oh, I can't wait for the story!"

"The story *won't* tell," said Douglas; "not in any literal, vulgar way."

"More's the pity, then. That's the only way I ever understand."

"Won't *you* tell, Douglas?" somebody else inquired.

He sprang to his feet again. "Yes—tomorrow. Now I must go to bed. Good night." And quickly catching up a candlestick, he left us slightly bewildered. From our end of the great brown hall we heard his step on the stair; whereupon Mrs. Griffin spoke. "Well, if I don't know who she was in love with, I know who *he* was."

"She was ten years older," said her husband.

"*Raison de plus*—at that age! But it's rather nice, his long reticence."

"Forty years!" Griffin put in.

"With this outbreak at last."

"The outbreak," I returned, "will make a tremendous occasion of Thursday night"; and everyone so agreed with me that, in the light of it, we lost all attention for everything else. The last story, however incomplete and like the mere opening of a serial, had been told; we handshook and "candlestuck," as somebody said, and went to bed.

I knew the next day that a letter containing the key had, by the first post, gone off to his London apartments; but in spite of—or perhaps just on account of—the eventual diffusion of this knowledge we quite let him alone till after dinner, till such an hour of the evening, in fact, as might best accord with the kind of emotion on which our hopes were fixed. Then he became as communicative as we could desire and indeed gave us his best reason for being so. We had it from him again before the fire in the hall, as we had had our mild wonders of the previous night. It appeared that the narrative he had promised to read us really required for a proper intelligence a few words of prologue. Let me say here distinctly, to have done with it, that this narrative, from an exact transcript of my own made much later, is what I shall presently give. Poor Douglas, before his death—when it was in sight—committed to me the manuscript that reached him on the third of these days and that, on the same spot, with immense effect, he began to read to our hushed little circle on the night of the fourth. The departing ladies who had said they would stay didn't, of course, thank heaven, stay: they departed, in consequence of arrangements made, in a rage of curiosity, as they professed, produced by the touches with which he had already worked us up. But that only made his little final auditory more compact and select, kept it, round the hearth, subject to a common thrill.

The first of these touches conveyed that the written statement took up the tale at a point after it had, in a manner, begun. The fact to be in possession of was therefore that his old friend, the youngest of several daughters of a poor country parson, had, at the age of twenty, on taking service for the first time in the schoolroom, come up to London, in trepidation, to answer in person an advertisement that had already placed her in brief correspondence with the advertiser. This person proved, on her presenting herself, for judgment, at a house in Harley Street, that impressed her as vast and imposing—this prospective patron proved a gentleman, a bachelor in the prime of life, such a figure as had never risen, save in a dream or an old novel, before a fluttered, anxious girl out of a Hampshire vicarage. One could easily fix his type; it never, happily, dies out. He was handsome and bold and pleasant, offhand and gay and kind. He struck her, inevitably, as gallant and splendid, but what took her most of all and gave her the courage she afterward showed was that he put the whole thing to her as a kind of favor, an obligation he should gratefully incur. She conceived him as rich, but as fearfully extravagant—saw him all in a glow of high fashion, of good looks, of expensive habits, of charming ways with women. He had for his own town residence a big house filled with the spoils of travel and the trophies of the chase; but it was to his country home, an old family place in Essex, that he wished her immediately to proceed.

He had been left, by the death of their parents in India, guardian to a small nephew and a small niece, children of a younger, a military brother, whom he had lost two years before. These children were, by the strangest of chances for a man in his position—a lone man without the right sort of experience or a grain of patience—very heavily on his hands. It had all been a great worry and, on his own part doubtless, a series of blunders, but he immensely pitied the poor chicks and had done all he could; had in particular sent them down to his other house, the proper place for them being of course the country, and kept them there, from the first, with the best people he could find to look after them, parting even with his own servants to wait on them and going down himself, whenever he might, to see how they were doing. The awkward thing was that they had practically no other relations and that his own affairs took up all his time. He had put them in possession of Bly, which was healthy and secure, and had placed at the head of their little establishment—but below stairs only—an excellent woman, Mrs. Grose, whom he was sure his visitor would like and who had formerly been maid to his mother. She was now housekeeper and was also acting for the time as superintendent to the little girl, of whom, without children of her own, she was, by good luck, extremely fond. There were plenty of people to help, but of course the young lady who should go down as governess would be in supreme authority. She would also have, in holidays, to look after the small boy, who had been for a term at school—young as he was to be sent, but what else could be done?—and who, as the holidays were about to begin, would be back from one day to the other. There had been for the two children at first a young lady whom they had had the misfortune to lose. She had done for them quite beautifully—she was a most respectable person—till her death, the great awkwardness of which had, precisely, left no alternative but the school for little Miles. Mrs. Grose, since then, in the way of manners and things, had done as she could for

Flora; and there were, further, a cook, a housemaid, a dairywoman, an old pony, an old groom, and an old gardener, all likewise thoroughly respectable.

So far had Douglas presented his picture when someone put a question. "And what did the former governess die of?—of so much respectability?"

Our friend's answer was prompt. "That will come out. I don't anticipate."

"Excuse me—I thought that was just what you *are* doing."

"In her successor's place," I suggested, "I should have wished to learn if the office brought with it——"

"Necessary danger to life?" Douglas completed my thought. "She did wish to learn, and she did learn. You shall hear tomorrow what she learned. Meanwhile, of course, the prospect struck her as slightly grim. She was young, untried, nervous: it was a vision of serious duties and little company, of really great loneliness. She hesitated—took a couple of days to consult and consider. But the salary offered much exceeded her modest measure, and on a second interview she faced the music, she engaged." And Douglas, with this, made a pause that, for the benefit of the company, moved me to throw in—

"The moral of which was of course the seduction exercised by the splendid young man. She succumbed to it."

He got up and, as he had done the night before, went to the fire, gave a stir to a log with his foot, then stood a moment with his back to us. "She saw him only twice."

"Yes, but that's just the beauty of her passion."

A little to my surprise, on this, Douglas turned round to me. "It *was* the beauty of it. There were others," he went on, "who hadn't succumbed. He told her frankly all his difficulty—that for several applicants the conditions had been prohibitive. They were, somehow, simply afraid. It sounded dull—it sounded strange; and all the more so because of his main condition."

"Which was——?"

"That she should never trouble him—but never, never: neither appeal nor complain nor write about anything; only meet all questions herself, receive all moneys from

his solicitor, take the whole thing over and let him alone.
She promised to do this, and she mentioned to me that
when, for a moment, disburdened, delighted, he held her
hand, thanking her for the sacrifice, she already felt rewarded."

"But was that all her reward?" one of the ladies asked.

"She never saw him again."

"Oh!" said the lady; which, as our friend immediately
left us again, was the only other word of importance
contributed to the subject till, the next night, by the corner of the hearth, in the best chair, he opened the faded
red cover of a thin old-fashioned gilt-edged album. The
whole thing took indeed more nights than one, but on the
first occasion the same lady put another question. "What
is your title?"

"I haven't one."

"Oh, *I* have!" I said. But Douglas, without heeding
me, had begun to read with a fine clearness that was like
a rendering to the ear of the beauty of his author's hand.

I

I remember the whole beginning as a succession of
flights and drops, a little seesaw of the right throbs and
the wrong. After rising, in town, to meet his appeal, I
had at all events a couple of very bad days—found myself doubtful again, felt indeed sure I had made a mistake. In this state of mind I spent the long hours of
bumping, swinging coach that carried me to the stopping
place at which I was to be met by a vehicle from the
house. This convenience, I was told, had been ordered,
and I found, toward the close of the June afternoon, a
commodious fly in waiting for me. Driving at that hour,
on a lovely day, through a country to which the summer
sweetness seemed to offer me a friendly welcome, my
fortitude mounted afresh and, as we turned into the avenue, encountered a reprieve that was probably but a

proof of the point to which it had sunk. I suppose I had expected, or had dreaded, something so melancholy that what greeted me was a good surprise. I remember as a most pleasant impression the broad, clear front, its open windows and fresh curtains and the pair of maids looking out; I remember the lawn and the bright flowers and the crunch of my wheels on the gravel and the clustered treetops over which the rooks circled and cawed in the golden sky. The scene had a greatness that made it a different affair from my own scant home, and there immediately appeared at the door, with a little girl in her hand, a civil person who dropped me as decent a curtsy as if I had been the mistress or a distinguished visitor. I had received in Harley Street a narrower notion of the place, and that, as I recalled it, made me think the proprietor still more of a gentleman, suggested that what I was to enjoy might be something beyond his promise.

I had no drop again till the next day, for I was carried triumphantly through the following hours by my introduction to the younger of my pupils. The little girl who accompanied Mrs. Grose appeared to me on the spot a creature so charming as to make it a great fortune to have to do with her. She was the most beautiful child I had ever seen, and I afterward wondered that my employer had not told me more of her. I slept little that night—I was too much excited; and this astonished me, too, I recollect, remained with me, adding to my sense of the liberality with which I was treated. The large, impressive room, one of the best in the house, the great state bed, as I almost felt it, the full, figured draperies, the long glasses in which, for the first time, I could see myself from head to foot, all struck me—like the extraordinary charm of my small charge—as so many things thrown in. It was thrown in as well, from the first moment, that I should get on with Mrs. Grose in a relation over which, on my way, in the coach, I fear I had rather brooded. The only thing indeed that in this early outlook might have made me shrink again was the clear circumstance of her being so glad to see me. I perceived within half an hour that she was so glad—stout, simple, plain, clean, wholesome woman—as to be positively on her guard against showing it too much. I wondered even

then a little why she should wish not to show it, and
that, with reflection, with suspicion, might of course have
made me uneasy.

But it was a comfort that there could be no uneasiness in a connection with anything so beatific as the radiant image of my little girl, the vision of whose angelic
beauty had probably more than anything else to do with
the restlessness that, before morning, made me several
times rise and wander about my room to take in the
whole picture and prospect; to watch, from my open
window, the faint summer dawn, to look at such portions
of the rest of the house as I could catch, and to listen,
while, in the fading dusk, the first birds began to twitter,
for the possible recurrence of a sound or two, less natural and not without, but within, that I had fancied I
heard. There had been a moment when I believed I recognized, faint and far, the cry of a child; there had been
another when I found myself just consciously starting as
at the passage, before my door, of a light footstep. But
these fancies were not marked enough not to be thrown
off, and it is only in the light, or the gloom, I should
rather say, of other and subsequent matters that they
now come back to me. To watch, teach, "form" little
Flora would too evidently be the making of a happy and
useful life. It had been agreed between us downstairs
that after this first occasion I should have her as a matter of course at night, her small white bed being already
arranged, to that end, in my room. What I had undertaken was the whole care of her, and she had remained,
just this last time, with Mrs. Grose only as an effect of
our consideration for my inevitable strangeness and her
natural timidity. In spite of this timidity—which the
child herself, in the oddest way in the world, had been
perfectly frank and brave about, allowing it, without a
sign of uncomfortable consciousness, with the deep,
sweet serenity indeed of one of Raphael's holy infants,
to be discussed, to be imputed to her, and to determine
us—I felt quite sure she would presently like me. It was
part of what I already liked Mrs. Grose herself for, the
pleasure I could see her feel in my admiration and wonder as I sat at supper with four tall candles and with my
pupil, in a high chair and a bib, brightly facing me, be-

tween them, over bread and milk. There were naturally things that in Flora's presence could pass between us only as prodigious and gratified looks, obscure and roundabout allusions.

"And the little boy—does he look like her? Is he too so very remarkable?"

One wouldn't flatter a child. "Oh, miss, *most* remarkable. If you think well of this one!"—and she stood there with a plate in her hand, beaming at our companion, who looked from one of us to the other with placid heavenly eyes that contained nothing to check us.

"Yes; if I do——?"

"You *will* be carried away by the little gentleman!"

"Well, that, I think, is what I came for—to be carried away. I'm afraid, however," I remember feeling the impulse to add, "I'm rather easily carried away. I was carried away in London!"

I can still see Mrs. Grose's broad face as she took this in. "In Harley Street?"

"In Harley Street."

"Well, miss, you're not the first—and you won't be the last."

"Oh, I've no pretension," I could laugh, "to being the only one. My other pupil, at any rate, as I understand, comes back tomorrow?"

"Not tomorrow—Friday, miss. He arrives, as you did, by the coach, under care of the guard, and is to be met by the same carriage."

I forthwith expressed that the proper as well as the pleasant and friendly thing would be therefore that on the arrival of the public conveyance I should be in waiting for him with his little sister; an idea in which Mrs. Grose concurred so heartily that I somehow took her manner as a kind of comforting pledge—never falsified, thank heaven!—that we should on every question be quite at one. Oh, she was glad I was there!

What I felt the next day was, I suppose, nothing that could be fairly called a reaction from the cheer of my arrival; it was probably at the most only a slight oppression produced by a fuller measure of the scale, as I walked round them, gazed up at them, took them in, of my new circumstances. They had, as it were, an extent and mass for which I had not been prepared and in the presence of which I found myself, freshly, a little scared as well as a little proud. Lessons, in this agitation, certainly suffered some delay; I reflected that my first duty was, by the gentlest arts I could contrive, to win the child into the sense of knowing me. I spent the day with her out-of-doors; I arranged with her, to her great satisfaction, that it should be she, she only, who might show me the place. She showed it step by step and room by room and secret by secret, with droll, delightful, childish talk about it and with the result, in half an hour, of our becoming immense friends. Young as she was, I was struck, throughout our little tour, with her confidence and courage with the way, in empty chambers and dull corridors, on crooked staircases that made me pause and even on the summit of an old machicolated square tower that made me dizzy, her morning music, her disposition to tell me so many more things than she asked, rang out and led me on. I have not seen Bly since the day I left it, and I daresay that to my older and more informed eyes it would now appear sufficiently contracted. But as my little conductress, with her hair of gold and her frock of blue, danced before me round corners and pattered down passages, I had the view of a castle of romance inhabited by a rosy sprite, such a place as would somehow, for diversion of the young idea, take all color out of storybooks and fairytales. Wasn't it just a storybook over which I had fallen adoze and adream? No; it was a big, ugly, antique, but convenient house, embodying a few features of a building still older, half-replaced and half-utilized, in which I had the fancy of our being almost as lost as a handful of passengers in a great drifting ship. Well, I was, strangely, at the helm!

II

This came home to me when, two days later, I drove over with Flora to meet, as Mrs. Grose said, the little gentleman; and all the more for an incident that, presenting itself the second evening, had deeply disconcerted me. The first day had been, on the whole, as I have expressed, reassuring; but I was to see it wind up in keen apprehension. The postbag, that evening—it came late—contained a letter for me, which, however, in the hand of my employer, I found to be composed but of a few words enclosing another, addressed to himself, with a seal still unbroken. "This, I recognize, is from the headmaster, and the headmaster's an awful bore. Read him, please; deal with him; but mind you don't report. Not a word. I'm off!" I broke the seal with a great effort —so great a one that I was a long time coming to it; took the unopened missive at last up to my room and only attacked it just before going to bed. I had better have let it wait till morning, for it gave me a second sleepless night. With no counsel to take, the next day, I was full of distress; and it finally got so the better of me that I determined to open myself at least to Mrs. Grose.

"What does it mean? The child's dismissed his school."

She gave me a look that I remarked at the moment; then, visibly, with a quick blankness, seemed to try to take it back. "But aren't they all——?"

"Sent home—yes. But only for the holidays. Miles may never go back at all."

Consciously, under my attention, she reddened. "They won't take him?"

"They absolutely decline."

At this she raised her eyes, which she had turned from me; I saw them fill with good tears. "What has he done?"

I hesitated; then I judged best simply to hand her my letter—which, however, had the effect of making her, without taking it, simply put her hands behind her. She shook her bead sadly. "Such things are not for me, miss."

My counselor couldn't read! I winced at my mistake, which I attenuated as I could, and opened my letter again to repeat it to her; then, faltering in the act and folding it up once more, I put it back in my pocket. "Is he really *bad?*"

The tears were still in her eyes. "Do the gentlemen say so?"

"They go into no particulars. They simply express their regret that it should be impossible to keep him. That can have only one meaning." Mrs. Grose listened with dumb emotion; she forbore to ask me what this meaning might be; so that, presently, to put the thing with some coherence and with the mere aid of her presence to my own mind, I went on: "That he's an injury to the others."

At this, with one of the quick turns of simple folk, she suddenly flamed up. "Master Miles! *him* an injury?"

There was such a flood of good faith in it that, though I had not yet seen the child, my very fears made me jump to the absurdity of the idea. I found myself, to meet my friend the better, offering it, on the spot, sarcastically. "To his poor little innocent mates!"

"It's too dreadful," cried Mrs. Grose, "to say such cruel things! Why, he's scarce ten years old."

"Yes, yes; it would be incredible."

She was evidently grateful for such a profession. "See him, miss, first. *Then* believe it!" I felt forthwith a new impatience to see him; it was the beginning of a curiosity that, for all the next hours, was to deepen almost to pain. Mrs. Grose was aware, I could judge, of what she had produced in me, and she followed it up with assurance. "You might as well believe it of the little lady. Bless her," she added the next moment—"*look* at her!"

I turned and saw that Flora, whom, ten minutes before, I had established in the schoolroom with a sheet of white paper, a pencil, and a copy of nice "round o's," now presented herself to view at the open door. She expressed in her little way an extraordinary detachment from disagreeable duties, looking to me, however, with a great childish light that seemed to offer it as a mere result of the affection she had conceived for my person,

which had rendered necessary that she should follow me.
I needed nothing more than this to feel the full force of
Mrs. Grose's comparison, and, catching my pupil in my
arms, covered her with kisses in which there was a sob
of atonement.

Nonetheless, the rest of the day I watched for further
occasion to approach my colleague, especially as, toward evening, I began to fancy she rather sought to
avoid me. I overtook her, I remember, on the staircase;
we went down together, and at the bottom I detained
her, holding her there with a hand on her arm. "I take
what you said to me at noon as a declaration that *you've*
never known him to be bad."

She threw back her head; she had clearly, by this
time, and very honestly, adopted an attitude. "Oh, never
known him—I don't pretend *that!*"

I was upset again. "Then you *have* known him——?"

"Yes indeed, miss, thank God!"

On reflection I accepted this. "You mean that a boy
who never is——?"

"Is no boy for *me!*"

I held her tighter. "You like them with the spirit to be
naughty?" Then, keeping pace with her answer, "So do
I!" I eagerly brought out. "But not to the degree to contaminate——"

"To contaminate?"—my big word left her at a loss. I
explained it. "To corrupt."

She stared, taking my meaning in; but it produced in
her an odd laugh. "Are you afraid he'll corrupt *you?*"
She put the question with such a fine bold humor that,
with a laugh, a little silly doubtless, to match her own, I
gave way for the time to the apprehension of ridicule.

But the next day, as the hour for my drive approached,
I cropped up in another place. "What was the lady who
was here before?"

"The last governess? She was also young and pretty—
almost as young and almost as pretty, miss, even as you."

"Ah, then, I hope her youth and her beauty helped
her!" I recollect throwing off. "He seems to like us young
and pretty!"

"Oh, he *did*," Mrs. Grose assented: "it was the way he
liked everyone!" She had no sooner spoken indeed than

she caught herself up. "I mean that's *his* way—the master's."

I was struck. "But of whom did you speak first?"

She looked blank, but she colored. "Why, of *him*."

"Of the master?"

"Of who else?"

There was so obviously no one else that the next moment I had lost my impression of her having accidentally said more than she meant; and I merely asked what I wanted to know. "Did *she* see anything in the boy——?"

"That wasn't right? She never told me."

I had a scruple, but I overcame it. "Was she careful—particular?"

Mrs. Grose appeared to try to be conscientious. "About some things—yes."

"But not about all?"

Again she considered. "Well, miss—she's gone. I won't tell tales."

"I quite understand your feeling," I hastened to reply; but I thought it, after an instant, not opposed to this concession to pursue: "Did she die here?"

"No—she went off."

I don't know what there was in this brevity of Mrs. Grose's that struck me as ambiguous. "Went off to die?" Mrs. Grose looked straight out of the window, but I felt that, hypothetically, I had a right to know what young persons engaged for Bly were expected to do. "She was taken ill, you mean, and went home?"

"She was not taken ill, so far as appeared, in this house. She left it, at the end of the year, to go home, as she said, for a short holiday, to which the time she had put in had certainly given her a right. We had then a young woman—a nursemaid who had stayed on and who was a good girl and clever; and *she* took the children altogether for the interval. But our young lady never came back, and at the very moment I was expecting her I heard from the master that she was dead."

I turned this over. "But of what?"

"He never told me! But please, miss," said Mrs. Grose, "I must get to my work."

III

Her thus turning her back on me was fortunately not, for my just preoccupations, a snub that could check the growth of our mutual esteem. We met, after I had brought home little Miles, more intimately than ever on the ground of my stupefaction, my general emotion: so monstrous was I then ready to pronounce it that such a child as had now been revealed to me should be under an interdict. I was a little late on the scene, and I felt, as he stood wistfully looking out for me before the door of the inn at which the coach had put him down, that I had seen him, on the instant, without and within, in the great glow of freshness, the same positive fragrance of purity, in which I had, from the first moment, seen his little sister. He was incredibly beautiful, and Mrs. Grose had put her finger on it: everything but a sort of passion of tenderness for him was swept away by his presence. What I then and there took him to my heart for was something divine that I have never found to the same degree in any child—his indescribable little air of knowing nothing in the world but love. It would have been impossible to carry a bad name with a greater sweetness of innocence, and by the time I had got back to Bly with him I remained merely bewildered—so far, that is, as I was not outraged by the sense of the horrible letter locked up in my room, in a drawer. As soon as I could compass a private word with Mrs. Grose I declared to her that it was grotesque.

She promptly understood me. "You mean the cruel charge——?"

"It doesn't live an instant. My dear woman, *look* at him!"

She smiled at my pretention to have discovered his charm. "I assure you, miss, I do nothing else! What will you say, then?" she immediately added.

"In answer to the letter?" I had made up my mind. "Nothing."

"And to his uncle?"

I was incisive. "Nothing."

"And to the boy himself?"

I was wonderful. "Nothing."

She gave with her apron a great wipe to her mouth. "Then I'll stand by you. We'll see it out."

"We'll see it out!" I ardently echoed, giving her my hand to make it a vow.

She held me there a moment, then whisked up her apron again with her detached hand. "Would you mind, miss, if I used the freedom—"

"To kiss me? No!" I took the good creature in my arms and, after we had embraced like sisters, felt still more fortified and indignant.

This, at all events, was for the time: a time so full that, as I recall the way it went, it reminds me of all the art I now need to make it a little distinct. What I look back at with amazement is the situation I accepted. I had undertaken, with my companion, to see it out, and I was under a charm, apparently, that could smooth away the extent and the far and difficult connections of such an effort. I was lifted aloft on a great wave of infatuation and pity. I found it simple, in my ignorance, my confusion, and perhaps my conceit, to assume that I could deal with a boy whose education for the world was all on the point of beginning. I am unable even to remember at this day what proposal I framed for the end of his holidays and the resumption of his studies. Lessons with me, indeed, that charming summer, we all had a theory that he was to have; but I now feel that, for weeks, the lessons must have been rather my own. I learned something—at first, certainly—that had not been one of the teachings of my small, smothered life; learned to be amused, and even amusing, and not to think for the morrow. It was the first time, in a manner, that I had known space and air and freedom, all the music of summer and all the mystery of nature. And then there was consideration—and consideration was sweet. Oh, it was a trap—not designed, but deep—to my imagination, to my delicacy, perhaps to my vanity; to whatever, in me, was

most excitable. The best way to picture it all is to say
that I was off my guard. They gave me so little trouble—
they were of a gentleness so extraordinary. I used to
speculate—but even this with a dim disconnectedness—
as to how the rough future (for all futures are rough!)
would handle them and might bruise them. They had the
bloom of health and happiness; and yet, as if I had been
in charge of a pair of little grandees, of princes of the
blood, for whom everything, to be right, would have to
be enclosed and protected, the only form that, in my
fancy, the afteryears could take for them was that of a
romantic, a really royal extension of the garden and the
park. It may be, of course, above all, that what suddenly
broke into this gives the previous time a charm of stillness—that hush in which something gathers or crouches.
The change was actually like the spring of a beast.

In the first weeks the days were long; they often, at
their finest, gave me what I used to call my own hour, the
hour when, for my pupils, teatime and bedtime having
come and gone, I had, before my final retirement, a small
interval alone. Much as I liked my companions, this hour
was the thing in the day I liked most; and I liked it
best of all when, as the light faded—or rather, I should
say, the day lingered and the last calls of the last birds
sounded, in a flushed sky, from the old trees—I could
take a turn into the grounds and enjoy, almost with a
sense of property that amused and flattered me, the
beauty and dignity of the place. It was a pleasure at these
moments to feel myself tranquil and justified; doubtless,
perhaps, also to reflect that by my discretion, my quiet
good sense and general high propriety, I was giving
pleasure—if he ever thought of it!—to the person to
whose pressure I had responded. What I was doing was
what he had earnestly hoped and directly asked of me,
and that I could, after all, do it proved even a greater
joy than I had expected. I daresay I fancied myself, in
short, a remarkable young woman and took comfort in
the faith that this would more publicly appear. Well, I
needed to be remarkable to offer a front to the remarkable things that presently gave their first sign.

It was plump, one afternoon, in the middle of my
very hour: the children were tucked away, and I had

come out for my stroll. One of the thoughts that, as I
don't in the least shrink now from noting, used to be with
me in these wanderings was that it would be as charming
as a charming story suddenly to meet someone. Someone
would appear there at the turn of a path and would
stand before me and smile and approve. I didn't ask
more than that—I only asked that he should *know;*
and the only way to be sure he knew would be to see it,
and the kind light of it, in his handsome face. That was
exactly present to me—by which I mean the face was—
when, on the first of these occasions, at the end of a
long June day, I stopped short on emerging from one of
the plantations and coming into view of the house. What
arrested me on the spot—and with a shock much greater
than any vision had allowed for—was the sense that my
imagination had, in a flash, turned real. He did stand
there!—but high up, beyond the lawn and at the very top
of the tower to which, on that first morning, little Flora
had conducted me. This tower was one of a pair—
square, incongruous, crenelated structures—that were
distinguished, for some reason, though I could see little
difference, as the new and the old. They flanked opposite
ends of the house and were probably architectural ab-
surdities, redeemed in a measure indeed by not being
wholly disengaged nor of a height too pretentious, dating,
in their gingerbread antiquity, from a romantic revival
that was already a respectable past. I admired them, had
fancies about them, for we could all profit in a degree,
especially when they loomed through the dusk, by the
grandeur of their actual battlements; yet it was not at
such an elevation that the figure I had so often invoked
seemed most in place.

It produced in me, this figure, in the clear twilight, I
remember, two distinct gasps of emotion, which were,
sharply, the shock of my first and that of my second
surprise. My second was a violent perception of the mistake of my first: the man who met my eyes was not the
person I had precipitately supposed. There came to me
thus a bewilderment of vision of which, after these years,
there is no living view that I can hope to give. An unknown man in a lonely place is a permitted object of fear
to a young woman privately bred; and the figure that

faced me was—a few more seconds assured me—as little anyone else I knew as it was the image that had been in my mind. I had not seen it in Harley Street—I had not seen it anywhere. The place, moreover, in the strangest way in the world, had, on the instant, and by the very fact of its appearance, become a solitude. To me at least, making my statement here with a deliberation with which I have never made it, the whole feeling of the moment returns. It was as if, while I took in—what I did take in —all the rest of the scene had been stricken with death. I can hear again, as I write, the intense hush in which the sounds of evening dropped. The rooks stopped cawing in the golden sky, and the friendly hour lost, for the minute, all its voice. But there was no other change in nature, unless indeed it were a change that I saw with a stranger sharpness. The gold was still in the sky, the clearness in the air, and the man who looked at me over the battlements was as definite as a picture in a frame. That's how I thought, with extraordinary quickness, of each person that he might have been and that he was not. We were confronted across our distance quite long enough for me to ask myself with intensity who then he was and to feel, as an effect of my inability to say, a wonder that in a few instants more became intense.

The great question, or one of these, is, afterward, I know, with regard to certain matters, the question of how long they have lasted. Well, this matter of mine, think what you will of it, lasted while I caught at a dozen possibilities, none of which made a difference for the better, that I could see, in there having been in the house—and for how long, above all?—a person of whom I was in ignorance. It lasted while I just bridled a little with the sense that my office demanded that there should be no such ignorance and no such person. It lasted while this visitant, at all events—and there was a touch of the strange freedom, as I remember, in the sign of familiarity of his wearing no hat—seemed to fix me, from his position, with just the question, just the scrutiny through the fading light, that his own presence provoked. We were too far apart to call to each other, but there was a moment at which, at shorter range, some challenge between us, breaking the hush, would have been the right result

of our straight mutual stare. He was in one of the
angles, the one away from the house, very erect, as it
struck me, and with both hands on the ledge. So I saw
him as I see the letters I form on this page; then, exactly,
after a minute, as if to add to the spectacle, he slowly
changed his place—passed, looking at me hard all the
while, to the opposite corner of the platform. Yes, I had
the sharpest sense that during this transit he never took
his eyes from me, and I can see at this moment the way
his hand, as he went, passed from one of the crenelations
to the next. He stopped at the other corner, but less
long, and even as he turned away still markedly fixed me.
He turned away; that was all I knew.

IV

It was not that I didn't wait, on this occasion, for
more, for I was rooted as deeply as I was shaken. Was
there a "secret" at Bly—a mystery of Udolpho or an insane, an unmentionable relative kept in unsuspected confinement? I can't say how long I turned it over, or how
long, in a confusion of curiosity and dread, I remained
where I had had my collision; I only recall that when I
re-entered the house darkness had quite closed in. Agitation, in the interval, certainly had held me and driven me,
for I must, in circling about the place, have walked three
miles; but I was to be, later on, so much more overwhelmed that this mere dawn of alarm was a comparatively human chill. The most singular part of it, in fact—
singular as the rest had been—was the part I became, in
the hall, aware of in meeting Mrs. Grose. This picture
comes back to me in the general train—the impression,
as I received it on my return, of the wide white panelled
space, bright in the lamplight and with its portraits and
red carpet, and of the good surprised look of my friend,
which immediately told me she had missed me. It came
to me straightway, under her contact, that, with plain

heartiness, mere relieved anxiety at my appearance, she knew nothing whatever that could bear upon the incident I had there ready for her. I had not suspected in advance that her comfortable face would pull me up, and I somehow measured the importance of what I had seen by my thus finding myself hesitate to mention it. Scarce anything in the whole history seems to me so odd as this fact that my real beginning of fear was one, as I may say, with the instinct of sparing my companion. On the spot, accordingly, in the pleasant hall and with her eyes on me, I, for a reason that I couldn't then have phrased, achieved an inward resolution—offered a vague pretext for my lateness and, with the plea of the beauty of the night and of the heavy dew and wet feet, went as soon as possible to my room.

Here it was another affair; here, for many days after, it was a queer affair enough. There were hours, from day to day—or at least there were moments, snatched even from clear duties—when I had to shut myself up to think. It was not so much yet that I was more nervous than I could bear to be as that I was remarkably afraid of becoming so; for the truth I had now to turn over was, simply and clearly, the truth that I could arrive at no account whatever of the visitor with whom I had been so inexplicably and yet, as it seemed to me, so intimately concerned. It took little time to see that I could sound without forms of inquiry and without exciting remark any domestic complication. The shock I had suffered must have sharpened all my senses; I felt sure, at the end of three days and as the result of mere closer attention, that I had not been practiced upon by the servants nor made the object of any "game." Of whatever it was that I knew, nothing was known around me. There was but one sane inference: someone had taken a liberty rather gross. That was what, repeatedly, I dipped into my room and locked the door to say to myself. We had been, collectively, subject to an intrusion; some unscrupulous traveler, curious in old houses, had made his way in unobserved, enjoyed the prospect from the best point of view, and then stolen out as he came. If he had given me such a bold hard stare, that was but a part of his indiscretion. The good thing, after all, was that we should surely see no more of him.

This was not so good a thing, I admit, as not to leave me to judge that what, essentially, made nothing else much signify was simply my charming work. My charming work was just my life with Miles and Flora, and through nothing could I so like it as through feeling that I could throw myself into it in trouble. The attraction of my small charges was a constant joy, leading me to wonder afresh at the vanity of my original fears, the distaste I had begun by entertaining for the probable gray prose of my office. There was to be no gray prose, it appeared, and no long grind; so how could work not be charming that presented itself as daily beauty? It was all the romance of the nursery and the poetry of the school-room. I don't mean by this, of course, that we studied only fiction and verse; I mean I can express no otherwise the sort of interest my companions inspired. How can I describe that except by saying that instead of growing used to them—and it's a marvel for a governess: I call the sisterhood to witness!—I made constant fresh discoveries. There was one direction, assuredly, in which these discoveries stopped: deep obscurity continued to cover the region of the boy's conduct at school. It had been promptly given me, I have noted, to face that mystery without a pang. Perhaps even it would be nearer the truth to say that—without a word—he himself had cleared it up. He had made the whole charge absurd. My conclusion bloomed there with the real rose flush of his innocence: he was only too fine and fair for the little horrid, unclean school world, and he had paid a price for it. I reflected acutely that the sense of such differences, such superiorities of quality, always, on the part of the majority—which could include even stupid, sordid head-masters—turns infallibly to the vindictive.

Both the children had a gentleness (it was their only fault, and it never made Miles a muff) that kept them—how shall I express it?—almost impersonal and certainly quite unpunishable. They were like the cherubs of the anecdote, who had—morally, at any rate—nothing to whack! I remember feeling with Miles in especial as if he had had, as it were, no history. We expect of a small child a scant one, but there was in this beautiful little boy something extraordinarily sensitive, yet extraordinarily happy, that, more than in any creature of his age I have seen, struck me as beginning anew each day. He had never for a second suffered. I took this as a direct disproof of his having really been chastised. If he had been wicked he would have "caught" it, and I should have caught it by the rebound—I should have found the trace. I found nothing at all, and he was therefore an angel. He never spoke of his school, never mentioned a comrade or a master; and I, for my part, was quite too much disgusted to allude to them. Of course I was under the spell, and the wonderful part is that, even at the time, I perfectly knew I was. But I gave myself up to it; it was an antidote to any pain, and I had more pains than one. I was in receipt in these days of disturbing letters from home, where things were not going well. But with my children, what things in the world mattered? That was the question I used to put to my scrappy retirements. I was dazzled by their loveliness.

There was a Sunday—to get on—when it rained with such force and for so many hours that there could be no procession to church; in consequence of which, as the day declined, I had arranged with Mrs. Grose that, should the evening show improvement, we would attend together the late service. The rain happily stopped, and I prepared for our walk, which, through the park and by the good road to the village, would be a matter of twenty minutes. Coming downstairs to meet my colleague in the hall, I remembered a pair of gloves that had required three stitches and that had received them—with a publicity perhaps not edifying—while I sat with the children at their tea, served on Sundays, by exception, in that cold, clean temple of mahogany and brass, the "grown-up" dining room. The gloves had been dropped there, and I turned in to recover them. The day was gray enough, but the afternoon light still lingered, and it enabled me, on crossing the threshold, not only to recognize, on a chair near the wide window, then closed, the articles I wanted, but to become aware of a person on the other side of the window and looking straight in. One step into the room had sufficed; my vision was instantaneous; it was all there. The person looking straight in was the person who had already appeared to me. He appeared thus again with I won't say greater distinctness, for that was impossible, but with a nearness that represented a forward stride in our intercourse and made me, as I met him, catch my breath and turn cold. He was the same—he was the same, and seen, this time, as he had been seen before, from the waist up, the window, though the dining room was on the ground floor, not going down to the terrace on which he stood. His face was close to the glass, yet the effect of this better view was, strangely, only to show me how intense the former had been. He remained but a few seconds—long enough to convince me he also saw and recognized; but it was as if I had been looking at him for years and had known him always. Something, however, happened this time that had not happened before; his stare into my face, through the glass and across the room, was as deep and hard as then, but it quitted me for a moment during which I could still watch it, see it fix successively several other things. On the spot there came to me the added shock of a certitude that it was not for me he had come there. He had come for someone else.

The flash of this knowledge—for it was knowledge in the midst of dread—produced in me the most extraordinary effect, started, as I stood there, a sudden vibration of duty and courage. I say courage because I was beyond all doubt already far gone. I bounded straight out of the door again, reached that of the house, got, in an instant, upon the drive, and, passing along the terrace as fast as I could rush, turned a corner and came full in sight. But it was in sight of nothing now—my visitor had vanished. I stopped, I almost dropped, with the real relief of this; but I took in the whole scene—I gave him time to reappear. I call it time, but how long was it? I can't speak to the purpose today of the duration of these things. That kind of measure must have left me: they couldn't have lasted as they actually appeared to me to last. The terrace and the whole place, the lawn and the garden beyond it, all I could see of the park, were empty with a great emptiness. There were shrubberies and big trees, but I remember the clear assurance

I felt that none of them concealed him. He was there or
was not there: not there if I didn't see him. I got hold of
this; then, instinctively, instead of returning as I had
come, went to the window. It was confusedly present
to me that I ought to place myself where he had stood.
I did so; I applied my face to the pane and looked, as
he had looked, into the room. As if, at this moment, to
show me exactly what his range had been, Mrs. Grose,
as I had done for himself just before, came in from the
hall. With this I had the full image of a repetition of
what had already occurred. She saw me as I had seen
my own visitant; she pulled up short as I had done; I
gave her something of the shock that I had received.
She turned white, and this made me ask myself if I had
blanched as much. She stared, in short, and retreated
on just *my* lines, and I knew she had then passed out
and come round to me and that I should presently meet
her. I remained where I was, and while I waited I thought
of more things than one. But there's only one I take
space to mention. I wondered why *she* should be scared.

V

Oh, she let me know as soon as, round the corner of
the house, she loomed again into view. "What in the name
of goodness is the matter——?" She was now flushed
and out of breath.

I said nothing till she came quite near. "With me?" I
must have made a wonderful face. "Do I show it?"

"You're as white as a sheet. You look awful."

I considered; I could meet on this, without scruple,
any innocence. My need to respect the bloom of Mrs.
Grose's had dropped, without a rustle, from my shoulders, and if I wavered for the instant it was not with
what I kept back. I put out my hand to her and she
took it; I held her hard a little, liking to feel her close
to me. There was a kind of support in the shy heave of

her surprise. "You came for me for church, of course, but I can't go."

"Has anything happened?"

"Yes. You must know now. Did I look very queer?"

"Through this window? Dreadful!"

"Well," I said, "I've been frightened." Mrs. Grose's eyes expressed plainly that *she* had no wish to be, yet also that she knew too well her place not to be ready to share with me any marked inconvenience. Oh, it was quite settled that she *must* share! "Just what you saw from the dining room a minute ago was the effect of that. What *I* saw—just before—was much worse."

Her hand tightened. "What was it?"

"An extraordinary man. Looking in."

"What extraordinary man?"

"I haven't the least idea."

Mrs. Grose gazed round us in vain. "Then where is he gone?"

"I know still less."

"Have you seen him before?"

"Yes—once. On the old tower."

She could, only look at me harder. "Do you mean he's a stranger?"

"Oh, very much!"

"Yet you didn't tell me?"

"No—for reasons. But now that you've guessed——"

Mrs. Grose's round eyes encountered this charge. "Ah, I haven't guessed!" she said very simply. "How can I if *you* don't imagine?"

"I don't in the very least."

"You've seen him nowhere but on the tower?"

"And on this spot just now."

Mrs. Grose looked round again. "What was he doing on the tower?"

"Only standing there and looking down at me."

She thought a minute. "Was he a gentleman?"

I found I had no need to think. "No." She gazed in deeper wonder. "No."

"Then nobody about the place? Nobody from the village?"

"Nobody—nobody. I didn't tell you, but I made sure."

She breathed a vague relief: this was, oddly, so much

to the good. It only went indeed a little way. "But if he isn't a gentleman——"

"What *is* he? He's a horror."

"A horror?"

"He's—God help me if I know *what* he is!"

Mrs. Grose looked round once more; she fixed her eyes on the duskier distance, then, pulling herself together, turned to me with abrupt inconsequence. "It's time we should be at church."

"Oh, I'm not fit for church!"

"Won't it do you good?"

"It won't do *them*——!" I nodded at the house.

"The children?"

"I can't leave them now."

"You're afraid——?"

I spoke boldly. "I'm afraid of *him*."

Mrs. Grose's large face showed me, at this, for the first time, the faraway faint glimmer of a consciousness more acute: I somehow made out in it the delayed dawn of an idea I myself had not given her and that was as yet quite obscure to me. It comes back to me that I thought instantly of this as something I could get from her; and I felt it to be connected with the desire she presently showed to know more. "When was it—on the tower?"

"About the middle of the month. At this same hour."

"Almost at dark," said Mrs. Grose.

"Oh, no, not nearly. I saw him as I see you."

"Then how did he get in?"

"And how did he get out?" I laughed. "I had no opportunity to ask him! This evening, you see," I pursued, "he has not been able to get in."

"He only peeps?"

"I hope it will be confined to that!" She had now let go my hand; she turned away a little. I waited an instant; then I brought out: "Go to church. Goodbye. I must watch."

Slowly she faced me again. "Do you fear for them?"

We met in another long look. "Don't *you?*" Instead of answering she came nearer to the window and, for a minute, applied her face to the glass. "You see how he could see," I meanwhile went on.

She didn't move. "How long was he here?"

"Till I came out. I came to meet him."

Mrs. Grose at last turned round, and there was still more in her face. "*I* couldn't have come out."

"Neither could I!" I laughed again. "But I did come. I have my duty."

"So have I mine," she replied; after which she added: "What is he like?"

"I've been dying to tell you. But he's like nobody."

"Nobody?" she echoed.

"He has no hat." Then seeing in her face that she already, in this, with a deeper dismay, found a touch of picture, I quickly added stroke to stroke. "He has red hair, very red, close-curling, and a pale face, long in shape, with straight, good features and little, rather queer whiskers that are as red as his hair. His eyebrows are, somehow, darker; they look particularly arched and as if they might move a good deal. His eyes are sharp, strange—awfully; but I only know clearly that they're rather small and very fixed. His mouth's wide, and his lips are thin, and except for his little whiskers he's quite clean-shaven. He gives me a sort of sense of looking like an actor."

"An actor!" It was impossible to resemble one less, at least, than Mrs. Grose at that moment.

"I've never seen one, but so I suppose them. He's tall, active, erect," I continued, "but never—no, never! —a gentleman."

My companion's face had blanched as I went on; her round eyes started and her mild mouth gaped. "A gentleman?" she gasped, confounded, stupefied: "a gentleman *he*?"

"You know him then?"

She visibly tried to hold herself. "But he *is* handsome?"

I saw the way to help her. "Remarkably!"

"And dressed——?"

"In somebody's clothes. They're smart, but they're not his own."

She broke into a breathless affirmative groan: "They're the master's!"

I caught it up. "You *do* know him?"

She faltered but a second. "Quint!" she cried.

"Quint?"

"Peter Quint—his own man, his valet, when he was here!"

"When the master was?"

Gaping still, but meeting me, she pieced it all together. "He never wore his hat, but he did wear—well, there were waistcoats missed. They were both here—last year. Then the master went, and Quint was alone."

I followed, but halting a little. "Alone?"

"Alone with *us*." Then, as from a deeper depth, "In charge," she added.

"And what became of him?"

She hung fire so long that I was still more mystified. "He went, too," she brought out at last.

"Went where?"

Her expression, at this, became extraordinary. "God knows where! He died."

"Died?" I almost shrieked.

She seemed fairly to square herself, plant herself more firmly to utter the wonder of it. "Yes. Mr. Quint is dead."

VI

It took of course more than that particular passage to place us together in presence of what we had now to live with as we could—my dreadful liability to impressions of the order so vividly exemplified, and my companion's knowledge, henceforth—a knowledge half consternation and half compassion—of that liability. There had been, this evening, after the revelation that left me, for an hour, so prostrate—there had been, for either of us, no attendance on any service but a little service of tears and vows, of prayers and promises, a climax to the series of mutual challenges and pledges that had straightway ensued on our retreating together to the schoolroom and shutting ourselves up there to have everything out. The result of our having everything out was simply to reduce our situation to the last rigor of its elements. She herself had seen nothing, not the shadow of a shadow, and nobody in the house but the governess was in the governess's plight; yet she accepted without directly impugning my sanity the truth as I gave it to her, and ended by showing me, on this ground, an awestricken tenderness, an expression of the sense of my more than questionable privilege, of which the very breath has remained with me as that of the sweetest of human charities.

What was settled between us, accordingly, that night, was that we thought we might bear things together; and I was not even sure that, in spite of her exemption, it was she who had the best of the burden. I knew at this hour, I think, as well as I knew later, what I was capable of meeting to shelter my pupils; but it took me some time to be wholly sure of what my honest ally was prepared for to keep terms with so compromising a contract. I was queer company enough—quite as queer as the company I received; but as I trace over what we went through I see how much common ground we must have found in the one idea that, by good fortune, *could* steady us. It was the idea, the second movement, that led me straight out, as I may say, of the inner chamber of my dread. I could take the air in the court, at least, and there Mrs. Grose could join me. Perfectly can I recall now the particular way strength came to me before we separated for the night. We had gone over and over every feature of what I had seen.

"He was looking for someone else, you say—someone who was not you?"

"He was looking for little Miles." A portentous clearness now possessed me. "*That's* whom he was looking for."

"But how do you know?"

"I know, I know, I know!" My exaltation grew. "And you know, my dear!"

She didn't deny this, but I required, I felt, not even so much telling as that. She resumed in a moment, at any rate: "What if *he* should see him?"

"Little Miles? That's what he wants!"

She looked immensely scared again. "The child?"

"Heaven forbid! The man. He wants to appear to *them*." That he might was an awful conception, and yet, somehow, I could keep it at bay; which, moreover, as we lingered there, was what I succeeded in practically proving. I had an absolute certainty that I should see again what I had already seen, but something within me said that by offering myself bravely as the sole subject of such experience, by accepting, by inviting, by surmounting it all, I should serve as an expiatory victim and guard the tranquility of my companions. The children, in especial, I should thus fence about and absolutely save. I recall one of the last things I said that night to Mrs. Grose.

"It does strike me that my pupils have never mentioned——"

She looked at me hard as I musingly pulled up. "His having been here and the time they were with him?"

"The time they were with him, and his name, his presence, his history, in any way."

"Oh, the little lady doesn't remember. She never heard or knew."

"The circumstances of his death?" I thought with some intensity. "Perhaps not. But Miles would remember—Miles would know."

"Ah, don't try him!" broke from Mrs. Grose.

I returned her the look she had given me. "Don't be afraid." I continued to think. "It *is* rather odd."

"That he has never spoken of him?"

"Never by the least allusion. And you tell me they were 'great friends'?"

"Oh, it wasn't *him!*" Mrs. Grose with emphasis declared. "It was Quint's own fancy. To play with him, I mean—to spoil him." She paused a moment; then she added: "Quint was much too free."

This gave me, straight from my vision of his face—*such* a face!—a sudden sickness of disgust. "Too free with *my* boy?"

"Too free with everyone!"

I forbore, for the moment, to analyze this description further than by the reflection that a part of it applied to several of the members of the household, of the half-dozen maids and men who were still of our small colony. But there was everything, for our apprehension, in the lucky fact that no discomfortable legend, no perturbation of scullions, had ever, within anyone's memory attached to the kind old place. It had neither bad name nor ill fame, and Mrs. Grose, most apparently, only desired to cling to me and to quake in silence. I even put her, the very last thing of all, to the test. It was when, at midnight, she had her hand on the schoolroom door to take leave. "I have it from you then—for it's of great importance—that he was definitely and admittedly bad?"

"Oh, not admittedly. *I* knew it—but the master didn't."

"And you never told him?"

"Well, he didn't like tale-bearing—he hated complaints. He was terribly short with anything of that kind, and if people were all right to *him*——"

"He wouldn't be bothered with more?" This squared well enough with my impression of him: he was not a trouble-loving gentleman, nor so very particular perhaps about some of the company *he* kept. All the same, I pressed my interlocutress. "I promise you *I* would have told!"

She felt my discrimination. "I daresay I was wrong. But, really, I was afraid."

"Afraid of what?"

"Of things that man could do. Quint was so clever—he was so deep."

I took this in still more than, probably, I showed. "You weren't afraid of anything else? Not of his effect——?"

"His effect?" she repeated with a face of anguish and waiting while I faltered.

"On innocent little precious lives. They were in your charge."

"No, they were not in mine!" she roundly and distressfully returned. "The master believed in him and placed him here because he was supposed not to be well and the country air so good for him. So he had everything to say. Yes"—she let me have it—"even about *them*."

"Them—that creature?" I had to smother a kind of howl. "And you could bear it!"

"No. I couldn't—and I can't now!" And the poor woman burst into tears.

A rigid control, from the next day, was, as I have said,

to follow them; yet how often and how passionately, for a week, we came back together to the subject! Much as we had discussed it that Sunday night, I was, in the immediate later hours in especial—for it may be imagined whether I slept—still haunted with the shadow of something she had not told me. I myself had kept back nothing, but there was a word Mrs. Grose had kept back. I was sure, moreover, by morning, that this was not from a failure of frankness, but because on every side there were fears. It seems to me indeed, in retrospect, that by the time the morrow's sun was high I had restlessly read into the fact before us almost all the meaning they were to receive from subsequent and more cruel occurrences. What they gave me above all was just the sinister figure of the living man—the dead one would keep awhile!—and of the months he had continuously passed at Bly, which, added up, made a formidable stretch. The limit of this evil time had arrived only when, on the dawn of a winter's morning, Peter Quint was found, by a laborer going to early work, stone dead on the road from the village: a catastrophe explained—superficially at least—by a visible wound to his head; such a wound as might have been produced—and as, on the final evidence, *had* been—by a fatal slip, in the dark and after leaving the public house, on the steepish icy slope, a wrong path altogether, at the bottom of which he lay. The icy slope, the turn mistaken at night and in liquor, accounted for much—practically, in the end and after the inquest and boundless chatter, for everything; but there had been matters in his life—strange passages and perils, secret disorders, vices more than suspected—that would have accounted for a good deal more.

I scarce know how to put my story into words that shall be a credible picture of my state of mind; but I was in these days literally able to find a joy in the extraordinary flight of heroism the occasion demanded of me. I now saw that I had been asked for a service admirable and difficult; and there would be a greatness in letting it be seen—oh, in the right quarter!—that I could succeed where many another girl might have failed. It was an immense help to me—I confess I rather applaud myself as I look back!—that I saw my service so strongly and so simply. I was there to protect and defend the little creatures in the world the most bereaved and the most lovable, the appeal of whose helplessness had suddenly become only too explicit, a deep, constant ache of one's own committed heart. We were cut off, really, together; we were united in our danger. They had nothing but me, and I—well, I had *them*. It was in short a magnificent chance. This chance presented itself to me in an image richly material. I was a screen—I was to stand before them. The more I saw, the less they would. I began to watch them in a stifled suspense, a disguised excitement that might well, had it continued too long, have turned to something like madness. What saved me, as I now see, was that it turned to something else altogether. It didn't last as suspense—it was superseded by horrible proofs. Proofs, I say, yes—from the moment I really took hold.

This moment dated from an afternoon hour that I happened to spend in the grounds with the younger of my pupils alone. We had left Miles indoors, on the red cushion of a deep window seat; he had wished to finish a book, and I had been glad to encourage a purpose so laudable in a young man whose only defect was an occasional excess of the restless. His sister, on the contrary, had been alert to come out, and I strolled with her half an hour, seeking the shade, for the sun was still high and the day exceptionally warm. I was aware afresh, with her, as we went, of how, like her brother, she contrived—it was the charming thing in both children—to let me alone without appearing to drop me and to accompany me without appearing to surround. They were never importunate and yet never listless. My attention to them all really went to seeing them amuse themselves immensely without me: this was a spectacle they seemed actively to prepare and that engaged me as an active admirer. I walked in a world of their invention—they had no occasion whatever to draw upon mine; so that my time was taken only with being, for them, some remarkable person or thing that the game of the moment required and that was merely, thanks to my superior, my exalted stamp, a happy and highly distinguished sinecure. I forget what I was on the present occasion; I only remember that I was something very important and very quiet and that Flora was playing very hard. We were on the edge of the lake, and, as we had lately begun geography, the lake was the Sea of Azof.

Suddenly, in these circumstances, I became aware that, on the other side of the Sea of Azof, we had an interested spectator. The way this knowledge gathered in me was the strangest thing in the world—the strangest, that is, except the very much stranger in which it quickly merged itself. I had sat down with a piece of work—for I was something or other that could sit—on the old stone bench which overlooked the pond; and in this position I began to take in with certitude, and yet without direct vision, the presence, at a distance, of a third person. The old trees, the thick shrubbery, made a great and pleasant shade, but it was all suffused with the brightness of the hot, still hour. There was no ambiguity in anything; none whatever, at least, in the conviction I from one moment to another found myself forming as to what I should see straight before me and across the lake as a consequence of raising my eyes. They were attached at this juncture to the stitching in which I was engaged, and I can feel once more the spasm of my effort not to move them till I should so have steadied myself as to be able to make up my mind what to do. There was an alien object in view— a figure whose right of presence I instantly, passionately questioned. I recollect counting over perfectly the possibilities, reminding myself that nothing was more natural, for instance, than the appearance of one of the men about the place, or even of a messenger, a postman, or a tradesman's boy, from the village. That reminder had as little effect on my practical certitude as I was conscious —still even without looking—of its having upon the character and attitude of our visitor. Nothing was more natural than that these things should be the other things that they absolutely were not.

Of the positive identity of the apparition I would assure myself as soon as the small clock of my courage should have ticked out the right second; meanwhile, with an effort that was already sharp enough, I transferred my eyes straight to little Flora, who, at the moment, was about ten yards away. My heart had stood still for an instant with the wonder and terror of the question whether she too would see; and I held my breath while I waited for what a cry from her, what some sudden innocent sign either of interest or of alarm, would tell me. I waited, but nothing came; then, in the first place—and there is something more dire in this, I feel, than in anything I have to relate—I was determined by a sense that, within a minute, all sounds from her had previously dropped; and, in the second, by the circumstance that, also within the minute, she had, in her play, turned her back to the water. This was her attitude when I at last looked at her—looked with the confirmed conviction that we were still, together, under direct personal notice. She had picked up a small flat piece of wood, which happened to have in it a little hole that had evidently suggested to her the idea of sticking in another fragment that might figure as a mast and make the thing a boat. This second morsel, as I watched her, she was very markedly and intently attempting to tighten in its place. My apprehension of what she was doing sustained me so that after some seconds I felt I was ready for more. Then I again shifted my eyes—I faced what I had to face.

VII

I got hold of Mrs. Grose as soon after this as I could; and I can give no intelligible account of how I fought out the interval. Yet I still hear myself cry as I fairly threw myself into her arms: "They *know*—it's too monstrous: they know, they know!"

"And what on earth——?" I felt her incredulity as she held me.

"Why, all that we know—and heaven knows what else besides!" Then, as she released me, I made it out to her, made it out perhaps only now with full coherency even to myself. "Two hours ago, in the garden"—I could scarce articulate—"Flora *saw!*"

Mrs. Grose took it as she might have taken a blow in the stomach. "She has told you?" she panted.

"Not a word—that's the horror. She kept it to herself! The child of eight, *that* child!" Unutterable still, for me, was the stupefaction of it.

Mrs. Grose, of course, could only gape the wider. "Then how do you know?"

"I was there—I saw with my eyes: saw that she was perfectly aware."

"Do you mean aware of *him?*"

"No—of *her.*" I was conscious as I spoke that I looked prodigious things, for I got the slow reflection of them in my companion's face. "Another person—this time; but a figure of quite as unmistakable horror and evil: a woman in black, pale and dreadful—with such an air also, and such a face!—on the other side of the lake. I was there with the child—quiet for the hour; and in the midst of it she came."

"Came how—from where?"

"From where they come from! She just appeared and stood there—but not so near."

"And without coming nearer?"

"Oh, for the effect and the feeling, she might have been as close as you!"

My friend, with an odd impulse, fell back a step. "Was she someone you've never seen?"

"Yes. But someone the child has. Someone *you* have." Then, to show how I had thought it all out: "My predecessor—the one who died."

"Miss Jessel?"

"Miss Jessel. You don't believe me?" I pressed.

She turned right and left in her distress. "How can you be sure?"

This drew from me, in the state of my nerves, a flash of impatience. "Then ask Flora—*she's* sure!" But I had no sooner spoken than I caught myself up. "No, for God's sake, *don't!* She'll say she isn't—she'll lie!"

Mrs. Grose was not too bewildered instinctively to protest. "Ah, how *can* you?"

"Because I'm clear. Flora doesn't want me to know."

"It's only then to spare you."

"No, no—there are depths, depths! The more I go over

it, the more I see in it, and the more I see in it, the more I fear. I don't know what I *don't* see—what I *don't* fear!"

Mrs. Grose tried to keep up with me. "You mean you're afraid of seeing her again?"

"Oh, no; that's nothing—now!" Then I explained "It's of *not* seeing her."

But my companion only looked wan. "I don't understand you."

"Why, it's that the child may keep it up—and that the child assuredly *will*—without my knowing it."

At the image of this possibility Mrs. Grose for a moment collapsed, yet presently to pull herself together again, as if from the positive force of the sense of what, should we yield an inch, there would really be to give way to. "Dear, dear—we must keep our heads! And after all, if she doesn't mind it—!" She even tried a grim joke. "Perhaps she likes it!"

"Likes *such* things—a scrap of an infant!"

"Isn't it just a proof of her blessed innocence?" my friend bravely inquired.

She brought me, for the instant, almost round. "Oh, we must clutch at *that*—we must cling to it! If it isn't a proof of what you say, it's a proof of—God knows what! For the woman's a horror of horrors."

Mrs. Grose, at this, fixed her eyes a minute on the ground; then at last raising them, "Tell me how you know," she said.

"Then you admit it's what she was?" I cried.

"Tell me how you know," my friend simply repeated.

"Know? By seeing her! By the way she looked."

"At you, do you mean—so wickedly?"

"Dear me, no—I could have borne that. She gave me never a glance. She only fixed the child."

Mrs. Grose tried to see it. "Fixed her?"

"Ah, with such awful eyes!"

She stared at mine as if they might really have resembled them. "Do you mean of dislike?"

"God help us, no. Of something much worse."

"Worse than dislike?"—this left her indeed at a loss.

"With a determination—indescribable. With a kind of fury of intention."

I made her turn pale. "Intention?"

"To get hold of her." Mrs. Grose—her eyes just linger-ing on mine—gave a shudder and walked to the window; and while she stood there looking out I completed my statement. "*That's* what Flora knows."

After a little she turned round. "The person was in black, you say?"

"In mourning—rather poor, almost shabby. But—yes —with extraordinary beauty." I now recognized to what I had at last, stroke by stroke, brought the victim of my confidence, for she quite visibly weighed this. "Oh, hand-some—very, very," I insisted; "wonderfully handsome. But infamous."

She slowly came back to me. "Miss Jessel—*was* in-famous." She once more took my hand in both her own, holding it as tight as if to fortify me against the increase of alarm I might draw from this disclosure. "They were both infamous," she finally said.

So, for a little, we faced it once more together; and I found absolutely a degree of help in seeing it now so straight. "I appreciate," I said, "the great decency of your not having hitherto spoken; but the time has certainly come to give me the whole thing." She appeared to as-sent to this, but still only in silence; seeing which I went on: "I must have it now. Of what did she die? Come, there was something between them."

"There was everything."

"In spite of the difference——?"

"Oh, of their rank, their condition"—she brought it woefully out. "*She* was a lady."

I turned it over; I again saw. "Yes—she was a lady."

"And he so dreadfully below," said Mrs. Grose.

I felt that I doubtless needn't press too hard, in such company, on the place of a servant in the scale; but there was nothing to prevent an acceptance of my companion's own measure of my predecessor's abasement. There was a way to deal with that, and I dealt; the more readily for my full vision—on the evidence—of our employer's late clever, good-looking "own" man; impudent, assured, spoiled, depraved. "The fellow was a hound."

Mrs. Grose considered as if it were perhaps a little a case for a sense of shades. "I've never seen one like him. He did what he wished."

"With *her?*"

"With them all."

It was as if now in my friend's own eyes Miss Jessel had again appeared. I seemed at any rate, for an instant, to see their evocation of her as distinctly as I had seen her by the pond; and I brought out with decision: "It must have been also what *she* wished!"

Mrs. Grose's face signified that it had been indeed, but she said at the same time: "Poor woman—she paid for it!"

"Then you do know what she died of?" I asked.

"No—I know nothing. I wanted not to know; I was glad enough I didn't; and I thanked heaven she was well out of this!"

"Yet you had, then, your idea——"

"Of her real reason for leaving? Oh, yes—as to that. She couldn't have stayed. Fancy it here—for a governess! And afterward I imagined—and I still imagine. And what I imagine is dreadful."

"Not so dreadful as what *I* do," I replied; on which I must have shown her—as I was indeed but too conscious —a front of miserable defeat. It brought out again all her compassion for me, and at the renewed touch of her kindness my power to resist broke down. I burst, as I had, the other time, made her burst, into tears; she took me to her motherly breast, and my lamentation overflowed. "I don't do it!" I sobbed in despair; "I don't save or shield them! It's far worse than I dreamed—they're lost!"

VIII

What I had said to Mrs. Grose was true enough: there were in the matter I had put before her depths and possibilities that I lacked resolution to sound; so that when we met once more in the wonder of it we were of a common mind about the duty of resistance to extravagant fancies. We were to keep our heads if we should keep nothing else—difficult indeed as that might be in the face of what, in our prodigious experience, was least to be questioned. Late that night, while the house slept, we had another talk in my room, when she went all the way with me as to its being beyond doubt that I had seen exactly what I had seen. To hold her perfectly in the pinch of that, I found I had only to ask her how, if I had "made it up," I came to be able to give, of each of the persons appearing to me, a picture disclosing, to the last detail, their special marks—a portrait on the exhibition of which she had instantly recognized and named them. She wished of course—small blame to her!—to sink the whole subject; and I was quick to assure her that my own interest in it had now violently taken the form of a search for the way to escape from it. I encountered her on the ground of a probability that with recurrence—for recurrence we took for granted—I should get used to my danger, distinctly professing that my personal exposure had suddenly become the least of my discomforts. It was my new suspicion that was intolerable; and yet even to this complication the later hours of the day had brought a little ease.

On leaving her, after my first outbreak, I had of course returned to my pupils, associating the right remedy for my dismay with that sense of their charm which I had already found to be a thing I could positively cultivate and which had never failed me yet. I had simply, in other words, plunged afresh into Flora's special society and there become aware—it was almost a luxury!—that she could put her little conscious hand straight upon the spot that ached. She had looked at me in sweet speculation and then had accused me to my face of having "cried." I had supposed I had brushed away the ugly signs: but I could literally—for the time, at all events—rejoice, under this fathomless charity, that they had not entirely disappeared. To gaze into the depths of blue of the child's eyes and pronounce their loveliness a trick of premature cunning was to be guilty of a cynicism in preference to which I naturally preferred to abjure my judgment and, so far as might be, my agitation. I couldn't abjure for merely wanting to, but I could repeat to Mrs. Grose—as I did there, over and over, in the small hours—that with their voices in the air, their pressure on one's heart, and their fragrant faces against one's cheek, everything fell to the ground but their incapacity and their beauty. It was a pity that, somehow, to settle this once for all, I had equally to re-enumerate the signs of subtlety that, in the afternoon, by the lake, had made a miracle of my show of self-possession. It was a pity to be obliged to reinvestigate the certitude of the moment itself and repeat how it had come to me as a revelation that the inconceivable communion I then surprised was a matter, for either party, of habit. It was a pity that I should have had to quaver out again the reasons for my not having, in my delusion, so much as questioned that the little girl saw our visitant even as I actually saw Mrs. Grose herself, and that she wanted, by just so much as she did thus see, to make me suppose she didn't, and at the same time, without showing anything, arrive at a guess as to whether I myself did! It was a pity that I needed once more to describe the portentous little activity by which she sought to divert my attention—the perceptible increase of movement, the greater intensity of play, the singing, the gabbling of nonsense, and the invitation to romp.

Yet if I had not indulged, to prove there was nothing in it, in this review, I should have missed the two or three dim elements of comfort that still remained to me. I should not for instance have been able to asseverate to my friend that I was certain—which was so much to the good—that *I* at least had not betrayed myself. I should not have been prompted, by stress of need, by desperation of mind—I scarce know what to call it—to invoke such further aid to intelligence as might spring from pushing my colleague fairly to the wall. She had told me, bit by bit, under pressure, a great deal; but a small shifty spot on the wrong side of it all still sometimes brushed my brow like the wing of a bat; and I remember how on this occasion—for the sleeping house and the concentration alike of our danger and our watch seemed to help—I felt the importance of giving the last jerk to the curtain. "I don't believe anything so horrible," I recollect saying; "no, let us put it definitely, my dear, that I don't. But if I did, you know, there's a thing I should require now, just without sparing you the least bit more—oh, not a scrap, come!—to get out of you. What was it you had in mind when, in our distress, before Miles came back, over the letter from his school, you said, under my insistence, that you didn't pretend for him that he had not literally *ever* been 'bad'? He has *not* literally 'ever,' in these weeks that I myself have lived with him and so closely watched him; he has been an imperturbable little prodigy of delightful, lovable goodness. Therefore you might perfectly have made the claim for him if you had not, as it happened, seen an exception to take. What was your exception, and to what passage in your personal observation of him did you refer?"

It was a dreadfully austere inquiry, but levity was not our note, and, at any rate, before the gray dawn admonished us to separate I had got my answer. What my friend had had in mind proved to be immensely to the purpose. It was neither more nor less than the circumstance that for a period of several months Quint and the boy had been perpetually together. It was in fact the very appropriate truth that she had ventured to criticize the propriety, to hint at the incongruity, of so close an alliance, and even to go so far on the subject as a frank overture to Miss Jessel. Miss Jessel had, with a most strange manner, requested her to mind her business, and the good woman had, on this, directly approached little Miles. What she had said to him, since I pressed, was that *she* liked to see young gentlemen not forget their station.

I pressed again, of course, at this. "You reminded him that Quint was only a base menial?"

"As you might say! And it was his answer, for one thing, that was bad."

"And for another thing?" I waited. "He repeated your words to Quint?"

"No, not that. It's just what he *wouldn't*!" she could still impress upon me. "I was sure, at any rate," she added, "that he didn't. But he denied certain occasions."

"What occasions?"

"When they had been about together quite as if Quint were his tutor—and a very grand one—and Miss Jessel only for the little lady. When he had gone off with the fellow, I mean, and spent hours with him.'

"He then prevaricated about it—he said he hadn't?" Her assent was clear enough to cause me to add in a moment: "I see. He lied."

"Oh!" Mrs. Grose mumbled. This was a suggestion that it didn't matter; which indeed she backed up by a further remark. "You see, after all, Miss Jessel didn't mind. She didn't forbid him."

I considered. "Did he put that to you as a justification?"

At this she dropped again. "No, he never spoke of it."

"Never mentioned her in connection with Quint?"

She saw, visibly flushing, where I was coming out. "Well, he didn't show anything. He denied," she repeated; "he denied."

Lord, how I pressed her now! "So that you could see he knew what was between the two wretches?"

"I don't know—I don't know!" the poor woman groaned.

"You do know, you dear thing," I replied; "only you haven't my dreadful boldness of mind, and you keep back, out of timidity and modesty and delicacy, even the impression that, in the past, when you had, without my aid, to flounder about in silence, most of all made you miserable. But I shall get it out of you yet! There was something in the boy that suggested to you," I continued, "that he covered and concealed their relation."

"Oh, he couldn't prevent——"

"Your learning the truth? I daresay! But, heavens," I fell, with vehemence, athinking, "what it shows that they must, to that extent, have succeeded in making of him!"

"An, nothing that's not nice *now!*" Mrs. Grose lugubriously pleaded.

"I don't wonder you looked queer," I persisted, "when I mentioned to you the letter from his school!"

"I doubt if I looked as queer as you!" she retorted with homely force. "And if he was so bad then as that comes to, how is he such an angel now?"

"Yes, indeed—and if he was a fiend at school! How, how, how? Well," I said in my torment, "you must put it to me again, but I shall not be able to tell you for some days. Only, put it to me again!" I cried in a way that made my friend stare. "There are directions in which I must not for the present let myself go." Meanwhile I returned to her first example—the one to which she had just previously referred—of the boy's happy capacity for an occasional slip. "If Quint—on your remonstrance at the time you speak of—was a base menial, one of the things Miles said to you, I find myself guessing, was that you were another." Again her admission was so adequate that I continued: "And you forgave him that?"

"Wouldn't *you?*"

"Oh, yes!" And we exchanged there, in the stillness, a sound of the oddest amusement. Then I went on: "At all events, while he was with the man——"

"Miss Flora was with the woman. It suited them all!"

It suited me, too, I felt, only too well; by which I mean that it suited exactly the particularly deadly view I was in the very act of forbidding myself to entertain. But I so far succeeded in checking the expression of this view that I will throw, just here, no further light on it than may be offered by the mention of my final observation to Mrs. Grose. "His having lied and been impudent are, I confess, less engaging specimens than I had hoped to have from you of the outbreak in him of the little natural man. Still," I mused, "They must do, for they make me feel more than ever that I must watch."

It made me blush, the next minute, to see in my friend's face how much more unreservedly she had forgiven him than her anecdote struck me as presenting to my own tenderness an occasion for doing. This came out when, at the schoolroom door, she quitted me. "Surely you don't accuse *him*——"

"Of carrying on an intercourse that he conceals from me? Ah, remember that, until further evidence, I now accuse nobody." Then, before shutting her out to go, by another passage, to her own place, "I must just wait," I wound up.

IX

I waited and waited, and the days, as they elapsed, took something from my consternation. A very few of them, in fact, passing, in constant sight of my pupils, without a fresh incident, sufficed to give to grievous fancies and even to odious memories a kind of brush of the sponge. I have spoken of the surrender to their extraordinary childish grace as a thing I could actively cultivate, and it may be imagined if I neglected now to address myself to this source for whatever it would yield. Stranger than I can express, certainly, was the effort to struggle against my new lights; it would doubtless have been, however, a greater tension still had it not been so frequently successful. I used to wonder how my little charges could help guessing that I thought strange things about them; and the circumstance that these things only made them more interesting was not by itself a direct aid to keeping them in the dark. I trembled lest they should see that they *were* so immensely more interesting. Putting things at the worst, at all events, as in meditation I so often did, any clouding of their innocence could only be—blameless and foredoomed as they were —a reason the more for taking risks. There were moments when, by an irresistible impulse, I found myself catching them up and pressing them to my heart. As soon as I had done so I used to say to myself: "What will they think of that? Doesn't it betray too much?" It would have been easy to get into a sad, wild tangle about how much I might betray; but the real account, I feel, of the hours of peace that I could still enjoy was that the immediate charm of my companions was a beguilement still effective even under the shadow of the possibility that it was studied. For if it occurred to me that I might occasionally excite suspicion by the little outbreaks of my sharper passion for them, so too I remember wondering if I mightn't see a queerness in the traceable increase of their own demonstrations.

They were at this period extravagantly and preternaturally fond of me; which, after all, I could reflect, was no more than a graceful response in children perpetually bowed over and hugged. The homage of which they were so lavish succeeded, in truth, for my nerves, quite as well as if I never appeared to myself, as I may say, literally to catch them at a purpose in it. They had never, I think, wanted to do so many things for their poor protectress; I mean—though they got their lessons better and better, which was naturally what would please her most—in the way of diverting, entertaining, surprising her; reading her passages, telling her stories, acting her charades, pouncing out at her, in disguises, as animals and historical characters, and above all astonishing her by the "pieces" they had secretly got by heart and could interminably recite. I should never get to the bottom—were I to let myself go even now—of the prodigious private commentary, all under still more private correction, with which, in these days, I overscored their full hours. They had shown me from the first a facility for everything, a general faculty which, taking a fresh start, achieved remarkable flights. They got their little tasks as if they loved them, and indulged, from the mere exuberance of the gift, in the most unimposed little miracles of memory. They not only popped out at me as tigers and as Romans, but as Shakespeareans, astronomers, and navigators. This was so singularly the case that it had presumably much to do with the fact as to which, at the present day, I am at a loss for a different explanation: I allude to my unnatural composure on the subject of another school for Miles. What I remember is that I was content not, for the time, to open the question, and that contentment must have sprung from the sense of his perpetually striking show of cleverness. He was too clever for a bad governess, for a parson's daughter, to spoil; and the strangest if not the brightest thread in the pensive embroidery I just spoke of was the impression I might have got, if I had dared to work it out, that he was under some influence operating in his small intellectual life as a tremendous incitement.

If it was easy to reflect, however, that such a boy could postpone school, it was at least as marked that for such a boy to have been "kicked out" by a school-master was a mystification without end. Let me add that in their company now—and I was careful almost never to be out of it—I could follow no scent very far. We lived in a cloud of music and love and success and private theatricals. The musical sense in each of the children was of the quickest, but the elder in especial had a marvelous knack of catching and repeating. The schoolroom piano broke into all gruesome fancies; and when that failed there were confabulations in corners, with a sequel of one of them going out in the highest spirits in order to "come in" as something new. I had had brothers myself, and it was no revelation to me that little girls could be slavish idolaters of little boys. What surpassed every-thing was that there was a little boy in the world who could have for the inferior age, sex, and intelligence so fine a consideration. They were extraordinarily at one, and to say that they never either quarreled or complained is to make the note of praise coarse for their quality of sweetness. Sometimes, indeed, when I dropped into coarseness, I perhaps came across traces of little under-standings between them by which one of them should keep me occupied while the other slipped away. There is a *naïve* side, I suppose, in all diplomacy; but if my pupils practiced upon me, it was surely with the minimum of grossness. It was all in the other quarter that, after a lull, the grossness broke out.

I find that I really hang back; but I must take my plunge. In going on with the record of what was hideous at Bly, I not only challenge the most liberal faith—for which I little care; but—and this is another matter—I re-new what I myself suffered, I again push my way through it to the end. There came suddenly an hour after which, as I look back, the affair seems to me to have been all pure suffering; but I have at least reached the heart of it, and the straightest road out is doubtless to advance. One evening—with nothing to lead up or to prepare it—I felt the cold touch of the impression that had breathed on me the night of my arrival and which, much lighter then, as I have mentioned, I should probably have made little of in memory had my subsequent sojourn been less agitated. I had not gone to bed; I sat reading by a couple of candles. There was a roomful of old books at Bly—last-century fiction, some of it, which, to the extent of a distinctly deprecated renown, but never to so much as that of a stray specimen, had reached the sequestered home and appealed to the unavowed curiosity of my youth. I remember that the book I had in my hand was Fielding's *Amelia;* also that I was wholly awake. I recall further both a general conviction that it was horribly late and a particular objection to looking at my watch. I figure, finally, that the white curtain draping, in the fashion of those days, the head of Flora's little bed, shrouded, as I had assured myself long before, the perfection of childish rest. I recollect in short. that, though I was deeply interested in my author, I found myself, at the turn of a page and with his spell all scattered, looking straight up from him and hard at the door of my room. There was a moment during which I listened, reminded of the faint sense I had had, the first night, of there being something undefinably astir in the house, and noted the soft breath of the open casement just move the half-drawn blind. Then, with all the marks of a deliberation that must have seemed magnificent had there been anyone to admire it, I laid down my book, rose to my feet, and, taking a candle, went straight out of the room and, from the passage, on which my light made little impression, noiselessly closed and locked the door.

I can say now neither what determined nor what guided me, but I went straight along the lobby, holding my candle high, till I came within sight of the tall window that presided over the great turn of the staircase. At this point I precipitately found myself aware of three things. They were practically simultaneous, yet they had flashes of succession. My candle, under a bold flourish, went out, and I perceived, by the uncovered window, that the yielding dusk of earliest morning rendered it unnecessary. Without it, the next instant, I saw that there was someone on the stair. I speak of sequences, but I required no lapse of seconds to stiffen myself for a third encounter with Quint. The apparition had reached the landing halfway up and was therefore on the spot nearest the window, where at sight of me, it stopped short and fixed me exactly as it had fixed me from the tower and from the garden. He knew me as well as I knew him; and so, in the cold, faint twilight, with a glimmer in the high glass and another on the polish of the oak stair below, we faced each other in our common intensity. He was absolutely, on this occasion, a living, detestable, dangerous presence. But that was not the wonder of wonders; I reserve this distinction for quite another circumstance: the circumstance that dread had unmistakably quitted me and that there was nothing in me there that didn't meet and measure him.

I had plenty of anguish after that extraordinary moment, but I had, thank God, no terror. And he knew I had not—I found myself at the end of an instant magnificently aware of this. I felt, in a fierce rigor of confidence, that if I stood my ground a minute I should cease—for the time, at least—to have him to reckon with; and during the minute, accordingly, the thing was as human and hideous as a real interview: hideous just because it was human, as human as to have met alone, in the small hours, in a sleeping house, some enemy, some adventurer, some criminal. It was the dead silence of our long gaze at such close quarters that gave the whole horror, huge as it was, its only note of the unnatural. If I had met a murderer in such a place and at such an hour, we still at least would have spoken. Something would have passed, in life, between us; if nothing had passed, one of us would have moved. The moment was so prolonged that it would have taken but little more to make me doubt if even *I* were in life. I can't express what followed it save by saying that the silence itself which was indeed in a manner an attestation of my strength—became the element into which I saw the figure disappear; in which I definitely saw it turn as I might have seen the low wretch to which it had once belonged turn on receipt of an order, and pass, with my eyes on the villainous back that no hunch could have more disfigured, straight down the staircase and into the darkness in which the next bend was lost.

X

I remained awhile at the top of the stair, but with the effect presently of understanding that when my visitor had gone, he had gone: then I returned to my room. The foremost thing I saw there by the light of the candle I had left burning was that Flora's little bed was empty; and on this I caught my breath with all the terror that, five minutes before, I had been able to resist. I dashed at the place in which I had left her lying and over which (for the small silk counterpane and the sheets were disarranged) the white curtains had been deceivingly pulled forward; then my step, to my unutterable relief, produced an answering sound: I perceived an agitation of the window blind, and the child, ducking down, emerged rosily from the other side of it. She stood there in so much of her candor and so little of her nightgown, with her pink bare feet and the golden glow of her curls. She looked intensely grave, and I had never had such a sense of losing an advantage acquired (the thrill of which had just been so prodigious) as on my consciousness that she addressed me with a reproach. "You naughty: where *have* you been?"—instead of challenging her own irregularity I found myself arraigned and explaining. She herself explained, for that matter, with the loveliest, eagerest simplicity. She had known suddenly, as she lay there, that I was out of the room, and had jumped up to see what had become of me. I had dropped, with the joy of her reappearance, back into my chair—feeling then, and then only, a little faint; and she had pattered straight over to me, thrown herself upon my knee, given herself to be held with the flame of the candle full in the wonderful little face that was still flushed with sleep. I remember closing my eyes an instant, yieldingly, consciously, as before the excess of something beautiful that shone out of the blue of her own. "You were looking for me out of the window?" I said. "You thought I might be walking in the grounds?"

"Well, you know, I thought someone was"—she never blanched as she smiled out that at me.

Oh, how I looked at her now! "And did you see any-one?"

"Ah, *no!*" she returned, almost with the full privilege of childish inconsequence, resentfully, though with a long sweetness in her little drawl of the negative.

At that moment, in the state of my nerves, I absolutely believed she lied; and if I once more closed my eyes it was before the dazzle of the three or four possible ways in which I might take this up. One of these, for a moment, tempted me with such singular intensity that, to withstand it, I must have gripped my little girl with a spasm that, wonderfully, she submitted to without a cry or a sign of fright. Why not break out at her on the spot and have it all over?—give it to her straight in her lovely little lighted face? "You see, you see, you *know* that you do and that you already quite suspect I believe it; therefore, why not frankly confess it to me, so that we may at least live with it together and learn perhaps, in the strangeness of our fate, where we are and what it means?" This solicitation dropped, alas, as it came: if I could immediately have succumbed to it I might have spared myself—well, you'll see what. Instead of succumbing I sprang again to my feet, looked at her bed, and took a helpless middle way. "Why did you pull the curtain over the place to make me think you were still there?"

Flora luminously considered; after which, with her little divine smile: "Because I don't like to frighten you!"

"But if I had, by your idea, gone out——?"

She absolutely declined to be puzzled; she turned her eyes to the flame of the candle as if the question were as irrelevant, or at any rate as impersonal, as Mrs. Marcet or nine-times-nine. "Oh, but you know," she quite adequately answered, "that you might come back, you dear, and that you *have!*" And after a little, when she had got into bed, I had, for a long time, by almost sitting on her to hold her hand, to prove that I recognized the pertinence of my return.

You may imagine the general complexion, from that moment, of my nights. I repeatedly sat up till I didn't know when; I selected moments when my roommate unmistakably slept, and, stealing out, took noiseless turns in the passage and even pushed as far as to where I had last met Quint. But I never met him there again; and I may as well say at once that I on no other occasion saw him in the house. I just missed, on the staircase, on the other hand, a different adventure. Looking down it from the top I once recognized the presence of a woman seated on one of the lower steps with her back presented to me, her body half-bowed and her head, in an attitude of woe, in her hands. I had been there but an instant, however, when she vanished without looking round at me. I knew, nonetheless, exactly what dreadful face she had to show; and I wondered whether, if instead of being above I had been below, I should have had, for going up, the same nerve I had lately shown Quint. Well, there continued to be plenty of chance for nerve. On the eleventh night after my latest encounter with that gentleman—they were all numbered now—I had an alarm that perilously skirted it and that indeed, from the particular quality of its unexpectedness, proved quite my sharpest shock. It was precisely the first night during this series that, weary with watching, I had felt that I might again without laxity lay myself down at my old hour. I slept immediately and, as I afterward knew, till about one o'clock; but when I woke it was to sit straight up, as completely roused as if a hand had shook me. I had left a light burning, but it was now out, and I felt an instant certainty that Flora had extinguished it. This brought me to my feet and straight, in the darkness, to her bed, which I found she had left. A glance at the window enlightened me further, and the striking of a match completed the picture.

The child had again got up—this time blowing out the taper, and had again, for some purpose of observation or response, squeezed in behind the blind and was peering out into the night. That she now saw—as she had not, I had satisfied myself, the previous time—was proved to me by the fact that she was disturbed neither by my reillumination nor by the haste I made to get into slippers and into a wrap. Hidden, protected, absorbed, she evi-

dently rested on the sill—the casement opened forward
—and gave herself up. There was a great still moon to
help her, and this fact had counted in my quick decision.
She was face to face with the apparition we had met at
the lake, and could now communicate with it as she had
not then been able to do. What I, on my side, had to
care for was, without disturbing her, to reach, from the
corridor, some other window in the same quarter. I got
to the door without her hearing me; I got out of it, closed
it, and listened, from the other side, for some sound from
her. While I stood in the passage I had my eyes on her
brother's door, which was but ten steps off and which, in-
describably, produced in me a renewal of the strange
impulse that I lately spoke of as my temptation. what if
I should go straight in and march to his window?—what
if, by risking to his boyish bewilderment a revelation of
my motive, I should throw across the rest of the mystery
the long halter of my boldness?

This thought held me sufficiently to make me cross
to his threshold and pause again. I preternaturally listened; I figured to myself what might portentously be; I
wondered if his bed were also empty and he too were
secretly at watch. It was a deep, soundless minute, at the
end of which my impulse failed. He was quiet; he might
be innocent; the risk was hideous; I turned away. There
was a figure in the grounds—a figure prowling for a sight,
the visitor with whom Flora was engaged; but it was not
the visitor most concerned with my boy. I hesitated
afresh, but on other grounds and only a few seconds;
then I had made my choice. There were empty rooms at
Bly, and it was only a question of choosing the right one.
The right one suddenly presented itself to me as the lower
one—though high above the gardens—in the solid corner
of the house that I have spoken of as the old tower. This
was a large, square chamber, arranged with some
state as a bedroom, the extravagant size of which made it
so inconvenient that it had not for years, though kept
by Mrs. Grose in exemplary order, been occupied. I had
often admired it and I knew my way about in it; I had
only, after just faltering at the first chill gloom of its
disuse, to pass across it and unbolt as quietly as I could
one of the shutters. Achieving this transit, I uncovered

the glass without a sound and, applying my face to the pane, was able, the darkness without being much less than within, to see that I commanded the right direction. Then I saw something more. The moon made the night extraordinarily penetrable and showed me on the lawn a person, diminished by distance, who stood there motionless and as if fascinated, looking up to where I had appeared—looking, that is, not so much straight at me as at something that was apparently above me. There was clearly another person above me—there was a person on the tower; but the presence on the lawn was not in the least what I had conceived and had confidently hurried to meet. The presence on the lawn—I felt sick as I made it out—was poor little Miles himself.

XI

It was not till late next day that I spoke to Mrs. Grose; the rigor with which I kept my pupils in sight making it often difficult to meet her privately, and the more as we each felt the importance of not provoking —on the part of the servants quite as much as on that of the children—any suspicion of a secret flurry or of a discussion of mysteries. I drew a great security in this particular from her mere smooth aspect. There was nothing in her fresh face to pass on to others my horrible confidences. She believed me, I was sure, absolutely: if she hadn't I don't know what would have become of me, for I couldn't have borne the business alone. But she was a magnificent monument to the blessing of a want of imagination, and if she could see in our little charges nothing but their beauty and amiability, their happiness and cleverness, she had no direct communication with the sources of my trouble. If they had been at all visibly blighted or battered, she would doubtless have grown, on tracing it back, haggard enough to match them; as matters stood, however, I could feel her, when she surveyed them, with her large white arms folded and the habit of serenity in all her look, thank the Lord's mercy that if they were ruined the pieces would still serve. Flights of fancy gave place, in her mind, to a steady fireside glow, and I had already begun to perceive how, with the development of the conviction that—as time went on without a public accident—our young things could, after all, look out for themselves, she addressed her greatest solicitude to the sad case presented by their instructress. That, for myself, was a sound simplification: I could engage that, to the world, my face should tell no tales, but it would have been, in the conditions, an immense added strain to find myself anxious about hers.

At the hour I now speak of she had joined me, under pressure, on the terrace, where, with the lapse of the season, the afternoon sun was now agreeable; and we sat there together while, before us, at a distance, but within call if we wished, the children strolled to and fro in one of their most manageable moods. They moved slowly, in unison, below us, over the lawn, the boy, as they went, reading aloud from a storybook and passing his arm round his sister to keep her quite in touch. Mrs. Grose watched them with positive placidity; then I caught the suppressed intellectual creak with which she conscientiously turned to take from me a view of the back of the tapestry. I had made her a receptacle of lurid things, but there was an odd recognition of my superiority—my accomplishments and my function—in her patience under my pain. She offered her mind to my disclosures as, had I wished to mix a witch's broth and proposed it with assurance, she would have held out a large clean saucepan. This had become thoroughly her attitude by the time that, in my recital of the events of the night, I reached the point of what Miles had said to me when, after seeing him, at such a monstrous hour, almost on the very spot where he happened now to be, I had gone down to bring him in; choosing then, at the window, with a concentrated need of not alarming the house, rather that method than a signal more resonant. I had left her meanwhile in little doubt of my small hope of representing with success even to her actual sympathy my sense of the real splendor of the little inspiration with which, after I had got him into the house, the boy met my final articulate challenge. As soon as I appeared in the moonlight on the terrace, he had come to me as straight as possible; on which I had taken his hand without a word and led him, through the dark spaces, up the staircase where Quint had so hungrily hovered for him, along the lobby where I had listened and trembled, and so to his forsaken room.

Not a sound, on the way, had passed between us, and I had wondered—oh, *how* I had wondered!—if he were groping about in his little mind for something plausible and not too grotesque. It would tax his invention, certainly, and I felt, this time, over his real embarrassment, a curious thrill of triumph. It was a sharp trap for the inscrutable! He couldn't play any longer at innocence; so how the deuce would he get out of it? There beat in me indeed, with the passionate throb of this question, an equal dumb appeal as to how the deuce *I* should. I was confronted at last, as never yet, with all the risk attached even now to sounding my own horrid note. I remember in fact that as we pushed into his little chamber, where the bed had not been slept in at all and the window, uncovered to the moonlight, made the place so clear that there was no need of striking a match—I remember how I suddenly dropped, sank upon the edge of the bed from the force of the idea that he must know how he really, as they say, "had" me. He could do what he liked, with all his cleverness to help him, so long as I should continue to defer to the old tradition of the criminality of those caretakers of the young who minister to superstitions and fears. He "had" me indeed, and in a cleft stick; for who would ever absolve me, who would consent that I should go unhung, if, by the faintest tremor of an overture, I were the first to introduce into our perfect intercourse an element so dire? No, no: it was useless to attempt to convey to Mrs. Grose, just as it is scarcely less so to attempt to suggest here, how, in our short, stiff brush in the dark, he fairly shook me with admiration. I was of course thoroughly kind and merciful; never, never yet had I placed on his little shoulders hands of such tenderness as those with which, while I rested against the bed, I held him there well under fire.

I had no alternative but, in form at least, to put it to him.

"You must tell me now—and all the truth. What did you go out for? What were you doing there?"

I can still see his wonderful smile, the whites of his beautiful eyes, and the uncovering of his little teeth shine to me in the dusk. "If I tell you why, will you understand?" My heart, at this, leaped into my mouth. *Would* he tell me why? I found no sound on my lips to press it, and I was aware of replying only with a vague, repeated, grimacing nod. He was gentleness itself, and while I wagged my head at him he stood there more than ever a little fairy prince. It was his brightness indeed that gave me a respite. Would it be so great if he were really going to tell me? "Well," he said at last, "just exactly in order that you should do this."

"Do what?"

"Think me—for a change—*bad!*" I shall never forget the sweetness and gaiety with which he brought out the word, nor how, on top of it, he bent forward and kissed me. It was practically the end of everything. I met his kiss and I had to make, while I folded him for a minute in my arms, the most stupendous effort not to cry. He had given exactly the account of himself that permitted least of my going behind it, and it was only with the effect of confirming my acceptance of it that, as I presently glanced about the room, I could say—

"Then you didn't undress at all?"

He fairly glittered in the gloom. "Not at all. I sat up and read."

"And when did you go down?"

"At midnight. When I'm bad I *am* bad!"

"I see, I see—it's charming. But how could you be sure I would know it?"

"Oh, I arranged that with Flora." His answers rang out with a readiness! "She was to get up and look out."

"Which is what she did do." It was I who fell into the trap!

"So she disturbed you, and, to see what she was looking at, you also looked—you saw."

"While you," I concurred, "caught your death in the night air!"

He literally bloomed so from this exploit that he could

afford radiantly to assent. "How otherwise should I have been bad enough?" he asked. Then, after another embrace, the incident and our interview closed on my recognition of all the reserves of goodness that, for his joke, he had been able to draw upon.

XII

The particular impression I had received proved in the morning light, I repeat, not quite successfully presentable to Mrs. Grose, though I reinforced it with the mention of still another remark that he had made before we separated. "It all lies in half a dozen words," I said to her, "words that really settle the matter. 'Think, you know, what I *might* do!' He threw that off to show me how good he is. He knows down to the ground what he 'might' do. That's what he gave them a taste of at school."

"Lord, you do change!" cried my friend.

"I don't change—I simply make it out. The four, depend upon it, perpetually meet. If on either of these last nights you had been with either child, you would clearly have understood. The more I've watched and waited the more I've felt that if there were nothing else to make it sure it would be made so by the systematic silence of each. *Never,* by a slip of the tongue, have they so much as alluded to either of their old friends, any more than Miles has alluded to his expulsion. Oh, yes, we may sit here and look at them, and they may show off to us there to their fill; but even while they pretend to be lost in their fairytale they're steeped in their vision of the dead restored. He's not reading to her," I declared; "they're talking of *them*—they're talking horrors! I go on, I know, as if I were crazy; and it's a wonder I'm not. What I've seen would have made *you* so; but it has only made me more lucid, made me get hold of still other things."

My lucidity must have seemed awful, but the charming creatures who were victims of it, passing and repassing in their interlocked sweetness, gave my colleague something to hold on by; and I felt how tight she held as, without stirring in the breath of my passion, she covered them still with her eyes. "Of what other things have you got hold?"

"Why, of the very things that have delighted, fascinated, and yet, at bottom, as I now so strangely see, mystified and troubled me. Their more than earthly beauty, their absolutely unnatural goodness. It's a game," I went on; "it's a policy and a fraud!"

"On the part of little darlings——?"

"As yet mere lovely babies? Yes, mad as that seems!" The very act of bringing it out really helped me to trace it—follow it all up and piece it all together. "They haven't been good—they've only been absent. It has been easy to live with them, because they're simply leading a life of their own. They're not mine—they're not ours. They're his and they're hers!"

"Quint's and that woman's?"

"Quint's and that woman's. They want to get to them."

Oh, how, at this, poor Mrs. Grose appeared to study them! "But for what?"

"For the love of all the evil that, in those dreadful days, the pair put into them. And to ply them with that evil still, to keep up the work of demons, is what brings the others back."

"Laws!" said my friend under her breath. The exclamation was homely, but it revealed a real acceptance of my further proof of what, in the bad time—for there had been a worse even than this!—must have occurred. There could have been no such justification for me as the plain assent of her experience to whatever depth of depravity I found credible in our brace of scoundrels. It was in obvious submission of memory that she brought out after a moment: "They *were* rascals! But what can they now do?" she pursued.

"Do?" I echoed so loud that Miles and Flora, as they passed at their distance, paused an instant in their walk and looked at us. "Don't they do enough?" I demanded in a lower tone, while the children, having smiled and nodded and kissed hands to us, resumed their exhibition. We were held by it a minute; then I answered: "They can destroy them!" At this my companion did turn, but the inquiry she launched was a silent one, the effect of which was to make me more explicit. "They don't know, as yet, quite how—but they're trying hard. They're seen only across, as it were, and beyond—in strange places and on high places, the top of towers, the roof of houses, the outside of windows, the further edge of pools; but there's a deep design, on either side, to shorten the distance and overcome the obstacle; and the success of the tempters is only a question of time. They've only to keep to their suggestions of danger."

"For the children to come?"

"And perish in the attempt!" Mrs. Grose slowly got up, and I scrupulously added: "Unless, of course, we can prevent!"

Standing there before me while I kept my seat, she visibly turned things over. "Their uncle must do the preventing. He must take them away."

"And who's to make him?"

She had been scanning the distance, but she now dropped on me a foolish face. "You, miss."

"By writing to him that his house is poisoned and his little nephew and niece mad?"

"But if they *are,* miss?"

"And if I am myself, you mean? That's charming news to be sent him by a governess whose prime undertaking was to give him no worry."

Mrs. Grose considered, following the children again. "Yes, he do hate worry. That was the great reason——"

"Why those fiends took him in so long? No doubt, though his indifference must have been awful. As I'm not a fiend, at any rate, I shouldn't take him in."

My companion, after an instant and for all answer, sat down again and grasped my arm. "Make him at any rate come to you."

I stared. "To *me?*" I had a sudden fear of what she might do. "'Him'?"

"He ought to *be* here—he ought to help."

I quickly rose, and I think I must have shown her a queerer face than ever yet. "You see me asking him for a visit?" No, with her eyes on my face she evidently couldn't. Instead of it even—as a woman reads another

—she could see what I myself saw: his derision, his amusement, his contempt for the breakdown of my resignation at being left alone and for the fine machinery I had set in motion to attract his attention to my slighted charms. She didn't know—no one knew—how proud I had been to serve him and to stick to our terms; yet she nonetheless took the measure, I think, of the warning I now gave her. "If you should so lose your head as to appeal to him for me——"

She was really frightened. "Yes, miss?"

"I would leave, on the spot, both him and you."

XIII

It was all very well to join them, but speaking to them proved quite as much as ever an effort beyond my strength—offered, in close quarters, difficulties as insurmountable as before. This situation continued a month, and with new aggravations and particular notes, the note above all, sharper and sharper, of the small ironic consciousness on the part of my pupils. It was not, I am as sure today as I was sure then, my mere infernal imagination: it was absolutely traceable that they were aware of my predicament and that this strange relation made, in a manner, for a long time, the air in which we moved. I don't mean that they had their tongues in their cheeks or did anything vulgar, for that was not one of their dangers: I do mean, on the other hand, that the element of the unnamed and untouched became, between us, greater than any other, and that so much avoidance could not have been so successfully effected without a great deal of tacit arrangement. It was as if, at moments, we were perpetually coming into sight of subjects before which we must stop short, turning suddenly out of alleys that we perceived to be blind, closing with a little bang that made us look at each other—for, like all bangs, it was something louder than we had intended—the doors we had indiscreetly opened. All roads lead to Rome, and there were times when it might have struck us that almost every branch of study or subject of conversation skirted forbidden ground. Forbidden ground was the question of the return of the dead in general and of whatever, in especial, might survive, in memory, of the friends little children had lost. There were days when I could have sworn that one of them had, with a small invisible nudge, said to the other: "She thinks she'll do it this time—but she *won't!*" To "do it" would have been to indulge for instance—and for once in a way—in some direct reference to the lady who had prepared them for my discipline. They had a delightful endless appetite for passages in my own history, to which I had again and again treated them; they were in possession of everything that had ever happened to me, had had, with every circumstance the story of my smallest adventures and of those of my brothers and sisters and of the cat and the dog at home, as well as many particulars of the eccentric nature of my father, of the furniture and arrangement of our house, and of the conversation of the old women of our village. There were things enough, taking one with another, to chatter about, if one went very fast and knew by instinct when to go round. They pulled with an art of their own the strings of my invention and my memory; and nothing else perhaps, when I thought of such occasions afterward, gave me so the suspicion of being watched from under cover. It was in any case over *my* life, *my* past, and *my* friends alone that we could take anything like our ease—a state of affairs that led them sometimes without the least pertinence to break out into sociable reminders. I was invited—with no visible connection—to repeat afresh Goody Gosling's celebrated *mot* or to confirm the details already supplied as to the cleverness of the vicarage pony.

It was partly at such junctures as these and partly at quite different ones that, with the turn my matters had now taken, my predicament, as I have called it, grew most sensible. The fact that the days passed for me without another encounter ought, it would have appeared, to have done something toward soothing my nerves. Since the light brush, that second night on the upper landing, of the presence of a woman at the foot of the stair, I had seen nothing, whether in or out of the house, that one had better not have seen. There was many a corner round which I expected to come upon Quint, and many a situation that, in a merely sinister way, would have favored the appearance of Miss Jessel. The summer had turned, the summer had gone; the autumn had dropped upon Bly and had blown out half our lights. The place, with its gray sky and withered garlands, its bared spaces and scattered dead leaves, was like a theater after the performance—all strewn with crumpled playbills. There were exactly states of the air, conditions of sound and of stillness, unspeakable impressions of the *kind* of ministering moment, that brought back to me, long enough to catch it, the feeling of the medium in which, that June evening out of doors, I had had my first sight of Quint, and in which, too, at those other instants, I had, after seeing him through the window, looked for him in vain in the circle of shrubbery. I recognized the signs, the portents—I recognized the moment, the spot. But they remained unaccompanied and empty, and I continued unmolested; if unmolested one could call a young woman whose sensibility had, in the most extraordinary fashion, not declined but deepened. I had said in my talk with Mrs. Grose on that horrid scene of Flora's by the lake—and had perplexed her by so saying—that it would from that moment distress me much more to lose my power than to keep it. I had then expressed what was vividly in my mind: the truth that, whether the children really saw or not—since, that is, it was not yet definitely proved—I greatly preferred, as a safeguard, the fullness of my own exposure. I was ready to know the very worst that was to be known. What I had then had an ugly glimpse of was that my eyes might be sealed just while theirs were most opened. Well, my eyes *were* sealed, it appeared, at present—a consummation for which it seemed blasphemous not to thank God. There was, alas, a difficulty about that: I would have thanked him with all my soul had I not had in a proportionate measure this conviction of the secret of my pupils.

How can I retrace today the strange steps of my obsession? There were times of our being together when I would have been ready to swear that, literally, in my presence, but with my direct sense of it closed, they had visitors who were known and were welcome. Then it was that, had I not been deterred by the very chance that such an injury might prove greater than the injury to be averted, my exultation would have broken out. "They're here, they're here, you little wretches," I would have cried, "and you can't deny it now!" The little wretches denied it with all the added volume of their sociability and their tenderness, in just the crystal depths of which—like the flash of a fish in a stream—the mockery of their advantage peeped up. The shock, in truth, had sunk into me still deeper than I knew on the night when, looking out to see either Quint or Miss Jessel under the stars, I had beheld the boy over whose rest I watched and who had immediately brought in with him—had straightway, there, turned it on me—the lovely upward look with which, from the battlements above me, the hideous apparition of Quint had played. If it was a question of a scare, my discovery on this occasion had scared me more than any other, and it was in the condition of nerves produced by it that I made my actual inductions. They harassed me so that sometimes, at odd moments, I shut myself up audibly to rehearse—it was at once a fantastic relief and a renewed despair—the manner in which I might come to the point. I approached it from one side and the other while, in my room, I flung myself about, but I always broke down in the monstrous utterance of names. As they died away on my lips, I said to myself that I should indeed help them to represent something infamous if, by pronouncing them, I should violate as rare a little case of instinctive delicacy as any schoolroom, probably, had ever known. When I said to myself: "*They* have the manners to be silent, and you, trusted as you are, the baseness to speak!" I felt myself crimson and I covered my face with my hands. After these secret scenes I chattered more than ever, going on volubly enough till one of our prodigious, palpable hushes occurred—I can call them nothing else—the strange, dizzy lift or swim (I try for terms!) into a stillness, a pause of all life, that had nothing to do with the more or less noise that at the moment we might be engaged in making and that I could hear through any deepened exhilaration or quickened recitation or louder strum of the piano. Then it was that the others, the outsiders, were there. Though they were not angels, they "passed," as the French say, causing me, while they stayed, to tremble with the fear of their addressing to their younger victims some yet more infernal message or more vivid image than they had thought good enough for myself.

What it was most impossible to get rid of was the cruel idea that, whatever I had seen, Miles and Flora saw *more*—things terrible and unguessable and that sprang from dreadful passages of intercourse in the past. Such things naturally left on the surface, for the time, a chill which we vociferously denied that we felt; and we had, all three, with repetition, got into such splendid training that we went, each time, almost automatically, to mark the close of the incident, through the very same movements. It was striking of the children, at all events, to kiss me inveterately with a kind of wild irrelevance and never to fail—one or the other—of the precious question that had helped us through many a peril. "When do you think he *will* come? Don't you think we *ought* to write?"—there was nothing like that inquiry, we found by experience, for carrying off an awkwardness. "He" of course was their uncle in Harley Street; and we lived in much profusion of theory that he might at any moment arrive to mingle in our circle. It was impossible to have given less encouragement than he had done to such a doctrine, but if we had not had the doctrine to fall back upon we should have deprived each other of some of our finest exhibitions. He never wrote to them—that may have been selfish, but it was a part of the flattery of his trust of me; for the way in which a man pays his highest tribute to a woman is apt to be but by the more festal celebration of one of the sacred laws of his comfort; and I held that I carried out the spirit of the pledge given not to appeal to him when I let my charges understand that their own letters were but charming literary exercises. They were too beautiful to be posted; I kept them myself; I have them all to this hour. This was a rule indeed which only added to the satiric effect of my being plied with the supposition that he might at any moment be among us. It was exactly as if my charges knew how almost more awkward than anything else that might be for me. There appears to me, moreover, as I look back, no note in all this more extraordinary than the mere fact that, in spite of my tension and of their triumph, I never lost patience with them. Adorable they must in truth have been, I now reflect, that I didn't in these days hate them! Would exasperation, however, if relief had longer been postponed, finally have betrayed me? It little matters, for relief arrived. I call it relief, though it was only the relief that a snap brings to a strain or the burst of a thunderstorm to a day of suffocation. It was at least change, and it came with a rush.

XIV

Walking to church a certain Sunday morning, I had little Miles at my side and his sister, in advance of us and at Mrs. Grose's, well in sight. It was a crisp, clear day, the first of its order for some time; the night had brought a touch of frost, and the autumn air, bright and sharp, made the church bells almost gay. It was an odd accident of thought that I should have happened at such a moment to be particularly and very gratefully struck with the obedience of my little charges. Why did they never resent my inexorable, my perpetual society? Something or other had brought nearer home to me that I had all but pinned the boy to my shawl and that, in the way our companions were marshaled before me, I might have appeared to provide against some danger of rebellion. I was like a gaoler with an eye to possible surprises and escapes. But all this belonged—I mean their magnificent little surrender—just to the special array of the facts that were most abysmal. Turned out for Sunday by his uncle's tailor, who had had a free hand and a notion of pretty waistcoats and of his grand little air, Miles's whole title to independence, the rights of his sex and situation, were so stamped upon him that if he had suddenly struck for freedom I should have had nothing to say. I was by the strangest of chances wondering how I should meet him when the revolution unmistakably occurred. I call it a revolution because I now see how, with the word he spoke, the curtain rose on the last act of my dreadful drama, and the catastrophe was precipitated. "Look here, my dear, you know," he charmingly said, "when in the world, please, am I going back to school?"

Transcribed here the speech sounds harmless enough, particularly as uttered in the sweet, high, casual pipe with which, at all interlocutors, but above all at his eternal governess, he threw off intonations as if he were tossing roses. There was something in them that always made one "catch," and I caught, at any rate, now so effectually that I stopped as short as if one of the trees of the park had fallen across the road. There was something new, on the spot, between us, and he was perfectly aware that I recognized it, though, to enable me to do so, he had no need to look a whit less candid and charming than usual. I could feel in him how he already, from my at first finding nothing to reply, perceived the advantage he had gained. I was so slow to find anything that he had plenty of time, after a minute, to continue with his suggestive but inconclusive smile: "You know, my dear, that for a fellow to be with a lady *always*——!" His "my dear" was constantly on his lips for me, and nothing could have expressed more the exact shade of the sentiment with which I desired to inspire my pupils than its fond familiarity. It was so respectfully easy.

But, oh, how I felt that at present I must pick my own phrases! I remember that, to gain time, I tried to laugh, and I seemed to see in the beautiful face with which he watched me how ugly and queer I looked. "And always with the same lady?" I returned.

He neither blanched nor winked. The whole thing was virtually out between us. "Ah, of course, she's a jolly, 'perfect' lady; but, after all, I'm a fellow, don't you see? that's—well, getting on."

I lingered there with him an instant ever so kindly. "Yes, you're getting on." Oh, but I felt helpless!

I have kept to this day the heartbreaking little idea of

how he seemed to know that and to play with it. "And you can't say I've not been awfully good, can you?"

I laid my hand on his shoulder, for, though I felt how much better it would have been to walk on, I was not yet quite able. "No, I can't say that, Miles."

"Except just that one night, you know——!"

"That one night?" I couldn't look as straight as he.

"Why, when I went down—went out of the house."

"Oh, yes. But I forget what you did it for."

"You forget?"—he spoke with the sweet extravagance of childish reproach. "Why, it was to show you I could!"

"Oh, yes, you could."

"And I can again."

I felt that I might, perhaps, after all, succeed in keeping my wits about me. "Certainly. But you won't."

"No, not *that* again. It was nothing."

"It was nothing," I said. "But we must go on."

He resumed our walk with me, passing his hand into my arm. "Then when *am* I going back?"

I wore, in turning it over, my most responsible air. "Were you very happy at school?"

He just considered. "Oh, I'm happy enough anywhere!"

"Well, then," I quavered, "if you're just as happy here——!"

"Ah, but that isn't everything! Of course you know a lot——"

"But you hint that you know almost as much?" I risked as he paused.

"Not half I want to!" Miles honestly professed. "But it isn't so much that."

"What is it, then?"

"Well—I want to see more life."

"I see; I see." We had arrived within sight of the church and of various persons, including several of the household of Bly, on their way to it and clustered about the door to see us go in. I quickened our step; I wanted to get there before the question between us opened up much further; I reflected hungrily that, for more than an hour, he would have to be silent; and I thought with envy of the comparative dusk of the pew and of the almost spiritual help of the hassock on which I might bend my knees.

I seemed literally to be running a race with some confusion to which he was about to reduce me, but I felt that he had got in first when, before we had even entered the churchyard, he threw out—

"I want my own sort!"

It literally made me bound forward. "There are not many of your own sort, Miles!" I laughed. "Unless perhaps dear little Flora!"

"You really compare me to a baby girl?"

This found me singularly weak. "Don't you, then, *love* our sweet Flora?"

"If I didn't—and you, too; if I didn't——!" he repeated as if retreating for a jump, yet leaving his thought so unfinished that, after we had come into the gate, another stop, which he imposed on me by the pressure of his arm, had become inevitable. Mrs. Grose and Flora had passed into the church, the other worshippers had followed, and we were, for the minute, alone among the old, thick graves. We had paused, on the path from the gate, by a low, oblong, tablelike tomb.

"Yes, if you didn't——?"

He looked, while I waited, about at the graves. "Well, you know what!" But he didn't move, and he presently produced something that made me drop straight down on the stone slab, as if suddenly to rest. "Does my uncle think what *you* think?"

I markedly rested. "How do you know what I think?"

"Ah, well, of course I don't; for it strikes me you never tell me. But I mean does *he* know?"

"Know what, Miles?"

"Why, the way I'm going on."

I perceived quickly enough that I could make, to this inquiry, no answer that would not involve something of a sacrifice of my employer. Yet it appeared to me that we were all, at Bly, sufficiently sacrificed to make that venial. "I don't think your uncle much cares."

Miles, on this, stood looking at me. "Then don't you think he can be made to?"

"In what way?"

"Why, by his coming down."

"But who'll get him to come down?"

"*I* will!" the boy said with extraordinary brightness and emphasis. He gave me another look charged with that expression and then marched off alone into church.

XV

The business was practically settled from the moment I never followed him. It was a pitiful surrender to agitation, but my being aware of this had somehow no power to restore me. I only sat there on my tomb and read into what my little friend had said to me the fullness of its meaning; by the time I had grasped the whole of which I had also embraced, for absence, the pretext that I was ashamed to offer my pupils and the rest of the congregation such an example of delay. What I said to myself above all was that Miles had got something out of me and that the proof of it, for him, would be just this awkward collapse. He had got out of me that there was something I was much afraid of and that he should probably be able to make use of my fear to gain, for his own purpose, more freedom. My fear was of having to deal with the intolerable question of the grounds of his dismissal from school, for that was really but the question of the horrors gathered behind. That his uncle should arrive to treat with me of these things was a solution that, strictly speaking, I ought now to have desired to bring on; but I could so little face the ugliness and the pain of it that I simply procrastinated and lived from hand to mouth. The boy, to my deep discomposure, was immensely in the right, was in a position to say to me: "Either you clear up with my guardian the mystery of this interruption of my studies, or you cease to expect me to lead with you a life that's so unnatural for a boy." What was so unnatural for the particular boy I was concerned with was this sudden revelation of a consciousness and a plan.

That was what really overcame me, what prevented my going in. I walked round the church, hesitating, hovering; I reflected that I had already, with him, hurt myself beyond repair. Therefore I could patch up nothing, and it was too extreme an effort to squeeze beside him into the pew: he would be so much more sure than ever to pass his arm into mine and make me sit there for an hour in close, silent contact with his commentary on our talk. For the first minute since his arrival I wanted to get away from him. As I paused beneath the high east window and listened to the sounds of worship, I was taken with an impulse that might master me, I felt, completely should I give it the least encouragement. I might easily put an end to my predicament by getting away altogether. Here was my chance; there was no one to stop me; I could give the whole thing up—turn my back and retreat. It was only a question of hurrying again, for a few preparations, to the house which the attendance at church of so many of the servants would practically have left unoccupied. No one, in short, could blame me if I should just drive desperately off. What was it to get away if I got away only till dinner? That would be in a couple of hours, at the end of which—I had the acute prevision—my little pupils would play at innocent wonder about my nonappearance in their train.

"What *did* you do, you naughty, bad thing? Why in the world, to worry us so—and take our thoughts off, too, don't you know?—did you desert us at the very door?" I couldn't meet such questions nor, as they asked them, their false little lovely eyes; yet it was all so exactly what I should have to meet that, as the prospect grew sharp to me, I at last let myself go.

I got, so far as the immediate moment was concerned, away; I came straight out of the churchyard and, thinking hard, retraced my steps through the park. It seemed to me that by the time I reached the house I had made up my mind I would fly. The Sunday stillness both of the approaches and of the interior, in which I met no one, fairly excited me with a sense of opportunity. Were I to get off quickly, this way, I should get off without a scene, without a word. My quickness would have to be remarkable, however, and the question of a conveyance was the great one to settle. Tormented, in the hall, with difficulties and obstacles, I remember sinking down at the foot of the staircase—suddenly collapsing there on the lowest step and then, with a revulsion, recalling that it was exactly where more than a month before, in the darkness of night and just so bowed with evil things, I had seen the specter of the most horrible of women. At this I was able to straighten myself; I went the rest of the way up; I made, in my bewilderment, for the schoolroom, where there were objects belonging to me that I should have to take. But I opened the door to find again, in a flash, my eyes unsealed. In the presence of what I saw I reeled straight back upon my resistance.

Seated at my own table in clear noonday light I saw a person whom, without my previous experience, I should have taken at the first blush for some housemaid who might have stayed at home to look after the place and who, availing herself of rare relief from observation and of the schoolroom table and my pens, ink, and paper, had applied herself to the considerable effort of a letter to her sweetheart. There was an effort in the way that, while her arms rested on the table, her hands with evident weariness supported her head; but at the moment I took this in I had already become aware that, in spite of my entrance, her attitude strangely persisted. Then it was—with the very act of its announcing itself— that her identity flared up in a change of posture. She rose, not as if she had heard me, but with an indescribable grand melancholy of indifference and detachment, and, within a dozen feet of me, stood there as my vile predecessor. Dishonored and tragic, she was all before me; but even as I fixed and, for memory, secured it, the awful image passed away. Dark as midnight in her black dress, her haggard beauty and her unutterable woe, she had looked at me long enough to appear to say that her right to sit at my table was as good as mine to sit at hers. While these instants lasted, indeed, I had the extraordinary chill of feeling that it was I who was the intruder. It was as a wild protest against it that, actually addressing her—"You terrible, miserable woman!"—I heard myself break into a sound that, by the open door, rang through the long passage and the empty house. She looked at me as if she heard me, but I had recovered myself and cleared the air. There was nothing in the room the next minute but the sunshine and a sense that I must stay.

XVI

I had so perfectly expected that the return of my pupils would be marked by a demonstration that I was freshly upset at having to take into account that they were dumb about my absence. Instead of gaily denouncing and caressing me, they made no allusion to my having failed them, and I was left, for the time, on perceiving that she too said nothing, to study Mrs. Grose's odd face. I did this to such purpose that I made sure they had in some way bribed her to silence; a silence that, however, I would engage to break down on the first private opportunity. This opportunity came before tea: I secured five minutes with her in the housekeeper's room, where, in the twilight, amid a smell of lately baked bread, but with the place all swept and garnished, I found her sitting in pained placidity before the fire. So I see her still, so I see her best: facing the flame from her straight chair in the dusky, shining room, a large clean image of the "put away"—of drawers closed and locked and rest without a remedy.

"Oh, yes, they asked me to say nothing; and to please them—so long as they were there—of course I promised. But what had happened to you?"

"I only went with you for the walk," I said. "I had then to come back to meet a friend."

She showed her surprise. "A friend—*you?*"

"Oh, yes, I have a couple!" I laughed. "But did the children give you a reason?"

"For not alluding to your leaving us? Yes; they said you would like it better. Do you like it better?"

My face had made her rueful. "No, I like it worse!" But after an instant I added: "Did they say why I should like it better?"

"No; Master Miles only said, 'We must do nothing but what she likes!'"

"I wish indeed he would! And what did Flora say?"

"Miss Flora was too sweet. She said, 'Oh, of course, of course!'—and I said the same."

I thought a moment. "You were too sweet, too—I can hear you all. But nonetheless, between Miles and me, it's now all out."

"All out?" My companion stared. "But what, miss?"

"Everything. It doesn't matter. I've made up my mind. I came, home, my dear," I went on, "for a talk with Miss Jessel."

I had by this time formed the habit of having Mrs. Grose literally well in hand in advance of my sounding that note; so that even now, as she bravely blinked under the signal of my word, I could keep her comparatively firm. "A talk! Do you mean she spoke?"

"It came to that. I found her, on my return, in the schoolroom."

"And what did she say?" I can hear the good woman still, and the candor of her stupefaction.

"That she suffers the torments——!"

It was this, of a truth, that made her, as she filled out my picture, gape. "Do you mean," she faltered, "—of the lost?"

"Of the lost. Of the damned. And that's why, to share them——" I faltered myself with the horror of it.

But my companion, with less imagination, kept me up. "To share them——?"

"She wants Flora." Mrs. Grose might, as I gave it to her, fairly have fallen away from me had I not been prepared. I still held her there, to show I was. "As I've told you, however, it doesn't matter."

"Because you've, made up your mind? But to what?"

"To everything."

"And what do you call 'everything'?"

"Why, sending for their uncle."

"Oh, miss, in pity do," my friend broke out.

"Ah, but I will, I will! I see it's the only way. What's 'out,' as I told you, with Miles is that if he thinks I'm afraid to—and has ideas of what he gains by that—he shall see he's mistaken. Yes, yes; his uncle shall have it here from me on the spot (and before the boy himself, if necessary) that if I'm to be reproached with having done nothing again about more school——"

"Yes, miss——" my companion pressed me.

"Well, there's that awful reason."

There were now clearly so many of these for my poor colleague that she was excusable for being vague. But —a—which?"

"Why, the letter from his old place."

"You'll show it to the master?"

"I ought to have done so on the instant."

"Oh, no!" said Mrs. Grose with decision.

"I'll put it before him," I went on inexorably, "that I can't undertake to work the question on behalf of a child who has been expelled——"

"For we've never in the least known what!" Mrs. Grose declared.

"For wickedness. For what else—when he's so clever and beautiful and perfect? Is he stupid? Is he untidy? Is he infirm? Is he ill-natured? He's exquisite—so it can be only *that;* and that would open up the whole thing. After all," I said, "it's their uncle's fault. If he left here such people——!"

"He didn't really in the least know them. The fault's mine." She had turned quite pale.

"Well, you shan't suffer," I answered.

"The children shan't!" she emphatically returned.

I was silent awhile; we looked at each other. "Then what am I to tell him?"

"You needn't tell him anything. *I'll* tell him."

I measured this. "Do you mean you'll write——?" Remembering she couldn't, I caught myself up. "How do you communicate?"

"I tell the bailiff. *He* writes."

"And should you like him to write our story?"

My question had a sarcastic force that I had not fully intended, and it made her, after a moment, inconsequently break down. The tears were again in her eyes. "Ah, miss, you write!"

"Well—tonight," I at last answered; and on this we separated.

XVII

I went so far, in the evening, as to make a beginning. The weather had changed back, a great wind was abroad, and beneath the lamp, in my room, with Flora at peace beside me, I sat for a long time before a blank sheet of paper and listened to the lash of the rain and the batter of the gusts. Finally I went out, taking a candle; I crossed the passage and listened a minute at Miles's door. What, under my endless obsession, I had been impelled to listen for was some betrayal of his not being at rest, and I presently caught one, but not in the form I had expected. His voice tinkled out. "I say, you there—come in." It was a gaiety in the gloom!

I went in with my light and found him, in bed, very wide awake, but very much at his ease. "Well, what are you up to?" he asked with a grace of sociability in which it occurred to me that Mrs. Grose, had she been present, might have looked in vain for proof that anything was "out."

I stood over him with my candle. "How did you know I was there?"

"Why, of course I heard you. Did you fancy you made no noise? You're like a troop of cavalry!" he beautifully laughed.

"Then you weren't asleep?"

"Not much! I lie awake and think."

I had put my candle, designedly, a short way off, and then, as he held out his friendly old hand to me, had sat down on the edge of his bed. "What is it," I asked, "that you think of?"

"What in the world, my dear, but *you?*"

"Ah, the pride I take in your appreciation doesn't insist on that! I had so far rather you slept."

"Well, I think also, you know, of this queer business of ours."

I marked the coolness of his firm little hand. "Of what queer business, Miles?"

"Why, the way you bring me up. And all the rest!"

I fairly held my breath a minute, and even from my glimmering taper there was light enough to show how he smiled up at me from his pillow. "What do you mean by all the rest?"

"Oh, you know, you know!"

I could say nothing for a minute, though I felt, as I held his hand and our eyes continued to meet, that my silence had all the air of admitting his charge and that nothing in the whole world of reality was perhaps at that moment so fabulous as our actual relation. "Certainly you shall go back to school," I said, "if it be that that troubles you. But not to the old place—we must find another, a better. How could I know it did trouble you, this question, when you never told me so, never spoke of it at all?" His clear, listening face, framed in its smooth whiteness, made him for the minute as appealing as some wistful patient in a children's hospital; and I would have given, as the resemblance came to me, all I possessed on earth really to be the nurse or the sister of charity who might have helped to cure him. Well, even as it was, I perhaps might help! "Do you know you've never said a word to me about your school—I mean the old one; never mentioned it in any way?"

He seemed to wonder; he smiled with the same loveliness. But he clearly gained time; he waited, he called for guidance. "Haven't I?" It wasn't for *me* to help him—it was for the thing I had met!

Something in his tone and the expression of his face, as I got this from him, set my heart aching with such a pang as it had never yet known; so unutterably touching was it to see his little brain puzzled and his little resources taxed to play, under the spell laid on him, a part of innocence and consistency. "No, never—from the hour you came back. You've never mentioned to me one of your masters, one of your comrades, nor the least little thing that ever happened to you at school. Never, little Miles—no, never—have you given me an inkling of anything that *may* have happened there. Therefore you can fancy how much I'm in the dark. Until you came out, that way, this morning, you had, since the first hour I saw you, scarce even made a reference to anything in your previous life. You seemed so perfectly to accept the present." It was extraordinary how my absolute conviction of his secret precocity (or whatever I might call the poison of an influence that I dared but half to phrase) made him, in spite of the faint breath of his inward trouble, appear as accessible as an older person —imposed him almost as an intellectual equal. "I thought you wanted to go on as you are."

It struck me that at this he just faintly colored. He gave, at any rate, like a convalescent slightly fatigued, a languid shake of his head. "I don't—I don't. I want to get away."

"You're tired of Bly?"

"Oh, no, I like Bly."

"Well, then——?"

"Oh, *you* know what a boy wants!"

I felt that I didn't know so well as Miles, and I took temporary refuge. "You want to go to your uncle?"

Again, at this, with his sweet ironic face, he made a movement on the pillow. "Ah, you can't get off with that!"

I was silent a little, and it was I, now, I think, who changed color. "My dear, I don't want to get off!"

"You can't, even if you do. You can't, you can't!"— he lay beautifully staring. "My uncle must come down, and you must completely settle things."

"If we do," I returned with some spirit, "you may be sure it will be to take you quite away."

"Well, don't you understand that that's exactly what I'm working for? You'll have to tell him—about the way you've let it all drop: you'll have to tell him a tremendous lot!"

The exultation with which he uttered this helped me somehow, for the instant, to meet him rather more. "And how much will *you*, Miles, have to tell him? There are things he'll ask you!"

He turned it over. "Very likely. But what things?"

"The things you've never told me. To make up his mind what to do with you. He can't send you back——"

"Oh, I don't want to go back!" he broke in. "I want a new field."

He said it with admirable serenity, with positive unimpeachable gaiety; and doubtless it was that very note that most evoked for me the poignancy, the unnatural childish tragedy, of his probable reappearance at the end of three months with all this bravado and still more dishonor. It overwhelmed me now that I should never be able to bear that, and it made me let myself go. I threw myself upon him and in the tenderness of my pity I embraced him. "Dear little Miles, dear little Miles——!"

My face was close to his, and he let me kiss him, simply taking it with indulgent good humor. "Well, old lady?"

"Is there nothing—nothing at all that you want to tell me?"

He turned off a little, facing round toward the wall and holding up his hand to look at as one had seen sick children look. "I've told you—I told you this morning."

Oh, I was sorry for him! "That you just want me not to worry you?"

He looked round at me now, as if in recognition of my understanding him; then ever so gently, "To let me alone," he replied.

There was even a singular little dignity in it, something that made me release him, yet, when I had slowly risen, linger beside him. God knows I never wished to harass him, but I felt that merely, at this, to turn my back on him was to abandon or, to put it more truly, to lose him. "I've just begun a letter to your uncle," I said.

"Well, then, finish it!"

I waited a minute. "What happened before?"

He gazed up at me again. "Before what?"

"Before you came back. And before you went away."

For some time he was silent, but he continued to meet my eyes. "What happened?"

It made me, the sound of the words, in which it seemed to me that I caught for the very first time a small faint quaver of consenting consciousness—it made me drop on my knees beside the bed and seize once more the chance of possessing him. "Dear little Miles, dear little Miles, if you *knew* how I want to help you! It's only that, it's nothing but that, and I'd rather die than give you a pain or do you a wrong—I'd rather die than hurt a hair of you. Dear little Miles"—oh, I brought it out now even if I *should* go too far—"I just want you to help me to save you!" But I knew in a moment after this that I had gone too far. The answer to my appeal was instantaneous, but it came in the form of an extraordinary blast and chill, a gust of frozen air, and a shake of the room as great as if, in the wild wind, the casement had crashed in. The boy gave a loud, high shriek, which, lost in the rest of the shock of sound, might have seemed, indistinctly, though I was so close to him, a note either of jubilation or of terror. I jumped to my feet again and was conscious of darkness. So for a moment we remained, while I stared about me and saw that the drawn curtains were unstirred and the window tight. "Why, the candle's out!" I then cried.

"It was I who blew it, dear!" said Miles.

XVIII

The next day, after lessons, Mrs. Grose found a moment to say to me quietly: "Have you written, miss?"

"Yes—I've written." But I didn't add—for the hour—that my letter, sealed and directed, was still in my pocket. There would be time enough to send it before the messenger should go to the village. Meanwhile there had been, on the part of my pupils, no more brilliant, more exemplary morning. It was exactly as if they had both had at heart to gloss over any recent little friction. They performed the dizziest feats of arithmetic, soaring quite out of *my* feeble range, and perpetrated, in higher spirits than ever, geographical and historical jokes. It was conspicuous of course in Miles in particular that he appeared to wish to show how easily he could let me down. This child, to my memory, really lives in a setting of beauty and misery that no words can translate; there was a distinction all his own in every impulse he revealed; never was a small natural creature, to the uninitiated eye all frankness and freedom, a more ingenious, a more extraordinary little gentleman. I had perpetually to guard against the wonder of contemplation into which my initiated view betrayed me; to check the irrelevant gaze and discouraged sigh in which I constantly both attacked and renounced the enigma of what such a little gentleman could have done that deserved a penalty. Say that, by the dark prodigy I knew, the imagination of all evil *had* been opened up to him: all the justice within me ached for the proof that it could ever have flowered into an act.

He had never, at any rate, been such a little gentleman as when, after our early dinner on this dreadful day, he came round to me and asked if I shouldn't like him, for half an hour, to play to me. David playing to Saul could never have shown a finer sense of the occasion. It was literally a charming exhibition of tact, of magnanimity, and quite tantamount to his saying outright: "The true knights we love to read about never push an advantage too far. I know what you mean now: you mean that—to be let alone yourself and not followed up—you'll cease to worry and spy upon me, won't keep me so close to you, will let me go and come. Well, I 'come,' you see—but I don't go! There'll be plenty of time for that. I do really delight in your society, and I only want to show you that I contended for a principle." It may be imagined whether I resisted this appeal or failed to accompany him again, hand in hand, to the schoolroom. He sat down at the old piano and played as he had never played; and if there are those who think he had better have been kicking a football I can only say that I wholly agree with them. For at the end of a time that under his influence I had quite ceased to measure, I started up with a strange sense of having literally slept at my post. It was after luncheon, and by the schoolroom fire, and yet I hadn't really, in the least, slept: I had only done something much worse —I had forgotten. Where, all this time, was Flora? When I put the question to Miles, he played on a minute before answering and then could only say: "Why, my dear, how do *I* know?"—breaking moreover into a happy laugh which, immediately after, as if it were a vocal accompaniment, he prolonged into incoherent, extravagant song.

I went straight to my room, but his sister was not there; then, before going downstairs, I looked into several others. As she was nowhere about she would surely be with Mrs. Grose, whom, in the comfort of that theory, I accordingly proceeded in quest of. I found her where I had found her the evening before, but she met my quick challenge with blank, scared ignorance. She had only supposed that, after the repast, I had carried off both the children; as to which she was quite in her right, for it was the very first time I had allowed the little girl out of my sight without some special provision. Of course now indeed she might be with the maids, so that the immediate thing was to look for her without an air of alarm. This we promptly arranged between us; but when, ten minutes later and in pursuance of our arrangement, we met in the hall, it was only to report on either side that after guarded inquiries we had altogether failed to trace her. For a minute there, apart from observation, we exchanged mute alarms, and I could feel with what high interest my friend returned me all those I had from the first given her.

"She'll be above," she presently said—"in one of the rooms you haven't searched."

"No; she's at a distance." I had made up my mind. "She has gone out."

Mrs. Grose stared. "Without a hat?"

I naturally also looked volumes. "Isn't that woman always without one?"

"She's with *her?*"

"She's with *her!*" I declared. "We must find them."

My hand was on my friend's arm, but she failed for the moment, confronted with such an account of the matter, to respond to my pressure. She communed, on the contrary, on the spot, with her uneasiness. "And where's Master Miles?"

"Oh, *he's* with Quint. They're in the schoolroom."

"Lord, miss!" My view, I was myself aware—and therefore I suppose my tone—had never yet reached so calm an assurance.

"The trick's played," I went on; "they've successfully worked their plan. He found the most divine little way to keep me quiet while she went off."

"Divine?" Mrs. Grose bewilderedly echoed.

"Infernal, then!" I almost cheerfully rejoined. "He has provided for himself as well. But come!"

She had helplessly gloomed at the upper regions. "You leave him——?"

"So long with Quint? Yes—I don't mind that now."

She always ended, at these moments, by getting possession of my hand, and in this manner she could at present still stay me. But after gasping an instant at my sudden resignation, "Because of your letter?" she eagerly brought out.

I quickly, by way of answer, felt for my letter, drew it forth, held it up, and then, freeing myself, went and laid it on the great hall table. "Luke will take it," I said as I came back. I reached the house door and opened it; I was already on the steps.

My companion still demurred: the storm of the night and the early morning had dropped, but the afternoon was damp and gray. I came down to the drive while she stood in the doorway. "You go with nothing on?"

"What do I care when the child has nothing? I can't wait to dress," I cried, "and if you must do so, I leave you. Try meanwhile, yourself, upstairs."

"With *them?*" Oh, on this, the poor woman promptly joined me!

XIX

We went straight to the lake, as it was called at Bly, and I daresay rightly called, though I reflect that it may in fact have been a sheet of water less remarkable than it appeared to my untraveled eyes. My acquaintance with

sheets of water was small, and the pool of Bly, at all
events on the few occasions of my consenting, under the
protection of my pupils, to affront its surface in the old
flat-bottomed boat moored there for our use, had impressed me both with its extent and its agitation. The
usual place of embarkation was half a mile from the
house, but I had an intimate conviction that, wherever
Flora might be, she was not near home. She had not
given me the slip for any small adventure, and, since the
day of the very great one that I had shared with her by
the pond, I had been aware, in our walks, of the quarter
to which she most inclined. This was why I had now given
to Mrs. Grose's steps so marked a direction—a direction
that made her, when she perceived it, oppose a resistance
that showed me she was freshly mystified. "You're going
to the water, Miss?—you think she's *in*——?"

"She may be, though the depth is, I believe, nowhere
very great. But what I judge most likely is that she's on
the spot from which, the other day, we saw together what
I told you."

"When she pretended not to see——?"

"With that astounding self-possession? I've always been
sure she wanted to go back alone. And now her brother
has managed it for her."

Mrs. Grose still stood where she had stopped. "You
suppose they really *talk* of them?"

I could meet this with a confidence! "They say things
that, if we heard them, would simply appal us."

"And if she *is* there——?"

"Yes?"

"Then Miss Jessel is?"

"Beyond a doubt. You shall see."

"Oh, thank you!" my friend cried, planted so firm that,
taking it in, I went straight on without her. By the time I
reached the pool, however, she was close behind me, and
I knew that, whatever, to her apprehension, might befall
me, the exposure of my society struck her as her least
danger. She exhaled a moan of relief as we at last came
in sight of the greater part of the water without a sight
of the child. There was no trace of Flora on that nearer
side of the bank where my observation of her had been
most startling, and none on the opposite edge, where,

save for a margin of some twenty yards, a thick copse
came down to the water. The pond, oblong in shape, had
a width so scant compared to its length that, with its
ends out of view, it might have been taken for a scant
river. We looked at the empty expanse, and then I felt
the suggestion of my friend's eyes. I knew what she meant
and I replied with a negative headshake.

"No, no; wait! She has taken the boat."

My companion stared at the vacant mooring place and
then again across the lake. "Then where is it?"

"Our not seeing it is the strongest of proofs. She has
used it to go over, and then has managed to hide it."

"All alone—that child?"

"She's not alone, and at such times she's not a child:
she's an old, old woman." I scanned all the visible shore
while Mrs. Grose took again, into the queer element I
offered her, one of her plunges of submission; then I
pointed out that the boat might perfectly be in a small
refuge formed by one of the recesses of the pool, an
indentation masked, for the hither side, by a projection of
the bank and by a clump of trees growing close to the
water.

"But if the boat's there, where on earth's *she?*" my
colleague anxiously asked.

"That's exactly what we must learn." And I started
to walk further.

"By going all the way round?"

"Certainly, far as it is. It will take us but ten minutes,
but it's far enough to have made the child prefer not to
walk. She went straight over."

"Laws!" cried my friend again; the chain of my logic
was ever too much for her. It dragged her at my heels
even now, and when we had got halfway round—a
devious, tiresome process, on ground much broken and
by a path choked with overgrowth—I paused to give her
breath. I sustained her with a grateful arm, assuring her
that she might hugely help me; and this started us afresh,
so that in the course of but few minutes more we reached
a point from which we found the boat to be where I
had supposed it. It had been intentionally left as much as
possible out of sight and was tied to one of the stakes of
a fence that came, just there, down to the brink and that

had been an assistance to disembarking. I recognized, as I looked at the pair of short, thick oars, quite safely drawn up, the prodigious character of the feat for a little girl; but I had lived, by this time, too long among wonders and had panted to too many livelier measures. There was a gate in the fence, through which we passed, and that brought us, after a trifling interval, more into the open. Then, "There she is!" we both exclaimed at once.

Flora, a short way off, stood before us on the grass and smiled as if her performance was now complete. The next thing she did, however, was to stoop straight down and pluck—quite as if it were all she was there for—a big, ugly spray of withered fern. I instantly became sure she had just come out of the copse. She waited for us, not herself taking a step, and I was conscious of the rare solemnity with which we presently approached her. She smiled and smiled, and we met; but it was all done in a silence by this time flagrantly ominous. Mrs. Grose was the first to break the spell: she threw herself on her knees and, drawing the child to her breast, clasped in a long embrace the little tender, yielding body. While this dumb convulsion lasted I could only watch it—which I did the more intently when I saw Flora's face peep at me over our companion's shoulder. It was serious now—the flicker had left it; but it strengthened the pang with which I at that moment envied Mrs. Grose the simplicity of *her* relation. Still, all this while, nothing more passed between us save that Flora had let her foolish fern again drop to the ground. What she and I had virtually said to each other was that pretexts were useless now. When Mrs. Grose finally got up she kept the child's hand, so that the two were still before me; and the singular reticence of our communion was even more marked in the frank look she launched me. "I'll be hanged," it said, "if *I'll* speak!"

It was Flora who, gazing all over me in candid wonder, was the first. She was struck with our bareheaded aspect. "Why, where are your things?"

"Where yours are, my dear!" I promptly returned.

She had already got back her gaiety, and appeared to take this as an answer quite sufficient. "And where's Miles?" she went on.

There was something in the small valor of it that quite

finished me: these three words from her were, in a flash like the glitter of a drawn blade, the jostle of the cup that my hand, for weeks and weeks, had held high and full to the brim and that now, even before speaking, I felt overflow in a deluge. "I'll tell you if you'll tell *me*——" I heard myself say, then heard the tremor in which it broke.

"Well, what?"

Mrs. Grose's suspense blazed at me, but it was too late now, and I brought the thing out handsomely. "Where, my pet, is Miss Jessel?"

XX

Just as in the churchyard with Miles, the whole thing was upon us. Much as I had made of the fact that this name had never once, between us, been sounded, the quick, smitten glare with which the child's face now received it fairly likened my breach of the silence to the smash of a pane of glass. It added to the interposing cry, as if to stay the blow, that Mrs. Grose, at the same instant, uttered over my violence—the shriek of a creature scared, or rather wounded, which, in turn, within a few seconds, was completed by a gasp of my own. I seized my colleague's arm. "She's there, she's there!"

Miss Jessel stood before us on the opposite bank exactly as she had stood the other time, and I remember, strangely, as the first feeling now produced in me, my thrill of joy at having brought on a proof. She was there, and I was justified; she was there, and I was neither cruel nor mad. She was there for poor scared Mrs. Grose, but she was there most for Flora; and no moment of my monstrous time was perhaps so extraordinary as that in which I consciously threw out to her—with the sense that, pale and ravenous demon as she was, she would catch and understand it—an inarticulate message of gratitude. She rose erect on the spot my friend and I had lately quitted, and there was not, in all the long reach of her

desire, an inch of her evil that fell short. This first vividness of vision and emotion were things of a few seconds,
during which Mrs. Grose's dazed blink across to where I
pointed struck me as a sovereign sign that she too at last
saw, just as it carried my own eyes precipitately to the
child. The revelation then of the manner in which Flora
was affected startled me, in truth, far more than it would
have done to find her also merely agitated, for direct dismay was of course not what I had expected. Prepared
and on her guard as our pursuit had actually made her,
she would repress every betrayal; and I was therefore
shaken, on the spot, by my first glimpse of the particular
one for which I had not allowed. To see her, without a
convulsion of her small pink face, not even feign to glance
in the direction of the prodigy I announced, but only, instead of that, turn at *me* an expression of hard, still
gravity, an expression absolutely new and unprecedented
and that appeared to read and accuse and judge me—
this was a stroke that somehow converted the little girl
herself into the very presence that could make me quail.
I quailed even though my certitude that she thoroughly
saw was never greater than at that instant, and in the
immediate need to defend myself I called it passionately
to witness. "She's there, you little unhappy thing—there,
there, *there*, and you see her as well as you see me!" I
had said shortly before to Mrs. Grose that she was not at
these times a child, but an old, old woman, and that
description of her could not have been more strikingly
confirmed than in the way in which, for all answer to
this, she simply showed me, without a concession, an
admission, of her eyes, a countenance of deeper and deeper, of indeed suddenly quite fixed, reprobation. I was by
this time—if I can put the whole thing at all together—
more appalled at what I may properly call her manner
than at anything else, though it was simultaneously with
this that I became aware of having Mrs. Grose also, and
very formidably, to reckon with. My elder companion,
the next moment, at any rate, blotted out everything but
her own flushed face and her loud, shocked protest, a
burst of high disapproval. "What a dreadful turn, to be
sure, miss! Where on earth do you see anything?"
I could only grasp her more quickly yet, for even

while she spoke the hideous plain presence stood un-dimmed and undaunted. It had already lasted a minute, and it lasted while I continued, seizing my colleague, quite thrusting her at it and presenting her to it, to insist with my pointing hand. "You don't see her exactly as *we* see?—you mean to say you don't now—*now?* She's as big as a blazing fire! Only look, dearest woman, *look*——" She looked, even as I did, and gave me, with her deep groan of negation, repulsion, compassion—the mixture with her pity of her relief at her exemption—a sense, touching to me even then, that she would have backed me up if she could. I might well have needed that, for with this hard blow of the proof that her eyes were hopelessly sealed I felt my own situation horribly crumble, I felt—I saw—my livid predecessor press, from her position, on my defeat, and I was conscious, more than all, of what I should have from this instant to deal with in the astound-ing little attitude of Flora. Into this attitude Mrs. Grose immediately and violently entered, breaking, even while there pierced through my sense of ruin a prodigious pri-vate triumph, into breathless reassurance.

"She isn't there, little lady, and nobody's there—and you never see nothing, my sweet! How can poor Miss Jessel—when poor Miss Jessel's dead and buried? *We* know, don't we, love?"—and she appealed, blundering in, to the child. "It's all a mere mistake and a worry and a joke—and we'll go home as fast as we can!"

Our companion, on this, had responded with a strange, quick primness of propriety, and they were again, with Mrs. Grose on her feet, united, as it were, in pained opposition to me. Flora continued to fix me with her small mask of reprobation, and even at that minute I prayed God to forgive me for seeming to see that, as she stood there holding tight to our friend's dress, her in-comparable childish beauty had suddenly failed, had quite vanished. I've said it already—she was literally, she was hideously, hard; she had turned common and almost ugly. "I don't know what you mean. I see nobody. I see nothing. I never *have.* I think you're cruel. I don't like you!" Then, after this deliverance, which might have been that of a vulgarly pert little girl in the street, she hugged Mrs. Grose more closely and buried in her skirts the dreadful little face. In this position she produced an almost furious wail. "Take me away, take me away—oh, take me away from *her!*"

"From *me?*" I panted.

"From you—from you!" she cried.

Even Mrs. Grose looked across at me dismayed, while I had nothing to do but communicate again with the figure that, on the opposite bank, without a movement, as rigidly still as if catching, beyond the interval, our voices, was as vividly there for my disaster as it was not there for my service. The wretched child had spoken exactly as if she had got from some outside source each of her stabbing little words, and I could therefore, in the full despair of all I had to accept, but sadly shake my head at her. "If I had ever doubted, all my doubt would at present have gone. I've been living with the miserable truth, and now it has only too much closed round me. Of course I've lost you: I've interfered, and you've seen— under *her* dictation"—with which I faced, over the pool again, our infernal witness—"the easy and perfect way to meet it. I've done my best, but I've lost you. Goodbye." For Mrs. Grose I had an imperative, an almost frantic "Go, go!" before which, in infinite distress, but mutely possessed of the little girl and clearly convinced, in spite of her blindness, that something awful had occurred and some collapse engulfed us, she retreated, by the way we had come, as fast as she could move.

Of what first happened when I was left alone I had no subsequent memory. I only knew that at the end of, I suppose, a quarter of an hour, an odorous dampness and roughness, chilling and piercing my trouble, had made me understand that I must have thrown myself, on my face, on the ground and given way to a wildness of grief. I must have lain there long and cried and sobbed, for when I raised my head the day was almost done. I got up and looked a moment, through the twilight, at the gray pool and its blank, haunted edge, and then I took, back to the house, my dreary and difficult course. When I reached the gate in the fence the boat, to my surprise, was gone, so that I had a fresh reflection to make on Flora's extraordinary command of the situation. She passed that night, by the most tacit, and I should add, were not the word so grotesque a false note, the happiest of arrangements, with Mrs. Grose. I saw neither of them on my return, but, on the other hand, as by an ambiguous compensation, I saw a great deal of Miles. I saw—I can use no other phrase—so much of him that it was as if it were more than it had ever been. No evening I had passed at Bly had the portentous quality of this one; in spite of which—and in spite also of the deeper depths of consternation that had opened beneath my feet—there was literally, in the ebbing actual, an extraordinarily sweet sadness. On reaching the house I had never so much as looked for the boy; I had simply gone straight to my room to change what I was wearing and to take in, at a glance, much material testimony to Flora's rupture. Her little belongings had all been removed. When later, by the schoolroom fire, I was served with tea by the usual maid, I indulged, on the article of my other pupil, in no inquiry whatever. He had his freedom now—he might have it to the end! Well, he did have it; and it consisted—in part at least—of his coming in at about eight o'clock and sitting down with me in silence. On the removal of the tea things I had blown out the candles and drawn my chair closer: I was conscious of a mortal coldness and felt as if I should never again be warm. So, when he appeared, I was sitting in the glow with my thoughts. He paused a moment by the door as if to look at me; then—as if to share them—came to the other side of the hearth and sank into a chair. We sat there in absolute stillness; yet he wanted, I felt, to be with me.

XXI

Before a new day, in my room, had fully broken, my eyes opened to Mrs. Grose, who had come to my bedside with worse news. Flora was so markedly feverish that an illness was perhaps at hand; she had passed a night of extreme unrest, a night agitated above all by fears that had for their subject not in the least her former, but wholly her present, governess. It was not against the possible re-entrance of Miss Jessel on the scene that she protested—it was conspicuously and passionately against mine. I was promptly on my feet of course, and with an immense deal to ask; the more that my friend had discernibly now girded her loins to meet me once more. This I felt as soon as I had put to her the question of her sense of the child's sincerity as against my own. "She persists in denying to you that she saw, or has ever seen, anything?"

My visitor's trouble, truly, was great. "Ah, miss, it isn't a matter on which I can push her! Yet it isn't either, I must say, as if I much needed to. It has made her, every inch of her, quite old."

"Oh, I see her perfectly from here. She resents, for all the world like some high little personage, the imputation on her truthfulness and, as it were, her respectability. 'Miss Jessel indeed—*she!*' All, she's 'respectable,' the chit! The impression she gave me there yesterday was, I assure you, the very strangest of all; it was quite beyond any of the others. I *did* put my foot in it! She'll never speak to me again."

Hideous and obscure as it all was, it held Mrs. Grose briefly silent; then she granted my point with a frankness which, I made sure, had more behind it. "I think indeed, miss, she never will. She do have a grand manner about it!"

"And that manner"—I summed it up—"is practically what's the matter with her now!"

Oh, that manner, I could see in my visitor's face, and not a little else besides! "She asks me every three minutes if I think you're coming in."

"I see—I see." I, too, on my side, had so much more than worked it out. "Has she said to you since yesterday —except to repudiate her familiarity with anything so dreadful—a single other word about Miss Jessel?"

"Not one, miss. And of course you know," my friend added, "I took it from her, by the lake, that, just then and there at least, there *was* nobody."

"Rather! And, naturally, you take it from her still."

"I don't contradict her. What else can I do?"

"Nothing in the world! You've the cleverest little per-

son to deal with. They've made them—their two friends,
I mean—still cleverer even than nature did; for it was
wondrous material to play on! Flora has now her grievance, and she'll work it to the end."

"Yes, miss; but to *what* end?"

"Why, that of dealing with me to her uncle. She'll
make me out to him the lowest creature——!"

I winced at the fair show of the scene in Mrs. Grose's
face; she looked for a minute as if she sharply saw them
together. "And him who thinks so well of you!"

"He has an odd way—it comes over me now," I
laughed, "—of proving it! But that doesn't matter. What
Flora wants, of course, is to get rid of me."

My companion bravely concurred. "Never again to so
much as look at you."

"So that what you've come to me now for," I asked,
"is to speed me on my way?" Before she had time to
reply, however, I had her in check. "I've a better idea—
the result of my reflections. My going *would* seem the
right thing, and on Sunday I was terribly near it. Yet that
won't do. It's *you* who must go. You must take Flora."

My visitor, at this, did speculate. "But where in the
world——?"

"Away from here. Away from *them*. Away, even most
of all, now, from me. Straight to her uncle."

"Only to tell on you——?"

"No, not 'only'! To leave me, in addition, with my
remedy."

She was still vague. "And what *is* your remedy?"

"Your loyalty, to begin with. And then Miles's."

She looked at me hard. "Do you think he——?"

"Won't, if he has the chance, turn on me? Yes, I venture still to think it. At all events, I want to try. Get off
with his sister as soon as possible and leave me with
him alone." I was amazed, myself, at the spirit I had
still in reserve, and therefore perhaps a trifle the more
disconcerted at the way in which, in spite of this fine
example of it, she hesitated. "There's one thing, of
course," I went on: "they mustn't, before she goes, see
each other for three seconds." Then it came over me that,
in spite of Flora's presumable sequestration from the instant of her return from the pool, it might already be too

late. "Do you mean," I anxiously asked, "that they *have* met?"

At this she quite flushed. "Ah, miss, I'm not such a fool as that! If I've been obliged to leave her three or four times, it has been each time with one of the maids, and at present, though she's alone, she's locked in safe. And yet —and yet!" There were too many things.

"And yet what?"

"Well, are you so sure of the little gentleman?"

"I'm not sure of anything but *you*. But I have, since last evening, a new hope. I think he wants to give me an opening. I do believe that—poor little exquisite wretch!— he wants to speak. Last evening, in the firelight and the silence, he sat with me for two hours as if it were just coming."

Mrs. Grose looked hard, through the window, at the gray, gathering day. "And did it come?"

"No, though I waited and waited, I confess it didn't, and it was without a breach of the silence or so much as a faint allusion to his sister's condition and absence that we at last kissed for good night. All the same," I continued, "I can't, if her uncle sees her, consent to his seeing her brother without my having given the boy— and most of all because things have got so bad—a little more time."

My friend appeared on this ground more reluctant than I could quite understand. "What do you mean by more time?"

"Well, a day or two—really to bring it out. He'll then be on *my* side—of which you see the importance. If nothing comes, I shall only fail, and you will, at the worst, have helped me by doing, on your arrival in town, whatever you may have found possible." So I put it before her, but she continued for a little so inscrutably embarrassed that I came again to her aid. "Unless, indeed," I wound up, "you really want *not* to go."

I could see it, in her face, at last clear itself; she put out her hand to me as a pledge. "I'll go—I'll go. I'll go this morning."

I wanted to be very just. "If you *should* wish still to wait, I would engage she shouldn't see me."

"No, no: it's the place itself. She must leave it." She

held me a moment with heavy eyes, then brought out the rest. "Your idea's the right one. I myself, miss——"

"Well?"

"I can't stay."

The look she gave me with it made me jump at possibilities. "You mean that, since yesterday, you *have* seen——?"

She shook her head with dignity. "I've *heard*——!"

"Heard?"

"From that child—horrors! There!" she sighed with tragic relief. "On my honor, miss, she says things——!" But at this evocation she broke down; she dropped, with a sudden sob, upon my sofa and, as I had seen her do before, gave way to all the grief of it.

It was quite in another manner that I, for my part, let myself go. "Oh, thank God!"

She sprang up again at this, drying her eyes with a groan. 'Thank God'?"

"It so justifies me!"

"It does that, miss!"

I couldn't have desired more emphasis, but I just hesitated. "She's so horrible?"

I saw my colleague scarce knew how to put it. "Really shocking."

"And about me?"

"About you, miss—since you must have it. It's beyond everything, for a young lady; and I can't think wherever she must have picked up——"

"The appalling language she applied to me? I can, then!" I broke in with a laugh that was doubtless significant enough.

It only, in truth, left my friend still more grave. "Well, perhaps I ought to also—since I've heard some of it before! Yet I can't bear it," the poor woman went on while, with the same movement, she glanced, on my dressing table, at the face of my watch. "But I must go back."

I kept her, however. "Ah, if you can't bear it——!"

"How can I stop with her, you mean? Why, just *for* that: to get her away. Far from this," she pursued, "far from *them*——"

"She may be different? She may be free?" I seized her

almost with joy. "Then, in spite of yesterday, you *believe*—"

"In such doings?" Her simple description of them required, in the light of her expression, to be carried no further, and she gave me the whole thing as she had never done. "I believe."

Yes, it was a joy, and we were still shoulder to shoulder: if I might continue sure of that I should care but little what else happened. My support in the presence of disaster would be the same as it had been in my early need of confidence, and if my friend would answer for my honesty, I would answer for all the rest. On the point of taking leave of her, nonetheless, I was to some extent embarrassed. "There's one thing, of course—it occurs to me —to remember. My letter, giving the alarm, will have reached town before you."

I now perceived still more how she had been beating about the bush and how weary at last it had made her. "Your letter won't have got there. Your letter never went."

"What then became of it?"

"Goodness knows! Master Miles—"

"Do you mean *he* took it?" I gasped.

She hung fire, but she overcame her reluctance. "I mean that I saw yesterday, when I came back with Miss Flora, that it wasn't where you had put it. Later in the evening I had the chance to question Luke, and he declared that he had neither noticed nor touched it." We could only exchange, on this, one of our deeper mutual soundings, and it was Mrs. Grose who first brought up the plumb with an almost elated "You see!"

"Yes, I see that if Miles took it instead he probably will have read it and destroyed it."

"And don't you see anything else?"

I faced her a moment with a sad smile. "It strikes me that by this time your eyes are open even wider than mine."

They proved to be so indeed, but she could still blush, almost, to show it. "I make out now what he must have done at school." And she gave, in her simple sharpness, an almost droll disillusioned nod. "He stole!"

I turned it over—I tried to be more judicial. "Well—perhaps."

She looked as if she found me unexpectedly calm. "He stole *letters!*"

She couldn't know my reasons for a calmness after all pretty shallow; so I showed them off as I might. "I hope then it was to more purpose than in this case! The note, at any rate, that I put on the table yesterday," I pursued, "will have given him so scant an advantage—for it contained only the bare demand for an interview—that he is already much ashamed of having gone so far for so little, and that what he had on his mind last evening was precisely the need of confession." I seemed to myself, for the instant, to have mastered it, to see it all. "Leave us, leave us"—I was already, at the door, hurrying her off. "I'll get it out of him. He'll meet me—he'll confess. If he confesses, he's saved. And if he's saved——"

"Then *you* are?" The dear woman kissed me on this, and I took her farewell. "I'll save you without him!" she cried as she went.

XXII

Yet it was when she had got off—and I missed her on the spot—that the great pinch really came. If I had counted on what it would give me to find myself alone with Miles, I speedily perceived, at least, that it would give me a measure. No hour of my stay in fact was so assailed with apprehensions as that of my coming down to learn that the carriage containing Mrs. Grose and my younger pupil had already rolled out of the gates. Now I *was,* I said to myself, face to face with the elements, and for much of the rest of the day, while I fought my weakness, I could consider that I had been supremely rash. It was a tighter place still than I had yet turned round in; all the more that, for the first time, I could see in the aspect of others a confused reflection of the crisis.

What had happened naturally caused them all to stare; there was too little of the explained, throw out whatever we might, in the suddenness of my colleague's act. The maids and the men looked blank; the effect of which on my nerves was an aggravation until I saw the necessity of making it a positive aid. It was precisely, in short, by just clutching the helm that I avoided total wreck; and I dare say that, to bear up at all, I became, that morning, very grand and very dry. I welcomed the consciousness that I was charged with much to do, and I caused it to be known as well that, left thus to myself, I was quite remarkably firm. I wandered with that manner, for the next hour or two, all over the place and looked, I have no doubt, as if I were ready for any onset. So, for the benefit of whom it might concern, I paraded with a sick heart.

The person it appeared least to concern proved to be, till dinner, little Miles himself. My perambulations had given me, meanwhile, no glimpse of him, but they had tended to make more public the change taking place in our relation as a consequence of his having at the piano, the day before, kept me, in Flora's interest, so beguiled and befooled. The stamp of publicity had of course been fully given by her confinement and departure, and the change itself was now ushered in by our nonobservance of the regular custom of the schoolroom. He had already disappeared when, on my way down, I pushed open his door, and I learned below that he had breakfasted—in the presence of a couple of the maids—with Mrs. Grose and his sister. He had then gone out, as he said, for a stroll; than which nothing, I reflected, could better have expressed his frank view of the abrupt transformation of my office. What he would now permit this office to consist of was yet to be settled: there was a queer relief, at all events—I mean for myself in especial—in the renouncement of one pretension. If so much had sprung to the surface, I scarce put it too strongly in saying that what had perhaps sprung highest was the absurdity of our prolonging the fiction that I had anything more to teach him. It sufficiently stuck out that, by tacit little tricks in which even more than myself he carried out the care for my dignity, I had had to appeal to him to let me off straining to meet him on the ground of his true capacity.

He had at any rate his freedom now; I was never to touch it again; as I had amply shown, moreover, when, on his joining me in the schoolroom the previous night, I had uttered, on the subject of the interval just concluded, neither challenge nor hint. I had too much, from this moment, my other ideas. Yet when he at last arrived, the difficulty of applying them, the accumulations of my problem, were brought straight home to me by the beautiful little presence on which what had occurred had as yet, for the eye, dropped neither stain nor shadow.

To mark, for the house, the high state I cultivated I decreed that my meals with the boy should be served, as we called it, downstairs; so that I had been awaiting him in the ponderous pomp of the room outside of the window of which I had had from Mrs. Grose, that first scared Sunday, my flash of something it would scarce have done to call light. Here at present I felt afresh—for I had felt it again and again—how my equilibrium depended on the success of my rigid will, the will to shut my eyes as tight as possible to the truth that what I had to deal with was, revoltingly, against nature. I could only get on at all by taking "nature" into my confidence and my account, by treating my monstrous ordeal as a push in a direction unusual, of course, and unpleasant, but demanding, after all, for a fair front, only another turn of the screw of ordinary human virtue. No attempt, nonetheless, could well require more tact than just this attempt to supply, one's self, *all* the nature. How could I put even a little of that article into a suppression of reference to what had occurred? How, on the other hand, could I make reference without a new plunge into the hideous obscure? Well, a sort of answer, after a time, had come to me, and it was so far confirmed as that I was met, incontestably, by the quickened vision of what was rare in my little companion. It was indeed as if he had found even now—as he had so often found at lessons—still some other delicate way to ease me off. Wasn't there light in the fact which, as we shared our solitude, broke out with a specious glitter it had never yet quite worn? —the fact that (opportunity aiding, precious opportunity which had now come) it would be preposterous, with a child so endowed, to forego the help one might wrest from absolute intelligence? What had his intelligence been given him for but to save him? Mightn't one, to reach his mind, risk the stretch of an angular arm over his character? It was as if, when we were face to face in the dining room, he had literally shown me the way. The roast mutton was on the table, and I had dispensed with attendance. Miles, before he sat down, stood a moment with his hands in his pockets and looked at the joint, on which he seemed on the point of passing some humorous judgment. But what he presently produced was: "I say, my dear, is she really very awfully ill?"

"Little Flora? Not so bad but that she'll presently be better. London will set her up. Bly had ceased to agree with her. Come here and take your mutton."

He alertly obeyed me, carried the plate carefully to his seat, and, when he was established, went on. "Did Bly disagree with her so terribly suddenly?"

"Not so suddenly as you might think. One had seen it coming on."

"Then why didn't you get her off before?"

"Before what?"

"Before she became too ill to travel."

I found myself prompt. "She's *not* too ill to travel: she only might have become so if she had stayed. This was just the moment to seize. The journey will dissipate the influence"—oh, I was grand!—"and carry it off."

"I see, I see"—Miles, for that matter, was grand, too. He settled to his repast with the charming little "table manner" that, from the day of his arrival, had relieved me of all grossness of admonition. Whatever he had been driven from school for, it was not for ugly feeding. He was irreproachable, as always, today; but he was unmistakably more conscious. He was discernibly trying to take for granted more things than he found, without assistance, quite easy; and he dropped into peaceful silence while he felt his situation. Our meal was of the briefest—mine a vain pretense, and I had the things immediately removed. While this was done Miles stood again with his hands in his little pockets and his back to me—stood and looked out of the wide window through which, that other day, I had seen what pulled me up. We continued silent while the maid was with us—as silent, it whimsically occurred to me, as some young couple who, on their wedding journey, at the inn, feel shy in the presence of the waiter. He turned round only when the waiter had left us. "Well—so we're alone!"

XXIII

"Oh, more or less." I fancy my smile was pale. "Not absolutely. We shouldn't like that!" I went on.

"No—I suppose we shouldn't. Of course we have the others."

"We have the others—we have indeed the others," I concurred.

"Yet even though we have them," he returned, still with his hands in his pockets and planted there in front of me, "they don't much count, do they?"

I made the best of it, but I felt wan. "It depends on what you call 'much'!"

"Yes"—with all accommodation—"everything depends!" On this, however, he faced to the window again and presently reached it with his vague, restless, cogitating step. He remained there awhile, with his forehead against the glass, in contemplation of the stupid shrubs I knew and the dull things of November. I had always my hypocrisy of "work," behind which, now, I gained the sofa. Steadying myself with it there as I had repeatedly done at those moments of torment that I have described as the moments of my knowing the children to be given to something from which I was barred, I sufficiently obeyed my habit of being prepared for the worst. But an extraordinary impression dropped on me as I extracted a meaning from the boy's embarrassed back—none other than the impression that I was not barred now. This inference grew in a few minutes to sharp intensity and seemed bound up with the direct perception that it was positively he who was. The frames and squares of the great window were a kind of image, for him, of a kind of failure. I felt that I saw him, at any rate, shut in or shut out. He was admirable, but not comfortable: I took it in with a throb of hope. Wasn't he looking, through the haunted pane, for something he couldn't see?—and wasn't it the first time in the whole business that he had known such a lapse? The first, the very first: I found it a splendid portent. It made him anxious, though he watched himself; he had been anxious all day and, even while in his usual sweet little manner he sat at table, had needed all his small strange genius to give it a gloss. When he at last turned round to meet me, it was almost as if this genius had succumbed. "Well, I think I'm glad Bly agrees with *me!*"

"You would certainly seem to have seen, these twenty-four hours, a good deal more of it than for some time before. I hope," I went on bravely, "that you've been enjoying yourself."

"Oh, yes, I've been ever so far; all round about— miles and miles away. I've never been so free."

He had really a manner of his own, and I could only try to keep up with him. "Well, do you like it?"

He stood there smiling; then at last he put into two words—"Do *you?*"—more discrimination than I had ever heard two words contain. Before I had time to deal with that, however, he continued as if with the sense that this was an impertinence to be softened. "Nothing could be more charming than the way you take it, for of course if we're alone together now it's you that are alone most. But I hope," he threw in, "you don't particularly mind!"

"Having to do with you?" I asked. "My dear child, how can I help minding? Though I've renounced all claim to your company—you're so beyond me—I at least greatly enjoy it. What else should I stay on for?"

He looked at me more directly, and the expression of his face, graver now, struck me as the most beautiful I had ever found in it. "You stay on just for *that?*"

"Certainly. I stay on as your friend and from the tremendous interest I take in you till something can be done for you that may be more worth your while. That needn't surprise you." My voice trembled so that I felt it impossible to suppress the shake. "Don't you remember how I told you, when I came and sat on your bed the night of the storm, that there was nothing in the world I wouldn't do for you?"

"Yes, yes!" He, on his side, more and more visibly nervous, had a tone to master; but he was so much more successful than I that, laughing out through his gravity, he could pretend we were pleasantly jesting. "Only that, I think, was to get me to do something for *you!*"

"It was partly to get you to do something," I conceded. "But, you know, you didn't do it."

"Oh, yes," he said with the brightest superficial eagerness, "you wanted me to tell you something."

"That's it. Out, straight out. what you have on your mind, you know."

"Ah, then, is *that* what you've stayed over for?"

He spoke with a gaiety through which I could still catch the finest little quiver of resentful passion; but I can't begin to express the effect upon me of an implication of surrender even so faint. It was as if what I had yearned for had come at last only to astonish me. "Well, yes—I may as well make a clean breast of it. It was precisely for that."

He waited so long that I supposed it for the purpose of repudiating the assumption on which my action had been founded; but what he finally said was: "Do you mean now—here?"

"There couldn't be a better place or time." He looked round him uneasily, and I had the rare—oh, the queer!—impression of the very first symptom I had seen in him of the approach of immediate fear. It was as if he were suddenly afraid of me—which struck me indeed as perhaps the best thing to make him. Yet in the very pang of the effort I felt it vain to try sternness, and I heard myself the next instant so gentle as to be almost grotesque. "You want so to go out again?"

"Awfully!" He smiled at me heroically, and the touching little bravery of it was enhanced by his actually flushing with pain. He had picked up his hat, which he had brought in, and stood twirling it in a way that gave me, even as I was just nearly reaching port, a perverse horror of what I was doing. To do it in any way was an act of violence, for what did it consist of but the obtrusion of the idea of grossness and guilt on a small helpless creature who had been for me a revelation of the possibilities of beautiful intercourse? Wasn't it base to create for a being so exquisite a mere alien awkwardness? I suppose I now read into our situation a clearness it couldn't have had at the time, for I seem to see our poor eyes already lighted with some spark of a prevision of the anguish that was to come. So we circled about, with terrors and scruples, like fighters not daring to close. But it was for each other we feared! That kept us a little longer suspended and unbruised. "I'll tell you everything," Miles said—"I mean I'll tell you anything you like. You'll stay on with me, and we shall both be all right, and I *will* tell you—I *will*. But not now."

"Why not now?"

My insistence turned him from me and kept him once more at his window in a silence during which, between us, you might have heard a pin drop. Then he was before me again with the air of a person for whom, outside, someone who had frankly to be reckoned with was waiting. "I have to see Luke."

I had not yet reduced him to quite so vulgar a lie, and I felt proportionately ashamed. But, horrible as it was, his lies made up my truth. I achieved thoughtfully a few loops of my knitting. "Well, then, go to Luke, and I'll wait for what you promise. Only, in return for that, satisfy, before you leave me, one very much smaller request."

He looked as if he felt he had succeeded enough to be able still a little to bargain. "Very much smaller——?"

"Yes, a mere fraction of the whole. Tell me"—oh, my work preoccupied me, and I was offhand!—"if, yesterday afternoon, from the table in the hall, you took, you know, my letter."

XXIV

My sense of how he received this suffered for a minute
from something that I can describe only as a fierce split
of my attention—a stroke that at first, as I sprang
straight up, reduced me to the mere blind movement of
getting hold of him, drawing him close, and, while I just
fell for support against the nearest piece of furniture, instinctively keeping him with his back to the window. The
appearance was full upon us that I had already had to
deal with here: Peter Quint had come into view like a
sentinel before a prison. The next thing I saw was that,
from outside, he had reached the window, and then I
knew that, close to the glass and glaring in through it, he
offered once more to the room his white face of damnation. It represents but grossly what took place within me
at the sight to say that on the second my decision was
made; yet I believe that no woman so overwhelmed ever
in so short a time recovered her grasp of the act. It
came to me in the very horror of the immediate presence
that the act would be, seeing and facing what I saw and
faced, to keep the boy himself unaware. The inspiration
—I can call it by no other name—was that I felt how
voluntarily, how transcendently, I *might*. It was like fight-
ing with a demon for a human soul, and when I had
fairly so appraised it I saw how the human soul—held
out, in the tremor of my hands, at arm's length—had a
perfect dew of sweat on a lovely childish forehead. The
face that was close to mine was as white as the face
against the glass, and out of it presently came a sound,
not low nor weak, but as if from much further away, that
I drank like a waft of fragrance.

"Yes—I took it."

At this, with a moan of joy, I enfolded, I drew him
close; and while I held him to my breast, where I
could feel in the sudden fever of his little body the

tremendous pulse of his little heart, I kept my eyes on the thing at the window and saw it move and shift its posture. I have likened it to a sentinel, but its slow wheel, for a moment, was rather the prowl of a baffled beast. My present quickened courage, however, was such that, not too much to let it through, I had to shade, as it were, my flame. Meanwhile the glare of the face was again at the window, the scoundrel fixed as if to watch and wait. It was the very confidence that I might now defy him, as well as the positive certitude, by this time, of the child's unconsciousness, that made me go on. 'What did you take it for?"

"To see what you said about me."

"You opened the letter?"

"I opened it."

My eyes were now, as I held him off a little again, on Miles's own face, in which the collapse of mockery showed me how complete was the ravage of uneasiness. What was prodigious was that at last, by my success, his sense was sealed and his communication stopped: he knew that he was in presence, but knew not of what, and knew still less that I also was and that I did know. And what did this strain of trouble matter when my eyes went back to the window only to see that the air was clear again and—by my personal triumph— the influence quenched? There was nothing there. I felt that the cause was mine and that I should surely get *all*. "And you found nothing!"—I let my elation out.

He gave the most mournful, thoughtful little he ad-shake. "Nothing."

"Nothing, nothing!" I almost shouted in my joy.

"Nothing, nothing," he sadly repeated.

I kissed his forehead; it was drenched. "So what have you done with it?"

"I've burned it."

"Burned it?" It was now or never. "Is that what you did at school?"

Oh, what this brought up! "At school?"

"Did you take letters?—or other things?"

"Other things?" He appeared now to be thinking of something far off and that reached him only through the pressure of his anxiety. Yet it did reach him. "Did I *steal?*"

I felt myself redden to the roots of my hair as well as wonder if it were more strange to put to a gentleman such a question or to see him take it with allowances that gave the very distance of his fall in the world. "Was it for that you mightn't go back?"

The only thing he felt was rather a dreary little surprise. "Did you know I mightn't go back?"

"I know everything."

He gave me at this the longest and strangest look. "Everything?"

"Everything. Therefore *did* you——?" But I couldn't say it again.

Miles could, very simply. "No. I didn't steal."

My face must have shown him I believed him utterly; yet my hands—but it was for pure tenderness—shook him as if to ask him why, if it was all for nothing, he had condemned me to months of torment. "What then did you do?"

He looked in vague pain all round the top of the room and drew his breath, two or three times over, as if with difficulty. He might have been standing at the bottom of the sea and raising his eyes to some faint green twilight.

"Well—I said things."

"Only that?"

"They thought it was enough!"

"To turn you out for?"

Never, truly, had a person "turned out" shown so little to explain it as this little person! He appeared to weigh my question, but in a manner quite detached and almost helpless. "Well, I suppose I oughtn't."

"But to whom did you say them?"

He evidently tried to remember, but it dropped—he had lost it. "I don't know!"

He almost smiled at me in the desolation of his surrender, which was indeed practically, by this time, so complete that I ought to have left it there. But I was infatuated-I was blind with victory, though even then the very effect that was to have brought him so much nearer was already that of added separation. "Was it to everyone?" I asked.

"No; it was only to——" But he gave a sick little headshake. "I don't remember their names."

"Were they then so many?"

"No—only a few. Those I liked."

Those he liked? I seemed to float not into clearness, but into a darker obscure, and within a minute there had come to me out of my very pity the appalling alarm of his being perhaps innocent. It was for the instant confounding and bottomless, for if he were innocent, what then on earth was *I?* Paralyzed, while it lasted, by the mere brush of the question, I let him go a little, so that, with a deep-drawn sigh, he turned away from me again; which, as he faced toward the clear window, I suffered, feeling that I had nothing now there to keep him from. "And did they repeat what you said?" I went on after a moment.

He was soon at some distance from me, still breathing hard and again with the air, though now without anger for it, of being confined against his will. Once more, as he had done before, he looked up at the dim day as if, of what had hitherto sustained him, nothing was left but an unspeakable anxiety. "Oh, yes," he nevertheless replied—"they must have repeated them. To those *they* liked," he added.

There was, somehow, less of it than I had expected; but I turned it over. "And these things came round——?"

"To the masters? Oh, yes!" he answered very simply. "But I didn't know they'd tell."

"The masters? They didn't—they've never told. That's why I ask you."

He turned to me again his little beautiful fevered face. "Yes, it was too bad."

"Too bad?"

"What I suppose I sometimes said. To write home."

I can't name the exquisite pathos of the contradiction given to such a speech by such a speaker; I only know that the next instant I heard myself throw off with homely force: "Stuff and nonsense!" But the next after that I must have sounded stern enough. "What *were* these things?"

My sternness was all for his judge, his executioner; yet it made him avert himself again, and that movement made *me*, with a single bound and an irrepressible cry, spring straight upon him. For there again, against the glass, as if to blight his confession and stay his answer, was the hideous author of our woe—the white face of damnation. I felt a sick swim at the drop of my victory and all the return of my battle, so that the wildness of my veritable leap only served as a great betrayal. I saw him, from the midst of my act, meet it with a divination, and on the perception that even now he only guessed, and that the window was still to his own eyes free, I let the impulse flame up to convert the climax of his dismay into the very proof of his liberation. "No more, no more, no more!" I shrieked, as I tried to press him against me, to my visitant.

"Is she *here?*" Miles panted as he caught with his sealed eyes the direction of my words. Then as his strange "she" staggered me and, with a gasp, I echoed it, "Miss Jessel, Miss Jessel!" he with a sudden fury gave me back.

I seized, stupefied, his supposition—some sequel to what we had done to Flora, but this made me only want to show him that it was better still than that. "It's not Miss Jessel! But it's at the window—straight before us. It's *there*—the coward horror, there for the last time!"

At this, after a second in which his head made the movement of a baffled dog's on a scent and then gave a frantic little shake for air and light, he was at me in a white rage, bewildered, glaring vainly over the place and missing wholly, though it now, to my sense, filled the room like the taste of poison, the wide, overwhelming presence. "It's *he?*"

I was so determined to have all my proof that I flashed into ice to challenge him. "Whom do you mean by 'he'?"

"Peter Quint—you devil!" His face gave again, round the room, its convulsed supplication. "*Where?*"

They are in my ears still, his supreme surrender of the name and his tribute to my devotion. "What does he matter now, my own?—what will he ever matter? I have you," I launched at the beast, "but he has lost you forever!" Then, for the demonstration of my work, "There, *there!*" I said to Miles.

But he had already jerked straight round, stared, glared again, and seen but the quiet day. With the stroke of the loss I was so proud of he uttered the cry of a creature hurled over an abyss, and the grasp with which I recovered him might have been that of catching him in his fall. I caught him, yes, I held him—it may be imagined with what a passion; but at the end of a minute I began to feel what it truly was that I held. We were alone with the quiet day, and his little heart, dispossessed, had stopped.

THE BEAST IN THE JUNGLE

❦

I

What determined the speech that startled him in the course of their encounter scarcely matters, being probably but some words spoken by himself quite without intention—spoken as they lingered and slowly moved together after their renewal of acquaintance. He had been conveyed by friends, an hour or two before, to the house at which she was staying; the party of visitors at the other house, of whom he was one, and thanks to whom it was his theory, as always, that he was lost in the crowd, had been invited over to luncheon. There had been after luncheon much dispersal, all in the interest of the original motive, a view of Weatherend itself and the fine things, intrinsic features, pictures, heirlooms, treasures of all the arts, that made the place almost famous; and the great rooms were so numerous that guests could wander at their will, hang back from the principal group, and, in cases where they took such matters with the last seriousness, give themselves up to mysterious appreciations and measurements. There were persons to be observed, singly or in couples, bending toward objects in out-of-the-way corners with their hands on their knees and their heads nodding quite as with the emphasis of an excited sense of smell. When they were two they either mingled their sounds of ecstasy or melted into silences of even deeper import, so that there were aspects of the occasion that gave it for Marcher much the air of the "look round," previous to a sale highly advertised, that excites or quenches, as may be, the dream of acquisition.

The dream of acquisition at Weatherend would have had to be wild indeed, and John Marcher found himself, among such suggestions, disconcerted almost equally by the presence of those who knew too much and by that of those who knew nothing. The great rooms caused so much poetry and history to press upon him that he needed to wander apart to feel in a proper relation with them, though his doing so was not, as happened, like the gloating of some of his companions, to be compared to the movements of a dog sniffing a cupboard. It had an issue promptly enough in a direction that was not to have been calculated.

It led, in short, in the course of the October afternoon, to his closer meeting with May Bartram, whose face, a reminder, yet not quite a remembrance, as they sat, much separated, at a very long table, had begun merely by troubling him rather pleasantly. It affected him as the sequel of something of which he had lost the beginning. He knew it, and for the time quite welcomed it, as a continuation, but didn't know what it continued, which was an interest, or an amusement, the greater as he was also somehow aware—yet without a direct sign from her —that the young woman herself had not lost the thread. She had not lost it, but she wouldn't give it back to him, he saw, without some putting forth of his hand for it; and he not only saw that, but saw several things more, things odd enough in the light of the fact that at the moment some accident of grouping brought them face to face he was still merely fumbling with the idea that any contact between them in the past would have had no importance. If it had had no importance he scarcely knew why his actual impression of her should so seem to have so much; the answer to which, however, was that in such a life as they all appeared to be leading for the moment one could but take things as they came. He was satisfied, without in the least being able to say why, that this young lady might roughly have ranked in the house as a poor relation; satisfied also that she was not there on a brief visit, but was more or less a part of the establishment—almost a working, a remunerated part. Didn't she enjoy at periods a protection that she paid for by helping, among other services, to show the place and explain it, deal with the tiresome people, answer questions about the dates of the buildings, the styles of the furniture, the authorship of the pictures, the favorite haunts of the ghost? It wasn't that she looked as if you could have given her shillings—it was impossible to look less so. Yet when she finally drifted toward him, distinctly handsome, though ever so much older—older than when he had seen her before—it might have been as an effect of her guessing that he had, within the couple of hours, devoted more imagination to her than to all the others put together, and had thereby penetrated to a kind of truth that the others were too stupid for. She *was* there on harder terms than anyone; she was there as a consequence of things suffered, in one way and another, in the interval of years; and she remembered him very much as she was remembered—only a good deal better.

By the time they at last thus came to speech they were alone in one of the rooms—remarkable for a fine portrait over the chimney-place—out of which their friends had passed, and the charm of it was that even before they had spoken they had practically arranged with each other to stay behind for talk. The charm, happily, was in other things, too; it was partly in there being scarce a spot at Weatherend without something to stay behind for. It was in the way the autumn day looked into the high windows as it waned; in the way the red light, breaking at the close from under a low, somber sky, reached out in a long shaft and played over old wainscots, old tapestry, old gold, old color. It was most of all perhaps in the way she came to him as if, since she had been turned on to deal with the simpler sort, he might, should he choose to keep the whole thing down, just take her mild attention for a part of her general business. As soon as he heard her voice, however, the gap was filled up and the missing link supplied; the slight irony he divined in her attitude lost its advantage. He almost jumped at it to get there before her. "I met you years and years ago in Rome. I remember all about it." She confessed to disappointment—she had been so sure he didn't; and to prove how well he did he began to pour forth the particular recollections that popped up as he called for them. Her face and her voice, all at his service now, worked the miracle—the impression operating like the torch of a lamplighter who touches into flame, one by one, a long row of gas jets. Marcher flattered himself that the illumination was brilliant, yet he was really still more pleased on her showing him, with amusement, that in his haste to make everything right he had got most things rather wrong. It hadn't been at Rome—it had been at Naples; and it hadn't been seven years before—it had been more nearly ten. She hadn't been either with her uncle and aunt, but with her mother and her brother; in addition to which it was not with the Pembles that *he* had been, but with the Boyers, coming down in their company from Rome—a point on which she insisted, a little to his confusion, and as to which she had her evidence in hand. The Boyers she had known, but she didn't know the Pembles, though she had heard of them, and it was the people he was with who had made them acquainted. The incident of the thunderstorm that had raged round them with such violence as to drive them for refuge into an excavation—this incident had not occurred at the Palace of the Caesars, but at Pompeii, on an occasion when they had been present there at an important find.

He accepted her amendments, he enjoyed her corrections, though the moral of them was, she pointed out, that he *really* didn't remember the least thing about her; and he only felt it as a drawback that when all was made comfortable to the truth there didn't appear much of anything left. They lingered together still, she neglecting her office—for from the moment he was so clever she had no proper right to him—and both neglecting the house, just waiting as to see if a memory or two more wouldn't again breathe upon them. It had not taken them many minutes, after all, to put down on the table, like the cards of a pack, those that constituted their respective hands; only what came out was that the pack was unfortunately not perfect—that the past, invoked, invited, encouraged, could give them, naturally, no more than it had. It had made them meet her at twenty, him at twenty-five; but nothing was so strange, they seemed to say to each other, as that, while so occupied, it hadn't done a little more for them. They looked at each other as

with the feeling of an occasion missed; the present one
would have been so much better if the other, in the far
distance, in the foreign land, hadn't been so stupidly
meager. There weren't, apparently, all counted, more than
a dozen little old things that had succeeded in coming to
pass between them; trivialities of youth, simplicities of
freshness, stupidities of ignorance, small possible germs,
but too deeply buried—too deeply (didn't it seem?) to
sprout after so many years. Marcher said to himself that
he ought to have rendered her some service—saved her
from a capsized boat in the bay, or at least recovered her
dressing bag, filched from her cab, in the streets of Naples,
by a lazzarone with a stiletto. Or it would have been nice
if he could have been taken with fever, alone, at his
hotel, and she could have come to look after him, to
write to his people, to drive him out in convalescence.
Then they would be in possession of the something or
other that their actual show seemed to lack. It yet somehow presented itself, this show, as too good to be
spoiled; so that they were reduced for a few minutes more
to wondering a little helplessly why—since they seemed
to know a certain number of the same people—their
reunion had been so long averted. They didn't use that
name for it, but their delay from minute to minute to
join the others was a kind of confession that they didn't
quite want it to be a failure. Their attempted supposition
of reasons for their not having met but showed how little
they knew of each other. There came in fact a moment
when Marcher felt a positive pang. It was vain to pretend
she was an old friend, for all the communities were
wanting, in spite of which it was as an old friend that
he saw she would have suited him. He had new ones
enough—was surrounded with them, for instance, at that
hour at the other house; as a new one he probably
wouldn't have so much as noticed her. He would have
liked to invent something, get her to make believe with
him that some passage of a romantic or critical kind had
originally occurred. He was really almost reaching out in
imagination—as against time—for something that would
do, and saying to himself that if it didn't come this new
incident would simply and rather awkwardly close. They
would separate, and now for no second or for no third

chance. They would have tried and not succeeded. Then it was, just at the turn, as he afterward made it out to himself, that, everything else failing, she herself decided to take up the case and, as it were, save the situation. He felt as soon as she spoke that she had been consciously keeping back what she said and hoping to get on without it; a scruple in her that immensely touched him when, by the end of three or four minutes more, he was able to measure it. What she brought out, at any rate, quite cleared the air and supplied the link—the link it was such a mystery he should frivolously have managed to lose.

"You know you told me something that I've never forgotten and that again and again has made me think of you since; it was that tremendously hot day when we went to Sorrento, across the bay, for the breeze. What I allude to was what you said to me, on the way back as we sat, under the awning of the boat, enjoying the cool. Have you forgotten?"

He had forgotten, and he was even more surprised than ashamed. But the great thing was that he saw it was no vulgar reminder of any "sweet" speech. The vanity of women had long memories, but she was making no claim on him of a compliment or a mistake. With another woman, a totally different one, he might have feared the recall possibly even some imbecile "offer." So, in having to say that he had indeed forgotten, he was conscious rather of a loss than of a gain; he already saw an interest in the matter of her reference. "I try to think—but I give it up. Yet I remember the Sorrento day."

"I'm not very sure you do," May Bartram after a moment said; "and I'm not very sure I ought to want you to. It's dreadful to bring a person back, at any time, to what he was ten years before. If you've lived away from it," she smiled, "so much the better."

"Ah, if *you* haven't why should I?" he asked.

"Lived away, you mean, from what I myself was?"

"From what *I* was. I was of course an ass," Marcher went on; "but I would rather know from you just the sort of ass I was than—from the moment you have something in your mind—not know anything."

Still, however, she hesitated. "But if you've completely ceased to be that sort——?"

"Why, I can then just so all the more bear to know. Besides, perhaps I haven't."

"Perhaps. Yet if you haven't," she added, "I should suppose you would remember. Not indeed that I in the least connect with my impression the invidious name you use. If I had only thought you foolish," she explained, "the thing I speak of wouldn't so have remained with me. It was about yourself." She waited, as if it might come to him; but as, only meeting her eyes in wonder, he gave no sign, she burned her ships. "Has it ever happened?"

Then it was that, while he continued to stare, a light broke for him and the blood slowly came to his face, which began to burn with recognition. "Do you mean I told you——?" But he faltered, lest what came to him shouldn't be right, lest he should only give himself away.

"It was something about yourself that it was natural one shouldn't forget—that is if one remembered you at all. That's why I ask you," she smiled, "if the thing you then spoke of has ever come to pass?"

Oh, then he saw, but he was lost in wonder and found himself embarrassed. This, he also saw, made her sorry for him, as if her allusion had been a mistake. It took him but a moment, however, to feel that it had not been, much as it had been a surprise. After the first little shock of it her knowledge on the contrary began, even if rather strangely, to taste sweet to him. She was the only other person in the world then who would have it, and she had had it all these years, while the fact of his having so breathed his secret had unaccountably faded from him. No wonder they couldn't have met as if nothing had happened. "I judge," he finally said, "that I know what you mean. Only I had strangely enough lost the consciousness of having taken you so far into my confidence."

"Is it because you've taken so many others as well?"

"I've taken nobody. Not a creature since then."

"So that I'm the only person who knows?"

"The only person in the world."

"Well," she quickly replied, "I myself have never spoken. I've never, never repeated of you what you told me." She looked at him so that he perfectly believed her. Their eyes met over it in such a way that he was without a doubt. "And I never will."

She spoke with an earnestness that, as if almost excessive, put him at ease about her possible derision. Somehow the whole question was a new luxury to him—that is, from the moment she was in possession. If she didn't take the ironic view she clearly took the sympathetic, and that was what he had had, in all the long time, from no one whomsoever. What he felt was that he couldn't at present have begun to tell her and yet could profit perhaps exquisitely by the accident of having done so of old. "Please don't then. We're just right as it is."

"Oh, I am," she laughed, "if you are!" To which she added: "Then you do still feel in the same way?"

It was impossible to him not to take to himself that she was really interested, and it all kept coming as a sort of revelation. He had thought of himself so long as abominably alone, and, lo, he wasn't alone a bit. He hadn't been, it appeared, for an hour—since those moments on the Sorrento boat. It was *she* who had been, he seemed to see as he looked at her—she who had been made so by the graceless fact of his lapse of fidelity. To tell her what he had told her—what had it been but to ask something of her? something that she had given, in her charity, without his having, by a remembrance, by a return of the spirit, failing another encounter, so much as thanked her. What he had asked of her had been simply at first not to laugh at him. She had beautifully not done so for ten years, and she was not doing so now. So he had endless gratitude to make up. Only for that he must see just how he had figured to her. "What, exactly, was the account I gave——?"

"Of the way you did feel? Well, it was very simple. You said you had had from your earliest time, as the deepest thing within you, the sense of being kept for something rare and strange, possibly prodigious and terrible, that was sooner or later to happen to you, that you had in your bones the foreboding and the conviction of, and that would perhaps overwhelm you."

"Do you call that very simple?" John Marcher asked.

She thought a moment. "It was perhaps because I seemed, as you spoke, to understand it."

"You do understand it?" he eagerly asked.

Again she kept her kind eyes on him. "You still have the belief?"

"Oh!" he exclaimed helplessly. There was too much to say.

"Whatever it is to be," she clearly made out, "it hasn't yet come."

He shook his head in complete surrender now. "It hasn't yet come. Only, you know, it isn't anything I'm to *do*, to achieve in the world, to be distinguished or admired for. I'm not such an ass as *that*. It would be much better, no doubt, if I were."

"It's to be something you're merely to suffer?"

"Well, say to wait for—to have to meet, to face, to see suddenly break out in my life; possibly destroying all further consciousness, possibly annihilating me; possibly, on the other hand, only altering everything, striking at the root of all my world and leaving me to the consequences, however they shape themselves."

She took this in, but the light in her eyes continued for him not to be that of mockery. "Isn't what you describe perhaps but the expectation—or, at any rate, the sense of danger, familiar to so many people—of falling in love?"

John Marcher thought. "Did you ask me that before?"

"No—I wasn't so free and easy then. But it's what strikes me now."

"Of course," he said after a moment, "it strikes you. Of course it strikes *me*. Of course what's in store for me may be no more than that. The only thing is," he went on, "that I think that if it had been that, I should by this time know."

"Do you mean because you've *been* in love?" And then as he but looked at her in silence: "You've been in love, and it hasn't meant such a cataclysm, hasn't proved the great affair?"

"Here I am, you see. It hasn't been overwhelming."

"Then it hasn't been love," said May Bartram.

"Well, I at least thought it was. I took it for that—I've taken it till now. It was agreeable, it was delightful, it was miserable," he explained. "But it wasn't strange. It wasn't what *my* affair's to be."

"You want something all to yourself—something that nobody else knows or has known?"

"It isn't a question of what I 'want'—God knows I don't want anything. It's only a question of the apprehension that haunts me—that I live with day by day."

He said this so lucidly and consistently that, visibly, it further imposed itself. If she had not been interested before, she would have been interested now. "Is it a sense of coming violence?"

Evidently now, too, again, he liked to talk of it. "I don't know of it as—when it does come—necessarily violent. I only think of it as natural and as of course, above all, unmistakable. I think of it simply as *the* thing. *The* thing will of itself appear natural."

"Then how will it appear strange?"

Marcher bethought himself. "It won't—to me."

"To whom then?"

"Well," he replied, smiling at last, "say to you."

"Oh, then, I'm to be present?"

"Why, you *are* present—since you know."

"I see." She turned it over. "But I mean at the catastrophe."

At this, for a minute, their lightness gave way to their gravity; it was as if the long look they exchanged held them together. "It will only depend on yourself—if you'll watch with me."

"Are you afraid?" she asked.

"Don't leave me *now*," he went on.

"Are you afraid?" she repeated.

"Do you think me simply out of my mind?" he pursued instead of answering. "Do I merely strike you as a harmless lunatic?"

"No," said May Bartram. "I understand you. I believe you."

"You mean you feel how my obsession—poor old thing!—may correspond to some possible reality?"

"To some possible reality."

"Then you *will* watch with me?"

She hesitated, then for the third time put her question. "Are you afraid?"

"Did I tell you I was—at Naples?"

"No, you said nothing about it."

Then I don't know. And I should *like* to know," said
John Marcher. "You'll tell me yourself whether you
think so. If you'll watch with me, you'll see."

"Very good then." They had been moving by this time
across the room, and at the door, before passing out,
they paused as if for the full windup of their understanding. "I'll watch with you," said May Bartram.

II

The fact that she "knew"—knew and yet neither
chaffed him nor betrayed him—had in a short time begun
to constitute between them a sensible bond, which became more marked when, within the year that followed
their afternoon at Weatherend, the opportunities for
meeting multiplied. The event that thus promoted these occasions was the death of the ancient lady, her great-aunt,
under whose wing, since losing her mother, she had to
such an extent found shelter, and who, though but the
widowed mother of the new successor to the property, had
succeeded—thanks to a high tone and a high temper—in
not forfeiting the supreme position at the great house. The
deposition of this personage arrived but with her death,
which, followed by many changes, made in particular a
difference for the young woman in whom Marcher's expert attention had recognized from the first a dependent
with a pride that might ache though it didn't bristle. Nothing for a long time had made him easier than the thought
that the aching must have been much soothed by Miss
Bartram's now finding herself able to set up a small home
in London. She had acquired property, to an amount that
made that luxury just possible, under her aunt's extremely
complicated will, and when the whole matter began to be
straightened out, which indeed took time, she let him
know that the happy issue was at last in view. He had seen
her again before that day, both because she had more than
once accompanied the ancient lady to town and because

he had paid another visit to the friends who so conveniently made of Weatherend one of the charms of their own hospitality. These friends had taken him back there; he had achieved there again with Miss Bartram some quiet detachment; and he had in London succeeded in persuading her to more than one brief absence from her aunt. They went together, on these latter occasions, to the National Gallery and the South Kensington Museum, where, among vivid reminders, they talked of Italy at large—not now attempting to recover, as at first, the taste of their youth and their ignorance. That recovery, the first day at Weatherend, had served its purpose well, had given them quite enough; so that they were, to Marcher's sense, no longer hovering about the headwaters of their stream, but had felt their boat pushed sharply off and down the current.

They were literally afloat together; for our gentleman this was marked, quite as marked as that the fortunate cause of it was just the buried treasure of her knowledge. He had with his own hands dug up this little hoard, brought to light—that is to within reach of the dim day constituted by their discretions and privacies—the object of value the hiding place of which he had, after putting it into the ground himself, so strangely, so long forgotten. The exquisite luck of having again just stumbled on the spot made him indifferent to any other question; he would doubtless have devoted more time to the odd accident of his lapse of memory if he had not been moved to devote so much to the sweetness, the comfort, as he felt, for the future, that this accident itself had helped to keep fresh. It had never entered into his plan that anyone should "know," and mainly for the reason that it was not in him to tell anyone. That would have been impossible, since nothing but the amusement of a cold world would have waited on it. Since, however, a mysterious fate had opened his mouth in youth, inspite of him, he would count that a compensation and profit by it to the utmost. That the right person *should* know tempered the asperity of his secret more even than his shyness had permitted him to imagine; and May Bartram was clearly right, because—well, because there she was. Her knowledge simply settled it; he would have been

sure enough by this time had she been wrong. There was
that in his situation, no doubt, that disposed him too
much to see her as a mere confidante, taking all her
light for him from the fact—the fact only—of her interest in his predicament, from her mercy, sympathy,
seriousness, her consent not to regard him as the fun-
niest of the funny. Aware, in fine, that her price for him
was just in her giving him this constant sense of his being
admirably spared, he was careful to remember that she
had, after all, also a life of her own, with things that
might happen to *her,* things that in friendship one should
likewise take account of. Something fairly remarkable
came to pass with him, for that matter, in this connection
—something represented by a certain passage of his consciousness, in the suddenest way, from one extreme to the
other.

He had thought himself, so long as nobody knew, the
most disinterested person in the world, carrying his concentrated burden, his perpetual suspense, ever so quietly,
holding his tongue about it, giving others no glimpse of it
nor of its effect upon his life, asking of them no allowance
and only making on his side all those that were asked. He
had disturbed nobody with the queerness of having to
know a haunted man, though he had had moments of
rather special temptation on hearing people say that they
were "unsettled." If they were as unsettled as he was—
he who had never been settled for an hour in his life—
they would know what it meant. Yet it wasn't, all the
same, for him to make them, and he listened to them civilly
enough. This was why he had such good—though possibly
such rather colorless—manners; this was why, above all,
he could regard himself, in a greedy world, as decently—
as, in fact, perhaps even a little sublimely—unselfish. Our
point is accordingly that he valued this character quite
sufficiently to measure his present danger of letting it
lapse, against which he promised himself to be much on
his guard. He was quite ready, nonetheless, to be selfish
just a little, since, surely, no more charming occasion for
it had come to him. "Just a little," in a word, was just as
much as Miss Bartram, taking one day with another, would
let him. He never would be in the least coercive, and he
would keep well before him the lines on which considera-

tion for her—the very highest—ought to proceed. He
would thoroughly establish the heads under which her
affairs, her requirements, her peculiarities—he went so
far as to give them the latitude of that name—would
come into their intercourse. All this naturally was a
sign of how much he took the intercourse itself for
granted. There was nothing more to be done about *that*.
It simply existed; had sprung into being with her first penetrating question to him in the autumn light there at
Weatherend. The real form it should have taken on the
basis that stood out large was the form of their marrying.
But the devil in this was that the very basis itself put
marrying out of the question. His conviction, his apprehension, his obsession, in short, was not a condition
he could invite a woman to share; and that consequence
of it was precisely what was the matter with him. Something or other lay in wait for him, amid the twists and
the turns of the months and the years, like a crouching
Beast in the Jungle. It signified little whether the crouching Beast were destined to slay him or to be slain. The
definite point was the inevitable spring of the creature;
and the definite lesson from that was that a man of feeling didn't cause himself to be accompanied by a lady on
a tiger hunt. Such was the image under which he had
ended by figuring his life.

They had at first, nonetheless, in the scattered hours
spent together, made no allusion to that view of it; which
was a sign he was handsomely ready to give that he didn't
expect, that he in fact didn't care always to be talking
about it. Such a feature in one's outlook was really like
a hump on one's back. The difference it made every minute of the day existed quite independently of discussion.
One discussed, of course *like* a hunchback, for there was
always, if nothing else, the hunchback face. That
remained, and she was watching him; but people watched
best, as a general thing, in silence, so that such would
be predominantly the manner of their vigil. Yet he didn't
want, at the same time, to be solemn; solemn was what
he imagined he too much tended to be with other
people. The thing to be, with the one person who knew,
was easy and natural—to make the reference rather than
be seeming to avoid it, to avoid it rather than be seeming

to make it, and to keep it, in any case, familiar, facetious even, rather than pedantic and portentous. Some such consideration as the latter was doubtless in his mind, for instance, when he wrote pleasantly to Miss Bartram that perhaps the great thing he had so long felt as in the lap of the gods was no more than this circumstance, which touched him so nearly, of her acquiring a house in London. it was the first allusion they had yet again made, needing any other hitherto so little; but when she replied, after having given him the news, that she was by no means satisfied with such a trifle, as the climax to so special a suspense, she almost set him wondering if she hadn't even a larger conception of singularity for him than he had for himself. He was at all events destined to become aware little by little, as time went by, that she was all the while looking at his life, judging it, measuring it, in the light of the thing she knew, which grew to be at last, with the consecration of the years, never mentioned between them save as "the real truth" about him. That had always been his own form of reference to it, but she adopted the form so quietly that, looking back at the end of a period, he knew there was no moment at which it was traceable that she had, as he might say, got inside his condition, or exchanged the attitude of beautifully indulging for that of still more beautifully believing him.

it was always open to him to accuse her of seeing him but as the most harmless of maniacs, and this, in the long run—since it covered so much ground—was his easiest description of their friendship. He had a screw loose for her, but she liked him in spite of it, and was practically, against the rest of the world, his kind, wise keeper, unremunerated, but fairly amused and, in the absence of other near ties, not disreputably occupied. The rest of the world of course thought him queer, but she, she only, knew how, and above all why, queer; which was precisely what enabled her to dispose the concealing veil in the right folds. She took his gaiety from him since it had to pass with them for gaiety—as she took everything else; but she certainly so far justified by her unerring touch his finer sense of the degree to which he had ended by convincing her. *She* at least never spoke of the secret of his life except as "the real truth about you," and she had in fact a wonderful way of making it seem, as such, the secret of her own life too. That was in fine how he so constantly felt her as allowing for him; he couldn't on the whole call it anything else. He allowed for himself, but she, exactly, allowed still more; partly because, better placed for a sight of the matter, she traced his unhappy perversion through portions of its course into which he could scarce follow it. He knew how he felt, but, besides knowing that, she knew how he looked as well; he knew each of the things of importance he was insidiously kept from doing, but she could add up the amount they made, understand how much, with a lighter weight on his spirit, he might have done, and thereby establish how, clever as he was, he fell short. Above all she was in the secret of the difference between the forms he went through—those of his little office under government, those of caring for his modest patrimony, for his library, for his garden in the country, for the people in London whose invitations he accepted and repaid—and the detachment that reigned beneath them and that made of all behavior, all that could in the least be called behavior, a long act of dissimulation. What it had come to was that he wore a mask painted with the social simper, out of the eyeholes of which there looked eyes of an expression not in the least matching the other features. This the stupid world, even after years, had never more than half discovered. It was only May Bartram who had, and she achieved, by an art indescribable, the feat of at once—or perhaps it was only alternately—meeting the eyes from in front and mingling her own vision, as from over his shoulder, with their peep through the apertures.

So, while they grew older together, she did watch with him, and so she let this association give shape and color to her own existence. Beneath *her* forms as well detachment had learned to sit, and behavior had become for her, in the social sense, a false account of herself. There was but one account of her that would have been true all the while, and that she could give, directly, to nobody, least of all to John Marcher. Her whole attitude was a virtual statement, but the perception of that only seemed destined to take its place for him as one of the many things necessarily crowded out of his consciousness. If she had, moreover, like himself, to make sacrifices to their real truth, it was to be granted that her compensation might have affected her as more prompt and more natural. They had long periods, in this London time, during which, when they were together, a stranger might have listened to them without in the least pricking up his ears; on the other hand, the real truth was equally liable at any moment to rise to the surface, and the auditor would then have wondered indeed what they were talking about. They had from an early time made up their mind that society was, luckily, unintelligent, and the margin that this gave them had fairly become one of their commonplaces. Yet there were still moments when the situation turned almost fresh—usually under the effect of some expression drawn from herself. Her expressions doubtless repeated themselves, but her intervals were generous. "What saves us, you know, is that we answer so completely to so usual an appearance: that of the man and woman whose friendship has become such a daily habit, or almost, as to be at last indispensable." That, for instance, was a remark she had frequently enough had occasion to make, though she had given it at different times different developments. What we are especially concerned with is the turn it happened to take from her one afternoon when he had come to see her in honor of her birthday. This anniversary had fallen on a Sunday, at a season of thick fog and general outward gloom; but he had brought her his customary offering, having known her now long enough to have established a hundred little customs. It was one of his proofs to himself, the present he made her on her birthday, that he had not sunk into real selfishness. It was mostly nothing more than a small trinket, but it was always fine of its kind, and he was regularly careful to pay for it more than he thought he could afford. "Our habit saves you, at least, don't you see? because it makes you, after all, for the vulgar, indistinguishable from other men. What's the most inveterate mark of men in general? Why, the capacity to spend endless time with dull women—to spend it, I won't say without being bored, but without minding that they are, without being driven off at a tangent by it; which comes to the same thing. I'm your dull woman, a part of the daily bread for which you pray at church. That covers your tracks more than anything."

"And what covers yours?" asked Marcher, whom his dull woman could mostly to this extent amuse. "I see of course what you mean by your saving me, in one way and another, so far as other people are concerned—I've seen it all along. Only, what is it that saves *you?* I often think, you know, of that."

She looked as if she sometimes thought of that, too, but in rather a different way. "Where other people, you mean, are concerned?"

"Well, you're really so in with me, you know—as a sort of result of my being so in with yourself. I mean of my having such an immense regard for you, being so tremendously grateful for all you've done for me. I sometimes ask myself if it's quite fair. Fair I mean to have so involved and—since one may say it—interested you. I almost feel as if you hadn't really had time to do anything else."

"Anything else but be interested?" she asked. "Ah what else does one ever want to be? If I've been 'watching' with you, as we long ago agreed that I was to do, watching is always in itself an absorption."

"Oh, certainly," John Marcher said, "if you hadn't had your curiosity——! Only, doesn't it sometimes come to you, as time goes on, that your curiosity is not being particularly repaid?"

May Bartram had a pause. "Do you ask that, by any chance, because you feel at all that yours isn't? I mean because you have to wait so long."

Oh, he understood what she meant. "For the thing to happen that never does happen? For the beast to jump out? No, I'm just where I was about it. It isn't a matter as to which I can *choose,* I can decide for a change. It isn't one as to which there *can* be a change. It's in the lap of the gods. One's in the hands of one's law—there one is. As to the form the law will take, the way it will operate, that's its own affair."

"Yes," Miss Bartram replied; "of course one's fate is coming, of course it *has* come, in its own form and its own way, all the while. Only, you know, the form and the way in your case were to have been—well, something so exceptional and, as one may say, so particularly *your* own."

Something in this made him look at her with suspicion. "You say 'were to *have* been,' as if in your heart you had begun to doubt."

"Oh!" she vaguely protested.

"As if you believed," he went on, "that nothing will now take place."

She shook her head slowly, but rather inscrutably. "You're far from my thought."

He continued to look at her. "What then is the matter with you?"

"Well," she said after another wait, "the matter with me is simply that I'm more sure than ever my curiosity, as you call it, will be but too well repaid."

They were frankly grave now; he had got up from his seat, had turned once more about the little drawing room to which, year after year, he brought his inevitable topic; in which he had, as he might have said, tasted their intimate community with every sauce, where every object was as familiar to him as the things of his own house and the very carpets were worn with his fitful walk very much as the desks in old countinghouses are worn by the elbows of generations of clerks. The generations of his nervous moods had been at work there, and the place was the written history of his whole middle life. Under the impression of what his friend had just said he knew himself, for some reason, more aware of these things, which made him, after a moment, stop again before her. "Is it, possibly, that you've grown afraid?"

"Afraid?" He thought, as she repeated the word, that his question had made her, a little, change color; so that, lest he should have touched on a truth, he explained very kindly. "You remember that that was what you asked *me* long ago—that first day at Weatherend."

"Oh, yes, and you told me you didn't know—that I was to see for myself. We've said little about it since, even in so long a time."

"Precisely," Marcher interposed—"quite as if it were too delicate a matter for us to make free with. Quite as if we might find, on pressure, that I *am* afraid. For then," he said, "we shouldn't, should we? quite know what to do."

She had for the time no answer to this question. "There have been days when I thought you were. Only, of course," she added, "there have been days when we have thought almost anything."

"Everything. Oh!" Marcher softly groaned as with a gasp, half-spent, at the face, more uncovered just then than it had been for a long while, of the imagination always with them. It had always had its incalculable moments of glaring out, quite as with the very eyes of the very Beast, and, used as he was to them, they could still draw from him the tribute of a sigh that rose from the depths of his being. All that they had thought, first and last, rolled over him; the past seemed to have been reduced to mere barren speculation. This in fact was what the place had just struck him as so full of—the simplification of everything but the state of suspense. That remained only by seeming to hang in the void surrounding it. Even his original fear, if fear it had been, had lost itself in the desert. "I judge, however," he continued, "that you see I'm not afraid now."

"What I see is, as I make it out, that you've achieved something almost unprecedented in the way of getting used to danger. Living with it so long and so closely, you've lost your sense of it; you know it's there, but you're indifferent, and you cease even, as of old, to have to whistle in the dark. Considering what the danger is," May Bartram wound up, "I'm bound to say that I don't think your attitude could well be surpassed."

John Marcher faintly smiled. "It's heroic?"

"Certainly—call it that."

He considered. "I *am*, then, a man of courage?"

"That's what you were to show me."

He still, however, wondered. "But doesn't the man of courage know what he's afraid of—or *not* afraid of? I don't know that, you see. I don't focus it. I can't name it. I only know I'm exposed."

"Yes, but exposed—how shall I say?—so directly. So intimately. That's surely enough."

"Enough to make you feel, then—as what we may call the end of our watch—that I'm not afraid?"

"You're not afraid. But it isn't," she said, "the end of

our watch. That is it isn't the end of yours. You've everything still to see."

"Then why haven't *you?*" he asked. He had had, all along, today, the sense of her keeping something back, and he still had it. As this was his first impression of that, it made a kind of date. The case was the more marked as she didn't at first answer; which in turn made him go on. "You know something I don't." Then his voice, for that of a man of courage, trembled a little. "You know what's to happen." Her silence, with the face she showed, was almost a confession—it made him sure. "You know, and you're afraid to tell me. It's so bad that you're afraid I'll find out."

All this might be true, for she did look as if, unexpectedly to her, he had crossed some mystic line that she had secretly drawn round her. Yet she might, after all, not have worried; and the real upshot was that he himself, at all events, needn't. "You'll never find out."

III

It was all to have made, nonetheless, as I have said, a date; as came out in the fact that again and again, even after long intervals, other things that passed between them wore, in relation to this hour, but the character of recalls and results. Its immediate effect had been indeed rather to lighten insistence—almost to provoke a reaction; as if their topic had dropped by its own weight and as if moreover, for that matter, Marcher had been visited by one of his occasional warnings against egotism. He had kept up, he felt, and very decently on the whole, his consciousness of the importance of not being selfish, and it was true that he had never sinned in that direction without promptly enough trying to press the scales the other way. He often repaired his fault, the season permitting, by inviting his friend to accompany him to the opera; and it not infrequently thus happened that, to show he didn't

wish her to have but one sort of food for her mind, he
was the cause of her appearing there with him a dozen
nights in the month. It even happened that, seeing her
home at such times, he occasionally went in with her
to finish, as he called it, the evening, and, the better to
make his point, sat down to the frugal but always careful
little supper that awaited his pleasure. His point was made,
he thought, by his not eternally insisting with her on
himself; made for instance, at such hours, when it befell
that, her piano at hand and each of them familiar with it,
they went over passages of the opera together. It chanced
to be on one of these occasions, however, that he reminded her of her not having answered a certain question
he had put to her during the talk that had taken place
between them on her last birthday. "What is it that saves
you?"—saved her, he meant, from that appearance of
variation from the usual human type. If he had practically escaped remark, as she pretended, by doing, in
the most important particular, what most men do—find
the answer to life in patching up an alliance of a sort with
a woman no better than himself—how had she escaped
it, and how could the alliance, such as it was, since they
must suppose it had been more or less noticed, have
failed to make her rather positively talked about?

"I never said," May Bartram replied, "that it hadn't
made me talked about."

"Ah, well, then, you're not 'saved.'"

"It has not been a question for me. If you've had your
woman, I've had," she said, "my man."

"And you mean that makes you all right?"

She hesitated. "I don't know why it shouldn't make me
—humanly, which is what we're speaking of—as right as
it makes you."

"I see," Marcher returned. "'Humanly,' no doubt, as
showing that you're living for something. Not, that is, just
for me and my secret."

May Bartram smiled. "I don't pretend it exactly shows
that I'm not living for you. It's my intimacy with you
that's in question."

He laughed as he saw what she meant. "Yes, but since,
as you say, I'm only, so far as people make out, ordinary, you're—aren't you?—no more than ordinary either.

You help me to pass for a man like another. So if I *am*, as I understand you, you're not compromised. Is that it?"

She had another hesitation, but she spoke clearly enough. "That's it. It's all that concerns me—to help you to pass for a man like another."

He was careful to acknowledge the remark handsomely. "How kind, how beautiful, you are to me! How shall I ever repay you?"

She had her last grave pause, as if there might be a choice of ways. But she chose. "By going on as you are."

It was into this going on as he was that they relapsed, and really for so long a time that the day inevitably came for a further sounding of their depths. It was as if these depths, constantly bridged over by a structure that was firm enough in spite of its lightness and of its occasional oscillation in the somewhat vertiginous air, invited on occasion, in the interest of their nerves, a dropping of the plummet and a measurement of the abyss. A difference had been made moreover, once for all, by the fact that she had, all the while, not appeared to feel the need of rebutting his charge of an idea within her that she didn't dare to express, uttered just before one of the fullest of their later discussions ended. It had come up for him then that she "knew" something and that what she knew was bad—too bad to tell him. When he had spoken of it as visibly so bad that she was afraid he might find it out, her reply had left the matter too equivocal to be let alone and yet, for Marcher's special sensibility, almost too formidable again to touch. He circled about it at a distance that alternately narrowed and widened and that yet was not much affected by the consciousness in him that there was nothing she could "know," after all, any better than he did. She had no source of knowledge that he hadn't equally—except of course that she might have finer nerves. That was what women had where they were interested; they made out things, where people were concerned, that the people often couldn't have made out for themselves. Their nerves, their sensibility, their imagination, were conductors and revealers, and the beauty of May Bartram was in particular that she had given herself so to his case. He felt in these days what, oddly enough, he had never felt before, the growth of a dread of losing her by some catastrophe—some catastrophe that yet wouldn't at all be *the* catastrophe: partly because she had, almost of a sudden, begun to strike him as useful to him as never yet, and partly by reason of an appearance of uncertainty in her health, coincident and equally new. It was characteristic of the inner detachment he had hitherto so successfully cultivated and to which our whole account of him is a reference, it was characteristic that his complications, such as they were, had never yet seemed so as at this crisis to thicken about him, even to the point of making him ask himself if he were, by any chance, of a truth, within sight or sound, within touch or reach, within the immediate jurisdiction of the thing that waited.

When the day came, as come it had to, that his friend confessed to him her fear of a deep disorder in her blood, he felt somehow the shadow of a change and the chill of a shock. He immediately began to imagine aggravations and disasters, and above all to think of her peril as the direct menace for himself of personal privation. This indeed gave him one of those partial recoveries of equanimity that were agreeable to him—it showed him that what was still first in his mind was the loss she herself might suffer. "What if she should have to die before knowing, before seeing——?" It would have been brutal, in the early stages of her trouble, to put that question to her; but it had immediately sounded for him to his own concern, and the possibility was what most made him sorry for her. If she did "know," moreover, in the sense of her having had some—what should he think?—mystical, irresistible light, this would make the matter not better, but worse, inasmuch as her original adoption of his own curiosity had quite become the basis of her life. She had been living to see what would be to be seen, and it would be cruel to her to have to give up before the accomplishment of the vision. These reflections, as I say, refreshed his generosity; yet, make them as he might, he saw himself, with the lapse of the period, more and more disconcerted. It lapsed for him with a strange, steady sweep, and the oddest oddity was that it gave him, independently of the threat of much inconvenience, almost the only positive surprise his career, if career it could

be called, had yet offered him. She kept the house as she
had never done; he had to go to her to see her—
she could meet him nowhere now, though there was
scarce a corner of their loved old London in which she
had not in the past, at one time or another, done so;
and he found her always seated by her fire in the deep,
old-fashioned chair she was less and less able to leave.
He had been struck one day, after an absence exceeding
his usual measure, with her suddenly looking much
older to him than he had ever thought of her being; then
he recognized that the suddenness was all on his side—
he had just been suddenly struck. She looked older because inevitably, after so many years, she was old, or almost; which was of course true in still greater measure of
her companion. If she was old, or almost, John Marcher
assuredly was, and yet it was her showing of the lesson,
not his own, that brought the truth home to him. His
surprises began here; when once they had begun
they multiplied; they came rather with a rush: it was as if,
in the oddest way in the world, they had all been kept
back, sown in a thick cluster, for the late afternoon of
life, the time at which, for people in general, the unexpected has died out.

One of them was that he should have caught himself
—for he *had* so done—*really* wondering if the great accident would take form now as nothing more than his being
condemned to see this charming woman, this admirable
friend, pass away from him. He had never so unreservedly
qualified her as while confronted in thought with such a
possibility; in spite of which there was small doubt for
him that as an answer to his long riddle the mere efface-
ment of even so fine a feature of his situation would be
an abject anticlimax. It would represent, as connected
with his past attitude, a drop of dignity under the shadow of which his existence could only become the most
grotesque of failures. He had been far from holding it a
failure—long as he had waited for the appearance that
was to make it a success. He had waited for a quite other
thing, not for such a one as that. The breath of his good
faith came short, however, as he recognized how long he
had waited, or how long, at least, his companion had.
That she, at all events, might be recorded as having

waited in vain—this affected him sharply, and all the more because of his at first having done little more than amuse himself with the idea. It grew more grave as the gravity of her condition grew, and the state of mind it produced in him, which he ended by watching, himself, as if it had been some definite disfigurement of his outer person, may pass for another of his surprises. This conjoined itself still with another, the really stupefying consciousness of a question that he would have allowed to shape itself had he dared. What did everything mean—what, that is, did she mean, she and her vain waiting and her probable death and the soundless admonition of it all—unless that, at this time of day, it was simply, it was overwhelmingly too late? He had never, at any stage of his queer consciousness, admitted the whisper of such a correction; he had never, till within these last few months, been so false to his conviction as not to hold that what was to come to him had time, whether *he* struck himself as having it or not. That at last, at last, he certainly hadn't it, to speak of, or had it but in the scantiest measure—such, soon enough, as things went with him, became the inference with which his old obsession had to reckon: and this it was not helped to do by the more and more confirmed appearance that the great vagueness casting the long shadow in which he had lived had, to attest itself, almost no margin left. Since it was in Time that he was to have met his fate, so it was in Time that his fate was to have acted; and as he waked up to the sense of no longer being young, which was exactly the sense of being stale, just as that, in turn, was the sense of being weak, he waked up to another matter beside. It all hung together; they were subject, he and the great vagueness, to an equal and indivisible law. When the possibilities themselves had, accordingly, turned stale, when the secret of the gods had grown faint, had perhaps even quite evaporated, that, and that only, was failure. It wouldn't have been failure to be bankrupt, dishonored, pilloried, hanged; it was failure not to be anything. And so, in the dark valley into which his path had taken its unlooked-for twist, he wondered not a little as he groped. He didn't care what awful crash might overtake him, with what ignominy or what monstrosity he might yet be associated—since he wasn't, after all, too utterly

old to suffer—if it would only be decently proportionate
to the posture he had kept, all his life, in the promised
presence of it. He had but one desire left—that he
shouldn't have been "sold."

IV

Then it was that one afternoon, while the spring of
the year was young and new, she met, all in her own way,
his frankest betrayal of these alarms. He had gone in late
to see her, but evening had not settled, and she was
presented to him in that long, fresh light of waning
April days which affects us often with a sadness sharper
than the grayest hours of autumn. The week had been
warm, the spring was supposed to have begun early, and
May Bartram sat, for the first time in the year, without a
fire, a fact that, to Marcher's sense, gave the scene of
which she formed part a smooth and ultimate look,
an air of knowing, in its immaculate order and its cold,
meaningless cheer, that it would never see a fire again.
Her own aspect—he could scarce have said why—intensified this note. Almost as white as wax, with the
marks and signs in her face as numerous and as fine as
if they had been etched by a needle, with soft white
draperies relieved by a faded green scarf, the delicate
tone of which had been consecrated by the years, she
was the picture of a serene, exquisite, but impenetrable
sphinx, whose head, or indeed all whose person, might
have been powdered with silver. She was a sphinx, yet
with her white petals and green fronds she might have
been a lily, too—only an artificial lily, wonderfully
imitated and constantly kept, without dust or stain,
though not exempt from a slight droop and a complexity
of faint creases, under some clear glass bell. The perfection of household care, of high polish and finish, always
reigned in her rooms, but they especially looked to
Marcher at present as if everything had been wound

up, tucked in, put away, so that she might sit with folded hands and with nothing more to do. She was "out of it," to his vision; her work was over; she communicated with him as across some gulf, or from some island of rest that she had already reached, and it made him feel strangely abandoned. Was it—or, rather, wasn't it—that if for so long she had been watching with him the answer to their question had swum into her ken and taken on its name, so that her occupation was verily gone? He had as much as charged her with this in saying to her, many months before, that she even then knew something she was keeping from him. It was a point he had never since ventured to press, vaguely fearing, as he did, that it might become a difference, perhaps a disagreement, between them. He had in short, in this later time, turned nervous, which was what, in all the other years, he had never been; and the oddity was that his nervousness should have waited till he had begun to doubt, should have held off so long as he was sure. There was something, it seemed to him, that the wrong word would bring down on his head, something that would so at least put an end to his suspense. But he wanted not to speak the wrong word; that would make everything ugly. He wanted the knowledge he lacked to drop on him, if drop it could, by its own august weight. If she was to forsake him it was surely for her to take leave. This was why he didn't ask her again, directly, what she knew; but it was also why, approaching the matter from another side, he said to her in the course of his visit: "What do you regard as the very worst that, at this time of day, *can* happen to me?"

He had asked her that in the past often enough; they had, with the odd, irregular rhythm of their intensities and avoidances, exchanged ideas about it and then had seen the ideas washed away by cool intervals, washed like figures traced in sea sand. It had ever been the mark of their talk that the oldest allusions in it required but a little dismissal and reaction to come out again, sounding for the hour as new. She could thus at present meet his inquiry quite freshly and patiently. "Oh, yes, I've repeatedly thought, only it always seemed to me of old that I couldn't quite make up my mind. I thought of dreadful things, between which it was difficult to choose; and so must you have done."

"Rather! I feel now as if I had scarce done anything else. I appear to myself to have spent my life in thinking of nothing but dreadful things. A great many of them I've at different times named to you, but there were others I couldn't name."

"They were too, too dreadful?"

"Too, too dreadful—some of them."

She looked at him a minute, and there came to him as he met it an inconsequent sense that her eyes, when one got their full clearness, were still as beautiful as they had been in youth, only beautiful with a strange, cold light—a light that somehow was a part of the effect, if it wasn't rather a part of the cause, of the pale, hard sweetness of the season and the hour. "And yet," she said at last, "there are horrors we have mentioned."

It deepened the strangeness to see her, as such a figure in such a picture, talk of "horrors," but she was to do, in a few minutes, something stranger yet—though even of this he was to take the full measure but afterward—and the note of it was already in the air. It was, for the matter of that, one of the signs that her eyes were having again such a high flicker of their prime. He had to admit, however, what she said. "Oh, yes, there were times when we did go far." He caught himself in the act, speaking as if it all were over. Well, he wished it were; and the consummation depended, for him, clearly, more and more on his companion.

But she had now a soft smile. "Oh, far——!"

It was oddly ironic. "Do you mean you're prepared to go further?"

She was frail and ancient and charming as she continued to look at him, yet it was rather as if she had lost the thread. "Do you consider that we went so far?"

"Why, I thought it the point you were just making—that we *had* looked most things in the face."

"Including each other?" She still smiled. "But you're quite right. We've had together great imaginations, often great fears; but some of them have been unspoken."

"Then the worst—we haven't faced that. I *could* face it, I believe, if I knew what you think it. I feel," he explained, "as if I had lost my power to conceive such things." And he wondered if he looked as blank as he sounded. "It's spent."

"Then why do you assume," she asked, "that mine isn't?"

"Because you've given me signs to the contrary. It isn't a question for you of conceiving, imagining, comparing. It isn't a question now of choosing." At last he came out with it. "You know something that I don't. You've showed me that before."

These last words affected her, he could see in a moment, remarkably, and she spoke with firmness. "I've shown you, my dear, nothing."

He shook his head. "You can't hide it."

"Oh, oh!" May Bartram murmured over what she couldn't hide. It was almost a smothered groan.

"You admitted it months ago, when I spoke of it to you as of something you were afraid I would find out. Your answer was that I couldn't, that I wouldn't, and I don't pretend I have. But you had something therefore in mind, and I see now that it must have been, that it still is, the possibility that, of all possibilities, has settled itself for you as the worst. This," he went on, "is why I appeal to you. I'm only afraid of ignorance now—I'm not afraid of knowledge." And then as for a while she said nothing: "What makes me sure is that I see in your face and feel here, in this air and amid these appearances, that you're out of it. You've done. You've had your experience. You leave me to my fate."

Well, she listened, motionless and white in her chair, as if she had in fact a decision to make, so that her whole manner was a virtual confession, though still with a small, fine, inner stiffness, an imperfect surrender. "It *would* be the worst," she finally let herself say. "I mean the thing that I've never said."

It hushed him a moment. "More monstrous than all the monstrosities we've named?"

"More monstrous. Isn't that what you sufficiently express," she asked, "in calling it the worst?"

Marcher thought. "Assuredly—if you mean, as I do, something that includes all the loss and all the shame that are thinkable."

"It would if it *should* happen," said May Bartram. "What we're speaking of, remember, is only my idea."

"It's your belief," Marcher returned. "That's enough for me. I feel your beliefs are right. Therefore if, having this one, you give me no more light on it, you abandon me."

"No, no!" she repeated. "I'm with you don't you see? —still." And as if to make it more vivid to him she rose from her chair—a movement she seldom made in these days—and showed herself, all draped and all soft, in her fairness and slimness. "I haven't forsaken you."

It was really, in its effort against weakness, a generous assurance, and had the success of the impulse not, happily, been great, it would have touched him to pain more than to pleasure. But the cold charm in her eyes had spread, as she hovered before him, to all the rest of her person, so that it was, for the minute, almost like a recovery of youth. He couldn't pity her for that; he could only take her as she showed—as capable still of helping him. It was as if, at the same time, her light might at any instant go out; wherefore he must make the most of it. There passed before him with intensity the three or four things he wanted most to know; but the question that came of itself to his lips really covered the others. "Then tell me if I shall consciously suffer."

She promptly shook her head. "Never!"

It confirmed the authority he imputed to her, and it produced on him an extraordinary effect. "Well, what's better than that? Do you call that the worst?"

"You think nothing is better?" she asked.

She seemed to mean something so special that he again sharply wondered, though still with the dawn of a prospect of relief. "Why not, if one doesn't *know?*" After which, as their eyes, over his question, met in a silence, the dawn deepened and something to his purpose came, prodigiously, out of her very face. His own, as he took it in, suddenly flushed to the forehead, and he gasped with the force of a perception to which, on the instant, everything fitted. The sound of his gasp filled the air; then he became articulate. "I see—if I don't suffer!"

In her own look, however, was doubt. "You see what?"

"Why, what you mean—what you've always meant."

She again shook her head. "What I mean isn't what I've always meant. It's different."

"It's something new?"

She hesitated. "Something new. It's not what you think. I see what you think."

His divination drew breath then; only her correction might be wrong. "It isn't that I am a donkey?" he asked between faintness and grimness. "It isn't that it's all a mistake?"

"A mistake?" she pityingly echoed. *That* possibility, for her, he saw, would be monstrous; and if she guaranteed him the immunity from pain it would accordingly not be what she had in mind. "Oh, no," she declared; "it's nothing of that sort. You've been right."

Yet he couldn't help asking himself if she weren't, thus pressed, speaking but to save him. It seemed to him he should be most lost if his history should prove all a platitude. "Are you telling me the truth, so that I shan't have been a bigger idiot than I can bear to know? I *haven't* lived with a vain imagination, in the most besotted illusion? I haven't waited but to see the door shut in my face?"

She shook her head again. "However the case stands, *that* isn't the truth. Whatever the reality, it is a reality. The door isn't shut. The door's open," said May Bartram.

"Then something's to come?"

She waited once again, always with her cold, sweet eyes on him. "It's never too late." She had, with her gliding step, diminished the distance between them, and she stood nearer to him, close to him, a minute, as if still full of the unspoken. Her movement might have been for some finer emphasis of what she was at once hesitating and deciding to say. He had been standing by the chimney piece, fireless and sparely adorned, a small, perfect old French clock and two morsels of rosy Dresden constituting all its furniture; and her hand grasped the shelf while she kept him waiting, grasped it a little as for support and encouragement. She only kept him waiting, however; that is, he only waited. It had become suddenly, from her movement and attitude, beautiful and vivid to him that she had something more to give him; her wasted face delicately shone with it, and it glittered, almost as with the white luster of silver, in her expression. She was right, incontestably, for what he saw in her face was the truth, and strangely, without consequence, while their talk of it as dreadful was still in the air, she appeared to present it as inordinately soft. This, prompting bewilderment, made him but gape the more gratefully for her revelation, so that they continued for some minutes silent, her face shining at him, her contact imponderably pressing, and his stare all kind, but all expectant. The end, nonetheless, was that what he had expected failed to sound. Something else took place instead, which seemed to consist at first in the mere closing of her eyes. She gave way at the same instant to a slow, fine shudder, and though he remained staring—though he stared, in fact, but the harder—she turned off and regained her chair. It was the end of what she had been intending, but it left him thinking only of that.

"Well, you don't say——?"

She had touched in her passage a bell near the chimney and had sunk back, strangely pale. "I'm afraid I'm too ill."

"Too ill to tell me?" It sprang up sharp to him, and almost to his lips, the fear that she would die without giving him light. He checked himself in time from so expressing his question, but she answered as if she had heard the words.

"Don't you know—now?"

"'Now'——?" She had spoken as if something that had made a difference had come up within the moment. But her maid, quickly obedient to her bell, was already with them. "I know nothing." And he was afterward to say to himself that he must have spoken with odious impatience, such an impatience as to show that, supremely disconcerted, he washed his hands of the whole question.

"Oh!" said May Bartram.

"Are you in pain?" he asked as the woman went to her.

"No," said May Bartram.

Her maid, who had put an arm round her as if to take her to her room, fixed on him eyes that appealingly contradicted her; in spite of which, however, he showed once more his mystification. "What then has happened?"

She was once more, with her companion's help, on

her feet, and, feeling withdrawal imposed on him, he had found, blankly, his hat and gloves and had reached the door. Yet he waited for her answer. "What *was* to," she said.

V

He came back the next day, but she was then unable to see him, and as it was literally the first time this had occurred in the long stretch of their acquaintance he turned away, defeated and sore, almost angry—or feeling at least that such a break in their custom was really the beginning of the end—and wandered alone with his thoughts, especially with one of them that he was unable to keep down. She was dying, and he would lose her; she was dying, and his life would end. He stopped in the park, into which he had passed, and stared before him at his recurrent doubt. Away from her the doubt pressed again; in her presence he had believed her, but as he felt his forlornness he threw himself into the explanation that, nearest at hand, had most of a miserable warmth for him and least of a cold torment. She had deceived him to save him—to put him off with something in which he should be able to rest. What could the thing that was to happen to him be, after all, but just this thing that had begun to happen? Her dying, her death, his consequent solitude—*that* was what he had figured as the Beast in the Jungle, that was what had been in the lap of the gods. He had had her word for it as he left her; for what else, on earth, could she have meant? It wasn't a thing of a monstrous order; not a fate rare and distinguished; not a stroke of fortune that overwhelmed and immortalized; it had only the stamp of the common doom. But poor Marcher, at this hour, judged the common doom sufficient. It would serve his turn, and even as the consummation of infinite waiting he would bend his pride to accept it. He sat down on a bench in the twilight. He hadn't been a fool. Something had *been,* as she had said, to come. Before he rose indeed it had quite struck him that the final fact really matched with the long avenue through which he had had to reach it. As sharing his suspense, and as giving herself all, giving her life, to bring it to an end, she had come with him every step of the way. He had lived by her aid, and to leave her behind would be cruelly, damnably to miss her. What could be more overwhelming than that?

Well, he was to know within the week, for though she kept him a while at bay, left him restless and wretched during a series of days on each of which he asked about her only again to have to turn away, she ended his trial by receiving him where she had always received him. Yet she had been brought out at some hazard into the presence of so many of the things that were, consciously, vainly, half their past, and there was scant service left in the gentleness of her mere desire, all too visible, to check his obsession and wind up his long trouble. That was clearly what she wanted; the one thing more, for her own peace, while she could still put out her hand. He was so affected by her state that, once seated by her chair, he was moved to let everything go; it was she herself therefore who brought him back, took up again, before she dismissed him, her last word of the other time. She showed how she wished to leave their affair in order. "I'm not sure you understood. You've nothing to wait for more. It *has* come."

Oh, how he looked at her! "Really?"

"Really."

"The thing that, as you said, *was* to?"

"The thing that we began in our youth to watch for."

Face to face with her once more he believed her; it was a claim to which he had so abjectly little to oppose. "You mean that it has come as a positive, definite occurrence, with a name and a date?"

"Positive. Definite. I don't know about the 'name,' but, oh, with a date!"

He found himself again too helplessly at sea. "But come in the night—come and pass me by?"

May Bartram had her strange, faint smile. "Oh, no, it hasn't passed you by!"

"But if I haven't been aware of it, and it hasn't touched me——?"

"Ah, your not being aware of it," and she seemed to hesitate an instant to deal with this—"your not being aware of it is the strangeness *in* the strangeness. It's the wonder *of* the wonder." She spoke as with the softness almost of a sick child, yet now at last, at the end of all, with the perfect straightness of a sybil. She visibly knew that she knew, and the effect on him was of something co-ordinate, in its high character, with the law that had ruled him. It was the true voice of the law; so on her lips would the law itself have sounded. "It *has* touched you," she went on. "It has done its office. It has made you all its own."

"So utterly without my knowing it?"

"So utterly without your knowing it." His hand, as he leaned to her, was on the arm of her chair, and, dimly smiling always now, she placed her own on it. "It's enough if *I* know it."

"Oh!" he confusedly sounded, as she herself of late so often had done.

"What I long ago said is true. You'll never know now, and I think you ought to be content. You've *had* it," said May Bartram.

"But had what?"

"Why, what was to have marked you out. The proof of your law. It has acted. I'm too glad," she then bravely added, "to have been able to see what it's *not.*"

He continued to attach his eyes to her, and with the sense that it was all beyond him, and that *she* was too, he would still have sharply challenged her, had he not felt it an abuse of her weakness to do more than take devoutly what she gave him, take it as hushed as to a revelation. If he did speak, it was out of the foreknowledge of his loneliness to come. "If you're glad of what it's 'not,' it might then have been worse?"

She turned her eyes away, she looked straight before her with which, after a moment: "Well, you know our fears."

He wondered. "It's something then we never feared?"

On this, slowly, she turned to him. "Did we ever dream,

with all our dreams, that we should sit and talk of it thus?"

He tried for a little to make out if they had; but it was as if their dreams, numberless enough, were in solution in some thick, cold mist, in which thought lost itself. "It might have been that we couldn't talk?"

"Well"—she did her best for him—"not from this side. This, you see," she said, "is the *other* side."

"I think," poor Marcher returned, "that all sides are the same to me." Then, however, as she softly shook her head in correction: "We mightn't, as it were, have got across——?"

"To where we are—no. We're *here*"—she made her weak emphasis.

"And much good does it do us!" was her friend's frank comment.

"It does us the good it can. It does us the good that *it* isn't here. It's past. It's behind," said May Bartram. "Before——" but her voice dropped.

He had got up, not to tire her, but it was hard to combat his yearning. She after all told him nothing but that his light had failed—which he knew well enough without her. "Before——?" he blankly echoed.

"Before, you see, it was always to *come*. That kept it present."

"Oh, I don't care what comes now! Besides," Marcher added, "it seems to me I liked it better present, as you say, than I can like it absent with *your* absence."

"Oh, mine!"—and her pale hands made light of it.

"With the absence of everything." He had a dreadful sense of standing there before her for—so far as anything but this proved, this bottomless drop was concerned— the last time of their life. It rested on him with a weight he felt he could scarce bear, and this weight it apparently was that still pressed out what remained in him of speakable protest. "I believe you; but I can't begin to pretend I understand. *Nothing*, for me, is past; nothing *will* pass until I pass myself, which I pray my stars may be as soon as possible. Say, however," he added, "that I've eaten my cake, as you contend, to the last crumb— how can the thing I've never felt at all be the thing I was marked out to feel?"

She met him, perhaps, less directly, but she met him unperturbed. "You take your 'feelings' for granted. You were to suffer your fate. That was not necessarily to know it."

"How in the world—when what is such knowledge but suffering?"

She looked up at him a while, in silence. "No—you don't understand."

"I suffer," said John Marcher.

"Don't, don't!"

"How can I help at least *that?*"

"*Don't!*" May Bartram repeated.

She spoke it in a tone so special, in spite of her weakness, that he stared an instant—stared as if some light, hitherto hidden, had shimmered across his vision. Darkness again closed over it, but the gleam had already become for him an idea. "Because I haven't the right——?"

"Don't *know*—when you needn't," she mercifully urged. "You needn't—for we shouldn't."

"Shouldn't?" If he could but know what she meant!

"No—it's too much."

"Too much?" he still asked—but with a mystification that was the next moment, of a sudden, to give way. Her words, if they meant something, affected him in this light—the light also of her wasted face—as meaning all, and the sense of what knowledge had been for herself came over him with a rush which broke through into a question. "Is it of that, then, you're dying?"

She but watched him, gravely at first, as if to see, with this, where he was, and she might have seen something, or feared something, that moved her sympathy. "I would live for you still—if I could." Her eyes closed for a little, as if, withdrawn into herself, she were, for a last time, trying. "But I can't!" she said as she raised them again to take leave of him.

She couldn't indeed, as but too promptly and sharply appeared, and he had no vision of her after this that was anything but darkness and doom. They had parted forever in that strange talk; access to her chamber of pain, rigidly guarded, was almost wholly forbidden him; he was feeling now moreover, in the face of doctors, nurses, the two or three relatives attracted doubtless by the presumption of what she had to "leave," how few were the rights, as they were called in such cases, that he had to put forward, and how odd it might even seem that their intimacy shouldn't have given him more of them. The stupidest fourth cousin had more, even though she had been nothing in such a person's life. She had been a feature of features in *his*, for what else was it to have been so indispensable? Strange beyond saying were the ways of existence, baffling for him the anomaly of his lack, as he felt it to be, of producible claim. A woman might have been, as it were, everything to him, and it might yet present him in no connection that anyone appeared obliged to recognize. If this was the case in these closing weeks it was the case more sharply on the occasion of the last offices rendered, in the great gray London cemetery, to what had been mortal, to what had been precious, in his friend. The concourse at her grave was not numerous, but he saw himself treated as scarce more nearly concerned with it than if there had been a thousand others. He was in short from this moment face to face with the fact that he was to profit extraordinarily little by the interest May Bartram had taken in him. He couldn't quite have said what he expected, but he had somehow not expected this approach to a double privation. Not only had her interest failed him, but he seemed to feel himself unattended——and for a reason he couldn't sound—by the distinction, the dignity, the propriety, if nothing else, of the man markedly bereaved. It was as if, in the view of society, he had not *been* markedly bereaved, as if there still failed some sign or proof of it, and as if, nonetheless, his character could never be affirmed, nor the deficiency ever made up. There were moments, as the weeks went by, when he would have liked, by some almost aggressive act, to take his stand on the intimacy of his loss, in order that it *might* be questioned and his retort, to the relief of his spirit, so recorded; but the moments of an irritation more helpless followed fast on these, the moments during which, turning things over with a good conscience but with a bare horizon, he found himself wondering if he oughtn't to have begun, so to speak, further back.

He found himself wondering indeed at many things, and this last speculation had others to keep it company. What could he have done, after all, in her lifetime, without giving them both, as it were, away? He couldn't have made it known she was watching him, for that would have published the superstition of the Beast. This was what closed his mouth now—now that the Jungle had been threshed to vacancy and that the Beast had stolen away. It sounded too foolish and too flat; the difference for him in this particular, the extinction in his life of the element of suspense, was such in fact as to surprise him. He could scarce have said what the effect resembled; the abrupt cessation, the positive prohibition, of music perhaps, more than anything else, in some place all adjusted and all accustomed to sonority and to attention. If he could at any rate have conceived lifting the veil from his image at some moment of the past (what had he done, after all, if not lift it to *her?*) so to do this today, to talk to people at large of the jungle cleared and confide to them that he now felt it as safe, would have been not only to see them listen as to a goodwife's tale, but really to hear himself tell one. What it presently came to in truth was that poor Marcher waded through his beaten grass, where no life stirred, where no breath sounded, where no evil eye seemed to gleam from a possible lair, very much as if vaguely looking for the Beast, and still more as if missing it. He walked about in an existence that had grown strangely more spacious, and, stopping fitfully in places where the undergrowth of life struck him as closer, asked himself yearningly, wondered secretly and sorely, if it would have lurked here or there. It would have at all events *sprung;* what was at least complete was his belief in the truth itself of the assurance given him. The change from his old sense to his new was absolute and final: what was to happen *had* so absolutely and finally happened that he was as little able to know a fear for his future as to know a hope; so absent in short was any question of anything still to come. He was to live entirely with the other question, that of his unidentified past, that of his having to see his fortune impenetrably muffled and masked.

The torment of this vision became then his occupation;

he couldn't perhaps have consented to live but for the possibility of guessing. She had told him, his friend, not to guess; she had forbidden him, so far as he might, to know, and she had even in a sort denied the power in him to learn: which were so many things, precisely, to deprive him of rest. It wasn't that he wanted, he argued for fairness, that anything that had happened to him should happen over again; it was only that he shouldn't, as an anticlimax, have been taken sleeping so sound as not to be able to win back by an effort of thought the lost stuff of consciousness. He declared to himself at moments that he would either win it back or have done with consciousness forever; he made this idea his one motive, in fine, made it so much his passion that none other, to compare with it, seemed ever to have touched him. The lost stuff of consciousness became thus for him as a strayed or stolen child to an unappeasable father; he hunted it up and down very much as if he were knocking at doors and inquiring of the police. This was the spirit in which, inevitably, he set himself to travel; he started on a journey that was to be as long as he could make it; it danced before him that, as the other side of the globe couldn't possibly have less to say to him, it might, by a possibility of suggestion, have more. Before he quitted London, however, he made a pilgrimage to May Bartram's grave, took his way to it through the endless avenues of the grim suburban necropolis, sought it out in the wilderness of tombs, and, though he had come but for the renewal of the act of farewell, found himself, when he had at last stood by it, beguiled into long intensities. He stood for an hour, powerless to turn away and yet powerless to penetrate the darkness of death; fixing with his eyes her inscribed name and date, beating his forehead against the fact of the secret they kept, drawing his breath, while he waited as if, in pity of him, some sense would rise from the stones. He kneeled on the stones, however, in vain; they kept what they concealed; and if the face of the tomb did become a face for him it was because her two names were like a pair of eyes that didn't know him. He gave them a last long look, but no palest light broke.

VI

He stayed away, after this, for a year; he visited the depths of Asia, spending himself on scenes of romantic interest, of superlative sanctity; but what was present to him everywhere was that for a man who had known what he had known the world was vulgar and vain. The state of mind in which he had lived for so many years shone out to him, in reflection, as a light that colored and refined, a light beside which the glow of the East was garish, cheap, and thin. The terrible truth was that he had lost—with everything else—a distinction as well; the things he saw couldn't help being common when he had become common to look at them. He was simply now one of them himself—he was in the dust, without a peg for the sense of difference; and there were hours when, before the temples of gods and the sepulchers of kings, his spirit turned, for nobleness of association, to the barely discriminated slab in the London suburb. That had become for him, and more intensely with time and distance, his one witness of a past glory. It was all that was left to him for proof or pride, yet the past glories of pharaohs were nothing to him as he thought of it. Small wonder then that he came back to it on the morrow of his return. He was drawn there this time as irresistibly as the other, yet with a confidence, almost, that was doubtless the effect of the many months that had elapsed. He had lived, in spite of himself, into his change of feeling, and in wandering over the earth had wandered, as might be said, from the circumference to the center of his desert. He had settled to his safety and accepted perforce his extinction; figuring to himself, with some color, in the likeness of certain little old men he remembered to have seen, of whom, all meager and wizened as they might look, it was related that they had in their time fought twenty duels or been loved by ten princesses.

They indeed had been wondrous for others, while he was but wondrous for himself; which, however, was exactly the cause of his haste to renew the wonder by getting back, as he might put it, into his own presence. That had quickened his steps and checked his delay. If his visit was prompt it was because he had been separated so long from the part of himself that alone he now valued.

It is accordingly not false to say that he reached his goal with a certain elation, and stood there again with a certain assurance. The creature beneath the sod *knew* of his rare experience, so that, strangely now, the place had lost for him its mere blankness of expression. It met him in mildness—not, as before, in mockery; it wore for him the air of conscious greeting that we find, after absence, in things that have closely belonged to us and which seem to confess of themselves to the connection. The plot of ground, the graven tablet, the tended flowers affected him so as belonging to him that he quite felt for the hour like a contented landlord reviewing a piece of property. Whatever had happened—well, had happened. He had not come back this time with the vanity of that question, his former worrying, "What, *what?*" now practically so spent. Yet he would, nonetheless, never again so cut himself off from the spot; he would come back to it every month, for if he did nothing else by its aid he at least held up his head. It thus grew for him, in the oddest way, a positive resource; he carried out his idea of periodical returns, which took their place at last among the most inveterate of his habits. What it all amounted to, oddly enough, was that, in his now so simplified world, this garden of death gave him the few square feet of earth on which he could still most live. It was as if, being nothing anywhere else for anyone, nothing even for himself, he were just everything here, and if not for a crowd of witnesses, or indeed for any witness but John Marcher, then by clear right of the register that he could scan like an open page. The open page was the tomb of his friend, and *there* were the facts of the past, there the truth of his life, there the backward reaches in which he could lose himself. He did this, from time to time, with such effect that he seemed to wander through the old years with his hand in the arm of a companion who was, in the most extraordinary manner, his other, his younger self; and to wander, which was more extraordinary yet, round and round a third presence—not wandering she, but stationary, still, whose eyes, turning with his revolution, never ceased to follow him, and whose seat was his point, so to speak, of orientation. Thus in short he settled to live—feeding only on the sense that he once *had* lived, and dependent on it not only for a support but for an identity.

It sufficed him, in its way, for months, and the year elapsed; it would doubtless even have carried him further but for an accident, superficially slight, which moved him, in a quite other direction, with a force beyond any of his impressions of Egypt or of India. It was a thing of the merest chance—the turn, as he afterward felt, of a hair, though he was indeed to live to believe that if light hadn't come to him in this particular fashion it would still have come in another. He was to live to believe this, I say, though he was not to live, I may not less definitely mention, to do much else. We allow him at any rate the benefit of the conviction, struggling up for him at the end, that, whatever might have happened or not happened, he would have come round of himself to the light. The incident of an autumn day had put the match to the train laid from of old by his misery. With the light before him he knew that even of late his ache had only been smothered. It was strangely drugged, but it throbbed; at the touch it began to bleed. And the touch, in the event, was the face of a fellow mortal. This face, one gray afternoon when the leaves were thick in the alleys, looked into Marcher's own, at the cemetery, with an expression like the cut of a blade. He felt it, that is, so deep down that he winced at the steady thrust. The person who so mutely assaulted him was a figure he had noticed, on reaching his own goal, absorbed by a grave a short distance away, a grave apparently fresh, so that the emotion of the visitor would probably match it for frankness. This fact alone forbade further attention, though during the time he stayed he remained vaguely conscious of his neighbor, a middle-aged man apparently, in mourning, whose bowed back, among the clustered monuments and mor-

tuary yews, was constantly presented. Marcher's theory
that these were elements in contact with which he himself revived, had suffered, on this occasion, it may be
granted, a sensible though inscrutable check. The autumn
day was dire for him as none had recently been, and he
rested with a heaviness he had not yet known on the low
stone table that bore May Bartram's name. He rested
without power to move, as if some spring in him, some
spell vouchsafed, had suddenly been broken forever. If
he could have done that moment as he wanted he would
simply have stretched himself on the slab that was
ready to take him, treating it as a place prepared to receive his last sleep. What in all the wide world had
he now to keep awake for? He stared before him with
the question, and it was then that, as one of the cemetery
walks passed near him, he caught the shock of the face.

His neighbor at the other grave had withdrawn, as he
himself, with force in him to move, would have done by
now, and was advancing along the path on his way to
one of the gates. This brought him near, and his pace
was slow, so that—and all the more as there was a kind
of hunger in his look—the two men were for a minute directly confronted. Marcher felt him on the spot as one of
the deeply stricken—a perception so sharp that nothing
else in the picture lived for it, neither his dress, his age,
nor his presumable character and class; nothing lived but
the deep ravage of the features that he showed. He
showed them—that was the point; he was moved, as he
passed, by some impulse that was either a signal for sympathy or, more possibly, a challenge to another sorrow.
He might already have been aware of our friend, might,
at some previous hour, have noticed in him the smooth
habit of the scene, with which the state of his own senses
so scantily consorted, and might thereby have been
stirred as by a kind of overt discord. What Marcher was
at all events conscious of was, in the first place, that the
image of scarred passion presented to him was conscious,
too—of something that profaned the air; and, in the second, that, roused, startled, shocked, he was yet the next
moment looking after it, as it went, with envy. The most
extraordinary thing that had happened to him—though he

had given that name to other matters as well—took place, after his immediate vague stare, as a consequence of this impression. The stranger passed, but the raw glare of his grief remained, making our friend wonder in pity what wrong, what wound it expressed, what injury not to be healed. What had the man *had* to make him, by the loss of it, so bleed and yet live?

Something—and this reached him with a pang—that *he*, John Marcher, hadn't; the proof of which was precisely John Marcher's arid end. No passion had ever touched him, for this was what passion meant; he had survived and maundered and pined, but where had been *his* deep ravage? The extraordinary thing we speak of was the sudden rush of the result of this question. The sight that had just met his eyes named to him, as in letters of quick flame, something he had utterly, insanely missed, and what he had missed made these things a train of fire, made them mark themselves in an anguish of inward throbs. He had seen *outside* of his life, not learned it within, the way a woman was mourned when she had been loved for herself; such was the force of his conviction of the meaning of the stranger's face, which still flared for him like a smoky torch. It had not come to him, the knowledge, on the wings of experience; it had brushed him, jostled him, upset him, with the disrespect of chance, the insolence of an accident. Now that the illumination had begun, however, it blazed to the zenith, and what he presently stood there gazing at was the sounded void of his life. He gazed, he drew breath, in pain; he turned in his dismay, and, turning, he had before him in sharper incision than ever the open page of his story. The name on the table smote him as the passage of his neighbor had done, and what it said to him, full in the face, was that *she* was what he had missed. This was the awful thought, the answer to all the past, the vision at the dread clearness of which he turned as cold as the stone beneath him. Everything fell together, confessed, explained, overwhelmed; leaving him most of all stupefied at the blindness he had cherished. The fate he had been marked for he had met with a vengeance— he had emptied the cup to the lees; he had been the man

of his time, *the* man, to whom nothing on earth was to
have happened. That was the rare stroke—that was his
visitation. So he saw it, as we say, in pale horror, while
the pieces fitted and fitted. So *she* had seen it, while he
didn't, and so she served at this hour to drive the
truth home. It was the truth, vivid and monstrous, that
all the while he had waited the wait was itself his
portion. This the companion of his vigil had at a given moment perceived, and she had then offered him the chance
to baffle his doom. One's doom, however, was never
baffled, and on the day she had told him that his own had
come down she had seen him but stupidly stare at the
escape she offered him.

The escape would have been to love her; then, then
he would have lived. *She* had lived—who could say now
with what passion?—since she had loved him for himself;
whereas he had never thought of her (ah, how it hugely
glared at him!) but in the chill of his egotism and the
light of her use. Her spoken words came back to him,
and the chain stretched and stretched. The Beast had
lurked indeed, and the Beast, at its hour, had sprung; it
had sprung in that twilight of the cold April when, pale,
ill, wasted, but all beautiful, and perhaps even then re-
coverable, she had risen from her chair to stand before
him and let him imaginably guess. It had sprung as he
didn't guess; it had sprung as she hopelessly turned from
him, and the mark, by the time he left her, had fallen
where it *was* to fall. He had justified his fear and achieved
his fate; he had failed, with the last exactitude, of all he
was to fail of; and a moan now rose to his lips as he remembered she had prayed he mightn't know. This horror
of waking—*this* was knowledge, knowledge under the
breath of which the very tears in his eyes seemed to
freeze. Through them, nonetheless, he tried to fix it and
hold it; he kept it there before him so that he might
feel the pain. That at least, belated and bitter, had
something of the taste of life. But the bitterness suddenly
sickened him, and it was as if, horribly, he saw, in the
truth, in the cruelty of his image, what had been appointed
and done. He saw the Jungle of his life and saw the lurk-
ing Beast; then, while he looked, perceived it, as by a stir

of the air, rise, huge and hideous, for the leap that was to settle him. His eyes darkened—it was close; and, instinctively turning, in his hallucination, to avoid it, he flung himself, on his face, on the tomb.

SELECTED BIBLIOGRAPHY

WORKS BY HENRY JAMES

A Passionate Pilgrim and Other Tales, 1875 Tales
Transatlantic Sketches, 1875 Travel
Roderick Hudson, 1875 Novel
The American, 1877 Novel
French Poets and Novelists, 1878 Criticism
The Europeans, 1878 Novel (Meridian Classic 0452-010217)
Daisy Miller, 1878 Tale (Signet Classic 0451-605705)
Hawthorne, 1879 Criticism
Washington Square, 1880 Tale (Signet Classic 0451-524993)
The Portrait of a Lady, 1881 Novel (Signet Classic 0451-522885)
The Art of Fiction, 1884 Criticism
The Bostonians, 1886 Novel (Signet Classic 0451-525507)
The Princess Casamassima, 1886 Novel
Partial Portraits, 1888 Criticism
The Aspern Papers, 1888 Tale
The Tragic Muse, 1889 Novel
The Lesson of the Master and Other Stories, 1892 Tales
Embarrassments, 1896 Tales
The Spoils of Poynton, 1897 Novel
What Maisie Knew, 1897 Novel
The Two Magics, 1898 Tales
The Awkward Age, 1899 Novel
The Sacred Fount, 1901 Novel
The Wings of the Dove, 1902 Novel (Meridian Classic 0452-008581)
The Ambassadors, 1903 Novel (Signet Classic 0451-519892)
The Golden Bowl, 1904 Novel
The American Scene, 1907 Novel
The Finer Grain, 1910 Tales
A Small Boy and Others, 1913 Autobiography
Notes of a Son and Brother, 1914 Autobiography
Notes on Novelists, 1914 Criticism
The Middle Years, 1917, Unfinished Autobiography
The Art of the Novel, 1934 Critical Prefaces
The Notebooks of Henry James, 1947 Memoranda

SELECTED BIOGRAPHY AND CRITICISM

Anderson, Quentin. *The American Henry James.* New Brunswick, N.J.: Rutgers University Press, 1957.
Beach, Joseph Warren, *The Method of Henry James.* Rev. ed. Philadelphia: Alfred Saifer, 1954.

Bewley, Marius. *The Complex Fate: Hawthorne, Henry James, and Some Other American Writers*. London: Chatto & Windus, 1952.

Blackmur, Richard P. "Henry James." In *Literary History of the United States*, ed. Robert E. Spiller, et al, pp. 1039–64. New York: Macmillan, 1953.

Bloom, Harold, ed. *Modern Critical Interpretations: Henry James's 'Daisy Miller,' 'The Turn of the Screw,' and Other Tales*. New York: Chelsea House, 1987.

Bowden, Edwin T. *The Themes of Henry James: A System of Observation Through the Visual Arts*. New Haven: Yale University Press, 1956.

Buitenhaus, Peter. *The Grasping Imagination: The American Writings of Henry James*. Toronto: University of Toronto Press, 1970.

Cargill, Oscar. *The Novels of Henry James*. New York: Macmillan, 1961.

Crews, Frederick C. *The Tragedy of Manners: Moral Drama in the Later Novels of Henry James*. New Haven: Yale University Press, 1957.

Dupee, F. W. *Henry James*. Rev. ed. New York: Sloane, 1956.
———,ed. *The Question of Henry James*. New York: Holt, 1945.

Edel, Leon, *Henry James*. 5 vols. Philadelphia: Lippincott, 1953–1972.
———,ed. *Henry James: A Collection of Critical Essays*. Englewood Cliffs, N.J.: Prentice-Hall, 1963.

Gale, Robert L. *The Caught Image: Figurative Language in the Fiction of Henry James*. Chapel Hill: University of North Carolina Press, 1964.

Gard, Roger, ed. *Henry James: The Critical Heritage*. London: Routledge & Kegan Paul; New York: Barnes & Noble, 1968.

Goode, John, ed. *The Air of Reality: New Essays on Henry James*. London: Methuen, 1972.

Kaplan, Fred. *Henry James: The Imagination of a Genius: A Biography*. New York: William Morrow, 1992.

Kelley, Cornelia P. *The Early Development of Henry James*. Urbana: University of Illinois Press, 1930.

Krook, Dorothea. *The Ordeal of Consciousness in Henry James*. New York: Cambridge University Press, 1962.

Leavis, F. R. *The Great Tradition*. New York: George Stewart, 1949.

Lebowitz, Naomi, ed. *Discussions of Henry James*. Boston: Health, 1962.

McElderry, Bruce R. Jr. *Henry James*. New York: Twayne Publishers, 1965.

Matthiessen, F. O. *Henry James: The Major Phase*. New York: Oxford University Press, 1944.

―――, *The James Family*. New York: Knopf, 1947.

Moore, Harry T. *Henry James*. New York: Viking, 1974.

Perosa, Sergio. *Henry James and the Experimental Novel*. Charlottesville: University Press of Virginia, 1978.

Poirer, Richard. *The Comic Sense of Henry James*. New York: Oxford University Press, 1960.

Powers, Lyall H. *Henry James: An Introduction and Interpretation*. New York: Holt, Rinehart, and Winston, 1970.

Przybylowicz, Donna. *Desire and Repression: The Dialectic of Self and Other in the Late Works of Henry James*. Tuscaloosa: University of Alabama Press, 1986.

Sears, Sallie. *The Negative Imagination: Form and Perspective in the Novels of Henry James*. Ithaca, N.Y.: Cornell University Press, 1968.

Tanner, Tony, ed. *Henry James: Modern Judgments*. London: Macmillan, 1968.

Tompkins, Jane P., ed. *Twentieth-Century Interpretations of 'The Turn of the Screw' and Other Tales: A Collection of Critical Essays*. Englewood Cliffs, N.J.: Prentice-Hall, 1970.

Winner, Viola H. *Henry James and the Visual Arts*. Charlottesville: University of Virginia Press, 1970.

Yeazell, Ruth Bernard. *Language and Knowledge in the Late Novels of Henry James*. Chicago: University of Chicago Press, 1976.

A NOTE ON THE TEXT

The text of each of these novellas is that of the first American appearance in book form. These appearances are as follows:

Daisy Miller. A Study. New York: Harper & Brothers, 1819 [1878], No. 82 in Harper's Half-Hour Series.

An International Episode. New York: Harper & Brothers, 1879, No. 91 in Harper's Half-Hour Series.

"The Aspern Papers," in *The Aspern Papers. Louisa Pallant, The Modern Warning.* London and New York: Macmillan and Co., 1888.

"The Altar of the Dead," in *Terminations.* New York: Harper & Brothers, 1895.

"The Turn of the Screw," in *The Two Magics.* New York and London: The Macmillan Company, 1898.

"The Beast in the Jungle," in *The Better Sort.* New York: Charles Scribner's Sons, 1903.

Four of these novellas appeared in magazines prior to their publication in book form. These appearances are as follows:

"Daisy Miller," *Cornhill Magazine,* June–July 1878.

"An International Episode," *Cornhill Magazine,* Dec. 1878–Jan. 1879

"The Aspern Papers," *Atlantic Monthly,* March–May 1888.

"The Turn of the Screw," *Collier's Weekly,* Jan. 27–April 16, 1898.

Even in the short time which elapsed between magazine publication and the appearance in book form, James was able to correct errors and do some revising and polishing. The changes in "Daisy Miller" are slight. One important passage was added to "An International Episode"—the walk up Fifth Avenue by the two visiting Englishmen. There are many verbal revisions in "The Aspern Papers." They show James working, as always, to describe the place seen and the emotion felt as precisely as possible.